BREACH

BREACH

W. L. GOODWATER

ACE
NEW YORK

ACE
Published by Berkley
An imprint of Penguin Random House LLC
375 Hudson Street, New York, New York 10014

Library of Congress Cataloging-in-Publication Data

Names: Goodwater, W. L. author.
Title: Breach / W. L. Goodwater.
Description: First edition. | New York : ACE, 2018.
Identifiers: LCCN 2018005080| ISBN 9780451491039 (trade pbk.) |
ISBN 9780451491046 (ebook)
Subjects: LCSH: Magician—Fiction. | Cold War—Fiction. | GSAFD: Fantasy fiction
Classification: LCC PS3607.O592258 B74 2018 | DDC 813/.6—dc23
LC record available at https://lccn.loc.gov/2018005080

First Edition: November 2018

Printed in the United States of America
1   3   5   7   9   10   8   6   4   2

Cover design by Pete Garceau
Book design by Kristin del Rosario

For my wife

ACKNOWLEDGMENTS

They say it takes a village to raise a child; I've learned it takes a reasonably-sized suburb to publish a novel. I have many well-earned thanks to bestow:

To my agent, Jennifer Udden, and my editor, Rebecca Brewer, for taking a risk on *Breach* and its unknown author. I hope for all our sakes your faith is not misplaced. Jen, thanks for pointing out that it can be irresponsible to make monsters too sympathetic; and Rebecca, thanks for reminding me that characters still have emotions (and readers still care about them!) even in the Third Act.

To my wife, for giving me time and support while I played make-believe behind a keyboard. And to my baby son, who has guaranteed that all proceeds from this book will disappear into a black hole of college savings.

To my friends, family, and coworkers who didn't run in terror at the words, "Would you like to read my unpublished fantasy novel?" This list is humbling, long, and probably incomplete: Tyler, Aaron, Bovee, Margaret, Audrey, Pamela & Theo, Mike & Kristen, Gabe, Jeff, Chris, Chrissy, and Leon.

To the Jewish Federation of Greater Santa Barbara and all the rabbis and Yiddish experts that Pamela got to weigh in on the one Yiddish phrase in this book. As expected, opinions were varied. If I got it wrong, the fault is mine.

To the marketing and publicity teams at Ace who spread the word about *Breach* to all who would listen. And to the copyeditors, proofreaders, designers, and artists who worked hard to make this book all the better for being a collaboration. Thank you all for using your talents on my behalf.

And to you. Yes, you, the random reader who had no reasonable expectation of acknowledgment but still read this section of the book. Your dedication is remarkable. Keep reading—the rest of the book will be more interesting, I promise.

ONE

At a dimly lit street corner on Sebastianstraße, a few miles south of Checkpoint Charlie and uncomfortably close to the East German border, two men in government-issue over-coats warded off the autumn cold and tried their best not to look like Americans. Or spies.

"You know, I have a lighter," the shorter man said. His breath steamed.

"I don't need a lighter," the taller man said through lips clenched around a bobbing cigarette.

It was quiet, as expected. There would be more signs of life farther westward, where routine had mostly replaced rubble, but stillness usually prevailed along the border. For this evening's business, that was for the best. Overhead, a skeletal moon proved to be a disinterested accomplice, leaving the night dark even by West Berlin standards. The only other light came from the heavily curtained windows reluctantly overlooking the empty road. And, of course, from the otherworldly silver-white flicker of the Wall. Its magical threads pulsed softly and steadily, like breath.

The shorter man tilted back the brim of his hat. Dark curls

popped out over a pale forehead. "From where I'm standing, Jimbo, it looks like you need a lighter."

Jim frowned. "How about you worry less about me and more about watching for our guests, pal?"

"But watching your little show is far more interesting."

Ignoring his companion, Jim took in a slow breath through his nose. He concentrated, murmured the words he'd been taught as best as he could remember them, and snapped his fingers.

The sound echoed hollowly down the quiet street. The cigarette remained unlit.

"The ladies must love this."

"What would you know about ladies, Dennis?" What was the problem? This usually worked, though he had to admit it had been a long time since he'd failed out of St. Cyprian's University of the Arcane.

Dennis laughed. "I may not have your chiseled jawline, but I do have something you clearly lack."

"And what's that, pal?"

"Self-awareness."

In the gloom behind them, the "construction site" they had hastily thrown together looked more like a spent battlefield. Heavy green trucks (labeled US ARMY in a previous life) were parked at odd angles next to aged German civilian machinery. Mounds of torn-up asphalt had been piled nearby. It had been costly (and a little sad) to dig up a perfectly good road, especially when plenty of streets in Berlin were still pocked with the cratered reminders of the war, but everything had to look authentic. Thick canvas tarps had been erected around the most sensitive areas of the site, blocking whole sections of the glittering Wall from view, to dissuade their more curious neighbors. Some things might be hard to come by in West Berlin, but it never lacked for prying eyes.

Snap. And again, nothing.

"See," Dennis said, "this is why I, like most hardworking Americans, don't bother with magic."

"I thought that was because the examiners tested you and found you had no magical ability. Or charisma."

"I don't remember them testing for charisma."

"In your case, they didn't have to."

Dennis shrugged. "Well, we can't all be as magical as you, Jimbo, can we? Do that one again, where you snap your fingers and nothing happens. I love that one."

The magic spell he was trying to cast wasn't hard. Maybe he was mispronouncing the first word; Latin had never been Jim's strongest subject. He'd always thought magic would be a lot simpler if he could just say the incantations in plain English. His disappointed professors hadn't been very sympathetic to this point of view.

Was the accent on the first syllable or the last . . . ? He snapped his fingers again and this time was rewarded by a prickle across the back of his neck, and a tiny orange ember of flame hovering in the foggy air above his hand like a benevolent spirit.

"Huh," Dennis said. "Would you look at that?"

"What did I tell you?" Jim said. "Magic." He held up the tip of his cigarette to the floating fire and puffed his cigarette to life. He sucked in a long draw, the smooth, hot air filling his lungs. For a moment, he savored the acrid taste of the smoke and sweet flavor of victory. Then ducked as the flame suddenly exploded in an angry sunburst, like a journalist's flashbulb, if it had been designed in hell.

Dennis's eyes were wide. "Does that usually happen?"

A little singed and with the ruins of his cigarette crumbling through his fingers, Jim swore foully, first in English, then in German for good measure. "This damned city," he said, mostly to himself. "Nothing works right here, not even magic."

A surly voice surprised them out of the dark. "There's this concept in intelligence work you two knuckleheads might want to look up," it said. "It's called subtlety."

"Sorry, Chief," they said in unison as Arthur joined them. He looked annoyed, but then again, he always did. The head of Berlin Operating Base wore a scowl effortlessly, as though his face had been molded that way by a disgruntled sculptor. His brown suit, the one that seemed expertly tailored to fit poorly, was scarred with the usual unintentional creases. His tie, a stained, threadbare mistake, hung on for dear life.

"They're late," Arthur said.

"Not late, Chief," Jim said. "Just running on European time."

Arthur snorted, which could have been a laugh or a rebuke. "Just keep your eyes open and let me know when they get here," he said. "Oh, and Jim? Leave the magic to the professionals and the Commies."

"Yes, sir."

"Our wayward guests are causing enough stress on my ulcer without you—"

"A shod m'hot nisht geredt fun moshiach," Dennis said.

"In English, Dennis, or I'll—" Arthur began.

Dennis nodded toward the intersection ahead. Two cars, glossy with accumulated mist, were coming toward them. "You goyim would say: Speak of the Devil and he shall appear."

The British got out first and dutifully greeted Arthur with firm, terse handshakes. Their leader, a burly Scotsman named Alec with a dark wild forest of a beard, had to stoop when he made his greetings.

Shortly behind came the French, a smaller, more somber contingent. They spoke in low whispers with Arthur for a long minute before he led them within the tent.

They gathered behind the tarps and trucks, a knot of foreigners ruling over the land they had rightly and thoroughly conquered, silent in expectation. Silent, that is, until Alec spoke.

"Would you look at this lot? One well-tossed grenade over the Wall and half the brains in Western intelligence go up in smoke," said the big Scot, who nearly filled the cramped space by himself. He shoved an elbow into Jim's ribs. "And that's just if they get me."

Alec had been a guerrilla fighter in the Highlands during the German occupation and had the scars to prove it. Jim had always wanted to ask him about what it had been like, but Arthur had been quick to wave him off. Some things are better left where they lay, had been his advice. Some wounds don't heal right.

"Forgive me," said a thin, dark-haired man. His English was excellent though his French accent unmistakable. "You said 'brains' but I believe you meant 'fat.'"

Alec's laugh nearly knocked down one of the tarps. "Emile, you didn't tell me they'd started issuing you frogs a sense of humor."

Emile was something more of a mystery. Jim had read his file, if you could call it that: a single sheet of paper, barely half-filled, with the only interesting bit of intel being his preferred brand of cigarettes. His age was hard to guess, but everyone in France was a veteran of some kind or another.

"Alec, ask Jim to light a cigarette for you," Dennis added from a corner.

"Enough," Arthur said. He eyed the assembled men with the red-rimmed glare of the unwillingly sober. "It's late, I'm tired, and none of you are very fun to look at, so kindly shut up."

With all mouths closed and eyes turned toward him, Arthur grunted. "Let's get this over with so you can get back to your bosses and tell them we're not crazy." He motioned impatiently to one of his men standing by one of the trucks. "Just very unlucky." The agent untied a cord and pulled back the canvas sheet that had been drawn over this section of the Wall. The others pressed in.

It wasn't easy to see it, even when pointed out. Just a shadow, no more than an inch square, nestled in the shimmering weave that made up the Wall. But on closer inspection, it was more: a flaw, a withering of the magic.

A breach.

Alec spoke first. "That's it? That's what we're all getting so ruffled about? I could barely stick my wee finger in there. I don't see many East Germans or Soviet spies sneaking through, no matter how little they feed them."

"Are we certain this has not always been here?" Emile said quietly, his eyes never leaving it. With care, he touched the area around the breach, the soft crackle of the magic filling the silence.

"We are," Arthur said. "And there's more."

This was news to Jim. "More?"

Arthur nodded. "It's growing."

Alec lurched back, nearly knocking a few of the others down in the process. "Growing? You never said anything about growing."

Jim felt a little sick. Dennis wasn't looking much better. Suddenly their joking didn't seem as funny. They'd been briefed on the breach shortly after it had been found, but at that point there was still hope it wasn't as bad as they feared. But if it were growing . . .

"We couldn't confirm until a few minutes ago," Arthur said. "We took another measurement and . . ." He pulled a folded slip of paper from his pocket and scanned it. "Five percent growth since discovery."

"Five percent? That's . . ." Alec said.

"This is a more serious problem than we thought," Emile said. "I will need to send this information to Paris."

"With the utmost security," Arthur added.

"You do not think the Soviets already know?" Emile asked.

"It is their Wall, their magic," Arthur said. "But even if the hole went all the way through, there's not a lot of opportunity for them to examine it from their side, not unless they're using a spotlight at a hundred yards or a rifle scope." He rubbed his eyes. "And besides, even if they know, we don't want them to know we know."

"This is why we Americans build our walls out of bricks and concrete," Dennis said. "Not fairy dust."

Emile whispered to his companion, then said, "The timing of this concerns us."

"How so?" Jim asked.

"This breach is a potential crisis between East and West," he said, "and it comes only weeks after our governments began to rearm West Germany."

"Over Moscow's strenuous objections," Arthur said.

Alec regained his composure enough to speak. "Am I the only one thinking about what happens if that wee hole doesn't stop growing?"

"If the Reds keep their pants on, we can handle a limited breach," Arthur said. "Just another gate to watch."

"But what if it is more than that? What if the whole bloody thing comes down?"

It was Emile who answered. "We would have thousands of refugees attempting to cross the border within hours. The East Germans would be forced to stop them. The Soviets would assist, of course, and we would be required to match any show of force with our own."

"And suddenly we're all pointing guns at each other again," Arthur said.

"Not just guns," Jim added.

"A lot more than just guns," Arthur said. "With fifty thousand civilians right in the middle. Civilians, I might add, who will be stupid and brave enough to force the issue."

"It'll be another war," Alec said, the first quiet words out of his mouth.

"It'll be the last war," Arthur said. "We're getting too good at killing each other not to do it right this time."

"What is the United States going to do?" Alec asked.

"Ask Eisenhower. Ask the commandant in Zehlendorf," Arthur said. "I just gather intel."

"Arthur . . ."

"What do you want me to say? We're going to prepare," Arthur said. "Boys will start shining their combat boots, politicians will be polishing their sabers. The same dance with an updated tune."

"And what are *you* going to do?" Emile asked.

Arthur sighed. "What else?" he said. "Figure out a way to keep the whole damn roof from falling in. Any of you all know anything about magic?"

Jim tried not to laugh at the question. There weren't many people out there who could help with magic on this scale. After the German invasion, British magicians were an all but extinct species. The French were hardly in a better position. No, this one would fall to the US of A, no matter how little Mom and Pop America would like it.

"What about you, Jim?" Arthur said. "You went to school for this stuff. Can you offer any magical insight here?"

Jim stood by the breach. It didn't look much bigger than when he'd first seen it a day or two ago, but he didn't doubt the measurements. "Sorry, Chief," he said. "They kicked me out long before we covered magic like this."

He thought about St. Cyprian's, and about the fireball blowing up in his face. He was pretty sure his eyebrows were a little burned. Carefully, Jim put a finger into the breach and felt only the cold. "I think we're going to need to call in the experts for this one."

TWO

"Whatever you do," Karen said, "don't move."

"Why can't I move?"

"You're moving."

"I'm not moving."

"Your lips are moving."

"Why can't my lips move?"

"Because you're scaring Bing."

"I think that might be the scalpel."

"No, not Bing," Karen said. She stroked the rat's white fur and he looked up at her expectantly, tiny nose twitching. "He's proud to do his part for magical research. Now hold him steady."

Gerald held Bing in place while Karen made a shallow half-inch cut along the rat's right leg. The blood was bright and quick, as if dropped on snow.

"See? He didn't even feel it." Karen set the scalpel aside and reached for the first element of the spell: powdered goat's horn.

"Think this one will work?" Gerald asked.

"No idea," Karen said as she sprinkled the grayish powder.

"But we're trying it anyway?"

"That's why they call it research," Karen said. She handed him the transcription Allison had typed up. "Here," she said, "read this. Your pronunciation is better than mine."

"Come now," Gerald said, taking the paper reluctantly. "Your magic runs circles around most of the people in this building."

Karen smiled at that, though she didn't believe a word of it. "Go ahead," she said. "I want you to do it."

With Gerald's Midwestern accent droning two-thousand-year-old words in her ear, Karen set out the other prescribed magical reagents, making sure the dried hemlock didn't touch the salt of an inland sea. She wanted to roll her eyes; these complicated spells never worked. The extra details always struck her as someone trying too hard. Good magic didn't have to be so arcane.

"Ready?" Gerald asked.

"Let's make history," Karen replied.

His voice rose as he began the last stanza, an uncharacteristic dramatic flair for the owl-eyed magician from Topeka. But when you might be on the verge of the greatest magical breakthrough in human history, Karen figured a little showmanship wasn't a bad thing.

There was some magic in the spell; Karen felt its familiar whisper starting in the back of her mind. Something was happening; she just wasn't sure what. Neither, it seemed, was Bing, his round pink eyes darting about the room as unseen energy began to gather. Karen watched the cut, the blood already clotting, and willed it to close.

And then Gerald was finished. The silence that invaded the room held them all captive for the longest a single moment could be stretched.

And then the moment passed and the wound remained unchanged.

Bing sniffed the air and stared at them, as if to say, *What did you expect, a miracle?*

Gerald did not seemed surprised. "You know the old saying," he said with a shrug. "'You want to heal someone, call a doctor.'"

"'You want to kill someone, call a magician,'" she finished. She let out the breath she hadn't realized she was holding in and found her research notebook. She had a dozen of these, each full of similar failures. She read the title off the cover. "Sorry, Quintilianus the Great," she said, "but your spell 'Quicken the Mending of Mortal Flesh' would be better named 'Wasten the Time of Overworked Magicians.'"

"That's why they call it research, right?" Gerald asked as he wrapped medical tape around Bing's leg.

"Right," Karen said, forcing herself not to sigh. "If it were easy, everyone would be doing it, instead of just two of us." She scooped up the bandaged Bing and held him nose to quivering nose. "Your country thanks you, Bing the Rat, for your service." She carried him across the room to his cage, where his fellow rats were waiting. "Marlon, Bob, Jimmy, you leave Bing alone. He's had a rough day."

The door to the cramped lab opened slightly and a blond-bobbed head peered in. "Is it over?" Allison asked.

"The magic or the rat torture?" Gerald asked.

"Yuck," Allison said. "Both."

"It is safe to enter," Gerald said as Karen watched the rats plow through fresh sawdust. It was, she thought, a painfully apt metaphor for magicians: a simple, caged life-form digging ignorantly through the leavings of some complex, unknowable mind, hoping to find a treat.

"Miss O'Neil?" Allison said.

"Karen," she said, seemingly for the hundredth time. "Call me Karen." Allison was only a couple years younger than her, after all; such formality made Karen feel old. But Allison was a hard worker and fiercely loyal, which was always welcome in a world

haunted by government bureaucrats. Karen suspected family connections had gotten her the job in the OMRD to keep her out of
trouble until she found a good husband, which, as Karen guessed
from the lengthy gossip Allison often subjected her to, wouldn't
take long.

"Karen, right," Allison said, as if trying to commit the name to
memory. "Karen, you're late for your staff meeting."

Oh, hell. Speaking of bureaucrats.

"Times like these," Gerald said, not looking up from his notes,
"I sure am glad you run this department, not me."

Karen thrust her notebooks into a drawer. "I keep showing up
late to staff meetings and there might soon be an opening."

"No, thanks," Gerald said. "Uncle Sam couldn't pay me enough
to sit in a conference room with the director."

"Dr. Haupt?" Karen said. "He's a great magician."

Gerald snorted. "He's terrifying."

"Not if you get to know him."

Gerald shook his head. "I think the more I knew, the more terrified I'd be."

"It isn't the director I'm worried about," Karen said. "It's the
rest of those blowhards."

Gerald adjusted his glasses. "I won't argue, but to be safe, I
think I'll stay here and let you deal with the lot of them."

"And they say that chivalry is dead," Karen said. On her way
out the door, she knelt down and put her face up against the wire
bars of the rat cage. "Wish me luck, boys," she said. "Time for me
to get experimented on."

Though she was only a few minutes late, they hadn't waited for
her. She tried to slip into the wood-paneled conference room
as quietly as possible, even wondering if they'd notice if she used a

few discreet spells to hide her arrival. But as soon as she stepped inside, all eyes turned her way.

"Nice of you to join us," said Harold Wilkerson, the balding head of the Military Application Department. Harold seemed to barely tolerate her existence, but since he offered similar disdain to just about everyone at the OMRD she didn't take it too personally.

"Sorry I'm late," she said quietly as she hurried to her place at the long table.

"Actually," said Marvin Barth, an ample-girthed magician who ran the Environmental Magic Department, whatever that was, "since you're up, you know what would be swell? If you could get us some coffee."

Karen paused in front of her chair. "I don't drink coffee."

Barth hefted his jowls into a smile. "But the rest of us do. And it would be swell."

The rest of the room stared at her through the cigarette haze, a wall of unblinking masculine eyes, waiting for her to capitulate. Demanding her to.

"I'll be right back," she said, "but don't go too far without me." She hurried out into the hall. Before she closed the door, she heard someone say, "So where were we?"

The break room wasn't far. The disorganized cupboards stared back at her in silent mockery of her situation. *You'll get no help from us,* they seemed to say to her. *We're on their side.* Simple, immovable, and usually full of worthless junk: the cupboards did remind her of most of the men of the OMRD.

Why let them boss you around? Why isn't Fat Marvin in here making the coffee? Because he's a man, obviously. Such domestic work would be beneath him.

Karen mercilessly flung a few open until she found what she needed. Grabbing a metal pot, she filled it with water and set it on the counter. With a fingertip, she traced a symbol on the surface, and nothing happened.

Of course, she thought. The enchantment had been used up and no one had bothered to reapply it. Why should they, after all, when they had a woman magician in the building? Isn't that why God let women use magic, so they could power the household appliances? She should serve it to them cold. No, she should make it piping hot and pour it over their heads.

Enchantments had never been her strength, not in school and not after. They could be useful tools, certainly, but there was something macabre about it to her, infusing an object with your own energy. Like leaving behind a lock of hair. Or a fingernail clipping. She sighed. The damn coffee wasn't going to heat itself, so instead she touched the leather pouch around her neck, gripped the pot with her other hand, and whispered the necessary words. The power moved easily enough, bleeding from her palm into the metal, settling there comfortably. Karen shivered.

The coffee grounds too were aligned with her foes. How much was she supposed to use? Did it matter which kind? If her mother knew she was twenty-six and still couldn't brew a cup of coffee for her "handsome" coworkers, she'd probably have a heart attack. Who was she kidding? Her mother knew, but, as with everything else unpleasant in her world, just pretended not to.

When finished, Karen eyed her handiwork: it smelled like an ashtray and looked like mud. Perfect.

". . . this report comes in from Sparks, Nevada, says they have a bona fide werewolf on the loose," Karen heard as she reentered the meeting with the coffee on a tray. The speaker was Al Lambert, head of Public Inquiry, the group responsible for handling reports of errant magic anywhere in the US. They were the largest group in the OMRD, with more than two dozen magicians on staff, and always had the best stories.

"So you tell them there's no such thing as monsters?"

Al leaned back in his chair and adjusted his tie. "Oh, we told them. Ten or fifteen times. But the local police were insistent. You know how people get. Want to blame everything on magic. They hate us until they think they need us. So we had to send out a team."

One of the others asked, "And what was it?"

"A particularly cranky beagle." Laughs all around.

As they started to sip at her scalding-hot coffee, Karen did her best to hide a grin at their disgusted looks. Maybe they'd think twice before asking her to do it next time. After all, she didn't remember seeing table service on her job description.

"Alright," Wilkerson said, "who's next? I don't have all day for this status meeting."

Just keep your head down, she thought. Don't remind them you are crashing their good ol' boys club and maybe you can get back to work faster.

"I for one would be very curious to hear the latest from Theoretical Magic," said George Cabott, deputy to Harold over in Military.

Ugh, so much for keeping her head down.

"Thank you, George," Karen said. He smiled. Allison would have swooned; just about every woman who worked at OMRD headquarters would have. But Karen knew George's dark secret: he was unbearable. She didn't really blame him, though, as human empathy had been bred out of his Manhattan-dwelling family generations ago. She just wished she had known all that before she slept with him back in college.

"Yes, great idea," Barth said, straightening up a bit in his groaning chair. "We've heard enough about actually useful magic for one day."

Karen turned to face him. "I'm sorry, Marvin, did you have some compelling breakthrough to share with us instead? Some wonderful achievement from the third floor to justify your bloated"—she paused for just a fraction of a moment before finishing—"budget?"

Barth choked on his coffee. See, this was why she usually kept quiet. She had plenty to say, but it never came out quite as nicely as these old men wanted it.

"As I've mentioned before," she began before Barth could recover, noting then ignoring the rolled eyes from some of the assembled, "we have a number of exciting research projects ongoing. We were running tests this morning on healing magic, and then there is our continuing work on Universal Expression Theory—"

"Is this getting somewhere, honey?" Al Lambert asked. He'd lived in DC for twenty years but still sounded like he'd just walked off the ranch in Plano.

"I need resources," she said flatly. There were groans all around. "My whole department is two magicians and one secretary. You talk about the public hating magicians. What if we could finally learn how to heal people? And what if we didn't have to rely on spells, but could control magic directly—"

"And what if I had a unicorn that pissed gold dust?" Lambert said. "There are, what, a few thousand people in the whole country who can do decent magic? We can't waste them all on chasing fairy tales. Listen here, honey—"

"Yes, sweetheart?" This stopped the old Texan cold. Stopped the whole room, actually. "Oh, I'm sorry," Karen said, "I thought we were being familiar. My mistake." There was part of her that hated herself for stooping to their level. But if you wanted to be heard by men, you had to act like a man: rude, entitled, and not afraid to make enemies. "Your team is chasing beagles. My team is trying to change the world. All I'm asking for is a few more people to help."

"Young lady, I think—" Lambert never had the chance to finish his reply. The door to the meeting room swung open and the director of the Office of Magical Research and Deployment stood in the doorway.

Dr. Max Haupt was a small man, stooped by age and bent by war, with silver hair and a silver-tipped cane. He held the cane in front of him with his hands folded atop each other. His face wore his sixty years hard, the scars and wrinkles becoming nearly indistinguishable. His eyes narrowed behind his ever-thickening glasses and slowly interrogated each magician in the room.

"I trust," he said, his German accent clipping every word, "that I am not interrupting anything."

"No, sir," Wilkerson said, standing. "We were just finishing here."

"Good." His gaze settled on Lambert, who did not return it. "Mr. Cabott and Miss O'Neil, I would speak with you in my office."

Between the massive cherry-wood monolith that functioned as Dr. Haupt's desk and the cascade of books that threatened to overwhelm even the sturdy shelves along every wall, the director's office had little room for visitors. It was drafty and austere and smelled of old paper, and Karen loved it. Though she was curious about why they had been invited in, she really could only think about the weight of the old magic lingering in the Teutonic texts surrounding them.

Dr. Haupt sat behind his desk and for a moment said nothing. Karen had known him since her second year at St. Cyprian's when she'd taken his class on Magical Source Theory, despite having been warned by older students to avoid him. During the lectures, he rarely interacted with his students other than to rap his silver cane on the desk of anyone starting to nod off. But when she'd visited his office, one significantly smaller than his current one, he had been delighted. He had mentored her for the following years until receiving the summons from President Eisenhower to head up the newly formed Office of Magical Research and Deployment. Karen hadn't even bothered to apply anywhere else after graduation; she knew who she wanted to work for.

"Thank you both for coming," he said softly. He sounded tired. Karen imagined the responsibilities of OMRD director were far weightier than shepherding magical sophomores through their required coursework, but Dr. Haupt rarely showed any sign of strain. He was constant, immutable, like the laws of the universe, from his cane to his suits to his endless supply of books. Karen had known him for years now, but knew nothing of his life outside of work. They had made bets back in school to see if anyone could find an old picture of Dr. Haupt, or even one where he wasn't scowling. None had ever surfaced.

"What's wrong, sir?" she asked.

Dr. Haupt placed a darkly veined hand on a folder on his desk. "We have received a request from the State Department. A request for assistance." His fingers idly tapped the folder. "With some reluctance, they have admitted that the request originated with the Central Intelligence Agency in West Berlin. The details are . . . scarce. Almost nonexistent. I have pushed for more information, but they have not been forthcoming."

"Whatever the problem is, can't we just leave it to the Soviets?" George asked. "They seem to want Berlin more than we do."

"I doubt the people of Berlin would appreciate the nuance of your recommendation," Dr. Haupt replied. An edge had entered his tone. George was a self-centered buffoon who didn't have the history with Dr. Haupt that Karen did, but even he should have known to tread carefully on the subject of Germany with the director.

"Are we being sent to Berlin?" Karen asked.

Dr. Haupt looked at her almost as if he had forgotten she was there. His voice softened, as much as it could, and he said, "One of you is being sent to Berlin to gather information and to advise. The request was very clear on the number. The CIA believes too many magical assets on the ground would have 'destabilizing potential.'"

"What does that mean?" George said.

"It means they don't trust magicians," Karen replied.

"They are not alone," Dr. Haupt said, sighing. For a moment, he seemed to be lost in his own thoughts, as though he were suddenly someplace else entirely: memory or fantasy, Karen couldn't tell, but whatever he saw there didn't seem to please him.

George stepped forward. Karen hated the fact that he was nearly a foot taller than she was. "So who's going?" he asked.

Dr. Haupt picked up his hand sharply, as though the folder had caught fire. His distant thoughts appeared banished. "I have asked you to come because you were both considered for this assignment. We are stretched for resources here and can spare little, but this is a request we cannot afford to ignore. Your names reached the top of a carefully selected list. You are both bright and capable and either of you would serve this office proudly in this matter."

"But who is—"

"Miss O'Neil."

Karen was pretty sure she was the most surprised person in the room, but it was close. George had the family connections in DC, a year of seniority, and immense skill. The decision shouldn't have even been close.

"If I may ask, sir, why," George said, his voice slowing down like it always did when he was attempting to control his anger, "was she selected over me?"

"You may ask, Mr. Cabott. But I do not choose to answer."

Karen wished she could have enjoyed the color rising to George's neck and face, but her mind was too busy elsewhere for proper gloating. She was going to Berlin? On a request from the State Department? To work with the CIA?

"Sir," George said at last, saying the word through lips that were barely willing to open, "is that all?"

"There will be other assignments, Mr. Cabott. There is always work to be done."

"Is that all? Sir."

Dr. Haupt nodded, and George was gone.

"Thank you, sir," Karen said in the ensuing silence. "Thank you for this opportunity. I won't let you down."

"Yes," Dr. Haupt said absently, nearly lost again. "Yes, you are welcome, Miss O'Neil. Karen." He took off his heavy glasses and placed them on the desk. With fingers expert in magic Karen could still only fumble at, he rubbed his deep-set eyes as if warding off an old ache. "I hope I have not made you an enemy."

"George?" Karen said. "He'll get over it. Though," she added, "why did you ask him to come to your office, if he wasn't picked?"

"I decided Mr. Cabott would benefit from learning he was my second choice," he replied, his accent landing heavy on the word "second."

Karen couldn't hide a grin. "Thank you, sir."

Dr. Haupt only nodded.

"You are from Berlin originally, aren't you, sir?"

"Yes," he said with a curt nod. "It is a beautiful city with a rich history, and an unfortunate present."

"You didn't want to take this assignment yourself, have a chance to see your home again on Uncle Sam's dime?"

Dr. Haupt's eyes dropped and Karen instantly regretted her question. "There is nothing for me in Germany now, I'm afraid. I have only been back once, since the war," he said. "Official business. Unpleasant business. I am not eager to return."

"Sir, I'm sorry. I—"

He held up a hand. "Forgive an old man his regrets. But the United States is my home now. A place of new beginnings. I shall leave Germany's complexities to a younger generation. My generation has done enough damage."

"Any advice for my first visit?"

"I doubt you will have much time for sightseeing, though there is much to be seen," he said. His face turned a bit grim. "The best advice I can give is this: stay away from the Wall."

"I'll leave you, then," Karen said. "And thanks again, sir."

As she neared the door, he stopped her. "Karen?"

"Yes?"

"I am sorry I interrupted the meeting earlier. I am certain you would have been able to handle it on your own satisfactorily."

"Cranky men don't bother me, sir."

"Good," he said. "And good luck."

George was waiting for her when she reached the stairwell. "You sleep with him too?"

"Go to hell, George."

"Is that a yes?"

"That is a 'go to hell.'"

She made to move past him, suddenly not in the mood for banter, but he reached out an arm and blocked the narrow hallway.

"This is a serious assignment," he said. "Lives might be at stake. It is hard enough to get the government to recognize the importance of magic. We should be sending our best."

"According to the director, we are."

"No, we're sending someone we can spare. Since Theoretical Magic isn't actually accomplishing anything . . ."

"See, here I thought the 'R' in 'OMRD' stood for 'Research.' Silly me. Now, move."

He didn't. "You really think you're ready for this? You really think *you* are the best person for the job?"

"I think our boss thinks so."

"That kraut?"

"Should we invite him out here so you can call him that to his face?"

"I don't care what he thinks. I asked if you think you're ready for this."

Karen considered retreating back the way she had come, but doubted that would deter him. "What do you want to hear, George? That you're the greatest magician in the world and everyone else should bow down before you and kiss your saintly feet?"

He smirked. "That'd be a good start."

"Fine. You're the best. When I grow up I want to be just like you. And when I go to Berlin instead of you, I'll do my best to make you proud. That good enough?"

"No."

"Then what do you want?"

"A bout."

"What?"

He dropped his arm. "A bout. Like in college. Winner takes all."

Karen groaned. It was always the same with men like George. "You only ever think about using your magic to smash something," she said. "You might be surprised to learn it has other, less destructive uses."

"You sound afraid."

"I don't need to be afraid. Dr. Haupt has already made his decision."

"And if you walk back in there and tell him you think I should go, he'll change his decision."

"And why would I do that?"

"Because deep down," he said softly, "you know I'm right."

She'd never hated him more than in that moment. His arrogance, his snobbery, the way he strutted around the OMRD like it was his personal fiefdom: she could handle that. She'd grown accustomed to it, even. But this was worse. Much worse. Because she wasn't sure he was wrong. She loved magic and was damn good at it. But was she the magician you wanted on the front lines, with everything at stake? Was she really ready for that kind of responsibility? Would she ever be?

"En garde," she said, and tried to ignore how pleased he looked.

"One touch," he said, backing up to an appropriate distance.

She grabbed the leather pouch. She saw him begin to spin the chunky gold ring he always wore, a gift from his father, if she remembered correctly, embossed with the Cabott family crest: a thistle and a branch. Magic began to hum in the air. "May the best woman win," she said.

You can do this. He doesn't stand a chance.

She took a breath.

Just forget the fact that he was captain of the spell fencing team at St. Cyprian's three years running. And that he went undefeated in their last season, breaking the previous record that had been set by his father, the famous Stephen Cabott. Or the trophies; God, the trophies. Karen was pretty confident that George's real favorite pastime wasn't sport; it was gazing at his own reflection in polished brass.

But Karen knew that spell fencing, like its bladed cousin, was a sport of strategy. To win you certainly had to know your basic techniques: when to use a quick bolt of lightning or a slower burst of fire; which defensive auras could counter which attacks without leaving you without an offense of your own; when you could safely retreat and when to push back. But you had to do more than master your skills; you had to master your opponent. You had to make them think you wanted one thing when in fact you wanted something else entirely. You had to feint and anticipate and react before they even moved.

It was, simply put, a game far too subtle for a man.

"Fence!"

Typically the first moments of a spell fencing bout were less than spectacular to watch; magicians quickly threw up some basic defensive spells to keep from getting caught by a lucky blow early on. With the right shields in place, strategy took over. Do you take out your opponent's outer defenses with a spell of kinetic force? Or do you start to cast that spell, only to turn it to something that would cut deeper at the last minute? Or do you pretend to set more defenses in place, only to counterattack when your opponent tried to wind up for a big spell?

George did exactly what she knew he would. He was a good fencer, maybe great, but not an inventive one. She saw the blur of magical wards come to life as his lips murmured well-worn enchantments, spells that had stood the test of time. Getting through those barriers to hit his body would be difficult. Doing so while defending against his own attacks, which were sure to come any moment, might be impossible.

But since she had no intention of doing that, she wasn't bothered.

Magical defenses, especially the simple ones used in spell fencing, were very specific. It took a lot of energy to block an oncoming spell, so you didn't cast your shield over everything, just what you had to protect. So an attack to his chest would be like cutting through a concrete wall, but an attack elsewhere might be completely unhindered.

And, as it turned out, gold was a marvelous conductor for magical energy. And heat.

Karen finished her spell just as George was ready to start his attack. She could see the gleam in his eyes when he realized how few defenses she'd bothered to put up. This would be over soon, he surely thought, and then she'd know her place. Then the correct order of the universe, with George Alistair Cabott at the top, would be restored. And then . . .

And then his ring, the center of his magical focus, caught on fire.

George screamed and tried to tear the shimmering metal from his finger. In doing so, all his shields vanished in a puff. Karen immediately ceased her spell, or at least she meant to. But for a brief moment, she reveled in that feeling only her magic brought: soothing, yet bracing, like standing in a perfectly hot shower. From the very start, she had known this was what she was meant for.

Then she saw George was on his knees, doubled over in pain, and she cut the magic off in an instant.

It was quiet in the hallway for a moment. Karen was torn between a twinge of guilt at letting the spell go a little too long and the regret she always felt when she had to rein her magic in.

"That hurt." George was breathing heavy.

"I believe the word you are looking for," Karen said, her voice quavering a bit, "is 'touché.'"

"You cheated."

"I won."

His face twitched with a mix of anger and pain. "I shouldn't be surprised. This has always been your problem, in school, and now here. You think just because you're good that you're good enough."

"Which one of us is on the floor, George?"

"You're going to fail," he said, clenching his blistered hand. "You're going to get over there, in the middle of a world you don't understand, and you're going to fail. I only hope someone is there to pick up the pieces when you do."

Karen wanted more than anything to have a good reply, something witty and mean that would have made George think twice about doubting her. But her mind was blank. No words, witty or otherwise, materialized. Just the silence of the hallway, the sting of his rebuke, and the lingering cordite smell of spent magic.

Without a word, she walked past him and down the stairs.

THREE

It was achingly cold, but that came as no surprise. In such a place, comfort would be inappropriate. Comfort invited a man to let down his guard, and only dead men made that mistake here. The colonel waited, as was so often his duty, and listened to the pipes ticking overhead and the watch ticking in his palm. He flipped the watch open. It was a weakness to look, he knew, but he was old enough now not to care. He sighed. The steadily clicking hands were not kind: he would be late. She would, he hoped, forgive him.

The door at the far end of the room groaned and swung out.

Leonid brought their guest in, as requested. The last one for the day. His uniform was mussed, a button missing from his jacket. A struggle, perhaps? No, not from this small man shivering under Leonid's grip, the man with the broken lens in his glasses and the blood on his collar. This man had no fight in him. Perhaps he would not be so late after all.

"Thank you," the colonel said softly, motioning to a waiting chair. "I have a place for our comrade just here."

The man was talking before he had even been forced into his seat. "Comrade Colonel, I assure you—"

The colonel held up a hand and silenced him. Pain erupted just above his right eye at the sound of the man's quavering voice. The headaches were always bad on days such as these. It was too much for one man to take on himself. That sounded like his wife's voice: *You use too much of yourself. There must be others who can do this. Others they can call on instead of my husband.*

But there were no others. No one else who could do what he could.

"I am tired, Artyom Ivanovich. I am tired and I am running late. Let us therefore avoid unnecessary talk."

"Comrade Colonel, whatever has been said of me, I—"

"We have never met, you and I, correct? Yet I trust you know me, perhaps by reputation. This is true?"

Artyom glanced back at the looming shadow of Leonid and nodded. "Yes, Comrade Colonel. I know who you are."

"Good. Then you know by the fact that I am sitting across from you that certain options are now closed. This is not a time for bartering. This is a time to do what must be done. You understand."

"But—"

"This room, do you know what it is for? It is a place for remembering. At times, men must be reminded of the importance of duty. And so they come here. So I can help them. That is why we are here, together, you and I. To do our duty."

"I have done my duty. I always do my duty. I—"

"At the academy, they teach us that magic is nothing more than will." He tapped his temple. "Will. That is why some men can use magic and some cannot: they lack will. Will is what gives us power. Will is what helps us do our duty. Will keeps us from making mistakes."

He clicked open his pocket watch and watched the seconds tick by. "This watch belonged to my grandfather. It still keeps perfect time, even after all these years. It helps me to focus, to impose my will." His fingers snapped it shut, but he could still feel its pulse, that inexorable march. "Since you are lacking will of your own, Artyom Ivanovich, I will lend you some of mine."

Now the words, in tongues ancient and lost, a further focus. The spells, those he had seen done so poorly by those who considered themselves masters, were so simple with the right will.

So simple.

The screams echoed unheard down the long, empty hallways.

T he theater was dark when he entered quietly, the performance nearly complete. He had a ticket for a seat, somewhere near the front, but no way to find it. That did not matter, however, now that he had arrived. He stood invisible in the shadowed back of the theater as the final soloist took the stage.

She was young, yet already growing into the dancer's graceful form. Her golden hair was pulled back tight, her face a powdered porcelain mask. She was smiling, but he saw the determination written beneath. The music began. She moved across the stage, hesitant, slightly behind the music. Uncertain on pointe. No, no. Breathe, he thought. You are better than this. As you have been taught. Yes, like that. There is my daughter. There is my girl.

The first time he had seen her mother had been on a stage like this. She was part of the corps, not yet a soloist, but to him, she had been up there alone, dancing just for him. That had been a lifetime ago, longer perhaps.

Up now, turn and turn. Jump, then back. Yes, she had her steps now. The music was in her, animating her. Ah, a misstep, a near fall. Recovery, yes. Forget it, child. The flaw only makes them see the beauty of the rest.

The applause filled the theater as she took her bow and hurried to the wings on airy steps. He watched her go, content.

"Your daughter, yes?"

He had been distracted by the dance, more so than he would usually allow, and he had not noticed the gray-haired man standing at his side until he spoke.

"Yes," he said.

"She dances with skill," the gray-haired man said.

"Thank you, sir."

"Perhaps we should speak outside?"

They stepped out into the granite chill of a Moscow autumn. Cars passed them by, their drivers invisible behind yellow headlights. An early rain caused their tires to hiss. Old leaves tumbled along empty sidewalks. The colonel followed the gray-haired man to the alley that ran behind the theater and lit his cigarette before lighting one of his own.

"The work is done?" the gray-haired man asked.

"We finished with the list earlier tonight," he answered. "I expect you will find the results satisfactory."

"We always have." The gray-haired man coughed. "The Chairman himself would like to extend to you his thanks."

He bowed, just slightly. "I am honored to serve the Party."

"That is good to hear," the gray-haired man said. Those were his words, but the colonel knew that more than this was being said: in the way he held his dirty-white cigarette, the way his small eyes glanced off into the night, the way his arthritic hands trembled.

"I remain at the behest of the Party," he said. "And of the Chairman."

"Yes," the gray-haired man said, sucking on the cigarette like a man drowning. From his heavy woolen overcoat he produced an envelope and handed it across the stale alleyway air.

The colonel opened it and quickly read the terse documents it contained. "Berlin?"

The gray-haired man nodded, then crushed the half-spent cigarette under his shoe. "A filthy city full of ungrateful people," he said with a shudder. "But an important city as well. We recently received word from a well-placed friend that our adversaries in the city have made a . . . significant discovery. It is imperative that they do not hinder our existing plans. Too much work has already been done. This must be contained."

He tucked the envelope into his coat. Ahead, people had already begun to stream from the theater out into the streets. He took out his watch and checked the time. "You have my word," he said. "I will see this done."

"Yes," the gray-haired man said. "We know that you will. That is why we are sending the Nightingale."

FOUR

Karen touched the leather pouch around her neck. She wasn't sure if magic would help much in the fight to come, but she felt better knowing she could call on it if necessary. She looked up and down the street. Cute houses, trimmed lawns, white fences. Everything appeared safe, but Karen wasn't sure if appearances could be trusted. *If you have to engage the enemy, it is best to do so on favorable ground.* Did Helen's house count? Hard to tell; big sisters were tricky to pin down that way.

She closed her eyes and slowed her breathing. *If he starts yelling, I can just threaten to turn him into a newt.* If only that were a real spell; but then, he didn't know that. Magic to him was scary and unstable, something to be avoided at all costs. Not unlike his youngest daughter. Aware she couldn't hide in her car all afternoon, she turned off the grumbling engine and got out.

And was almost immediately assaulted by a roving band of nine-year-olds.

"Aunt Karen! You came! I told Mom you would!"

"The birthday girl's wish is my command," Karen said, peeling Martha's arms off her legs before they both fell into the street. She held out her gift: a rectangle wrapped hastily in plain brown paper. "Happy birthday."

"Thanks!" Martha said, taking the gift. "Will you do some magic for us? Please?" Martha's eyes were huge and bursting with childish glee; Karen suspected someone had been stealing frosting when her mother wasn't looking. The others, all similarly pigtailed and looking for trouble, added their assent in a high-pitched chorus.

"We'll see," Karen said.

"Mom says you are the greatest magician ever," Martha said eagerly. "Better than all the gross boy magicians."

Karen smirked. "I'm not the greatest yet," she said. "But I'm working on it."

"When you are the greatest, will you blast all the other magicians with fireballs?" Martha asked.

"Or lightning?" another girl chimed in.

"That sounds like something a gross boy magician would do," Karen said, playfully tugging Martha's pigtail. "I'd want to do something with fewer explosions. I'll show you some magic later, if your mom says it's okay."

With their demands for a performance agreed to, the gaggle let Karen pass unmolested. She wandered inside to the kitchen, where she found her sister looking oddly grown-up. Karen leaned against the doorjamb and said, "Remember when you used to try to get Mom and Dad to forbid me from coming to your birthday parties? Now you beg me to come to Martha's."

Helen dropped the sandwich she was hurriedly assembling and reached for a hug. "You made it," she said, sounding more than a bit relieved.

"The drive from the city wasn't bad."

"It wasn't the drive I was worried about."

"Fair enough," Karen replied, eyeing the white and pink cake for finger marks. "When are they supposed to get here?"

"Any minute now. You going to be alright?"

"Looks like you could use some help with those sandwiches."

Helen smiled; she looked a lot like their mom when she did that. When had that happened?

"You got a magic spell to make sandwiches?" Helen asked.

"I wish," Karen said, grabbing a knife and a slice of white bread. "If magicians could do that, we might have more fans."

"I'd certainly sign up," Helen said. After a pause, she asked, "This government job of yours, are they treating you alright? Seems like it might be a hard place to work for a woman. If you need me to go down and tell them to be nice to you . . ."

Karen stuck out her tongue. "I have a master's degree in theoretical magic, I have my own apartment, and sometimes I even do my own laundry. When should I expect you'll start treating me like an adult?"

"When you stop being my little sister," Helen said. "And you didn't answer my question."

"They treat me fine," Karen said. Slapping a sandwich together, she sighed. "When they aren't expecting me to be someone's secretary."

"Nothing wrong with being a secretary," Helen said.

"Nothing at all," Karen said, "if that's your actual job title."

"Good point," Helen said. "And how do you react when they behave like pigs?"

"By keeping my mouth shut," Karen said.

Helen's arched eyebrow was having none of it. "You would lie to me in my own kitchen?"

Karen rolled her eyes. ". . . or by shooting my mouth off until they get so angry you can see steam coming out of their ears."

"That sounds more like my little sister," Helen said. She wiped her hands on her apron and forced Karen to look at her. "You don't have to sink to their level, you know. I tell Martha all the time. Just because the boys are misbehaving doesn't give you the right to do the same."

"Thanks, Mom."

The doorbell chimed through the house. "You must have magic powers," Helen said, wriggling her fingers. "You speak the words and evil spirits materialize." Helen smiled again, but this time it was the wry grin Karen remembered from when they were kids. So there was still some of her sister wrapped in that apron after all.

"You have a back door, right? I can make a run for it?"

"You know the deal," Helen said, wiping her hands and heading for the door. "You tell him, or I will."

Karen could smell her mother's perfume as soon as the door opened. Hugging her was like holding on to a soft, fragrant cloud; hugging her father, rather, was like wrapping her arms around a bristling tree stump.

"Helen didn't tell us you were going to be here," her dad said.

"So what a wonderful surprise," her mom said, cutting in. "Isn't it, Roger? A wonderful surprise."

They were saved by the arrival of the birthday girl and her merry band and their unionized demands for cake and presents. After some tense negotiations, Helen brokered a deal for cake after lunch, but while they were waiting, couldn't Aunt Karen do some magic for them? Never one to defy the will of the people, Helen gave her sister an apologetic glance, then her blessing.

They assembled in the living room, the kids on the floor. Her mother, true to form, followed Helen into the kitchen and her dad, suddenly without an ally, settled alone onto the lime-green couch. Karen didn't bother to look at him; she knew what she'd see. Consistency had always been his prime virtue.

"Can you light something on fire?" one of the girls asked.

"Can you kill someone with magic?"

"Or make a boy like you?"

Karen rattled off quick answers: "Yes; I'm not going to answer that; and you're too young for that question." What could she show them that was just the right balance of impressive and safe? She could feel the heat of her father's scowl. To him, there was no such thing as safe magic. Roger O'Neil was wrong about a lot of things, but he might actually be right about that one.

"Alright girls, close your eyes," she said. She chose a simple spell, though even the easiest magic required a level of focus that could be difficult to muster while being scrutinized by a small child army. She touched the leather pouch and the familiar gesture calmed her. She breathed out, said the words of the spell, and flung her free hand into the air.

A dozen pinpricks of light, one for each partygoer, danced in the air above the woolly shag carpet. They were red and blue, purple, white, and green, all flickering and pulsing like distant stars, casting Independence Day colors across the living room.

The unanimous murmuring of astonishment proved the girls weren't very good at following directions but at least appreciated a good show.

Now this was the interesting part. She'd done this before, but never with an audience. *Ignore them. Focus.* Gripping the pouch a little harder, Karen closed her eyes. She didn't need to see the lights; she could feel them, minute extensions of her will. This part wasn't covered by Dr. Eckstein in Intro to Illumination Magic. This part wasn't in any of the textbooks either.

She reached out with her thoughts and touched the lights. Gently at first, until she held each one. Then, without words, without the confines of an age-old spell or timeworn incantation, she made them dance.

The lights swung wildly around the room like a confused meteor shower, spinning about each partygoer until she collapsed in dizziness or delight, then resting finally like a fairy crown on little Martha's radiant curls.

Karen opened her eyes. It had worked. It really worked. She knew it would; she had tried it enough times. But seeing it in action, magic as an act of will rather than correct recitation, never failed to make her heart soar.

Then she made the mistake of looking at her dad. That vein was throbbing on his forehead. His right hand clutched the arm of the couch in a death grip; his left kneaded the leg that had never been the same since it took a spray of shrapnel outside of Paris. He looked like he was back there, ready to fight, ready to defend what he loved against something he hated.

"My goodness!" Mom came in from the kitchen with a platter of sandwiches and nearly dropped them when she saw the scene. Karen's focus ruined, the lights popped into a shower of harmless sparks and the girls broke into applause.

Perhaps it was the applause that helped Karen recover. This was for Martha, after all; if Dad didn't like it, he knew where the door was.

"Remember, girls," Karen said to her rapt audience, "recent studies show that women have a fifteen percent higher chance of being born with magical ability and up to twenty percent higher magical aptitude, so make sure your parents let you take the tests."

"I want to be a magician!" one of the girls said.

Not to be outdone, the rest quickly agreed.

When Karen looked up, her dad was gone.

Helen appeared at her side. "Don't worry about him," she said quietly, "he'll be fine." She pressed a napkin into Karen's hand.

"What's this?"

Helen gestured covertly toward Karen's face just as she felt the blood. Karen quickly turned away and pressed the cloth to her nose. "Occupational hazard," she said with a laugh.

Helen tried to smile, but ended up looking concerned instead, and more like Mom than ever.

When Karen turned back toward the house after depositing the bags of garbage in the bins on the street, her dad was waiting on the porch.

"Your sister said you wanted to talk to me," he said, not looking at her.

"Did she," Karen said. "How sweet."

He said nothing: his default answer.

Karen sighed. Well, she'd delayed long enough. "They're sending me to West Germany, Dad. I'm already packed. I leave tomorrow."

"Germany," he said, suddenly feeling verbose.

"Berlin, actually."

"That's in East Germany."

"Only part of it is."

"This for that job of yours?"

"Yes, Dad. A request came in from the State Department for a magical expert and they're sending me."

"To Berlin."

"That is what I said."

"To do magic."

"Yes."

He blew out a mouthful of air and looked like he had nothing more to say.

"Look, I know how you feel—"

"This isn't about how I feel," he said. His face was getting red; the vein was returning to the surface. "This is about what's right."

"And what's that, Dad?"

"Karen, magic . . . it's just not right."

"Oh, yes, I remember: magic is for the krauts."

"Tell me I'm wrong," he said, a shaking finger solidifying his argument. "Tell me half the people you work for aren't krauts, or worse, just plain Nazis."

"I don't work for Nazis, Dad. I work for the government. Just because someone is from Germany doesn't mean they're—"

"You weren't there, young lady. You didn't see what I saw."

That didn't take long. "No, but I've heard about what you saw, many, many times, and I suspect I'm about to—"

"Good men died, even if you and your generation want to forget that. Good men were incinerated, blown to bits by your precious magic. You think it is all pretty lights and fun games, but I've seen what magic really does. I've seen what it's really for."

"You saw good men shot too, but I don't hear you trying to outlaw guns."

"Magic isn't American, Karen. We didn't use it and we won. Everybody else . . . see what good it did. The Germans used it and see what good they offered the world. The Japs and the Russians too. You tell me how they made this world a better place with magic."

This was why she hadn't wanted to come. People don't change, least of all old men who have to limp around on a daily reminder of the worst mankind has to offer. If she'd been in Europe during the war, maybe she would feel the same. But she couldn't live her father's life. "Dad, I wasn't looking for your permission. My country asked for my help and I'm going. I thought maybe you'd understand that."

At first she thought he wasn't even going to bother to reply. It might have been better if he hadn't. "There are ways for a woman to help her country," he said, "but this isn't one of them."

Karen shifted her weight back on her heels. "Is this because I'm a magician or because I'm a woman? Pick one prejudice and focus on that—it'll help you make your point better next time."

"Young lady—"

"Tell Helen it was a swell party. And tell Mom I'm proud of her for sticking it out with her close-minded bastard of a husband."

If he responded, she didn't hear it over the sound of her car door slamming or the engine roaring to life or the tires cheering like nine-year-old girls as she made her escape.

FIVE

The plane, like everything in this city, was late. The Germans were supposed to be the model of efficiency, but after two years stationed in Berlin, Jim was skeptical. At times he wondered if the ever-present delays and disruptions were the city's way of getting even with its conquerors: vengeance by way of bureaucracy. Or maybe bombing Germany back to the Stone Age had been more successful than anyone had realized.

". . . the Knights Templar, if you can believe it," Dennis was saying.

"What?"

"The Knights Templar," he repeated. "They owned all this. That's why they call it Tempelhof."

Jim frowned. "The Knights Templar owned an airport?"

"Sure," Dennis said. He was leaning against the car, his hat pushed back. "Of course, it was pretty hard to get a flight back then, since the airplane wouldn't be invented for another eight hundred years."

"And when were sarcastic little know-it-alls invented?"

"During the Renaissance, I believe."

"Is that why Arthur made me bring you?" Jim asked. "To bore me to death?"

"I think he sent me because he doesn't trust you alone with our visitor."

"What? I'm the perfect gentleman."

"Right," Dennis said. "So all those stories they tell back at HQ . . ."

"All lies, pal," Jim said. "Except the good ones."

He thought briefly (and maybe a little wistfully) about the girls he'd left behind. He doubted any would even remember him, gone these long years on his grand spy adventure overseas. He checked his watch. Some adventure. After failing out of magician school and scraping by at Harvard, he'd been awestruck by the Agency recruiter who had asked for a moment of his time. A real-life spy, he had thought. What they hadn't told him that day outside his dorm was that spying was less action and drama and more of this: waiting. Lots and lots of waiting.

Still, it wasn't like he had anything better to do, and being a spy, even a bored spy, was better than any other job opportunity back in Little Rock.

"What do you think about all this?" Jim asked.

"All what?"

He waved his hands to encompass their surroundings. "The hole in the Wall, us bringing over a magician from Stateside," he said. "Arthur seems crankier than usual, and I wasn't sure that was even possible."

"Of course he is. Like all real red-blooded Americans," Dennis said, "magic gives him the willies. Even worse that he had to ask for help from the OMRD. He'd rather ask Hitler's ghost."

"You really think the Reds will start something?"

"If that spell fails and yonder Wall comes tumbling down,"

Dennis said, "we're suddenly sitting on the most dangerous border in the world. You've seen the reports: those East Germans are killing themselves to get over the Wall now. What do you think they'll do if it suddenly vanishes in a puff of smoke?"

"Kill themselves all the same," Jim said, looking up at the stars beginning to dot the evening sky. "Just with a shorter jump at the end." He nodded up at a flashing set of lights descending from the heavens. "Make yourself presentable, pal; I believe our girl is here."

Jim snatched the file from the passenger seat and flipped it open as the plane came in overhead. There was a picture clipped to the file: young, cute, short brown hair, green eyes (the picture was black-and-white, but the dossier filled out the salient details). She'd been two years behind him at St. Cyprian's, but unlike him, had sailed through with enough honors and accolades to require two extra pages stapled behind. No criminal record, no improper political ties. A perfect all-American girl, except for the whole magic thing. Her parents (Roger and Doris, registered Democrats, married twenty-nine years) had probably wanted her to become something respectable, like a nurse or a secretary. Instead, right out of college she'd gone off and joined the bastard child of American government agencies: the OMRD. Probably a lot of weeping and gnashing of teeth over that decision.

The passengers were coming out now. Mostly military, some old fat men in suits, and then there she was. Wearing a loose-fitting knit sweater and pants (what would Doris think of that outfit?), she would have looked more natural on the Harvard quad than waiting for her CIA contact on the tarmac at Tempelhof.

"Miss O'Neil?" Jim said as they approached.

There was something lively about the way she looked at them, something he liked and something he wasn't sure he could handle. "You must be my contacts," she said.

"My name is James, but I insist that you call me Jim." He took her hand in both of his. "Welcome to Berlin. Thank you for coming to our aid in this time of crisis." Next to him, Dennis coughed and Jim fought back a glare. "Allow me to introduce Dennis, the tiny unpleasant fellow next to me."

"You can ignore most everything he says," Dennis said as he shook her hand. "We certainly do."

"Don't mind him," Jim said. "He didn't get his nap today." Before Dennis could offer his best attempt at a witty reply, Jim added, "Please, let me carry your bag for you."

"There's no need, James," she said, her mouth turned in a coy smile. She had something hanging around her neck, a well-worn leather pouch. She reached up and touched it, eyes slightly closed, and whispered a few words. A moment later, her heavy luggage began to hover off the tarmac.

Jim quickly grabbed it out of the air; it was heavier than it looked. "I appreciate your capabilities, Miss O'Neil," he said, trying not to sound like he was struggling with the weight of the bag, "but we'd rather not call attention to them in such a public space."

She glanced around, her sly grin gone, those green eyes suddenly very aware of their surroundings. "I'm sorry, I didn't . . ." She dropped her hand from the pouch and nodded. "Well, if you are going to carry my bag, you can call me Karen."

Jim hadn't been that impressed with Berlin when he'd first arrived (you've seen one big, dirty city, you've seen them all), but on the drive back from Tempelhof, Karen had the uninitiated's curiosity and a dozen questions about every landmark they passed. To him, they looked the same: gray buildings, cracked statues, empty churches. Not to mention the occasional blockade or tank.

Luckily Dennis could provide the running commentary, though that left Jim with uncomfortably little to add to the conversation.

"First time out of the country?" Jim asked during a brief lull in her inquiries.

"Is it that obvious?"

"Not at all," Jim said. "I'm a spy, after all. Reading people is my job." Dennis snorted, but Jim ignored him. "I remember my first time in Berlin. It was amazing. All this history—"

"You don't care about history," Dennis said.

"I care about history," Jim said. "Just not when you're talking about it."

"What about the Wall?" Karen asked. "Are we going to drive by it? Magic on that scale . . . it's almost unprecedented in human history. I've read the studies on it, but I'm sure that's nothing compared to seeing the real thing."

"Yeah," Jim said. "The Wall's great. But we should probably take you to see the boss first. He feels lonely when he's left out."

Karen seemed disappointed. For the first time since they'd started driving, she fell silent and took to staring out the window at the city flashing by.

"So," Jim said to fill the silence, "that pouch around your neck, that's your locus, right?"

A hand went protectively up. "You have magical training?"

"Jim here's a bona fide wizard," Dennis said with a chuckle. "He's got this fire spell that will knock your socks off, and if you're lucky, only figuratively."

"I took the tests in school," Jim said with a sour look lobbed at Dennis. The other agent didn't seem to notice. "I had enough aptitude to get into St. Cyprian's, but not enough to stay there. I never made it to the spells hard enough to require a locus. Just a few words in Latin or Late Middle Japanese and some fancy finger-wiggling."

"But it's all the same," Karen said, shifting in the seat toward Jim. "It's all about concentration and focus. That's what the locus is for: a talisman to help you channel that focus. But there's this idea, called Universal Expression Theory, which says that the spells and the hand waving, they aren't really necessary. It's all just to help us focus on what we want the spell to do. We don't need any of it."

A looker who was both smart and enthusiastic. Nothing like the usual dregs Washington sent over. Jim was fairly certain this was the best thing to happen to him during his entire tour in Berlin. "So what's the alternative?"

"Magic. Just magic. Not just repeating the same spells done by every magician since the dawn of time. Real magic as an expression of the magician, magic by thought, not recitation. I wrote my dissertation all about it. It isn't well regarded by the traditional . . ." She suddenly turned red. "Sorry, I didn't mean to babble. I just don't get a lot of chances to talk magic outside of work."

"Well, I never got far enough for any theories," Jim said. He felt less dumb when she was asking questions about Berlin history he didn't know. "Luckily the CIA doesn't care much if you can do magic. In fact, they probably prefer . . . I mean, not that . . ."

"No, go on, Jimbo," Dennis said. "Tell our guest here all about how the CIA loves and respects magical practitioners."

"I'm used to people wanting to burn me at the stake," Karen said. "Magic is just misunderstood, but that's changing. Americans need to realize that magic is part of this world, and if we want to compete with Russia, we've got to start caring about magical progress as much as technological."

"Until magic wins us a war like the bomb won the last one," Jim said, "I think that might be an uphill battle."

He was never good at identifying the wrong thing to say before he opened his mouth, but he had a talent for realizing it after the words came out. Karen turned away, her eyes drawn away from him and back to the dreary concrete and dead trees of Berlin.

"That's just it," she said, almost too quiet to hear over the sound of the car engine. "If we were any good with magic, we might not have needed the bomb. Think of the lives we might have spared."

Even Dennis didn't have a witty reply to that. Luckily they were saved by their arrival at headquarters.

"We've arrived at the next stop on our tour of the most boring landmarks in Berlin," Jim said as he put the car into park. "Let's go introduce you to BOB."

SIX

When Jim turned onto a quaint street called Föhrenweg on the western outskirts of Berlin and parked across from an unexceptional building, Karen couldn't help but be surprised. What had she expected? A bunker? A militarized compound with razor wire and guard towers? A glowing sign announcing the headquarters of the CIA in Berlin? Such ideas made her feel childish, but still she couldn't get over how normal it all appeared.

She followed her handlers inside. It looked like any other office building, except of course for the armed guard sitting behind bulletproof glass watching their arrival with professional skepticism. Karen could only see from the chest up, but his shoulders were linebacker wide and his neck bulged thicker than his bald head. He looked like a cross between a rhinoceros and a brick wall.

"Hey, Earl," Jim said cheerily. "How's the day shift?"

Earl grunted.

He checked identification for Jim and Dennis, then searched a clipboard for record of Karen's visit. After staring at her for what felt like a good five minutes, he pushed a red button with a hand that looked better suited for cracking skulls and as a buzzer sounded the door in front of them clanked open.

Past the main security entrance, her garrulous guides took her through a series of locked doors, some of which she sensed were magically warded, though she wondered if Jim or Dennis even knew. The wards were old, probably in place for five years or more, and not minor spells either; a serious magician had secured this otherwise innocuous-looking location against all manner of magical intrusion. Perhaps the Americans weren't so bad at putting magic to use after all. Or, more likely, they'd had help.

Berlin, after all, was buzzing with magic. She had felt it thrumming the moment the plane landed. Like white noise, like radio static, it could fade into the background, but when she focused on it, it was more like standing in the ocean rolling in at high tide. It had to be the Wall. Most major cities had all sorts of magical networks crisscrossing them like a street map, but no other city on earth could boast encapsulation by a twenty-foot-high barrier of pure magical energy. No wonder the magic was loud here; she'd be lucky to hear anything else.

Jim ducked his head in an open doorway. "And here you are, my dear June," he said, holding out the car keys with a flourish to a middle-aged woman in a floral-print dress. "With nary a scratch on it."

"And a full tank?" the woman—June—asked with a raised eyebrow.

"Karen," Jim said, "this is June, master of the CIA motor pool. If you ever need a vehicle, don't even think about asking her, because she'll just make you fill it up on your own dime. And on my meager salary!"

June held out a hand and Karen gently squeezed it. "Pleased to meet you," she said.

"A word of advice, dearie," June said through a slow Alabama drawl. "Just forget everything these two dummies tell you, and you'll do fine here."

"That seems to be common advice."

Dennis snorted. "You should probably listen to her."

"Ignore both of them," Jim said. "The tour continues."

On the second floor, they entered a large open room awash with noise and activity. "And this is the center of it all," Jim said. The far wall was nearly covered by a neatly annotated map of Berlin. Thin gray lines denoted the various districts, color-coded to show which occupying power held sway: in the north, blue for the French in Reinickendorf; in the west, brown for the British in Spandau and Charlottenburg; green in the south for the USA in Zehlendorf and Tempelhof; and of course red in the east for the USSR in Treptow, Auttenberg, and Pankow. A dark black outline hemmed in the Western districts on all sides. From this vantage, it was hard to see if the Wall was to keep them in or the Soviets out.

The center of the room was dominated by a large oak table flanked by hard-looking chairs and piled with informational detritus: files stuffed with documents blackened by the myriad of available typewriters lining the wall opposite the map; at least four separate telephones, each a different color and shape; grainy aerial photographs arrayed like a fan; notes and reports and dossiers and who knew what else. Karen wondered if there was some sort of mad organization to the mess. She doubted it.

Jim introduced her to a few of the people milling about, including the cadre of silver-haired women manning the typewriters. Most were American, but a few had a noticeable German accent. They were polite and looked at her with a mix of maternal warmth and pity.

"This is the bullpen," Jim said, taking the whole room in with a sweep of his hand. "All our operations start and end right here."

"It's a bit . . . chaotic," Karen said over the low hum of a dozen conversations and the metallic rainfall of the typewriters.

"Nothing good ever gets done without a little chaos," he said.

The door to an office attached at one side of the bullpen opened and a handful of men jostled out, each looking eager to escape. Most were of an age with Jim and Dennis, though a few were older. All of them had the blanched faces of the reprimanded.

"Rough meeting, Milt?" Jim asked the first man to pass them. He looked to Karen like a storm cloud: dark, puffy, and ready to ruin someone's picnic.

"Milton," he said slowly. "To you, Mr. Garriety or 'sir.' Is that understood?"

"Sure," Jim said as he put his hands up, adding, "sir."

His thunderhead eyes turned on Karen. "This the magician?"

"In the flesh, Mr. Garriety, sir," Jim said.

"Lovely," he said, rolling his sunken eyes. "Bad enough they have to send us a magician, and then they go and send us a woman. Lord help us." Before Jim could reply or Karen could set his tie on fire, he groaned and vanished out the door.

"Head of Espionage," Jim said when he was gone. "Wonderful man. Great with kids."

Karen decided Milt would get along splendidly with George Cabott.

"Bill!" Jim called as the rest of the agents filed past. "What's the story?"

A red-haired man with a boyish collection of freckles on his cheeks looked up and did his best to offer a smile. "Boss is on the rampage," he said before offering his hand to Karen. "Bill Holland. Sorry that you got assigned these jokers. All the real agents were too busy."

"Busy with what, exactly?" Dennis asked.

"Sitting on our hands, if you ask the boss. He thinks the Commies, German or Russian variety, are behind this Wall nonsense, and that they are up to something. Something big."

"And are they?"

"Who knows?" He let out a long sigh. "I guess we're supposed to find out."

Jim patted him on the shoulder. "Well, keep fighting the good fight, pal. Tell your lady friends I said hello."

"Sorry again," Bill said to Karen as he ducked out.

"Good spy," Jim said. "Specializes in getting hookers to inform on their johns."

"Hookers?" Karen said.

"Uh, you know," Jim said. "Prostitutes. Real fonts of intel. Men will say all sorts of things they aren't supposed to when they're . . . well . . ."

"Go on," Karen said, enjoying watching Jim's cheeks flush. "You were talking about men saying stupid things around women." She thought for a moment. "What did he mean by 'Wall nonsense'?"

"Right," Jim said. "That's why you're here. But we'd probably better let the chief explain that one."

The humming noise of the bullpen died down as one last man exited the office. He wore his middle age hard, not unlike the rumpled suit that hung badly from his shoulders and struggled to restrain an expanding gut. What remained of his grizzled hair was buzzed short in a style Karen recognized all too well; her father, even years out of the uniform, had never been comfortable with a civilian's haircut. This man had an alcoholic's nose, an insomniac's bruised eyes, and an old soldier's handshake.

"You must be our magician," he said.

"And you must be Bob," Karen replied, smiling.

Dennis and Jim snickered. They seemed nice enough, though she hadn't expected the first CIA agents she met to remind her so much of the preening boys she knew in middle school.

"The name's Arthur," he said. He wasn't laughing; he glanced at Jim and Dennis and then they weren't either. "This is BOB: Berlin Operating Base. CIA headquarters on our little island in the Red Sea. I thought they'd send your boss."

He was blunt for a spy. "Dr. Haupt felt," Karen said with a slight hesitation, "that I would be up to the task. Though, we weren't exactly provided with any details on what that task would be."

"Hazards of the job," Arthur said. "Everything we send over the wire has a chance of ending up in Moscow." He looked Karen over again, seemingly doubtful. "I also imagine Director Haupt wasn't too thrilled at the idea of a return trip to the Fatherland. Not with a history like his."

"I'm not sure what you . . ." Karen began, but Arthur wasn't listening.

He grabbed his coat and hat. "I'll have someone take your things to your quarters," he said, nodding at her suitcase. "Grab whatever you need and let's go save the free world."

"It's grown."

Dennis consulted a chart. "It's nearly two inches wide now."

Karen had been briefed about the breach on the drive over, and "brief" certainly seemed the right word to describe it. They didn't know much, and what they knew, they didn't like. She wondered if Dr. Haupt would have made a different choice if he had known why the OMRD'd been called in to consult.

"Has the area been swept for interference?" she asked as she knelt by the crackling Wall. So much energy. This was magic on a scale usually only theorized. "Or checked for disruption nets? At least purged of the latent magic bleed?"

"Umm . . ." Jim said, looking around.

"Magic is not our area of expertise, Miss O'Neil," Arthur said. With the wan light of the Wall reflecting on his skin, he looked to be made of melting wax. "That's why you're here. Tell us what you need and you'll have it. But this is your show."

Alright then. She did her best to force an image of a sneering George from her thoughts and focused on the task ahead. "What exactly are you hoping for me to do here?"

"Fix it," Arthur said. "Or at least tell us what, or who, is taking it down."

Right, she thought. Easy. Just fix some inexplicable problem with the most complex magic ever cast, and try not to cause a war while you're at it. Very helpful. She flipped open her satchel and rummaged around for the necessary tools: chalk for runes and marking any existing ley lines, pulverized lime for shielding, pencil and notepad to write down the hundred questions she already had, and an apple in case she got hungry.

"Settle in, gentlemen," she said without looking back at the agents watching her, "this is going to take a while."

Arthur made a noise that sounded like a snort then said, "Keep me posted." He ducked out of the makeshift tent.

Karen touched her locus and felt the nerves that had been warring in her stomach start to settle. The magic was there, just waiting for her to ask for it. The answers would be there too, she knew, if she just knew where to look. This was why she had worked so hard and put up with so much, so that she could use her gift to do something that mattered. Without that, magic was just a game and it had always been more than that to her. It was why she got out of bed in the morning, why she put up with condescending men and disapproving glances and the eye-watering headaches. Because with the right ingredients, the world bent to her will.

"Don't you boys have something better to do than supervise me? Catching Russian spies or something like that?"

Jim chuckled; he was probably checking her out while she worked. "Nope," he said. "Right now, this is the most important place in the world."

Thanks, she thought. No pressure.

SEVEN

The train groaned into the station at Friedrichstraße a few minutes after dawn, but despite the early hour, none of the men in the cabin slept. This was enemy territory after all, or near enough to it, and they were at war, no matter what the politicians might claim. And these men had been honed for war.

The colonel had taken his time when selecting his assistants. Weak links were no more acceptable than failure. There had been a few mistakes when he first began his work, but they had been identified and purged. Unworthy men always revealed themselves, in time.

Kirill sat by the door. He was a young man still, though with a face of indeterminate age. A war orphan, he had been enrolled at the People's Institute for Magical Instruction outside Murmansk when he crippled another student during magical combat training. He was expelled and sent to a labor camp. It was probably for the best; not knowing what to do with someone more powerful than them, his teachers had beat and bored him. The colonel traveled to the labor camp to meet the ill-fated boy, and had been impressed by his power and his capacity for hate. Both skills were useful and dangerous. He often found himself somewhat afraid of Kirill, which was how he knew Kirill was indispensable.

Across from him in the cramped compartment was Leonid, his solid arms crossed over his massive chest. They had met in the ruins of war. Germany's surprise suicidal invasion had burned across Russia for months but had mired in an unyielding Soviet winter. Despite presenting a temptingly large target for German snipers among the blasted rubble, Leonid had proven astonishingly difficult to kill. When the momentum swung back toward Berlin, the colonel and Leonid had ridden it together, and together had repaid in full measure the blood debt on Germany for its crimes. Leonid had no magical aptitude, but even Kirill gave the big man a wide berth. Across his cheek and nose, he wore a permanent reminder of those unpleasant days: a large curved scar, an unwelcome gift from a German bomb.

It was Leonid who broke the hours-long silence. "What do we do first?" he said. There was little formality among them. Rank had its uses, but his connection and control of his team went far deeper than any insignia on his collar could muster.

"Containment," he said. "The West knows little, and we must keep it that way."

The train shuddered and stopped. It could no longer be avoided: they were in Berlin. "Both of you go to Karlshorst and review their files on known Western agents operating in East Berlin. Monitor the checkpoints. They will come. They must. And when they do, you will be waiting. We will know what they know. And ensure they do not learn more."

Leonid grunted. "And where will you go?"

He looked out the window, nearly opaque with grime. "We are guests in a foreign land," he said. He recalled drinking fouled water from blasted craters, the whine of German artillery shells falling on a city they had already reduced mostly to char, and the first time he had seen German pyromancers at work on a squad of unprepared Russian infantry. It was the smell that lingered in his thoughts. He had not been able to eat meat since. "I will show our hosts the respect they are due."

"My apologies, Colonel, but we were not informed of your arrival. If the proper communication channels had been utilized, then we would be in a better position to offer assistance." The man who sat across the meager desk from him had a forgettable face, a perfunctory smile, and narrowed eyes that did not seem to blink. He spoke softly, but clearly enough to be heard. His hands were always in motion when he was speaking, but never enough to distract. His office was small, neat, and precise. He was, it seemed, perfectly suited to be the spymaster for the German Ministry of State Security.

"Perhaps," he continued, that smile almost a taunt, "I can contact my colleagues at the Administration for the Use of Magic and they will be able to offer their input into this matter." He reached for the flesh-colored telephone on his desk, but the colonel placed his hand on the receiver.

"I have been misunderstood," he said. He had not slept well on the train, though in truth he had not slept well in many nights. Sleep, it appeared, was only for the young. "I have not come to ask for your assistance. It was your *assistance* that has led us to this unfortunate situation."

The man's smile wavered. The eyes narrowed further. "Every report I have seen on this project shows it to be a remarkable success so far. We have every confidence. Every confidence. Besides, Colonel, need I remind you that this project belongs to the German Democratic Republic."

"As will the failures," he said. "And their consequences."

Nearly a minute came and went with only the dull buzz of the lightbulbs to disturb the silence. Then the director abandoned his smile and asked simply, "Then why are you here?"

"You and I met once before," the colonel said. "It was some years ago, in Moscow. Nineteen forty-nine. You had not yet completed your ascension to power, but I clearly remember you. It is said that you are elusive. It is said that you fashion yourself a man who stays in the shadows, a worker of string in a world of puppets. It is said that you are skilled. That your people fear you. That the West fears you."

He watched his words, no more magical than the headlines of *Pravda,* do their work on this great man of the German Democratic Republic. Magic was a vital tool, yet he would not walk into a building like House 1 of the Ministry of State Security, so interlaced with magical wards that it was difficult to breathe, without other tools at his disposal.

"I am afraid," the director said, those raptor eyes masking uncharacteristic unease, "that I do not remember you."

"Nor would I expect you to. I do not say that because I am a humble man nor because I believe myself unremarkable." The colonel leaned forward. He realized his hand was on his pocket watch, a reflex, but unnecessary here. "I say this to make a point: there are two types of forgettable men in this world, those who are elusive and those who are unknown. An elusive man can do many things, as I am certain you know. He can unseat kings. He can topple empires."

He felt the ticking of time against the palm of his hand. Now he allowed himself a smile. "But an unknown man," he said, "such a man can do anything."

He stood and turned for the door. Enough time wasted on politicians.

"Colonel, a moment." The director had let his voice take on the tone of a man who was unaccustomed to defiance. A weakness. "You did not answer my question. Why are you here?"

"Comrade Director," he said with a sigh, "let me speak plainly, for my time is valuable. I am here in Berlin to clean up your mess. I am here in your office to tell you to stay out of my way."

The apartment building was just far enough away from the Wall to have escaped the purge. Those too close to the Wall had been evacuated "for the protection and safety of its inhabitants" after a man died attempting to jump from a rooftop into West Berlin. Shortly thereafter, they had been demolished to make way for the guard towers and sandpits. But this building survived and to any observer (and in Berlin there were always observers) it was unremarkable. Men and women came and went. Lights in the windows turned on and off. Garbage accumulated in its alleys. It was nearly impossible to tell the upper floors were abandoned, the lower floors were occupied by security forces, and the basement area was a research facility for the East German Administration for the Use of Magic.

The colonel was ushered inside through a covered back entrance and quickly escorted to the basement. He did not speak to the guards, nor the assistants who met him at the rune-scrawled door. They were gears in the machine: vital but replaceable. They did not need to know him or his purpose.

"Colonel, welcome to our facility." The speaker was a trim, neatly groomed, tired-looking German man nearing sixty. His hands were steady, his eyes alert, his gait unhindered; unlike many men of his generation, he appeared to have survived Germany's wars unscathed. He spoke Russian with little trace of a German accent and did not bother to smile as he invited the colonel into a makeshift library.

"Comrade Ehle," the colonel said as he inspected the spines of the tomes neatly arranged on nearby shelves. "Your earlier work is known to me." Though his eyes were on the books, he did not fail to notice how his words landed hard on his host. For some men, their past was the heaviest burden they would ever bear.

"And your reputation is known to me, Colonel," Ehle said carefully. Interesting. He was well informed. The colonel wondered from where that information came.

"How progresses the operation here?" he asked, switching the conversation to German.

"Slowly," Ehle said. He stood near the center of the room, his arms at his sides. He was nervous but attempting not to show it. Something to hide? Or perhaps he knew more about the colonel's reputation than he should. "As I have clearly stated in my monthly reports. This is no small matter you have commissioned, Colonel. We did our original work well. You cannot expect us to undo it easily."

"I am here," he said as he extracted a book from the shelf, "because there is a concern that you have not reported everything, at least, not to Moscow." The book felt weighty in his hands. It was bound in leather and filled with old, thick paper, the way books ought to be made.

"Your support has been greatly appreciated in this effort," Ehle said. He was now staring at the book. "We have no reason to hide results from you."

"Perhaps not," he said. He opened the book to the title page. The book was an eighteenth-century treatise written by a German magician on the study of magical containment fields. "But perhaps you have a reason to hide failures."

"Failures? This project has been nothing but a series of failures since we began. I have not hidden this."

"Unintended successes then."

Before the colonel realized it, Ehle had crossed the distance between them and snatched the book from his hand, replacing it carefully on the shelf. "Colonel, you doubtlessly have many duties pressing on your time. Perhaps I can be of more assistance if you state your concerns directly."

The colonel did not trust this man. He was accustomed to distrusting anyone outside of his team, but something about Ehle sharpened that sense. At present he had no reason other than instinct, but at present, instinct was enough.

"The Wall, Comrade. The Wall which maintains order in this cursed city that is waiting to be ravaged again by war."

"I am familiar with the Wall, Colonel."

"There is a breach, Herr Ehle," he said. "Near Sebastianstraße. The West has discovered it. Now they are asking questions, questions that might lead them to look where they would otherwise not. Questions that will undermine this entire project before it can be brought to fruition."

The color drained from Ehle's face as the colonel spoke. If this was an act, he was a skilled performer. "A breach? Where?"

"Did you cause it?"

"No," he said, "it is not possible." The attempt at confidence was gone now. "Our work is progressing, both on the Wall and the barriers beyond it. But we have not . . . the Wall should not have been affected."

The colonel took out his pocket watch. The day was already half gone with little to show for it. These Germans may be content to waste their time and plead excuses, but not him. The Chairman would want to hear of results, of progress. He felt the magic stirring in his fingertips, felt it itching his tongue. He wondered how Ehle would respond to his spells. Their records stated he had been a great magician once; the colonel was not certain what he was now. A relic. A formality. But it did not matter. His services were required by the Party and so he was safe. Useful men, with few exceptions, were spared his severe attentions.

"Your task remains unchanged. The timeline, however, has accelerated. Slow progress and no progress are two paths to the same unpleasant destination. I am only interested in complete success, and I am *very* interested."

Ehle gathered himself. The colonel wondered what calculations this experienced mind had been doing. "We will redouble our efforts," Ehle said, speaking in Russian once again. "And we will keep Moscow informed on our swift progress."

"You will keep me informed," he said, in German. "I intend to remain to see this work to its end, Herr Ehle."

EIGHT

The American met her where he always did: along Oranienburgerstraße, not far from the river, just after 10:00 p.m. He
wore what he always wore: a long coat and a cheap red scarf
that matched his hair. He smiled, again like always, and when he
did he looked like he was ten years old. The other girls rolled their
eyes at his terrible German and laughed at him behind his back,
but she nodded and led him away, grateful to be out of the cold, if
only for a few minutes.

Her apartment was a single room. A curtain hid the toilet and
a threadbare quilt was draped over the ancient bed as though it
were covering a corpse. Unwelcome light snuck in from a street-
lamp by her tiny window. She did not bother to switch on her own
bulb. Instead she lit a cigarette in the semidark.

"Cold night," he said. He was barely visible in the gloom.

She exhaled gray smoke. "They are all cold nights."

He sat down on the edge of the bed. The springs complained
under even his slight weight. She stood with her back pressed
against the far wall. She did not fear him, but neither did she like
having him in her home.

"Your man can't keep you off the streets?"

"Which? I have many men," she said.

"You know who I mean. E.E."

"Ah, him. He cannot change reality any more than I can. Any more than you can."

"Have you seen him?"

She hated the taste of the cigarettes they sold in East Berlin. She had always hated it. It tasted like death, like the air when the bombs were falling. But when she tried to quit, her hands would shake, sometimes so hard she worried it would never stop.

"He came to me today," she said. "He had a message for you."

The bed creaked. "A message?"

"He wants out. He wants to go to the West."

"He told you this?"

"He told me to tell you."

"You told him you were giving me information?"

"No." It was the truth, though she would have lied if necessary. But he had just known. Held her in his arms and whispered her own darkest secrets into her ear. "But he knew."

"And he wants to defect? Why now?"

A dog barked somewhere outside. The sound echoed in the alleys before drowning in the hum of the streets. "He is afraid."

"Afraid? Of what? Did he tell you?"

Yes, he had told her. And trembled when he did. "A man has come from Moscow. He fears this man."

"Who is it? Did he tell you his name? The Russian's name."

"He does not have a proper name. But he said he is called the Nightingale."

She watched him over the warm light of her cigarette. He did not move or speak. Perhaps he was afraid too. All men were capable of terror. She knew this. Yet it often surprised her. She forgot sometimes that men were nothing more than boys wearing the mask of age.

"I have to go," he said. The bed protested as he stood, but he was already at the door. "I will get him out. I will get you out too. It isn't safe here anymore." He opened the door and went out into the hall. "Don't go out again," he said. "Not tonight." Then he was gone.

How neat and orderly, the minds of men. They feel the cold and think of shelter. They see danger and plan rescue. They believe tonight is different from any other night and that the men they fear do not already have a boot on their neck.

There was something red on the quilt: his forgotten scarf. Seeing it there felt scandalous, a feeling she had not experienced in a long while. She picked it up, ran it between her bone-thin fingers. It was cheaply made. She had thought it unsightly when he wore it, but it, like her, benefited from his absence. It was even still warm.

She tossed away her cigarette, wrapped the scarf around her neck, and went back out into the cold.

NINE

I t didn't make any sense.

Or, maybe it did make sense, but not the kind of sense you could wrap your head around.

At least, not the kind Karen could wrap her head around.

The Wall was everything she could have hoped for: a masterwork of interwoven magic, spells layered on spells, the complex intertwined with the impossible. When the Wall had first appeared one morning and split Berlin into two, everyone had wondered how the Soviets could dare. But having seen their work up close, Karen wondered if the better question was how they could manage. Russian magicians had always been among the best in the world, even after they purged some of the greatest in the fires of the Revolution. Grim stories were told of the Soviet magic wielded against Nazi Germany at the end of the war and to crush anti-Communist demonstrations in Hungary or Poland. They knew magic and, unlike America, had no qualms about using it.

But this magic was more than impressive; it was terrifying. If the Soviets could make the Wall, who knew what else they were capable of.

And it was impenetrable in more ways than one. It exuded so

much magical power that any test she tried to run was almost completely thwarted. If there was other magic at work, she might not even notice it. Making sense of it was like trying to hear your own breathing over the sound of an orchestra.

And then there was the flaw in this masterpiece: the breach.

A spell like the Wall should have lasted forever. And yet, it was withering. In the stillness of the office, she could just make out Professor Goldberg's squeaky lecturing from across the years since her sophomore class on magical theory:

Now, class, what is the best way to upset an existing magical spell? Forget its birthday!

Karen smiled at her teacher's dumb joke. The intervening years and the lack of sleep somehow made it seem funnier. The real answer was more complicated, but pretty much boiled down to two choices:

#1. Disrupt the spell with other magic.

Or #2. Exhaust the spell's source.

The first was harder than it sounded. Magic, once cast, was relentless. It was like gravity: with enough arm flapping, you might be able to stop it for a while, but really you'd better hope you had a parachute. Disrupting a spell usually required intimate knowledge of the spell's nature, how it was structured and what held it together, something usually only the original caster knew.

That left the second option. For the Wall, she couldn't even discover the source of magical energy. Most simple spells drew their power directly from the caster, which was the painful drawback to wielding the cosmic powers of the universe. Some magic was tied to a totem, a physical item that had been imbued with arcane energy. It was theorized that was partly how a magician's locus helped them cast stronger magic. But whatever was powering the Wall hid its tracks well. There was clearly some nearby source of magical energy, a big one, but her efforts to pin it down had been in vain.

In other words, she had no idea what was going on.

She didn't pretend to be an expert at the political minefield she'd volunteered to tiptoe through, but she knew enough to be scared. Lots of dangerous people had lots of dangerous ideas about how to run Berlin. And though she hadn't learned much so far, it was enough to convince her that there was more at work here than it appeared. Something was in the air, something intangible but undeniable. And so far, inexplicable.

"Well, it took some digging, but I think I found what you asked for," said a walking stack of books that suddenly appeared in the doorway. They had given Karen a temporary office on the second sublevel, saying that its usual occupant was "on assignment." It was cramped and a little damp, but she preferred to think of it as cozy.

"Really? That's great!" Thrilled to be distracted from her unhelpful notes, Karen jumped up and helped Jim arrange the musty old books into some semblance of organization on her severe metal desk.

"Every book of magic we've got," Jim said, dusting off his now rumpled shirt. "Which, now that I think about it, isn't a lot. I'm sure we've got more back in some secret library in Virginia, but getting any of those is above my pay grade."

Karen opened the book on top: *Majik ak Mistè*. It was written in what looked like Haitian Creole and was full of elaborate diagrams of animal dissections, occult symbols, and rambling, all written in a slightly reddish ink that looked a bit too much like blood. She doubted any of this old magic had made its way into the Wall spell. But even if it had, the book wouldn't prove to be terribly useful to her, as someone had gone through with a steady hand and a sharp knife and excised large sections of nearly every page.

She held up a page and glanced at Jim through one of the larger gaps. He smiled nervously.

"Sorry about that," he said with a boyish shrug. "Sometimes it seems like the 'C' in 'CIA' stands for 'Censoring.'"

Typical. How did these magiophobic lunkheads expect her to diagnose the problem with the Wall when their policy on magical intelligence seemed to be to destroy what they didn't understand? Winning the war against more magically inclined nations like Germany had left the US with the mistaken impression that magic was some European nuisance. It took an impressive kind of arrogance to dismiss one of mankind's greatest powers, but America was up to the task.

She chose, however, not to share these thoughts with the amiable CIA agent in her office deep beneath the Agency's Berlin headquarters. Instead, she said, "Thank you, Jim. I'm sure these will be very helpful."

"I also found these," Jim said, producing a thin folder and adding it to the pile. "Most of the Agency's files on the Wall are classified well above my pay grade, but there were a few available for general consumption."

Any excitement Karen might have felt at getting access to the CIA's files on the Wall was quickly doused as she flipped through the scant pages. Some of the words remained legible, even a sentence or two in some places, but mostly it was a sea of thick black bars, obliterating whatever information might have once been contained within.

Jim sighed. "We're nothing if not consistent."

"Why would the CIA be so secretive about the Wall?" Karen asked.

"The CIA is secretive about everything," Jim said. "I had to get a special clearance for them to tell me where the bathroom was on my first day."

Karen scanned the documents.

Findings of the ███████ on August██ 19██ only for ████████
████████

Conclusive evidence not███████████████████████████
magical asset confirmed████████████████████████
for████████ and the ████████████████████ if
████████ for which the ████████████████████

When reporting to ████████████████ which ████████
therefore ████████████

And on and on.

"I'm sure I can find something here that . . ." Her voice trailed off as she noticed something at the bottom of one of the pages that looked only partly censored. The rest of the documents were printed on blue paper; this one was green. She pointed. "What does this line mean?"

"Operation Hobnail?" Jim sounded as confused as she was. "I'm not sure—"

"This is dated from just before the Wall appeared," Karen said. She read aloud. "'Senior magical asset on ground reports success in initial development.' Black line, black line. 'Threat containment minimal. District still . . .'" And the document ended.

"I think she might have been misfiled," Jim said, removing it from the rest. He tried to smile, tried not to furrow his brow. "Happens all the time, I'm afraid. Don't tell the Soviets. BOB's a well-oiled machine, as far as they know."

Karen stared at him for a moment, wondering, but decided not to press for more information. She doubted he would be forthcoming, even if he knew anything. "Don't worry about me," she said. "Your secret is safe."

An awkward silence fell as he seemed to be desperately searching for something else to say and she was too tired to help him out. In the end, he offered to help her find anything else she needed, and then disappeared into the maze of BOB's halls and stairways.

Alone with incomplete books, insufficient notes, and infuriating questions, Karen collapsed into her chair. If George were here, she thought, he'd be just as lost as she was. And she doubted Jim would have been nearly as helpful. You can do this. You're smart, capable, and a damn good magician. Sure, the available information is absurdly limited, and the stakes laughably, world-shatteringly high, but that doesn't matter, because Karen J. O'Neil from Rockville, Maryland, is on the case.

Sighing like a rapidly deflating birthday balloon, she tapped her forehead against the sharp edge of the desk, and wondered how hard she'd have to hit it to knock herself out until this was all over.

TEN

The car pulled slowly up to the blockade at Checkpoint Charlie. It was late, though it was hard to tell with the floodlights whitewashing everything with an artificial noontime glare. Young men dressed in the dark uniform of the National People's Army stood watch with solemn faces and ready rifles. It was mostly for show. There had been incidents at the Wall, including a few at Checkpoint Charlie, but this was the gate for foreign diplomats and military. This was the gate where World War III could start. Accordingly, everyone was usually on their best behavior.

Bill Holland cranked down his window and handed his passport to the waiting soldier. He'd made this crossing countless times since being posted to Berlin, but tonight he couldn't keep his heart from racing just a little. His fingers drummed the wide steering wheel. He had news, after all. And not the good kind. The sooner he was back at BOB, the better.

He turned and looked out his open window. The soldier had handed his passport to another. A third was approaching.

"The stamp is there," Bill said in German, pointing a finger at his passport to show them where to look. "Right there. Just look."

The soldiers did not even glance in his direction. "Bunch of buffoons," he added, though quieter and in English.

Another man was there now, a strikingly big man with a serious scar across his face. Wearing a Soviet uniform. The other men showed the scarred newcomer his passport. Everyone knew the Soviets were the real power behind the German Democratic Republic, but they usually weren't so obvious about it.

Then Bill thought about what the prostitute had told him. The Nightingale was in Berlin.

He could see West Berlin not that far ahead of him. The car would never make it through the barrier, especially from a dead stop, but if he got out and ran, maybe he could get there. It was a straight line, completely exposed; the GDR snipers couldn't ask for an easier shot. But would they take it? Would they shoot an American government agent in full view of the world?

Maybe the better question was if he was ready to be the guy who started a war.

His hands gripped the steering wheel now. They were sweating.

They were coming back toward his car. The Soviet waited behind, but he was watching closely. Bill glanced over his shoulder. More soldiers were coming up from the other side.

You trained for this, he told himself. Do what you are supposed to do.

But whatever that was, he couldn't remember.

One of the Germans placed a hand on his car door. He'd left the window down. "Step out," the soldier said, in English. "Please."

ELEVEN

The spy game used to be simple. Or as simple as it could be in a city bisected by a magical wall and run by four separate foreign nations. Jim found himself thinking fondly of his early days with the CIA in Berlin. He'd been assigned to counterintelligence, so that just meant knowing who in West Berlin was working for the other side and how to keep them from finding out anything useful. Oh, and if possible, asking them if they'd be open to the idea of betraying their masters. You know, easy stuff.

But lately, things were all jumbled. The breach was certainly part of it, but it wasn't all. Berlin was rumbling, like a sleeping monster about to stir. His usual informers (the nosy garbage collectors, the observant street sweepers, the bored bartenders) had all gone silent. Known Soviet agents were changing apartments for no reason, some vanishing in the process. Suspected operatives suddenly stopped behaving suspiciously, as if they knew they were being watched. Birds were flying backward, lions and lambs were snuggling, water was turning to blood.

And then there was the Bill situation.

Bill Holland was one of those guys you could count on. He played by the rules, even when the boss wasn't looking, something

Jim certainly couldn't boast. That was why Bill was trusted with whore detail. He was a real company man, a straight shooter.

And now he was missing.

Dennis had been the one to tell him, right after lunch.

"Garriety's on the warpath," he had said, careful to keep his voice down. "Bill never checked in last night after going over the Wall."

"Maybe he finally succumbed to the wiles of one of his contacts," Jim offered, but both men knew that wasn't likely. And even if he had, he would have had the smarts to drag himself into work the next morning.

They hadn't said much else, just sat there. They knew, of course, that a job like theirs carried risks. They were spies, after all, working to thwart some very serious men. Among the paperwork and the boredom, it was sometimes easy to forget the danger. And then they'd be reminded. Jim had been working for the CIA for six months when he saw his first flag-covered coffin. He hadn't known the man well, and it had been an accident, not some foreign provocateur, but it had still hit Jim hard. For some time. And then routine, the real opiate of the masses, took over and he forgot life and death for a while, forgot about the monsters on the other side of the Wall, forgot that he wasn't immortal.

He checked in with their guest, the comely magician drowning in old books and redacted files down in the basement, but he didn't linger. She looked like she hadn't slept in a week and she'd only been there a few days. Her eyes had the desperate mania of the caged animal. He took that to mean the research was not going well.

So instead he drove around Berlin and checked in with a few of his remaining contacts, old friends he nearly trusted, and asked about any chatter over a missing American. They had heard none. Not even a peep. Sometimes, they said, people just disappear. He thanked them for being so unhelpful then drove out to Checkpoint Charlie for a while. People came and went through the narrow gap in the shimmering Wall, looking relieved (though not really that pleased) to be back in West Berlin. He watched the guards, young men enforcing the will of old ones. What sort of man would he have been if he'd been born in Germany? How would he carry the inherited shame of a defeated aggressor? How would he explain Auschwitz or Ravensbrück?

He drove back in silence. Normally he'd listen to the broadcast from Radio in the American Sector, but tonight he just needed to hear his own thoughts, as empty and uncomforting as they were.

If the worst happened to Bill . . . , his thoughts said, leaving the rest for his imagination.

This whole place is going up in flames, they whispered. You going with it?

A real man could do something about it, they hissed. What can you do?

And so it was with a clouded mind and an uncertain heart that Jim turned the car onto Föhrenweg, hoping to get a few hours of work in before he had to sleep, when he saw Bill Holland stumbling down the side of the road.

TWELVE

Karen jerked up at the sound. For an instant, she was hyper-aware of the gurgling pipes that ran across the ceiling of her office, of the stillness that had settled over BOB, of the tiny dark pool of drool that had accumulated on her notes while she napped. She dragged an awkward hand across her mouth. How long had she been asleep? It had to have been only a few minutes. Then why did her watch say over an hour had passed? Maybe it was lying. Maybe it was working for the Communists. The second hand was red, after all . . .

The room was thankfully empty; only the books stared at her in silent judgment. They had proven mostly useless anyway, so who cared what they thought?

Focus, Karen. Words . . . think words. Think anything. She rubbed her eyes. For just a moment, just a flash, she remembered scream-ing. In anger? In fear? A dream, already fading, already gone. Just the echo of the kind of scream that you can feel clawing violence in your throat, an ancestral, animal sound that requires a whole body to produce.

She blinked. Where was she? Right, her notes. She dabbed away the puddle and stared hard at her own handwriting. The last line started strong but had trailed off by the end into a drooping scrawl of fatigue's design. Something about the source . . . calculations about how the magic was working against itself . . .

Her conclusions, such as they were, didn't make any more sense after a nap. From her best calculations, the source of the Wall's magic remained strong. But the spell itself . . . it was almost like it was moving in reverse. Could a magic spell commit suicide? She suspected that somewhere in the pages and pages of her calculations, there was a mistake. Or ten.

Then she heard voices. That must have been what interrupted her impromptu nap. She checked the clock; it was late, too late for anyone to still be down here. The voices were too far away to make out what was being said. There was a spell she'd read about that supposedly increased one's hearing, but in testing back at the OMRD, it had usually just left her with ringing ears and an odd fruity taste in her mouth. So rather than risk a brain tumor, she got up, straightened her blouse, and went to eavesdrop the old-fashioned way.

The voices were coming from an empty conference room down the hall. As she neared, they became clearer. And more familiar.

". . . a plan, pal?"

". . . get him sober, fast."

"Before Garriety finds him."

"Before Garriety finds all of us."

She nudged the door open. It looked like a meeting room, with a few metal chairs and a sagging table pushed against one wall. Jim and Dennis were standing with their backs to her, jackets long since tossed aside, shirtsleeves rolled up. In front of them was another man, poured like lumpy gravy into a chair.

"Rough night?" she asked, and the two men almost hit the low ceiling.

When he saw who was standing in the doorway, Jim blew out

a long sigh of relief. "Sorry," Jim said. "We thought you were some-one else."

"What's . . . going . . . who's . . . where am I?" said the gravy puddle in a rumpled suit.

"Ol' Bill here just needs a minute to gather his thoughts," Jim said.

Karen came closer. She could smell the reek of alcohol even at a distance. "He's the one who went missing, right?"

"The prodigal returns," Dennis said. He was still watching the door. "Only slightly worse for wear."

Bill's eyes roved the room. He looked like she felt coming out of her nap: desperate to have a coherent thought, utterly unable to, and a little angry about it. She had her own fair share of experi-ences with alcohol at the university and they usually turned out alright in the end, but Bill seemed to be having a particularly tough time of it.

"This normal behavior for him?" she asked.

"Not really," Jim said as he pressed a mug of coffee to the pa-tient's lips. "Bill's usually on the straight and narrow, aren't you, pal? But today you decided to go nuts on us, right in the middle of crisis time. Drink up, before I pour this over your head."

Her brain was finally shaking off the postnap muddle and was telling her something wasn't right. She knelt down in front of Bill. His eyes looked everywhere else and then settled for a mo-ment on her face.

"You're . . . pretty," he said with a sloppy smile.

"Thank you, Bill," she said. She held up a finger. "Look here." He did, or at least attempted to, and she spoke the words to one of the first spells she'd ever learned: To Illuminate Magic. Magic could be subtle, but almost always left footprints behind, like an arrogant thief who just couldn't resist leaving a calling card. Magic, Karen always liked to think, was a bit of a show-off.

Bill's eyes, still vodka glazed, crackled brightly.

And then the door to the conference room slammed open the rest of the way.

"What is going on in here?" demanded Milton Garriety.

"Milt, calm down," Jim was saying, holding up the coffee mug like a shield. "We found him wandering on the side of the road. We were going to get him a little sobered up then bring him straight to you."

"Like hell you were," Garriety said. He pushed past Jim but stopped when he saw Karen. "What is she doing here?"

"I think," Karen said, her mind racing at the possibilities, "that he's been enchanted."

The room was silent for a moment. "What?" Jim asked.

"I'm not saying he doesn't smell like the bottom of a bottle," she said, standing up, "but there's magic at work here."

"Magic," Garriety said. "You expect me to . . . no." He shook his head as if trying to dislodge some unacceptable thought. He grabbed Bill's arm and forced him to his feet. "Come on, you coward. Time to face the firing squad."

"Milt," Jim said, trying to keep Bill from collapsing, "he can barely stand."

Garriety let Bill slump back to the chair and spun on Jim. "At the very least, this fool is guilty of dereliction of his duty. He might be guilty of treason. His career is over. You want to join him? Or is that what this is, you take him out on the town and get him drunk then try to get your little magician in a skirt to convince me, 'Oh, this isn't rank insubordination and stupidity; it's magic!'"

"Milt, it's like I said," Jim said. "We found him like this. Karen was just trying to—"

"I don't give a damn what 'Karen' was trying to do. What she is doing is interfering with Agency business." Now those baleful eyes fell on her. "I don't know what you are hoping to do here, but this is no place for you. Men are putting their lives on the line to defend their country and you're playing with your little magic tricks and trying to tell me what's going on with my agents. I think it's time you do everybody a favor and get on the next flight back home before your daddy realizes you're gone."

Then he was back on Jim, a finger thrust into his chest. "And if you call me 'Milt' one more time, you pathetic excuse for a man, I'll have Arthur sign your discharge order so fast it'll make your tiny head spin. In fact, why don't I just call him down right now?"

"There's no need," Arthur said from the doorway.

"Sir," Garriety said, his bluster deflated, but only for a moment. "I've found our missing agent. I was just about to bring him upstairs."

"I heard," Arthur said. He looked like he hadn't slept in days. "What's this about magic?"

Karen had barely been listening; it was taking all her willpower to fight back the stupid, unwanted tears Garriety's rant had summoned. She hated them, hated herself for being so weak, hated Garriety for knowing exactly what to say, like he'd been reciting a spell to rip her guts out.

"Magic," she said, before taking in a sharp breath. The sting behind her eyes was fading. "I detected magic on him. In him."

"What exactly," Arthur said slowly, "does that mean?"

Focus, Karen. Be the one adult in the room. "There are spells," she said carefully, "that affect our minds. I'm not talking about simple illusions. These spells work into your brain, harvesting or changing your memories, your personality. This magic is dangerous, even deadly. It is also illegal in the United States and banned by the Geneva Convention for the Use of Magic in War."

"So you are saying Bill isn't drunk; he's had his brain addled by magic?"

"He may be drunk," Karen said. "Or someone may have poured a bottle over his head. But before that someone definitely cast a spell over his mind."

No one said anything. This was a common reaction. Everyone knew that magic was serious, but for the non-magically-trained, it was also foreign. Sure, magic could make someone's head explode, but that could never happen to me. It was like the fear of the atomic bomb or of God: too terrifying to be anything other than abstract. So when people had to stare real magic in the face, they usually fell silent.

"Can you do anything for him?" Jim asked softly.

"No," Karen said. She wished for a different answer, but it was the only truthful one. She hadn't been trained to combat or reverse mental magic.

"Then what good are you?" Garriety asked.

"Milton," Arthur said, "get one of your boys to take Bill home. Get him cleaned up. And make sure someone stays with him."

"Arthur, I—"

"Just do it, Milton."

Garriety helped Bill to his feet, somewhat more gently this time, and walked him out the door toward the stairs.

"This magic," Arthur said when they were gone, "what else can you tell me?"

"It is difficult. Master-level magic. Stuff of legends more than reality."

"And who in the world knows how to use it?"

Karen shook her head. "I . . . I don't know."

"The Germans?"

"Possibly," she said. "But the Soviets are better magicians."

Arthur seemed to accept that, however reluctantly. He rasped a callused hand over his sandpaper cheek. To Karen, he looked dried out and worn thin, like he was in desperate need of a nap or a drink.

"What're you thinking, Chief?" Jim asked.

Arthur pulled at the discolored collar of his shirt and looked at Jim as if surprised to find him there. "See that Miss O'Neil gets some rest," he said. "Something we could all use a little more of." Then he ambled out, fists pushed halfway into his pockets.

"Well," Dennis said when the footsteps faded, "that could have gone worse."

"Don't mind Milt," Jim said. It took Karen a while to realize he was talking to her. "He's an ass. Can't help it. He comes from a long line of asses."

"Yeah," she said. Her voice sounded very far away in her head.

"I mean it," Jim said. He was staring at her. Could he see that she'd nearly been crying? "It's nice having you here. Good, I mean. Whatever's going on, I know we wouldn't want to deal with it without you. Without you we'd never have known what happened to Bill. Maybe it pays to have a magical expert around after all."

He was trying to be kind; she knew that. And Garriety was trying to be condescending and mean. It certainly wasn't her first encounter with men like that. She knew how to handle them, knew when to be mean right back. But when you took away the motivations, good or bad, and just looked at the facts, either the nice guy or the mean guy was right.

"Thank you," Karen said. "You've been great. You both have. But he wasn't wrong." Karen's thoughts turned on her, twisting in her head: You knew it would end this way. You knew before you even got on the plane that you'd never see this through to the end. "I'm not the right person for this job. I think it is time for me to go home."

THIRTEEN

I t seemed that no one wanted her.

The other girls, ones whose faces she knew if not their names, were nearly all gone. Some in fact had come back and left again while she just stood and shivered. The men who came down to the streets near Oranienburgerstraße were usually not so picky. They came to get what they wanted and did not bother to waste precious time deciding; making carefully considered decisions was not a core virtue among the men of the German Democratic Republic.

She pulled her red scarf tighter around her neck. Winter was insistent this year, unwilling to wait its turn. She tapped out a cigarette, her last. Another disappointment, though hardly surprising; life had taught her that the good things always left too soon.

A car drove past, headlights leaving embers in her vision. The driver was alone, older, well dressed but not that well. She struggled to smile, but the car didn't slow.

The men who came to Oranienburgerstraße often reminded her of her father. It was a perverse thought, especially in the creaking, grunting dark of her apartment, but she could not help it. She wondered if he had ever come to such a place, looked at the women the way these men did, made a faceless choice in the middle of a desperate night. Maybe he never had the chance, before the war carried him away and never brought him back.

It was bad now in the city: no money, no freedom, no hope. But it had been worse. Much worse. And she'd seen it. Felt it. Been scarred by it. The damned war. Hitler's war. The politicians' war. The rich men's war. They said it was against Europe, against Soviet Russia, against impurity. Lies. She knew better. It had been a war waged by Germany against Germany. A suicide. It would have been more efficient if the Chancellor had just lined up the German people in front of his tanks and kept the rest of the world out of it. Just a flash and then nothing, a clean death. Not like this.

In the past, she had told some of the other girls she was helping the Americans. She had not meant to, but when so much is taken from you without your consent, you had to choose to share something of yourself or you would go mad. Some called her a hero; the rest called her a fool. She no longer believed there was a distinction. They asked what the Americans gave her, or what she told them, or if they would take her to the West.

But they never asked her why she did it.

Because they all knew there was no Germany left to betray.

Another car was coming. She sucked the last smoke out of her cigarette and let it fall. The car was slowing down, pulling close to the side of the street. Just one tonight, she told herself. Maybe just one.

The headlights made it hard to see, but the man behind the wheel was big. He was stooped to fit inside the cabin. Big men came in two extremes: those who reveled in towering over the rest of humanity and those who apologized for it. When the car stopped in front of her and she could better see his face, with its large red scar, she knew he was one of the former. She also knew, even before he spoke, that he was Russian.

"Get in," he said. She had seen enough dead men to recognize the look in his eyes.

"No," she said, shocked to hear the sound of her own voice, let alone the word.

"Get," the scarred Russian said, his voice somehow completely empty of all tone, like it was the echo of some other man's voice, "in."

She started moving. Her shoes clicked on the chilly concrete. It was hard to walk fast and she doubted she even remembered how to run. A block away, she finally dared look back. The car had not moved. The man's silhouette still filled the space behind the window, impossibly large. She could not see his face but felt those awful corpse eyes crawling on her skin.

She reached her apartment in half the normal time. Her heart protested. Her lungs burned in defiance. But the car had not followed. The street was empty.

It felt somewhat odd to climb the stairs without the scrape of heavy boots behind her, like she was a ghost hovering over what had once been her life. Her fingers struggled with the key, scoring the metal as it fit into the old lock. She pushed the door open and then closed, the world and all its woe held at bay by that simple piece of wood.

It was when she unwound her scarf to hang it on a peg by the door that she realized she was not alone.

He sat on the far side of the little room. He was thin, with light hair, and a Soviet officer's uniform. He had been checking the time on a battered brass pocket watch. When he looked up, he did not seem pleased to see her, as though he were already anticipating some deep regret.

"Who are you?" Her voice felt as weak as her legs. "Why are you in my home?"

"I recently met an acquaintance of yours," the man said in precise German. "An American. A spy." His fingers rubbed the face of his pocket watch. "Please," the man said, "come and sit a moment with me."

FOURTEEN

The specter of George's smirking face kept Karen from sleeping. He wouldn't even have to say anything; he'd already said it, after all. He could just sit there and smirk while she explained to everyone back home how the Berlin mission had been just too complicated. Too difficult. Too real.

The only thing worse than the thought of George was Dr. Haupt. He'd taken a risk sending her, and she'd let him down.

Before she'd left to catch her flight to Berlin, she'd gone back to Dr. Haupt's office to thank him again for this opportunity. She knew it was a risk, sending a young woman on such a significant mission, but Dr. Haupt had never been one to care much for the politics of his job. He did what he thought was right and had the ability and seniority to get away with it.

"It is easy to lose your footing in a city like Berlin. The ground is always shifting," he had told her. "So trust your instincts and you will succeed, my dear. I have no doubt."

What if her instincts told her to quit?

"Have you ever thought of visiting Berlin again, sir?" she'd asked as he walked her to the door. "Any fond memories of home?"

He did not reply immediately. She knew he was reluctant to

discuss his personal history, but thought if he would share with anyone, it would be her. "This is my home now," Dr. Haupt said, patting her hand. "Berlin is my past. I prefer to focus on the future. As should you. Yours will be bright indeed, my dear. I have no doubt."

How could she go home and disappoint him now?

But what choice did she have? She could sit in the bowels of the Berlin Operating Base until she was withered and gray and still might not understand the complexity of the Wall magic, let alone whatever else was at work. Better to give up now and let someone more qualified come and solve this mess, before things got worse. Before someone got hurt.

Like Bill. Someone had taken a CIA agent and manipulated his mind using outlawed magic and then made it look like he was just drunk. The Germans? The Soviets? Maybe more importantly, why? What had Bill found out? Or what had they found out from him?

It chilled her to think about, but there was no use denying it: this was war and she had no business taking part in it. She'd be better off if . . .

Her eyes opened and she sat up.

Magic had been the first thing in her life that had made her feel like she was in control. Was she going to give that up, just because things had gotten hard?

As a junior at St. Cyprian's, she had found herself afloat. Many of her classmates already knew what they wanted after graduation: careers, marriage, the usual litany of life experiences when you are young and powerful. It wasn't that Karen didn't want any of those things, but every option, no matter how minor, seemed mired in so much uncertainty that she felt paralyzed. She'd no longer felt capable of knowing what she truly wanted.

So she had gone to see Dr. Haupt. He had listened carefully

and quietly as she described her malaise. The words all sounded so childish as she said them and she felt her face burn with shame. But he had been kind and told her the simple truth that uncertainty is unavoidable.

"If you are going to change the world, Karen," he had said, "you can never let yourself be overcome by your fears or by regret. Do what you believe is right. Trust your instincts, not your fears."

Trust your instincts, not your fears.

She dressed quickly in the dark, rummaging through already-packed bags for practical clothes: jeans, boots, a jacket. Her hair would be a mess, but that's why God invented ponytails. She found her notes, a map, and a flashlight. Lastly she hung her leather pouch around her neck. The weight there felt right, like it agreed with her plan.

Now she just needed a plan.

Stanley hated the night shift. He never had a problem staying awake; the Germans had no shortage of coffee. No, it was the opposite problem: he could never force himself to sleep when the sun was out. It was like his brain rebelled at the very thought. *It's daytime, dummy,* he heard it say when he'd toss and turn, *so get out there and do something.* It didn't matter that he couldn't keep his eyes open. Sleep just wasn't willing to change schedules.

But he had a hard time complaining. Here he was, right back in Germany, but he didn't mind it this time around. Fewer people were trying to kill him on this visit. Sure, he still carried a gun, but he never expected to use it. Who would be nuts enough to try to attack the CIA's Berlin headquarters? Even the Soviets weren't that crazy. So as jobs went, his was pretty swell.

He glanced at his watch: 3:17 A.M. Only a few hours left. Almost time for a sandwich.

Voices drifted in from the hallway behind him. That was odd; there were always people about in BOB, but usually pretty few at this hour. But his job was to keep the bad guys out and these were coming from inside, so he just shrugged.

". . . Stanley . . ." This made his ears perk up. Were they talking about him?

". . . spying . . ." another distant voice murmured. ". . . East Germans."

He sat up in his chair. What was that? Spying for the Germans? He quickly tried to think of another Stanley who worked at BOB, but came up blank. Who could they be talking about?

He got up as quietly as the old springs in the chair would allow and moved toward the door. Light from the hallway spilled into the guardroom, but he couldn't see anyone through the crack.

But Stanley heard the next word clear enough: ". . . traitor."

Now his heart was going. Why would he betray his country?

Enough of this, he thought, pushing the door open and barging out into the hall. Whoever had the nerve to question his loyalty in the middle of the office in the middle of the night, they were about to get a piece of his mind.

There was no one in the hall. He heard only the soft buzz of the lightbulbs.

Behind him, the door to the guardroom slid closed.

He spun and grabbed at the handle, but it was too late. He didn't remember leaving it locked, but it wasn't budging. "No, no, no," he said, rattling the knob. But there was no one to hear him, just his mind playing tricks and him playing along.

Worst of all, now he had to go wake Earl to unlock the door. He wasn't going to be happy. Earl was never happy, but he was going to be even less so at 3:21 A.M.

Sighing, Stanley hurried down the hall before anyone else noticed he was away from his post.

And so he missed the sound of the main door unlocking and the sight of the visiting magician slipping out into the cold Berlin darkness.

K aren had the taxi drop her off more than a mile from the breach site. No need to draw any more attention than necessary. Not to mention, the extra subterfuge made her feel more like a spy. She had been worried the CIA might have placed a guard on the site itself, but it looked abandoned. A guard would have drawn questions, questions no one wanted asked. She watched the quiet windows in the nearby apartments. Any one of them could hide some prying eyes, so she did her best to slip in quietly.

When she reached the tarp-covered area concealing the breach, she let out a gasp: the breach had grown, nearly doubling in size since her last visit. While she had been running and rerunning calculations, this crisis-in-the-making hadn't been idle. How much longer could they keep this hidden? And what would happen once people started to notice?

She set down her satchel and stared at the decaying magic. *Just you and me,* she thought. *Time to surrender your secrets.*

T wo hours later, she remembered why giving up had seemed so attractive.

There was just too much noise from the Wall to make sense of any measurement she could take. A spell like this was a diva, pushing all other magic aside for its time in the spotlight. Whatever else was involved was subtle, an assassin rather than an armored column, a slow poison rather than a gunshot.

A wind had started to pick up, snapping the tarp overhead, but she barely noticed until it spoke.

". . . hear me . . ." it said.

She stopped midspell. Was someone coming? The street still seemed empty.

The wind tugged again at the canvas. ". . . please . . ." it said. ". . . can you hear me . . ."

Okay, she thought, the universe is punishing me for the trick I played on poor Stanley. She had thought it a clever way to draw the guard away while she made her escape, funny even; it didn't seem so funny now.

But whereas Stanley was convinced the voices he heard were his colleagues, Karen knew magic when it whispered plaintively in her ear.

"Yes," she said, keeping her voice low. "I can hear you."

". . . do not have . . . much time . . ." said the wind. ". . . tell them . . . they must come . . . to East Berlin . . . I can help . . . with the Wall . . ."

I promise, if I make it back to BOB alive, I'll apologize to Stanley.

". . . tell them . . ." another gust said, stronger now, ". . . come tomorrow night . . . or do not come at all . . ."

"Who are you?" she asked, which seemed both a vital and a silly question to ask the wind.

". . . my name . . . is Erwin . . . Ehle . . ." the wind said. It was quieter now, its strength fading. ". . . you must lead them . . . when they come . . . you will know where . . . I will show you . . . convince them . . . convince them . . ." The wind stilled for a moment before, with its last breath, almost too soft for any to hear, it added, ". . . or flee."

FIFTEEN

"You lost me at the part where you violated this building's perimeter."

Jim was quick to interject. "In all fairness, she broke out, Chief, not in."

"Jim," Arthur said, speaking slowly, "this is one of those times when it is better to be seen and not heard."

"Boss—"

Karen interrupted; Jim was grateful, since he wasn't exactly sure how he would have finished that sentence anyway. "I'm sorry," she said. "I am. I just wanted another look at the Wall before . . . before I put in a request to go home."

"If you'd asked, we would have taken you," Arthur said.

"I know. But it was late and . . . I'm sorry."

Nicely done, Jim thought. Arthur could come down hard when he needed to (Jim certainly had experience with that), but even the boss couldn't much argue with a sincere apology. Especially when it came alongside a potential lead. Jim was just glad that Milt Garriety had so far kept quiet as he loomed in the corner.

"You're sure about the name?" Arthur asked, sighing.

"Erwin Ehle," she repeated. "Does that name mean anything to you?"

"That information," Arthur said, "is classified."

"Come on, Chief," Jim said before he remembered he was supposed to be quiet. "I think we're a little past ceremony now. She's on our side."

"Jim, don't—"

"I don't need to know the details," Karen said quickly. "Maybe I don't want to know. But this man said I needed to come, that he'd show me how to find him."

"That's assuming anyone goes," Arthur said.

"We can't just let this one slip through our fingers," Jim said; he'd never been good at keeping his mouth shut before, so why start now? "Not if he can help us. Not if he can explain what's going on around here."

Arthur rested his hands on his desk. The boss's office had always seemed small to Jim. He assumed Arthur liked it that way, liked his visitors to feel uncomfortable. Jim could attest that it was working.

"Milton," Arthur said, "what do you think?"

The glowering vampire who looked like he'd had maybe an hour of sleep the night before unfolded himself from his perch. "I think," he said, "that this is nonsense. And in choosing that word, I am being gracious. Otherwise, the word I might choose to describe sending agents into hostile territory on a moment's notice with no intel other than the word of an untested civilian magician would be 'suicidal.' I would forbid any of my agents from taking part."

"You heard him, Jim," Arthur said.

"You both are just going to pretend that this is a coincidence?" Jim stared at the two men. They both were sharing the same expression: the look you get when you see an insect you'd really like to crunch. "After what happened to Bill, suddenly this particular asset asks for us to meet him?"

"Did he?"

"Come on, Milt. How else did she know the man's name?"

"Not everyone in this room is cleared for this discussion," Garriety said.

"I'll leave," Karen said, "but I'll be on my way to East Berlin."

"Chief," Jim said, "we're in crisis mode. She can help. You tell her, or I will. You can fire me later." As the words were coming out of his mouth, part of Jim's brain wondered if he would be fighting so hard if their guest magician didn't have such a cute smile.

Arthur puffed out his cheeks then blew out a rush of frustrated air. "I wouldn't fire you," he said. "I'd send you to prison."

"Well," Jim said, that same part of his brain laughing at him now. Another fine mess, brought to you by the ladies. "What I meant was . . ."

"Shut up," Arthur said. "Miss O'Neil, have a seat."

"Arthur . . ." Garriety said.

"Erwin Ehle is a high-ranking East German magician," Arthur said as if he couldn't hear the espionage chief; Jim would have to learn that trick. "One of their top guys, if our intel is worth a damn. Most of said intel comes from a single source: a prostitute that Bill handled. He was going to meet with her the night he . . . got lost."

"Wow," Karen said, finally sitting in the offered chair. "That's quite the coincidence."

"Furthermore," Arthur said, "the best we can tell, this Ehle is one of the magicians who worked on the original Wall spell."

Karen was looking at Arthur, but Jim could see her magic wheels turning. If Arthur thought he could stop her from making contact now, he'd need to find an empty cell in the basement and throw away the key.

"Then we have to go," she said, as if it were the most obvious thing in the world. She leaned forward. "I won't lie to you, sir: I don't know what is wrong with the Wall. But it *is* getting worse. If Ehle wants to help, we have to go over there and talk to him."

"It is not that simple," Arthur said.

"I'm not CIA," she said. "I have a passport. I can go over, find him, find out what he knows, and be back before anyone is the wiser."

At this, Garriety laughed. It was about as patronizing a sound as a human was capable of making. "I don't know much about your little magic world," he said, for the first time addressing Karen directly. "But I do know mine. And while I'm not sure magic is all you magicians claim it to be, I know the Soviets and the East Germans are very careful about it. They have trained people watching the crossings. They'd know an American magician was entering East Berlin before you even got within a mile of Checkpoint Charlie."

It made Jim's skin crawl, but he had to agree with Garriety. "Someone knew to grab Bill, probably when he was trying to pass through the gate. They would see you coming."

"I snuck out of here easily enough," she said, daring the men to deny it.

Arthur didn't. "Don't remind me," he said. "But they're a lot less nice than we are."

"What I am hearing," Karen said, "is a bunch of excuses why we can't do something that we have to do." She wasn't smiling now. "Is this how intelligence work usually gets done? You guys have a little competition to see who can be the most useless?"

Jim could see Garriety's whole body tense, his knuckles white. Jim wasn't used to hearing women talk like Karen did, and he guessed Milt was far less accustomed and certainly less charmed by it. But he never got his chance to vent his bile, because of a strange sound emanating from the head of BOB: laughter. Jim wasn't sure if he'd ever heard the boss laugh before; it was unsettling.

"Actually, yes," Arthur said, still chuckling. "I'd say you got us pegged, Miss O'Neil. Don't you agree, boys?"

"Arthur," Garriety said, "I don't like this."

Mirth died painfully on Arthur's face, as if Garriety's voice reminded him of some bad news he had hoped to forget. "You don't like it? Big surprise. I haven't liked a single thing since I came to this dump," Arthur said. "The food, the weather, even the beer tastes like dirt. Luckily Uncle Sam didn't send us here for our well-being. He sent us here to do our damn jobs."

"Chief," Jim said. "You're a genius."

"What?"

"Dirt," Jim said, a grin stretching across his face. "I think I know how we can pay Mr. Ehle a visit."

SIXTEEN

ooking down into the tunnel was like staring into an open grave. Karen's whole body shuddered at the thought of disappearing through the narrow opening. And yet she couldn't deny that she felt compelled by it, like standing on a cliff's edge, afraid of the inexplicable instinct to jump.

"Claustrophobic?" Jim asked pleasantly.

"Never had the chance to find out," she answered.

She told herself she didn't have room to complain; she was, after all, the one who had demanded to go over. Plus, as dank earthen tunnels went, this one wasn't that bad. It had lights hung at somewhat steady intervals, and while it wasn't high enough to really stand up, she wasn't going to be sliding into East Berlin on her belly either. It had taken a lot of work to cut this path through the German soil and she ought to be grateful it had been made available to them.

She decided to save her gratitude for when she emerged safely on the other side.

Jim slid a dark glass bottle out from a nearby rack. "Good year," he said, eyeing the label. The tunnel had been dug into a wine cellar of a home near the Wall, carefully concealed among the rows of reds and whites. "A swig of this might help. Think they'll notice one missing?"

"You often get drunk before your secret spy missions?" Karen asked.

"Only the dangerous ones," said Jim.

"Well now," said a big voice behind her, "sure am glad you didn't ask me to come along on this wee adventure. I think you'd have to widen it a bit first." The voice belonged to a Scotsman called Alec, a senior member of British intelligence, Karen was told. Arthur had insisted that key representatives of the other Western powers be informed of their plan. The US had to be careful not to act like it was running the show, Arthur said, and never more so than when it actually was.

"I don't think they dig many tunnels your size," Jim said. He was dressed more casually than Karen had seen him before: gone were the suit and tie, replaced with coarse, colorless trousers and a slightly stained work shirt. He looked less like a CIA agent than a poor German laborer, but she guessed that was precisely the point. She had been a little flattered when he volunteered to go over with her, especially since she was short on escorts due to Garriety's refusal to risk any more of his agents.

"Looks roomy to me," said her other knight-in-homespun-armor, Dennis. He'd volunteered after Jim, maybe slightly more reluctantly, though he had seemed like he didn't want to miss the party. "My whole life has been leading up to this moment: I'm finally glad both my parents were short."

"It was not built for comfort." The speaker stood at the foot of the stairs that led down from the main house. He was dressed like Jim and Dennis, though the simple clothes hung less like a costume on his sturdy frame. His hair and eyes were dark, his expression dour, and when he looked at her, Karen had the sense that their presence in his tunnel was a sort of violation. "It was built for expedience."

"Thank you again, Dieter," Jim said, moving past the others to shake his hand. "The United States owes you a great debt."

"The United States can repay that debt," Dieter said, "by helping me save more of my people from Soviet-imposed captivity."

"We have," Jim said. "You know we have; that's why you're here."

"Every day that Wall stands," Dieter said, "more Germans starve. More Germans freeze. Every day you in the West allow the Soviets to remain, we suffer."

"We are grateful," Jim said, squeezing Dieter's arm. The German did not appear to appreciate the gesture. "And we'll hold up our end of the bargain: money and manpower for this and your other tunnels. We'll open the floodgates, pal. You'll see."

Karen wondered how much the digger had been told. Certainly he knew something of their mission; he would be coming with them for some of it, after all. But did he know that they were heading east in order to find someone to help keep the Wall standing? Not to keep the Germans in bondage to the USSR, but to prevent the chaos that would follow. Surely Dieter would understand. Surely Jim had made all that clear to him.

"We ready?" Dennis asked, eyeing his watch.

"Where's the frog?" Alec asked.

"I am here," said the last member of their party. The British had been content to be kept aware of the mission, with Alec acting as liaison between their governments. But the French were displeased by the whole idea and had required further coaxing. They had not wanted to "provoke" a response from the East Germans or worse, the Soviets, by an illegal crossing, especially when they were still ostensibly allowed access via the checkpoints. Arthur had prevailed eventually, but not before agreeing to allow a French agent to join them.

"Emile," Alec said, "you're looking chipper, as usual."

"I was in a wonderful mood," the Frenchman said, blowing out a cloud of cigarette smoke, "until they told me you were here." It sounded like a joke, just without any trace of humor in his tone. Karen hoped that had been lost in the translation. "Why are you here?"

"I'm providing valuable oversight," Alec said. "Someone has to make sure the Yanks don't start a war."

"We don't start wars," Jim said. "We just finish yours."

"Yes, your knack for involving yourself in the business of other nations is unparalleled," Emile said. Again, Karen couldn't tell if the Frenchman was bantering or truly held the rest of them in that much contempt.

"We'll remember you said that the next time Paris is getting bombed," Jim replied.

It seemed someone needed to remind them that they were on a mission. "While you boys are having your little geopolitical pissing contest, I think I'll just pop over to East Berlin for a bit," Karen said, starting for the ladder. "Don't wait up."

"Feisty," Alec said with an approving laugh. "You got Scottish blood?"

"Irish," Karen replied.

"Close enough," Alec said. He elbowed Jim in the ribs, nearly knocking him off his feet. "Take good care of her, gents. This one is a keeper."

Karen was still not sure if she was claustrophobic. She was fairly certain, however, that she hated being in a narrow tunnel deep underneath Berlin. The damp, stale air threatened to steal the breath from her lungs. *Run,* the fear whispered to her. *Run away, little girl.*

It was fortuitous, then, that the others were ahead of her and behind; she couldn't run even if she wanted to. And she didn't want to, not really. And not just to show these men that she was just as capable as them, and not to prove that magicians were not cowards who hid at a safe distance while real patriots did their duty. No, this wasn't about them; this was research. This mission was her laboratory and she was the test subject. She wanted to prove herself once and for all.

She did wish, however, that she had chosen an easier test to start with.

Dieter and Jim led the way and they stopped just as the tunnel widened into an antechamber. Battered shovels and picks were stacked in the corner. In the jaundiced light from the bulbs hung precariously along one wall, her companions looked ill and uneasy.

"The Wall is just ahead," Dieter whispered. "When we pass under it, you will know."

Jim raised his eyebrows at this, but for once, he made no reply. Karen chose to believe that was a good sign; he was taking this seriously. Though perhaps that meant the mission was more dangerous than she had realized.

They continued along the tunnel, hunched over and silent. *No, she told herself, it isn't getting narrower. It's all in your head. It's all . . .*

The magic of the Wall pushed suddenly down, as if it were trying to drown her. She stumbled and choked, her body burning. A hand went instinctively to her locus. A host of defensive spells jostled each other in her mind. This was no fencing match; this was a real magical assault, and yet she couldn't even control her thoughts long enough to cast the simplest of shielding spells. Her fingers clawed the soft sand of the tunnel floor, her voice dying silently in her throat.

Then a hand grabbed hers and pulled her forward. She scraped gracelessly along the dirt for a moment, and then the Wall's magic receded. She breathed deep of the moist, chthonic air, oddly surprised to be alive.

The Wall had been designed as a barrier; clearly the spell took that charge seriously.

Dieter's edged voice jangled in her ear. "It always affects magicians worse." He helped her to her feet. "I should have made my warning more precise."

She nodded, though not out of understanding. *I warned you*, the fear whispered with a laugh, but she just wiped the sand from her clothes. "I'm fine," she said. "Let's keep going."

The world was dark when they reached the tunnel's end. The lighting had stopped some ways back, but Dieter knew his way by feel and soon had them out of the earth and in some cramped basement on the Eastern side of the Wall. After a moment of fumbling in the black, he lit an oil lamp and hung it from a post.

"I have done what you asked," he said, speaking to Jim. "Though I wonder why you would want to come."

"Thank you," Jim replied, taking his hand, repeating it in German.

"You okay, Emile?" Dennis asked. The Frenchman did seem pale.

"I am fine," Emile replied, rubbing his forehead.

"Do what you came for," Dieter said, nodding to a set of stairs so steep and narrow it was at least half ladder. "So we can return home. Being in the East makes me feel like a bag will be pulled over my head at any moment."

The image made Karen's skin prickle.

"Right," Jim said, ignoring the grim German. "Dieter will stay here and watch the tunnel. Emile, you'll find a place up top to watch. Either of you see anything, you have your radio."

"If we see something," Emile said, "it will already be too late."

"That's what I like about you guys," Jim said. "Always looking on the bright side."

Dennis tapped his wrist. "Moonlight's burning, Jimbo."

Everyone turned toward Karen. Ehle had said that she would know the way when they came. She had assumed he would show her how to find him via some sort of spell, but the encounter at the Wall made it difficult to sense any magic in the air now. But they had done what he asked and she doubted he would fail on his end; even speaking through the wind, she had heard the desperation in his voice.

"Alright, Karen," Jim said. "Where to?"

SEVENTEEN

Her picture was still on his desk, where it had always been. Arthur couldn't quite say why he hadn't tossed it in the trash after she'd walked out on him. And then she'd gone off and died, giving him two perfectly good reasons to move on. He couldn't have asked for better excuses for a clean break. It wasn't like he hadn't tried. Leaving the wedding ring in a drawer hadn't been too hard. The skin worn smooth by twenty years of friction had even begun to take on a normal, healthy color. It was good, moving on. Natural. Expected.

But then there was the damn picture. Arthur picked it up. The frame had seen better days. Moving half a dozen times across Europe was bound to leave a mark, in more ways than one. She had enjoyed that at first: the intrigue, the mystery, the cloak-and-dagger, as she always called it. That hadn't lasted long. It wasn't the life he'd imagined when he signed on after the war. It certainly wasn't the life she had wanted when she put that ring on his finger. They'd been just kids then: dumb, happy kids.

She didn't look much older than that in the picture. Beautiful, full of life, beaming that irresistible smile over her shoulder, right at the camera. He was surprised she hadn't cheated on him sooner really, a woman like that, left alone, her smile like a candle drawing all the horny moths. One of them was bound to get through. A matter of time really.

He hated her, of course. That was only appropriate. But he didn't, couldn't hate the woman in the picture. He pitied her. He wished someone could go back and tell her not to marry such a deadbeat. Find a man who will cherish you, someone who wouldn't choose a job over being with you. Someone who'd sacrifice everything. Otherwise you'll end up becoming something no one ever would have guessed: ugly.

He set down the picture and found the scotch. He didn't like to drink at the office. Instead he usually saved it for the empty nights in his tiny apartment, when he could pretend for a moment that there was still a part of his life that wasn't promised to the Agency. That fiction was getting harder to swallow these days. He poured some and then poured some more.

The office was quiet, for once, since he'd sent most everyone home early. No sense in anyone else knowing what they were up to. Plausible deniability and all that. Would make things easier for the war crimes tribunal.

Now he was just being dramatic. They sent people over the border all the time to spy on the Commies. Sure, they didn't usually sneak in via illegal tunnels. And typically they weren't civilians or magicians. If word got out, he had no doubt it would have a negative impact on diplomatic relations, but that was a problem for the diplomats. His job was information, something he sorely lacked right now. Here was a question for those suits at the State Department: which was worse, violating the borders of the German Democratic Republic or letting that same border go all to hell when the Wall collapsed on his watch?

He tried to take a sip of scotch, but somehow his glass was already empty. He tilted the bottle, but it was nearly dry. He groaned. It was too early in the night to run out; they probably hadn't even violated any of the good international treaties yet.

There was noise out in the bullpen. He saw no one. Arthur drained the bottle and set it down slowly. The drawer he'd fished it out of was still open, so he retrieved what had been sitting next to it: a loaded Colt .45. Why so jumpy? The stentorian voice of his family's Methodist reverend came to him then: *The wicked flee when no man pursueth.*

Arthur worked the slide on the pistol. ". . . But the righteous are bold as a lion," he murmured.

"Chief?"

"Bill?" Arthur came out of his office, still holding the gun. Bill Holland was standing in the center of the room. He looked like he was suffering the worst hangover in history. His eyes were red with angry veins, his skin sallow and sweat sheened, and his knees boneless and uneasy. "What in the blue hell are you doing here? You're supposed to be resting."

"Sorry, Chief," Bill said, a hand pressed against his temple, presumably warding off one monster of a headache. "I . . . I just . . ."

"Get to bed, Bill," Arthur said, tucking the .45 in his waistband.

"I remembered something," Bill said.

That got Arthur's attention. He pulled out a chair before Bill's legs gave way. The spy slumped gratefully into the chair. "Alright, let's hear it, if it is so important."

"I don't remember much. It's all still such a blur," Bill said, grinding his fists into his eyes. "But something came to me. I was lying there and it just popped in my head. I don't remember why it matters, but I thought I needed to get down here and—"

"I'll tell you if it matters," Arthur said, "once you tell me what it is."

"Just a word," Bill said. "'Nightingale.' That mean anything to you, boss?"

Cold sweat prickled his forehead. The remnants of his scotch tasted suddenly sour in his mouth. "Oh, hell," Arthur said, wiping his face with a handkerchief. "Where's the damn phone?"

EIGHTEEN

East Berlin, for the most part, looked very much like West Berlin. They came up from underground far enough from the Wall to be out of sight of the guard towers and increased patrols, so all Karen saw was the same bleak landscape of lifeless buildings and potholed roads. Even the sky seemed unwilling to bother with the city, its face black-washed of any stars.

But there was something different here, even if it were just in the air: dread. Karen reminded herself that she'd asked for this, pushed for it. But now, facing down alleyways bound to conceal unfriendly eyes and waiting for the first Soviet tank to appear from around any corner, she started to think that maybe she should have become a dentist.

"I will wait for you there," Emile said softly, motioning with only his eyes toward a nearly empty parking lot within sight of the building that housed the tunnel's entrance. "If I see anything suspicious, I will use the radio."

"Sure you don't want to come with us?" Jim asked.

"I will wait," he replied. "But do not make me wait long."

"Roger that," Dennis said.

"Alright, Karen," Jim said. "Lead the way."

She closed her eyes. There was something else different on this side of the Wall, something that had been left for her to find. She felt the cold night wind on her face, heard a car a street or two over, smelled the wet dirt on their shoes. And then there it was again: a trace of magic, a faint signal on some metaphysical wavelength.

"This way," she said.

The metaphor was unflattering, but she felt like a bloodhound as Dennis and Jim followed her, oblivious to what only she could track. But was she the only one? Couldn't anyone attuned to magic find the signal if they knew to look? She stopped, the scent lost. *Focus, Karen. Forget the fact that you're probably walking into a trap. Forget the fact that you want to run and hide. Forget and focus.*

A moment later, her mind brushed up against it again and she took hold. She sensed the signal spooling out ahead of her, a delicate thread leading them toward the center of the labyrinth. "Come on," she said.

The signal stopped at an apartment building in Lichtenberg.

"You sure this is the place?" Jim asked, keeping his voice very low. They were deeper into the city now, and the farther they got from the Wall, the more people appeared. Few made eye contact or even looked in their direction, but that didn't mean they weren't listening.

Karen pressed hard on her locus. She could feel the familiar jagged edges against her palm. There was noise murmuring around her, the realities, magical and practical, of a city this big. And even this far east, the Wall droned in the distance, obscuring the signal. But it was still there, and it was coming from the fourth floor.

Not wanting to risk the foreign sounds of English, she nodded.

Dennis sighed and dug in his pockets for a cigarette. "I'll watch the street," he said, flicking his lighter. "But please hurry."

Jim patted him on the back and held the door open for Karen.

The stairs were old and protested their intrusion with every step, but they still seemed the safer choice than the wheezing elevator. The air inside the building smelled of mold and damp cigarettes. As they wound their way up, Karen found herself wondering if Jim was armed. If it were a trap waiting for them, she doubted even a gun could help them, but she still would feel safer if they weren't entirely reliant on her magic in case of danger.

She heard a creak behind them and turned, her lips already moving, but there was no one. Just a tired old building settling.

"You okay?" Jim asked from a few steps above her.

"Sure," she said. What if it had been a threat? What spell would she have cast to protect herself? Would it have been in time?

"Don't worry," Jim said. "I'm not going to let anything happen."

"Thanks," she said. "But I'm fine." *That's right, don't you worry: a man is here to keep you safe. Just keep your head down and let the men take care of everything.* Karen bit her cheek, hoping the pain would distract her accusing thoughts. It didn't. Of course she didn't need Jim to protect her; so then why did his confident smile make her feel protected?

Because you're a coward, afraid of your own shadow. Afraid of your own power.

The thought echoed and died and she had nothing to offer to rebut it.

"For the record," Jim said softly, "my dates are usually a bit classier than this."

The comment caught Karen off guard, but she found herself

smiling. "Is that what this is, then? A date? To a Communist country?"

"Anyone could take you out to dinner and dancing," Jim said. She couldn't see his face but could picture the pleased-with-himself smirk he was bound to be wearing. "I find dark tunnels and the threat of Soviet capture to be much more romantic."

"I suspect," Karen said, "that you don't find many girls who agree."

"That's the best part," he said. "My system filters out the boring ones."

Karen stared down each empty hallway they passed on their climb. "Shouldn't we be a bit more . . . secretive?"

Jim chuckled. "The Soviets are scary," he said, "but they aren't omniscient."

That did little to reassure her. She felt eyes on her, prying inside. "I suppose it's a little late to ask this," she said, "but are you actually any good at being a spy?"

That earned a louder laugh, loud enough to make Karen wince. "I have no idea," he said. "Let's just say I think being a spy and enjoying yourself shouldn't be mutually exclusive."

"I think I'll enjoy myself when we're back on the other side of the Wall."

"Amen to that," Jim said. Before she could make a reply, he went on. "Fourth floor. We still on the right track?"

It took Karen a moment to hear him. "Yes," she said eventually. "Yes. Down that way."

The last door at the end of the hall looked like all the others, except for a few extra scratches in the peeling paint. To the tenants of the building, they must have just seemed like the expected wear on a run-down apartment. But to Karen, they were proof they'd found the right place. They were crudely made, but purposefully so. They needed to look incidental, but they were anything but. Her fingers brushed them and tingled as the inherent magic buzzed.

"Runes," she said quietly. "Written magic. Usually for protection."

"I guess we found our guy," Jim said.

"I guess so."

"Then let's be friendly and introduce ourselves." He pulled off a glove and knocked on the flimsy door.

At first, there was silence. No movement behind the door, nothing in the hall. Had they come too late? Then the unmistakable sound of a working lock, and the click of tired hinges, and a man was standing in the doorway.

"Good," he said in accented English. "You were foolish enough to come."

NINETEEN

Erwin Ehle ushered them quickly inside. The apartment was tiny and cold. It barely looked lived in. There was a bed, but no pillow. No closet or dresser. A small iron stove in the corner, but no wood. And even in the little light offered, Jim could see the footprints left in the dust on the floor.

"Don't use this safe house often?"

"Observant," he said. He was an older man, well dressed, with hair that was graying and thinning. "I apologize for the precautions. I did not know where I would be if you came, so I was forced to become . . . creative."

His eyes moved from Jim to Karen, taking her in as if noticing her for the first time. "You . . ." he said, his voice faltering. He quickly threaded his fingers together, his skin turning white under the pressure. "You are the magician?"

"I am," she answered.

"I was . . . expecting a man."

Ouch, Jim thought. *Probably not the best way to make friends.*

"My apologies," Karen said. She sounded less than amused. "I'm not trying to be female, really. Just sort of came out this way."

Ehle's jaw twinged, muscles firing with some irrepressible

emotion. He released his hands but held them tightly against his legs, as though he didn't trust them not to move on their own. "I did not mean . . ." he said, but then trailed off. "I trust the magical trail was not difficult for you to follow."

"No," she said. "Though I haven't seen magic like this before."

"It is nothing," he said. He lifted a small stone carving from a dusty table. It looked like it was supposed to be some sort of four-legged animal, but Jim couldn't say if it was supposed to be a dachshund or a Holstein. "Just a trinket I enchanted, in another lifetime."

"And the spell you used to speak to me through the wind?"

Ehle almost smiled at that. He retrieved a leather bag from the floor by the door. It looked older than Karen and Jim both. The German pulled another small item from inside, this one a wooden flute. Well, almost a flute, but while it had a mouthpiece, it had no other holes to change notes. "I was quite proud of this one," he said. "I improved on an older design. The original used Norse runes, but I found the Arabic to be more suitable."

"May I see?" Karen asked.

He placed the strange flute in her hand, but shook his head as he did. "I expelled the last of its magic in contacting you. A pity."

"Mr. Ehle," Jim said, "I thought you were working for the GDR. But this looks like you're in hiding. What's going on?"

"Ah," Ehle said, smiling and looking sad at the same time. "So that explains why you still came. You do not know."

Jim's palms were beginning to sweat. He'd supported this crazy plan, he'd fought for it, put his career on the line for it, but it wasn't until they walked into this lifeless room that he'd begun to get nervous. "We don't know what?"

Ehle looked at them both in turn. "Yes," he said, "I am in hiding, but I do not expect to remain so for long. Either I will be found, or you will take me to the West. Tonight."

"Take you . . . you want to defect?" Jim said.

"That is why I asked you to come."

"Your message to Karen never said anything about defection," Jim said. "You said you had intel about the Wall. We came . . . we brought our magician so you two could—"

"I have information about the Wall," Ehle said, "and what is tearing it down. Information that I will give you when we are safe in West Berlin."

"Look, sir, I don't want—"

But Karen interrupted him. "Found by whom?"

Jim saw the brief flash of fear in Ehle's eyes. "The matter of the Wall," he said, "has drawn the attention of our masters in Moscow. They have sent someone here to control the problem and I believe he has decided I am not to be trusted. He is a KGB colonel. I do not know his true name, but in some circles he is known as the Nightingale."

"Hell," Jim said.

"I thought that you would have heard," Ehle said by way of apology.

"Who is the Nightingale?" Karen asked.

"The Boogeyman," Jim said. Now he felt the sweat creeping down his back. "He's the one mommies and daddies tell little spies will come gobble them up if they don't eat their vegetables."

"But he's real?"

"Very real," Jim said. "He was in Berlin years back, before my time. We lost three agents in an afternoon. Just gone. Empty coffins on the plane back to the States. And you say he's here? Because the Wall has a hole in it?"

"There is more," Ehle said calmly. "Which I will explain, when we have time."

"After we sneak you across the most secure border in the world."

"You found a way here," Ehle said. He pointed at Karen. "Certainly you did not bring her across at a checkpoint or you would not have made it this far. Judging by the sand you tracked into my apartment, I imagine the path was a bit cramped and dark, but I do not mind."

"Jim," Karen said. "What is the problem? He helped build the Wall in the first place. He can help us. We can't just leave him here for the Soviets to find."

Even after Ehle's crack about her being a woman, she was on his side (magician solidarity and all that). That was probably the real reason he had insisted on Karen coming with the team to meet with him. But they didn't understand the situation like he did. They took defections from the East, even spent countless hours and dollars to make them happen. And Ehle would be a high-value asset, being well placed in the GDR machine. But he was a magician and Washington wasn't the biggest fan of magicians, the Agency even less so. Sure, they'd take him, but they wouldn't be happy about it. Not one bit, and it would be Jim's name all over the recruitment paperwork.

But none of that mattered. What mattered now was getting back to the saner side of the Wall without anyone getting shot.

"Okay," Jim said. "Let's—"

The room filled with the sound of little bells, though for the life of him, Jim couldn't see any. Then the tinkling stopped. "What was that?" he asked.

"Were you followed?" Ehle demanded.

"No," Jim said. "Of course not."

"No one knows about this place," Ehle said. "They found the others but not this one, not until you arrived."

"No one knew we were coming," Jim said. "Even if they did, no one knew where. We weren't followed."

Ehle parted one of the heavy curtains blocking the window

that looked down to the street. "A car has circled the block three times," he said softly. "And now it is stopped by the entrance to the building."

"How could you know that?" Jim asked.

Ehle closed the curtain. "I am a magician working for the German Democratic Republic and the USSR who wants to defect to the West," he said. "I may be a fool, but I am not unprepared."

Now there was an indistinct murmur of static. Jim retrieved his radio from his jacket and turned up the volume. "Say again," he said into the receiver.

Dennis's voice came over the line. "You've got four guys who just pulled up. Dressed like regular folks, but haircuts say military."

"What are they doing?" Jim asked.

A pause. "Waiting. Watching the door you went in."

Jim turned to Ehle. "Is there another way out of the building?"

He shook his head.

"Can't you use some fancy magic spell to make a new door?"

The magicians shared a glance. Great, Jim thought. They knew each other for five minutes and were already bonding over their common distaste for nonmagical dummies like him.

"There are many things we could do with magic. But if they have a magician with them," Ehle said, "any significant magic we used could be easily detected."

Jim peeked through the curtains. He saw the car idling ominously.

"What about the roof? Anywhere we can go up there without drawing attention?"

"I am not yet a feeble old man," Ehle said, "but there are limits on how far these legs can jump."

Jim quickly assessed their dwindling options. The window was just big enough to squeeze through, but seeing if he could survive a four-story drop wasn't at the top of his to-do list. Maybe there was a sewer entrance in the basement, but he doubted it. If they couldn't sneak out, that left the more direct approach. He had a pistol strapped to his ankle and two magicians. Maybe if they—

"I've got an idea," Karen said. She turned to Ehle. "What else do you have in that bag?"

TWENTY

They sat in silence.

Three of the men had grown up together in Moscow, had fought in the war together, and had been on many similar operations together. On those nights, they had joked and laughed about memories old and exaggerated. On those nights, they had complained about the terrible weather and the worse cigarettes, the women who had left them and those who they wished would leave, and the food, always the food. But on those nights, they had been alone.

The fourth man in the car did not speak. He did not even look at them. He was young but carried himself with the arrogance of a senior general. They had only been told his first name: Kirill. Do whatever he tells you, their superiors had ordered. It will be better for you not to ask questions. They asked none. They were accustomed to following the commands of a man they feared.

"Something is happening," Kirill said suddenly.

"I see nothing," one of the others said, looking out the window at the apartment.

"Magic," Kirill said. "They are using magic."

They knew they were hunting a magician. Nothing scared

these men, not after Stalingrad, but magic certainly made them uneasy. Most of them wore the cheap baubles you could get from some gypsy to ward against evil spells. They did not believe they did anything, but that was hardly the point. You had to take precautions, and with magic, who knew what would work or what would not?

Kirill got out and two of the men followed, leaving only the driver. They entered the lobby and found it empty. "Up there," Kirill said, nodding toward the stairs. The other men reached into their jackets and slid out black pistols.

On the fourth floor, he stopped as if listening for something faint. Then he led them down a hallway to the last door. One of the others, the biggest man among them, started for it, but Kirill stopped him with a raised hand and cruel eyes. He ran his fingers across some meaningless scratches in the paint, whispering to himself. Then he stood back, lifted his hands, and blasted the door off its hinges with a single word.

The men with guns were in the room in an instant.

The apartment was empty. Their quarry was not here. The room was lit with a golden light that came from a glowing stone on a small table. The man called Kirill crossed the room and picked it up, and the light immediately died in his hands. A moment later, the stone burned to ash.

The only other sound in the room was the soft flutter of the curtains over an open window.

They hit the asphalt a little harder than Karen intended, but considering she didn't have much experience levitating three full-grown adults, it wasn't really that bad. Then again, this wasn't so much levitating as it was trying to fall at a nonlethal speed, and that was magic she could manage. More importantly, it wouldn't require so much energy as to overwhelm the distraction she had left behind in the apartment.

"It isn't that we can't use magic," she had said when quickly explaining her plan. "We just have to use so much of it that they don't know which to pay attention to." That was one of the problems with magical detection: easy to know that magic was at work, but hard to know exactly what it was doing. Ehle had offered the use of a sunstone, a straightforward enchantment useful for illuminating dark places, or blinding your enemies, depending on its strength.

"Well," she said as she tested her feet back on solid ground, "that could have been worse."

Then she heard a car door. One of their visitors had apparently stayed with the car and they'd just landed right in front of him. The man stepped out, his eyes wide with surprise. But even the shock of seeing humans falling from the sky wasn't slowing his hand as he reached into his jacket.

His eyes went even wider and then rolled back into his head. As he collapsed, Karen saw Dennis standing over him, his smashed radio crumbling in his fist.

"You people know how to make an entrance," he said, shaking out his hand.

Above them they heard a huge crash, like someone had blown a hole in a wall.

Jim reached into the car, grabbed the keys, and tossed them into a nearby drain. "Come on," he said. "Time to get out of here."

Emile was not at the parking lot where they left him. Jim risked using the radio but got only quiet static. There was no one in the streets, barely even any cars, like the world had moved on and left them behind. Karen realized her hand hadn't left her locus since they fled the apartment.

"I don't like this," Dennis said.

Karen wholeheartedly agreed with him but decided it was best to keep that to herself. She'd read enough scary stories as a kid to know the fastest way to summon a monster was to speak its name.

"Come on," Jim said. Karen could barely see his face in the dark but saw enough to know he was on edge.

When they neared the building that hid the tunnel entrance, Emile appeared out of the shadows. He was breathing a bit hard and Karen noted beads of sweat on his upper lip before he wiped them away.

"Where were you?" Jim said.

"Dieter is gone," Emile replied.

"What?"

"He left shortly after you did. I followed him for a bit, but lost him in the streets."

Karen glanced back the way they had come, suddenly even more wary. Had Dieter told the GDR where to find them? That didn't seem right; Dieter hated the East Germans more than any of them. But how well did she know him? How well did she know any of the men she was with? The breach, the message from Ehle at the Wall, the tunnel, the magical signal; it had all fallen into place so quickly that she'd never stopped to ask if any of this was a good idea or not.

"Why didn't you answer me?" Jim was asking Emile.

Emile fumbled for his radio. "My apologies. I didn't want the sound to alert him so I turned it down."

"And no one else came or left the building?" Jim asked.

"Not that I saw," Emile said.

Ehle said something to Emile in French. Emile responded and Ehle replied, but it did not sound like a pleasant exchange.

"No time for this now," Jim said. "Dieter knew the risks. I'm not going to put us all in danger waiting for him."

They crossed the deserted street and slipped inside, locking the door behind them. They went down the stairs to the cellar and found the entrance to the tunnel just as they had left it, only without Dieter standing guard.

"Alright," Jim said. "Emile, you first. Then Ehle, then Karen. Dennis and I will take up the rear. Let's go. Time to emigrate."

They went down the ladder and into the cold ground. This time, the constricting press of the tunnel felt comforting; it meant they were going back.

"Nice job tonight," Dennis said to Karen, his voice just above a whisper. "Arthur will be thrilled. We'll make a spy out of you yet."

When they neared the Wall, Karen felt its now familiar presence overhead. She'd almost forgotten about this part. Just keep moving, she told herself. Pretty soon, this will all be a happy memory of that time she pretended to be a CIA agent and snuck behind the Iron Curtain.

The pressure increased. Even knowing what was coming didn't seem to make it any easier to take. Before, the Wall had seemed so benign, despite its inhumane purpose. But now it felt like an intruder, a hostile presence seeping into territory where it did not belong. It wasn't just the assaulting magic; there was something behind it, something within it. An intelligence. An intent.

She reached out a hand and touched Ehle's shoulder. "I should warn you," she said softly. "Crossing under the Wall as a magician can be . . . painful."

"That is not unexpected," he whispered back. "That is how it was made. Our design was to . . ."

He kept going, but she stopped listening. A flicker of one of the tunnel lights cast an unexpected shadow along the wall. She reached out and brushed it and fresh dirt crumbled under her fingers. This hadn't been there before. Someone had been here since they had come through and carved something into the earth. Her thoughts raced back to Ehle's apartment and how they had used magic to conceal other magic, hiding a faint signal in a roar of noise.

Touching the locus around her neck, Karen whispered the words for To Illuminate Magic. A brief pause, and then the hidden runes written all along the tunnel began to glow.

"Run!" she yelled, throwing herself forward into Ehle just as everything exploded.

TWENTY-ONE

Karen woke to a memory of pain, like an ache in the back of her mind. She remembered the taste of blood and dirt, and the stab of ringing ears. She saw through muddy vision a hand reaching into the blasting light: her hand, empty. It took a few minutes before her eyes remembered how to open. Her mouth was dry and tasted terrible. She tried to breathe, but instead it came out as a weak moan.

"You're looking better," said a voice just at the edge of her blurred vision. A few blinks later the blur became Arthur, sitting at the foot of her bed, sipping a mug of coffee. There were a few other beds next to and across from hers—some kind of infirmary. The overhead lights glared off the starched white blankets and pale walls.

"Water," she croaked. He helped her drink something tepid from a paper cup. The room stank of ammonia.

"How are you feeling?" Arthur asked when she lay back.

"Like I was kicked in the head," she said, eyes pressed closed against the bright lights. "Did I survive or are you doing St. Peter's gig now?"

"You survived," he said.

"What happened?"

"I was hoping," he said, "that you could tell us."

It was coming back now, in tangled fragments. Ehle, the apartment, the Soviets. And the tunnel with its unexpected runes. The explosion. She tried to explain it the best she could, slowly, gingerly, like putting together a puzzle when you only barely knew what it was supposed to look like.

"They knew," she said with grim certainty. "They knew about Ehle's safe house. They came for him; they must have known he wanted to defect. He said no one knew."

"What about his prostitute?"

"What?"

"One of Bill's contacts," Arthur said. "She was feeding Bill info about Ehle. Bill met with her just before he got nabbed."

"So . . . the Soviets found her?"

"And from her, they discovered Ehle wasn't their man anymore."

"Ehle mentioned something about the Nightingale," she said.

If she was looking for a reaction, she got none; Arthur did not flinch or even blink when she said the name. He probably thought that would reassure her. Instead, it told her he already knew. "Don't worry about him," he said. "He isn't your problem to solve, not anymore."

She was suddenly fully awake. "Wait, why not?"

"Because I'm sending you home."

"Like hell you are."

"That is no way for a lady to talk."

"Noted," she said. "Why the hell are you sending me back?"

"Because your boss asked me to. He's worried about you."

Dr. Haupt. She'd only been in Berlin a few days, but already their last conversation seemed a lifetime ago. Normally, his concern would have touched her. If her own father wasn't going to bother acting paternal, at least she had someone who would. But now, she bristled at the thought. Why was Dr. Haupt intervening now? What did he know about what was going on? Why didn't he trust her judgment?

"What happened to everyone else?" she asked. "Why aren't they in here with me? Where's Jim? And Dennis? And Ehle?"

Arthur stood up. "You need rest."

"I need answers. I told you what you wanted to hear, now your turn."

"Mr. Ehle is safe," Arthur said. "He told us that you pushed him clear of the blast."

"What about Jim and Dennis?"

Arthur breathed out from his nose, seeming to shrink as the air was expelled. "If I told you not to worry about it, would that suffice?"

"What do you think?" she asked.

"Jim is MIA," he said while looking down at his scuffed shoes. "We've got people looking, but so far, we just don't know." Arthur exhaled. "And after we dug you out, we recovered Dennis's body from the tunnel."

The news pushed down on her like the weight of the Wall overhead, a suffocating black pressure. "No, not Dennis," she said, a weak protest against an uncaring universe.

"He was a good kid," Arthur said. "He knew the risks."

She could see Dennis's face haloed by the brim of his pushed-up hat: wry, amused by the world around him. His banter with Jim still danced in her ears. Did he have a family? A wife? Someone who would weep for him? "This is my fault," she said, blinking back tears. "I pushed for the mission. He agreed to go because . . ."

Arthur pressed a handkerchief into her hand. "This is the nature of our business, Miss O'Neil," he said. "Saying that doesn't bring anyone back. But it's the only way we can get through days like today."

Karen wiped her eyes but kept the smooth cloth bundled in her fist. Her face was hot and her cheeks trembled.

"And we have to get through days like today," Arthur said, "because we have to be ready for what comes next." He reached into a back pocket and took out a folded piece of paper. "Your mission mattered, Miss O'Neil. It came with a cost, but it mattered." He placed the paper on the table by her bed. "When you're ready," he said, then left her to her tears.

MEMORANDUM

SUBJECT: Expansion of Berlin Wall Collapse
TO: Director, Central Intelligence
FROM: Chief, Berlin Operating Base

Timeline of 8 November

[0130] Breach at original site growing.

[0145] Additional breaches discovered at Wilhelmsruh, by the river at Köpenicker, at Treptow, and at Hänselstraße.

[0150] Wall at original breach collapsed. Opening holding steady at twelve (12) meters wide.

[0210] Additional breaches' growth slowed. Wall gaps range from eight (8) to nineteen (19) meters wide.

[0300] One thousand one hundred (1100) refugees estimated to have crossed border at breach sites, requesting asylum.

[0315] GDR police units on-site at each breach location. National People's Army (NPA) units present at Hänselstraße and Treptow. Barricades erected. Refugees attempting to cross detained.

[0400] Commandant, Western Allied Forces, orders 3rd Battalion, 6th Infantry to breach sites to maintain order.

[0430] Crowds gathering on East and West sides at each site.

[0440] First sighting of Soviet military personnel at breach site at Wilhelmsruh.

[0500] Soviet infantry reinforcing NPA military and GDR police units at each breach site. Crowds estimated at ten thousand (10000) on East side of Wall.

[0525] First riot at Treptow site. Crowd attempts crossing barricade. Shots fired. Gas deployed. Crowd dispersed. Casualty figures unavailable.

[0605] Soviet armor units sighted.

[0615] Commandant, Western Allied Forces, orders 2nd Battalion, 6th Infantry to breach sites to maintain order. Commandant orders Company F, 40th Armor to breach sites. 4th Battalion, 18th Infantry; Battery C, 94th Field Artillery; 42nd Engineer Company put on alert.

[0650] Crowd attempts border crossing at Wilhelmsruh. Police and military units fire into crowd. Estimated casualties: ninety-five (95).

[0710] New breach site discovered near rail line at Kiefholzstraße. NPA units erect barricade.

[0930] All breach sites secured by NPA, GDR, and Red Army units. Refugees directed to Tempelhof for processing.

Crowds still gathered on East side of Wall. Presumed looking for opportunity to cross, either at existing site or at new breach. NPA and Red Army unit strength growing. Facing humanitarian, military, political crises.

Please advise.

"I'm not leaving."

As soon as her legs would carry her, she'd made her escape from the infirmary and hurried up to the bullpen, where she knew Arthur would be holding court. Every step she took hurt, and every ache or bruise reminded her that Dennis wasn't coming back, which made her walk even faster. She couldn't be sent home now, not before she made Dennis's sacrifice matter.

"Miss O'Neil," Arthur said, one hand cupped over the receiver on his phone. "Good to see you up and about so soon."

Karen glanced at the five other agents crowded into Arthur's office and ignored Garriety's scowl. "I know you have more important things to deal with right now," she said, getting her words out quickly before someone stopped her, "but I'm not leaving." She waved the memo. "If I can help, I want to."

Arthur preempted anyone else from speaking. "I've got a missing agent, a crumbling Wall, and World War Three all knocking on my door. If you can help with one of those problems, I'll inform Dr. Haupt that your transfer Stateside has been delayed."

"I can help," she said, "but I need to speak with Ehle."

"Fine," Arthur said. He rummaged around behind his desk and produced Ehle's battered leather bag. "Anything dangerous in here?"

Karen had no idea what other enchanted items the German magician had stored away. "Probably," she said.

"Anything that could help?"

"Possibly."

Arthur grunted, but passed the bag over to her anyway. "Just don't blow anything up."

TWENTY-TWO

A crackle in the receiver, and then the voice of the gray-haired man: "I trust I do not need to tell you that the Chairman is not pleased."

"No, sir. You do not."

"I thought not. However, I will tell you then that these developments in Berlin have left your reputation precariously placed. The Nightingale is still a name that signifies great honor among those few who know it, but that can change."

"I understand."

"Do you? I hope so. The Chairman hopes so." A pause. "When a man is known as someone who solves problems, he is an asset to the Party. He is honored and treated well. But once a man shows that he cannot solve problems, such a man is of little use to anyone."

"Please inform the Chairman that I remain committed to resolving this problem. These recent complications are a matter of the late hour in which I was asked to intervene, nothing more."

"Can the project recover?"

"The defector took his notes with him, but he was not working alone. I have been assured of the loyalty and competence of the remaining staff."

"And what have you learned of this defector?"

"He was a coward and a traitor and he frequented with whores. I suspect we will be better off without him."

"And the West? Will they be better off with him?"

"I am already considering how to resolve that particular complication, sir."

"I trust you are. However, results will be required."

"Yes, sir."

Another pause. Static on the line. "These are dangerous times. Only moments ago the Premier ordered two tank battalions to Berlin to help 'observe the crisis.' More will follow. We are preparing for war with the West. And the West, I am certain, is preparing for war with us."

"We will be victorious, sir."

"Of course we will. But before the shells start to fall, I want what is in Auttenberg. If it is to be war, I want every weapon on our side. Is that understood?"

"Yes, sir. I will see to it."

"Good. I will speak to you again when it is done."

"Very good, sir. I—" The line was already dead.

TWENTY-THREE

Karen found Ehle locked in a cell-like room in the bottom floor of the BOB building. To even get there she had to be escorted by an unsmiling agent with a gun on his hip, and they were then met by another armed guard at the door. Only with an order signed by Arthur's hand was she allowed inside and even then they remained separated by iron bars. She tried not to think about why the CIA needed a room like this in their Berlin headquarters.

"Your friends are slow to bestow trust," Ehle said as Karen entered. He was dressed in the same clothes he had escaped in, now muted with a fine layer of dust and slashed with deep wrinkles. "I am reminded of my experience with Soviet hospitality after the war. Though even they did not have such intricate magical disruption runes carved into the walls of my cell."

"Maybe they should have," Karen said as she approached the bars. Erwin Ehle had a plain face, neither handsome nor otherwise. It was the sort of face that might wear a smile, but always like an ill-fitting suit, like he had borrowed the gesture and wore it under duress.

"It is fine workmanship," he said as he traced the carvings with a fingernail. The air in the room smelled of rust. "But they need not have bothered. I do not cast magic anymore."

Karen raised an eyebrow and patted his bag, which she had slung over a shoulder. "Your enchantments?"

"Created a long time ago," he said. "That sort of magic was something of a diversion for me in my youth. Now these few items are all that remain."

She stared at him. No magic? That seemed an odd lie, and he did not look like a man who bothered with unnecessary lies. "You lost your locus?"

Now his eyebrows raised. "You are perceptive, for one so young."

"What happened to it?"

"I cast it away."

Her hand went protectively to her own locus around her neck. It was her connection to her magic, the channel for her focus. She would rather cut off a finger than lose it. It took years to craft a locus, and some magicians who lost theirs were never able to form an equal replacement. "You gave up your magic?" she said. "I don't understand."

His eyes fell. "I hope you never do." When he looked up at her a moment later, he said, "You do not believe me."

Karen had just been considering if she could buy such a story. It was unnerving to have him read her thoughts so easily. She doubted she'd ever make a good spy. "Have you given me any reason to trust you?"

"I abandoned my home to help you," he said.

"Help?" She felt color in her face, in her blood. She hadn't intended on getting angry or picking a fight; she wanted to help and needed Ehle to do so. But when she looked at him all she could see was Dennis and Jim. "How much more is this help going to cost us?"

"Ah," he said.

"What?"

"My interrogators have been so far reluctant to share," he replied. "I did not know the results of the explosion in the tunnel, but now I see not everyone escaped."

Now she flushed again, this time with embarrassment. She hadn't meant to give him details Arthur's people weren't willing to share. Talking to the German magician left her feeling exposed; she had to fight to keep from wrapping her arms around her body.

"Is there not another magician I could speak to?" he asked.

Karen laughed at this, though without pleasure. "You mean a man."

He said nothing. Disappointment that she was a woman seemed to transcend all ages, cultures, and languages.

"Sorry," she said. "But you're stuck with me."

"I did not mean—"

"You came to help us, right? No time like the present."

He paused as if uncertain how to move forward, like a man afraid of land mines. "I can help," he said. "And I will. But not from this cell."

"Help me first, and then they will have a reason to trust you."

"If I help you," he said, "I lose the only reason they have to release me."

The numbers she had read in that report Arthur gave her kept pulsing in her thoughts. Hundreds likely dead already. Thousands massed at the breaches. Soldiers and tanks on both sides of the border with guns pointed at the refugees and at each other. Everything she knew, her family, her studies and research: they all seemed so trivial now, compared to what she had fallen into here. The air was thick with war, not as some abstract concept, but bloody and immediate.

"They are killing people," she said. When she started to speak, she had wanted to say something more eloquent, but maybe straight-forward was the better approach. "Shooting them in the streets. It is only getting worse. We have to do something."

"What precisely would you do?" he asked, his eyes suddenly bright with anger. His question rang in Karen's ears. "Repair the Wall? What of all those people who see it every day and curse? What of the families that Wall separated? What of this city? If people are dying trying to cross the broken border, it is because they think it is worth the risk to come. Would you deny them that, American?"

Again she felt heat on her face. Had she really not stopped to ask if repairing the Wall was the right thing to do? The Soviets had put it in place, after all; if it fell, wouldn't that be a blow to them? Yet if the Wall fell entirely, it could be a massacre. And the West couldn't just let it happen. Could they?

"Forgive me. It is not my place to argue diplomacy," he said softly. Though his tone softened, the anger wasn't gone. She real-ized now that it had always been there, lurking behind everything he said, a slow-burning but well-fueled fire. "Leave that to the politicians and the generals. Let them decide the fates of thou-sands."

"I am sorry," she said. "I only want to help the people of Ber-lin." She neared the bars, but he suddenly pulled back, as if afraid she might touch him. The act was so instinctual that it seemed to surprise them both.

"As do I. And I will help," he said, pointing to the locked cell door, "when I am freed."

Karen nodded. "I will see what I can do."

"Thank you," he said. As she turned to go, he spoke again, sur-prising her. "I wonder why you are so eager for my help. What can I offer your efforts that you do not already have?"

"What do you mean? You worked on the Wall spell," she said.

"That expertise is invaluable. Without that, we're blindly guessing at what—"

"Ah," he said again.

"'Ah'? What does that mean?"

"Nothing," he said with a wave of his hand. "Nothing."

She approached the bars. "Tell me."

He stared at her. Despite what he had said back in his apartment, it was not the sort of look that men often gave her, the ones she was painfully used to by now. She knew how to respond to men who thought she was dumb, or pretty, or uppity. But this was different, harder to place. If she had to put a name to it, it would be pity.

"It means," he said, "that your superiors do not fully trust you either."

Karen heard it when she was still some distance away: a low, steady roar. It sounded like the ocean. She pictured the times her family had visited the beach when she was younger. Her sister had run straight into the surf, but she had held back. She'd been afraid. She remembered the sharp taste of that moment, could still see the blue-white waves. It had just been too big. Did her parents not see? How could her sister play in the water when it had no end?

This was no ocean, but the fear felt the same on her tongue. There must have been a thousand people, maybe more, their voices thrumming the ground. Beyond them a line of soldiers, some holding the people back, some watching across the border. Even more there: another endless sea, this time of humanity, breaking not on sand but on tanks and riot gear. Breaking now, but how long until the tide changed?

And then there was the Wall. It looked sick. Dying.

She had immediately gone to Arthur and reported about the conversation she'd had with Ehle, excluding for now his parting words to her. Had he been right? Were they keeping secrets from her about the Wall? Ehle was a stranger and she had no reason to trust him. She didn't know Arthur well, but he was one of the good guys; why should she believe an East German over the head of the CIA in Berlin?

Another voice in her head, the one that so often haunted her thoughts with the things she'd rather forget, whispered: *Why trust any of them?*

Arthur had nodded and absently ran a thick-fingered hand through thinning hair. "So unless we let him out," Arthur had said, "he'll keep his mouth shut."

"That seems to be the situation," she replied.

"And without him . . . ?" He looked at her expectantly.

"I can't stop it," she said. "You can get more magicians from the OMRD out here, maybe together we can figure something out, but they won't know anything more about the Wall than I do." She wondered now if that were true. Was that what Ehle was trying to say?

"Alright," Arthur said. "Thank you for speaking to him." He reached for his telephone. "I've got to make some calls, then I'll pay our guest a visit myself."

"Is there anything else I can do?"

"Don't wander off," he said, pointing the telephone's receiver at her. "And whatever you do, don't leave the building."

S he pushed into the crowd. The air was thick with the smell of sweat as she wound through the people. She did not understand the words they chanted, but the sentiment was universal. Young and old, men and women, they were angry. If the Wall had been made of brick and concrete, they would probably be armed with hammers. As it was, they shouted their defiance toward the breach, toward the men holding back the waves, toward their friends and family separated from them by politics and magic.

What would she do in their place? Would she brave the crossing? She had magic to protect her, though she didn't want to find out if it could stop a bullet. How much was a new life worth? How much was any life worth?

She hoped she would fight. She hoped she would try to fight for her future, or that of her family. She hoped she would be like those all around her who defied order and prudent diplomacy and made their voices heard in support of justice. She hoped . . . but something deep down told her she was kidding herself. *You'd hide,* it said. *You'd watch from a distant window, and you'd let someone else take the risk.*

Karen closed her eyes and focused on the voices of the people around her, letting them drown her unwanted thoughts. It didn't matter what she might or might not do with another life. It only mattered what she was doing with this one.

She had just started to turn to leave when she felt the hand clamp down on her elbow from behind.

TWENTY-FOUR

Use your own discretion, Arthur, they had said. Berlin was his area of operations, after all, so they agreed to defer to him. They wanted it to sound like they trusted him, but these were not men given to trusting others. So that only left one option: they were scared out of their damned minds and didn't have a clue what to do. It might say "In God We Trust" on the dollar, but the true motto of Washington, DC, was: "If you can't come up with a good idea, settle for a convenient scapegoat." That's where he came in.

"That's right, Mr. Senator," they'd say in the hearing. "He was acting on his own. Completely outside of our authority. A rogue element in the Agency. We never liked him anyway."

To hell with them. If they wanted to give him enough rope to hang himself, he'd see how many extra nooses he could fashion.

"Open up," Arthur said to the guard at the door. The kid's eyes bugged out seeing who was addressing him, but he quickly fumbled for his keys. "Time to pay my respects."

The asset was sitting in the cell, hands on his knees, watching the door. Like he was waiting for him. Like he knew Arthur was coming.

"They tell me," Arthur said as he dragged a metal chair across the floor to place in front of the cell's bars, "that you speak English."

"I do," the asset said. Arthur felt the weight of those eyes on him and wondered for the first time just how effective the magical wards they'd paid to have installed on that cell were. "Though I am not yet certain if I speak American."

"Oh, I think you'll find talking American isn't all that hard," Arthur said, leaning back in his chair. "It's like speaking English, but with the twist that we only hear what we want to hear."

Ehle smiled at that, though without as much as even a crease around his eyes. "What is it that you want to hear?"

"How to stop a war, for starters," Arthur said. "After that, things might get interesting."

"Ah," he said. The asset raised an eyebrow. "And what does a man like yourself," he asked, "find interesting?"

"Me? I have wide interests," Arthur said, coming forward. "One area in particular I enjoy is history. Do you like history? Europeans always do, since most of the good stuff is about you guys. Different empires, same wars, for a thousand years. But what I find so fascinating about history is how some things get left out. Facts sometimes just fade away. Have you ever seen this peculiar forgetfulness in action?"

Ehle sat perfectly still. A cool customer, this one. After a long silence, he spoke. "A true history," he said, "can be elusive. In my experience, therefore, it is prudent to judge a man by his present, not his past."

"See, now that's a fascinating theory," Arthur said. "It's one that I've heard before, usually championed by men with something in their history they'd rather forget."

"Every man I have ever known has something in his past he would rather forget."

"Someone once told me that life is just the accumulation of memories and regrets."

"A wise saying."

"Worst part is, the older I get, I forget about the memories, but those regrets tend to stick around," Arthur said. He shrugged. "That said, some men's regrets are bigger than others. I might say that I regret not making more time for my wife when we were married. She deserved better. But another man might say, for example, that he regrets being an active member of the Nazi Party and fervent supporter of the Third Reich in its attempt to conquer the world and purge it of impure races." He weighed both in upturned hands. "Not all regret is created equal."

To his credit, Ehle didn't even blink. "You do not know me," he said.

"It's my job to know you, Mr. Ehle," Arthur said. "It's also my job to help keep this part of the world from blowing itself up, and I take that job rather seriously." Arthur stood, the chair scraping. "Let's be clear: the fact that the evil a man does can be wiped away if he happens to have useful knowledge makes me sick. And I don't mean that figuratively. I mean I want to vomit, like I did when my battalion liberated Dachau. The very sight of you makes the bile rise in the back of my throat."

Arthur took the cell's key out of his pocket. "But see, you do have useful knowledge, and I've got a war to stop." He unlocked the door with a sharp metallic click. "So welcome to the West."

The asset stood and straightened his shirt. "Thank you."

"I'm not quite done," Arthur said, stopping him at the cell door. "I've got two conditions to your release. First, you promise me you'll keep the magician you're working with safe. I've seen enough people get hurt in this infernal city and I don't want her on my conscience. Got it?"

Ehle replied, "And the second condition?"

"You don't tell her the real reason for the Wall."

TWENTY-FIVE

"Stay very still," the voice in her ear said in English with a German accent. The grip on her arm was like steel. "They are watching you."

Her mind tripped over itself searching for and rejecting options: that spell was too dangerous in a crowd; this one was too dangerous at close range; another was far too dangerous with the Wall's disruption. *Come on, Karen, do something. Even just spin around and knee him in the groin.* That sort of magic always worked.

"I am not here to hurt you," the voice said and now, despite the constant buzz around them, it sounded familiar. "I need to speak to you."

"Dieter?"

"Do not turn," he said. "There are two men behind us, about thirty meters. They have been following you since you left the Americans' building."

"What happened when—"

"I will explain, but not here." His fingers relaxed on her arm. "South of here, three city blocks, there is an alleyway between two brick buildings. It appears to be a dead end, but there is another passage near the back. I will meet you there in ten minutes."

Then the hand was gone. She didn't look back. She was a little surprised that the CIA had sent minders for her, and more than a little surprised she hadn't noticed them herself. She supposed she still had a lot of work to do before she was a full-fledged international spy. No time like the present to start.

She stepped in front of a knot of particularly tall protestors and ducked low. She loosed her hair and let it fall down around her shoulders. Though the autumn air was cool, she took off her jacket and tied it around her waist, then started moving south, careful to keep her head down and her path jagged. The crowd thinned as she neared the buildings Dieter had told her about, so she stayed with the multitude as long as she could, constantly fighting the urge to look over her shoulder.

Just as she was about to make her break for the alley, she heard the first gunshot. The crowd went strangely quiet, as if under some mass spell. Then another shot rang out, and then the chattering of more, and the crowd came alive. Everyone ran, some away from the breach, others toward it. The guns didn't sound close; even though she couldn't see, Karen was certain they were coming from East Berlin.

Through the churn of limbs, she caught glimpses of the breach. For a moment, she saw men running, arms waving, rifles held to shoulders. Then smoke, so thick and roiling that she knew in an instant it was magical, poured in, clogging the gap, snatching all of the eastern side of the city from view.

More shots. Yelling. Someone ran past her, toward the soldiers, carrying a crude brick and shouting. Nearby, someone was screaming.

Move your legs, Karen. Now.

She reached the alley at a sprint and didn't bother to see if she was being watched. Down at the end, behind a stack of crumbling wet cardboard boxes, she found the other alleyway. This one seemed like a mistake in architecture. A few feet wide, barely enough to walk in, with the daylight from some other nameless street at the far end. She saw no one, but clutched her locus all the same.

Dieter appeared a moment later. He held up a finger and peered around the corner back up the alley.

"What happened out there?" Karen asked in a whisper.

"They have set up barricades on the Eastern side of the Wall, and someone tried to cross them," Dieter said, still looking away from her. "I do not think the crossing was successful."

Karen took a few steps back from Dieter. Where his jacket lifted away from his waist, she could see a sliver of dark metal tucked into his pants. She tried to control her breathing, her snare-drum heart, and summoned a kinetic shield between them.

Dieter turned. If he saw the shimmer of the barrier, she didn't know, but he did not try to approach and he kept his hands away from the gun.

"What happened to you? In East Berlin. Where did you go?"

"They came," he said in his harsh-sounding English. "As soon as you were out of sight, the Soviets came."

"You were in the basement," she said. "How did you know?"

"I am not a trusting man," he replied. "I went up and watched, and then when they arrived, I escaped. Only just."

"How did you get back to West Berlin?"

"I have resources," he said. "I have not wasted them all by sharing them with the Americans."

"The others thought . . ."

He sneered at that, a laugh dying stillborn on his lips. "They thought it was me? *Narren.* I risked everything by letting you use the tunnel. Do you know how many I could have saved with it? And now they think I betrayed them?"

"Come with me," she said. "We can explain. We can make them understand—"

He shook his head once, hard and final. "It is you that does not understand. The Soviets knew about your mission. Someone has betrayed you and they will do it again."

"It was Ehle," Karen said. "He told someone who was compromised by the Soviets."

"Ehle did not know about the tunnel," Dieter said. "Even if they followed you back from his apartment, they would not have had time to place their trap. They knew everything before we took our first step into East Berlin."

She felt stupid. Of course they'd known.

Why trust any of them? her mocking thoughts echoed.

Run away, they whispered. *Run before it is too late.*

"We have to do something," she said, hating how weak her voice sounded.

"It is about to get worse," he said, glancing back toward the Wall behind the building. "If the Wall falls, some will make it to safety. Many more will die. I will not do nothing."

"Is that why you found me? To warn me about the traitor?"

"No," Dieter said. "I came to tell you what I saw afterward."

"Afterward?"

"I watched," he said. "I watched them follow you into the building. I heard the explosion and felt my tunnel collapse. And after they were finished inside, I watched them drag someone out alive." Dieter's deep-set eyes dug into her. "It was James."

Jim. No.

"I thought you would like to know. *Auf Wiedersehen,*" he said, turning to go. "And good luck."

He left the way they had come and Karen had no wish to follow. She pressed her way through the narrow alley to the far exit.

The street beyond was mostly quiet. No more gunshots. No more screams. For now.

She ducked out and fell in behind a group of older men and women. One of them had a bloody rag pressed against a gash on his forehead. Another was held up by two companions as he nursed a swollen ankle. Minor wounds, she thought. West German wounds. She did not want to imagine what that choking fog had hidden, but could not stop herself.

Lost in these thoughts, she didn't notice the men behind her until they were already on either side, hemming her in. Plainly dressed but thickly built, they towered over her. She reached for her locus, but one of them quickly, efficiently, pinned her arm to her side.

"That won't be necessary, Miss O'Neil," he said without looking at her.

A car pulled up alongside them and they directed her toward an opening door. It was all over before she could even think to protest. Some spy she turned out to be. The car door slammed shut and tires squealed and she found herself sitting across from Milton Garriety.

"You've been a busy girl," he said softly.

TWENTY-SIX

His head hurt. He was fairly certain other things hurt too, but right now his focus was on his head. Busted ribs would heal. Cuts would close and bruises fade, but only if he could think. Only if he could remember. If he kept his wits, if his head would stop pounding for one moment and let him think, then maybe he could stay alive.

She had yelled something. It was hard to hear in the tunnel over his own breathing, but he had heard something. Then a flash of light, dust and sand in his eyes, in his mouth. Then nothing.

Then this room.

He did not think he had been here before. The walls were gray, the floor concrete. There were no windows and one door (with no handle).

His chair was bolted to the floor. There was a table and then another chair across from him. Empty. He wasn't tied up or chained down, but his legs felt too weak to stand.

The tunnel. Why were they in the tunnel? Where were they going? Every time he tried to remember, the pain started in, blacking his vision, burning up his skin.

A wall. Something about a wall . . .

The door opened. How long had he been waiting for the damned door to just open? A man walked inside and sat in the chair across from him. He was dressed in a military uniform. Soviet? GDR? GRU? KGB? Letters swam in his vision as he tried to focus on the man's face, on his insignia.

A green jacket. Golden leaf on both shoulders. Holy hell. This guy was army. US Army.

"Major," he said, trying out his voice (it wasn't pretty). "Where am I?"

The major placed a blue folder on the table and flipped it open. He could see photographs, typed pages, marked up with red pencil. A map of Berlin, a dark black line outlining the Wall.

"What is this about?"

"Treason," the major answered, his eyes on the pages as he thumbed through them.

"Treason?" His voice was working, but maybe his ears had failed. "What do you mean, treason? Is this some sort of joke?"

The major's eyes snapped up and met his. "Am I laughing?"

"No, sir," he said, flinching away from his gaze. "I just—"

"James Fletcher Jr., born 9 August 1936 to Elizabeth and James Sr. Recruited into Central Intelligence out of college, completed training in Virginia, transferred to Berlin Operating Base to work in counterintelligence. Currently in third year of deployment, where you have served without distinction."

"Hey now," Jim said, the words, the facts, jumbling up in his skull. "I—"

The major closed the folder. "Agent Fletcher, why do you think we are here?"

"I . . . I don't . . ." It was like the memories wanted to crack their way out of his head and had found a crowbar to make it happen.

"Do you remember illegally crossing the border into the German Democratic Republic?"

"We had to use the tunnel," he said, squeezing his eyes shut. "The Soviets would have identified us if we crossed at a checkpoint."

"Do you remember authorizing the unplanned extraction of a German asset code-named Yellowjacket?"

"Ehle?" Jim could see now: the dusty apartment, the men in the car, falling out the window. "We needed his help. He was going to help us fix the Wall."

"That is what this . . ." His voice trailed off as he consulted the folder's contents again. "Karen O'Neil told you? That this Ehle would help you fix the Wall?"

"Yes," Jim said. "Yes, she said he . . . that he contacted her." Something was wrong. Why was he answering questions? He didn't know where he was, who he was really talking to. Remember your training, he told himself. "Listen, I need to speak to my boss. Is he here?"

"What else did she tell you?"

"What else . . ." Jim felt his hands gripping the arms of his chair. "What kinds of questions are these? You know what, I need to speak to Arthur before I answer any more of your questions. Get him in here and then we'll talk."

The major sighed. Jim tried to focus on his face, make out any detail. Was he older, graying? Were those glasses? His head was pounding. When had the lights gotten so bright?

"Agent Fletcher," the major said, "I do not believe you have the proper perspective."

"Is that so, pal? Well, why don't you—"

"The Berlin Wall is gone, Mr. Fletcher. The entire thing disappeared the night you crossed into East Berlin. Thousands are dead, shot trying to cross the border. Soviet and East German military units have surrounded West Berlin and cut off all communication and supply. We are looking at the start to a world war and Washington is looking for someone to blame."

"Blame? For the Wall? You don't mean—"

The major folded his hands on the table in front of him. "Tell me what you know about Karen O'Neil."

"Karen? What's she got to do with—"

"Agent Fletcher," the major said abruptly, cutting Jim off. "The situation is dire. It is time to start answering questions, not asking them. If you are going to save yourself, it is time to become helpful."

No, this wasn't right. He knew it wasn't. Don't talk, don't give away information. They covered this in training. Don't give away intel to the enemy. But this wasn't the enemy; this was his own people. The training didn't apply. If only he could think. If only his head would stop threatening to explode.

"You were in love with her?"

"What?"

The major drummed his fingers. "With Miss O'Neil."

"I just met her. Why would you even ask—"

The major pulled an off-white paper from his folder. He looked at it briefly before passing it across the table to Jim. He did not bother to hide his disgust.

"If you weren't in love with her," the major said as Jim picked up the paper, "why did you buy her an engagement ring?"

There was a picture of a ring clipped to the paper. It was simple, a solid gold band with a small diamond in the center. It reminded him of the one his mother wore even long after the news about his father had come. Behind the picture were copies of receipts, amounts in different currencies, the name of a jeweler in the American sector, and a signature, undeniably his.

"I don't remember any of this," Jim said, mostly to himself. He felt faint. His hands were as white as the paper they shakily held.

"A pretty girl," the major said. Jim could feel the man's eyes on him, eyes he couldn't meet. "Great smile. Smart, pleasant, all-American type. Easy to fall for her. Who wouldn't, in your shoes?"

No, it wasn't like that. Sure, she was a looker, and he liked making her laugh, but marriage? "There was a problem at the Wall," he said. The words came out slowly, but the cadence helped him think. "We asked for help. We needed a magician. And the OMRD sent Karen. She was a colleague. Maybe we were friendly, but I don't remember a ring."

"How familiar are you with magic, Mr. Fletcher?"

"A little," Jim said. "I studied it for a bit, had some knack but not enough." This answer came out before he even realized it. *Slow it down, Jimbo. Think. Don't give away information.*

"In your studies, did they teach you about magical emotional manipulation?"

"Magical emotional . . ." The pain was swelling again. The words rattled around like rusty nails in an old tin can. "Are you saying . . . she cast a love spell on me?"

"Do you have another explanation why a trained intelligence operative of the United States government spent three months' salary on a diamond ring for a girl he just met? And then accompanied that girl across an international border so she could meet up with a known Communist magician for some unknown purpose? And then when these two magicians were under the Wall, in a secret tunnel the CIA provided for this purpose, it just so happens that the Wall spell failed and put us on the road to total war?"

The major leaned forward. He seemed bigger, or the room smaller. Jim couldn't breathe, couldn't think. The man's face, unknowable but everywhere, loomed over him as he shrank into himself.

"Because if you've got another explanation, son," the major said, his voice grinding inside Jim's head, "you better start talking. You'll find me a better listener than the firing squad."

TWENTY-SEVEN

"Was I unclear?"

"No, sir, but—"

"Did I mumble?"

"No, I—"

"Stutter?"

Karen licked her lips. "I just wanted—"

"So you understood; you just chose to disobey my direct order."

"I wasn't in any danger."

Arthur slammed his fist down on his desk. The sudden but brief explosion of violence left the room utterly silent. "You have no idea if you were in danger or not," he said, jabbing a blunt finger toward Karen. "You have no damned idea. You know how I know that? Because I don't know. I have no idea what is going on out there, and if I don't know, you sure as hell don't either."

Karen swallowed. Her mouth was dry and her palms moist. She had assumed the worst when Garriety's thugs threw her in the car: they were going to drive her out to the woods, or some abandoned factory, or just toss her in the river, like some loose end to be tied up before the bombs started falling. Instead they had driven her back to BOB in silence, which may have been a worse fate than the grim ones she'd imagined.

"I wanted to see the Wall," she said. Garriety was behind her, watching, breathing softly, but she tried to ignore him and just focus on calming Arthur. "I needed to see what state it was in. Everyone here had more important things to do than play tour guide, so I went out. I'm sorry."

Arthur looked at her like she had lost her mind. He placed his hands flat on his desk as if steadying it. Bright, ugly veins stood out like scars on his nostrils.

"Miss O'Neil," he said, like he was the principal and she was the disappointing sixth grader, "it's going to hell out there. I've got generals, senators on the line calling me. Between politicians and reporters and refugees, there are more eyes on Berlin right now than anywhere on God's green earth. I don't have time to . . ." He stopped himself, forced himself to breathe.

"I'm sorry," Karen said, almost as a reflex, but Arthur held up a hand.

"You're wrong about something," he said. "You said people around here have better things to do than look after you but you're dead wrong. That Wall going back up, as painful as that might be, is the only chance we've got to calm this hornet's nest down, and you're our best bet at that happening. There's nothing more important than repairing the Wall, got it? So when I give an order about your safety, I'm not being difficult and I'm not trying to be your father; I'm trying to keep Europe from burning down."

Karen felt a lump in her throat, but she wasn't about to show even a glimpse of a tear to these old men. "Yes, sir."

"I've released your friend the German magician," Arthur said. "See what help he can offer, but don't trust a word he says."

"So go ask him for help, but don't believe what he tells me?"

"Welcome to the intelligence game."

"Arthur," she said, hesitant. Her hands balled into fists. "There's more."

"More," he said. It wasn't a question; she wasn't sure he even realized he had said anything. He looked blank, like an unwritten page, offering nothing to the reader.

"Can I tell you in private?" she asked. Garriety snorted, but she pressed on. "It is important."

"You don't trust Milton?" Arthur asked, almost amused.

"I don't trust any of you." She had meant it to sound like banter, like a joke she might have thrown at Jim and Dennis, but when it came out, her voice sounded hard and sharp, like cracked marble, and she realized she meant every word.

Arthur didn't laugh. The empty page of his face filled in with dark black lines of some ancient, universal script. "Milt," he said, "give us a moment."

"Wait now," Garriety said. "Arthur, if she—"

"Out."

The door slammed a little when he left. Karen tried not to smirk.

"Dieter found me at the Wall," she said. Arthur hadn't been playing before; she'd crossed a line by disobeying him. But at the mention of Dieter's name, his mood somehow turned darker.

He listened without interruption as she explained what had happened at the Wall and what Dieter had told her. She honestly didn't know if what she'd learned was good news or bad, but in the end it was information, and that was Arthur's business.

"Why did he go to you?" the chief asked when she was done.

"He said . . . he doesn't trust us," Karen answered. "He thinks there's a traitor. Someone working for the Soviets."

Arthur nodded. "And you don't think it's me?"

Karen finally laughed at that. "Dieter trusted me because he had to trust someone. Now I'm trusting you."

"Thank you for that," he replied. He was silent for a long time, his gaze moving through her and through the walls and out to the uncertain sky.

"You don't look surprised."

"Few things surprise me anymore, Miss O'Neil."

"You knew?"

"Suspected." He paused, drumming his heavy fingers on his desk. "The tunnel. They got to it while you were gathering Mr. Ehle. That means someone has been telling tales out of school."

"Can you get Jim back?" she asked.

"I can try."

Karen nodded. "Being a spy seems like a lonely job," she said softly.

"You get used to it," Arthur said.

"Is it worth it?"

"On the good days it is," he said.

"And on the bad?"

"I'm here for the good days. The bad ones . . . they'll figure themselves out." He tried to smile, but abandoned the gesture quickly. "I meant what I said before. We need you to solve this thing."

"I'll go speak to Ehle now, sir." Whether he likes it or not.

"Actually, before you do that," he said, rummaging through a pile on his desk until he uncovered a pink note, "you need to call home."

She took the paper. Dr. Haupt wanted her to contact the OMRD immediately.

"Just make the call," Arthur said. "You have my leave to stay here until we're all on airplanes to Bonn. But make the call."

"Yes, sir."

"Good." He stood up. "Because I've got work of my own to do."

When Dr. Haupt answered, his voice was metallic and very small. "Karen? Karen, is that you?"

"Yes, Doctor," she said. She wondered what she sounded like to him on the other side of the world.

"Oh, my dear, it is so good to hear from you," Dr. Haupt said. "I was so worried when I heard what is happening there. Terrible, just terrible. If I had known I was sending you into a war zone . . . I am just so relieved you are well."

But you don't know if I'm well, do you?

"I'm safe," she decided to say, hoping it was actually true. "But the situation here is serious."

"That is what I feared," he said. "I believe it is time for you to come home."

"No, Doctor," she said. "I can't leave now. They need me."

"Karen, I—"

"I need your help, sir," she said quickly, before he could finish. Did she trust Dr. Haupt? Did she truly know him? She continually replayed Ehle's words in her head: *Your superiors do not fully trust you either.* There was something they were keeping from her, something about the Wall. They knew more about it than they were letting on. "Doctor," she said carefully, "can you tell me anything more about the Wall spell?"

There was a long stillness on the line, only the cicada buzz of static. If anyone in the US knew more about the Wall, it had to be Dr. Haupt; he had forgotten more about magic than most American magicians combined ever knew. But why wasn't he in Berlin then instead of her?

"The Wall was raised after I left Germany for the United States," came the eventual tinny reply. "There's nothing I can tell you."

She remembered that "misfiled" document Jim had given her,

dated from just before the Wall cut Berlin in half. "What do you know about Operation Hobnail?"

"Karen," he said, his voice suddenly louder, surprising her, "where are these questions coming from?" There was something in his tone, barely translated across the Atlantic but still unmistakable, that she had never heard before. "To whom have you been speaking?"

The question landed hard. It was not the sort of question a man without secrets would even think to ask. And the edge to his words, like the crack of his silver cane on marble, said a great deal about how he felt about having such secrets exposed.

"Dr. Haupt," she said, heart thumping, "did the US have something to do with the Wall?"

"I think it is time you came home, my dear. It is not safe for you there anymore. I will send—"

She dropped the telephone back into its cradle. It wasn't the most eloquent way to end the conversation, but it was the best she could manage. Something else was at work here. Layers upon layers, endless staircases to dark basements that she wasn't supposed to peek into. And yet . . . wasn't that exactly what Arthur had told her to do? Solve the mystery of the Wall. Figure out the magic.

Prevent World War III.

And that was just what she was going to do.

TWENTY-EIGHT

There was nothing quite like a German butcher shop. There wasn't much they did right, but the krauts knew their meat. Shops like this one, more plentiful in less bellicose times, always reminded Arthur of Christmas, with the stacks of hocks and chops wrapped in paper and twine for all the good little boys and girls, and sausages hanging in the windows like garlands. It was an innocuous place, somewhere everyone in the neighborhood eventually visited but no one really noticed or thought much about.

In other words, a perfect place for a spy.

Arthur pulled the list out of his jacket pocket. The crumpled paper had only one name left on it. Just this stop, and then one more errand after that. He replaced the list and found the flask in the same pocket. Never too early for a pick-me-up. He patted his driver on the shoulder and said, "Circle the block a few times. This shouldn't take long."

The bell over the front door jangled as he entered. He held the door for a tiny old woman carrying a wrapped hunk of meat bigger than her whole torso, then approached the counter.

"One moment," came the call from the back room. Arthur

took off his gloves. The shop smelled of blood and old wood, comforting smells, if you were the right sort of man.

The knobby bald head of the butcher appeared around a corner. "Welcome," he said. His thick, bristled body followed slowly, carrying the burden of Germany's many momentous years with each step. He had the look of someone who earned his living with his hands, not his words.

"Do you speak English?" Arthur asked.

The man nodded. "Yes," he said. "I speak some."

"Wonderful," Arthur said. "We Americans appreciate you Europeans learning our language. Makes traveling abroad so much simpler." He offered a broad smile. "I've thought about learning another language, maybe picking up some German, but if you learn English and I learn German, well, one of us is wasting his time, isn't he?"

The butcher blinked small dark eyes. "How may I help you today?" His English wasn't bad, maybe a bit too British.

"This is a nice shop you have here," Arthur said, looking around. "Sorry, I didn't catch your name."

"Otto."

"Otto," Arthur said. "Pleased to meet you, Otto. How long have you had this shop?"

His eyes flickered a moment as he reached for the word. "Many generations," he said at last. "My father's shop, his father's before that."

"Your father taught you the trade?"

Otto nodded. "I learned what I could."

"And your sons?" Arthur asked. "You teach them as well?"

Now the butcher's face darkened. New lines creased his jowly face. "I lost my sons," Otto said. "To the war."

"Germany does seem to have an acute shortage of sons these

days," Arthur said. "But I guess that's the cost of trying to burn the world down."

Otto's cleaver hands twitched. "How," he said slowly, "may I help you today?"

"Peter," Arthur said. "Your eldest. He died in France during that first push to Paris. Weren't many casualties for you lot then, since the rest of us weren't quite ready for you, but poor Peter just caught an unlucky bullet."

"Who are—?"

"Edmund lasted a bit longer," Arthur said, shaking his head. "Almost went the distance, but his battalion got hit by bombers just outside of Berlin during the retreat. Never really had a chance."

"You must leave," Otto said. His hands had become fists. "Now."

Arthur pulled his Colt .45 from his jacket and set it on the counter with a solid clunk that ended all other sounds in the butcher shop. Otto was perfectly still. In nearly flawless German, Arthur said, "I never had sons myself. But I believe I can understand. If I had sons, and the Allies killed them, I too might have betrayed my country as you have."

The fury died in the butcher's face, replaced with wary confusion. "I have betrayed no one."

"It is a problem of geography," Arthur said, drumming his fingers softly on the grip of his .45. "If you were in East Berlin, gathering intelligence for the Soviets would make you a hero, not a traitor. But we are not in East Berlin, are we, Otto?"

"Who are you?"

"The answer to that depends on the day, Otto," Arthur said. "Today, I am the trashman. I am sweeping garbage out of West Berlin."

"You must have me confused," the butcher said. He tried to

keep his eyes on Arthur, but gravity kept pulling them downward, toward the barrel of the pistol. "You have come to the wrong—"

Arthur held up a hand and sighed. "I am a busy man, so you must forgive me for being direct. I have visited with a number of your colleagues today." He pulled out his list and started reading. "Karl Müller, over in Wilmersdorf. Then Rolf Baumann, a tailor in Charlottenburg. I just came from meeting a Mr. Oskar Beck— now he was a cranky little fellow, not pleasant to work with at all." He put the list away. "Need I go on? I have a dozen or so more."

The butcher said nothing.

"I had each of them arrested for a myriad of crimes, some they had even committed. They will stay in jail at my pleasure. But you, Otto, you are lucky. I am going to solve your problem of geography."

"You are sending me to East Berlin?"

"Yes, I am, but not because I am a gracious man. I need you to deliver a message for me. When you return to Karlshorst for your debriefing, there will be a colonel there newly arrived from Moscow. This colonel, some call him the Nightingale. He has something of mine that I want back: an agent named Jim. Every day I have to wait, I will send another of his spies back to him. At first I will send them walking. Then I will become creative. When I am finished, there will be no such thing as a Soviet intelligence network in West Germany. Am I making myself understood to you, Otto?"

The butcher was silent for a long time. Arthur did not press him. Otto's entire life, what was left of it after the war took its due, was crumbling around him. He could spare a moment's reflection for a broken man.

"Yes," Otto said at last. "I understand."

"Splendid," Arthur said in English, sweeping up his gun and tucking it away in his jacket. "And while you're at it, I'll take a package of those delicious-looking sausages."

TWENTY-NINE

Ehle was waiting for Karen when she returned to her cramped office. He was sitting behind her desk, her notes spread out in front of him in a disarray so complete it had to be either utter chaos or genius. At first it felt like a trespass; this guy was a prisoner of the state five minutes ago and now they just let him dig through her stuff? But then she reminded herself that he had been freed on her request and that if she wanted him to help with her research, the first thing she'd have to do was share.

"This is impressive," Ehle said without looking up. "You have been here a short while and yet have already made important discoveries."

She leaned against the hard concrete wall and watched him. "Not bad for a woman."

Now he met her eyes. "I did not doubt your magical ability."

"What then? My upper-body strength? My capacity for rational thought?"

"It is complicated." The anger was back, or at least more obvious.

"What is complicated?"

"My history with women."

"Right," Karen replied. She didn't care if he was angry. She was angry; let him deal with that. "Men. Why are you so bothered by the weaker sex? Sorry that we keep getting in the way. It's just hard, you know, staying hidden when you are half the world's population."

He let the paper in his hands flutter to the desk. His fingers were trembling; he balled them into tight fists, blue veins jagged and clear against white skin. He wouldn't, couldn't look at her. In fact he suddenly seemed far away, like his mind was making a hasty retreat from whatever was clouding his thoughts.

"I . . ." he started, his voice soft, his eyes gouging the desk's surface, "apologize."

"Okay," Karen said. Her anger was long gone now, forgotten by what she saw coiled up inside this man. Rage, yes. But also pain. And an exhausting force of will keeping it all in check.

"I told you before that I discarded my locus," he said. He still couldn't look at her.

"Yes," she said. "You haven't done any real magic since."

"Indeed," he said wistfully. "You did not believe me, and I do not blame you. What magician would throw away such an item? Not only the source of our talent, but also of unmatched personal value. It was not easy."

"You don't have to tell me," she said.

"You should know," he said. He breathed deep and then continued. "As a young magician, I had skill but not enough focus. I tried a number of items as my locus, but nothing seemed to fit. It was only as a man, with a wife and child, that I loved something enough to find the necessary will."

He held out an empty hand. "It was a locket. Silver, with a picture of my wife and my daughter. I can still see their faces now. My Karoline, and sweet Liesel. She was a lucky girl; she looked like her mother." A tear hinted at the edge of an eye and he quickly brushed the intrusion away. "With such a talisman, my magic knew no bounds."

"What happened to them?" Karen asked with the scratch of a dry tongue.

"The war took them as it took so many others," Ehle answered after a long pause. "I could not bear the weight of that locket around my neck. And so I threw it into a pile of rubble." He sighed, a bone-deep sound of relief. "Even now, it is difficult for me. Liesel would be about your age."

For the first time since she'd heard his voice on the wind near the Wall, she faced the reality that Ehle wasn't the means to an end or the answer to her prayers. He was a man: troubled, tired, and weak. Not just a man, a father. She saw her own father in him, not the stubborn taskmaster of her childhood or the scowling crank he'd become, but the silent, hollowed man he'd been in those first weeks after returning from the war. Both men had faced the worst, and somehow, both men had survived. But not without cost.

"I am sorry," she said. The words were too easy, but all she could offer.

"Thank you." His shoulders lowered a little and his fists became hands again.

Karen took the pouch from around her neck and emptied it on the desk. A tangle of little silver stars, like three-dimensional asterisks, tumbled out onto the smooth surface. "It took me a long time to choose a locus," she said. "Our professors told us to pick something 'imbued with resonant emotion,' whatever that means. I tried jewelry, like some of the other girls in my class. The guys mostly went for manly things: pocketknives, flip lighters, wristwatches. One guy made himself a crown, an actual golden crown." She laughed at the memory. Crown Guy had failed out in their junior year.

"But nothing really stuck for me," she said, poking at the metal stars. "I played this game with my sister when we were kids. Mom called it knucklebones. We just called it jacks. It was silly, just something to pass the time when Dad wanted us out of the way. But when I feel these little guys in my hand, it makes me think of those days, when everything was just easier."

"You find comfort in your past," Ehle said. The thought sounded impossible to him.

"It makes me feel safe," she said. "It reminds me that the world doesn't have to be so complicated."

"Ah," he said.

Karen heard something in the tone of his voice. "You disagree?"

Ehle shook his head. "Your locus is yours alone. Whatever it is, it must be important to you, beyond everything else."

"But?"

He hesitated, but she just stared at him until he blinked. "But," he said, "sometimes, the world does have to be complicated."

Karen gathered up the jacks and put them back into the pouch. "I think we have work to do," she said.

"Yes," Ehle replied. "To work. There is much to be done."

She slid his leather satchel across the desk to him. "Can you be trusted with these?"

Ehle nearly reached for the strap, but then seemed to decide against it. "Please," he said, "keep it for me. For now. Perhaps my trinkets can be of use to you, somehow."

Karen watched him a moment, then took back the bag of enchanted items. She rummaged through her notes until she found what she was looking for. "What can you tell me about the Wall?"

"What would you like to know?"

"The magic's impressive, no question," she said. "When I first started examining it, I was frankly in awe of it. I've never seen power on that scale. Just standing near it is . . . deafening."

His face was impassive. "It is the masterwork of the best magicians in a generation. I only wish such talent had been put toward more positive ends."

"But that's just it," Karen said, pointing to the numbers she had hastily scribbled on the page. "This is legendary magic. It should also be elegant, but it isn't."

At this, Ehle offered a sliver of a smile. "You offered me asylum in the West so you might critique my craftsmanship?"

"Not at all," she said. "Just your honesty. You and everyone who built the Wall."

The smile shriveled, but was replaced with something more interesting. For the first time, Ehle looked engaged. "Go on, Miss O'Neil," he said quietly.

"Like I said, the Wall puts out so much noise," she said. "No magician could even hear themselves think near it. All that noise is wasted energy. Inefficient magic. I couldn't figure out why such masterful magicians would cast such a rough spell, until we went over to East Berlin. Until our escape from your apartment."

"Your distraction," Ehle said.

"Yes," Karen said. "Magic hiding other magic. The same thing happened in the tunnel. The Soviets carved explosive runes in the dirt, but we didn't notice them until it was too late because of the Wall."

"Do you have a hypothesis?"

"No," she answered. "Just a question: what's the Wall hiding?"

He was silent. She could read nothing from his expression. It was almost as if she had not even spoken.

"Mr. Ehle, our time is short and I—"

"Do you know Righetto's Silence?"

Karen blinked. "Yes, I think so."

"Would you show me? Please."

The spell took a few moments to prepare. Luckily she had some chalk, an excellent memory, and passable Etruscan pronunciation. When she finished, she felt the silence settle in around them like a shroud. It was as if they were in the center of the earth, buffeted by miles of rock, isolated entirely.

Ehle nodded approval. "Well done," he said, his restless hands reaching out to touch the shimmer that marked the limits of the silencing spell.

"Why did you have me cast it?" she asked. "No one is listening in. They're too busy."

"You should know better the men for whom you work," Ehle said. "You have not experienced an unrecorded moment since you arrived."

That was an unpleasant thought, but she brushed it quickly aside. "I have nothing to hide. I'm trying to help them."

"As am I."

"So why did—"

"Because I am going to trust you," Ehle said. He took the chair out from behind the desk and moved it closer so that they could both sit facing one another. "And in doing so, risk my freedom."

Karen sat. It dawned on her, as she did, that with the spell in place she was truly alone with this man. She slid the chair back a few inches and tried not to reach for her locus.

"Why," she said, swallowing, "is your freedom at risk?"

"Because a condition of my release was that I not tell you the Wall's true purpose," he said, folding his hands in his lap. "And I intend to violate that condition."

Karen's fingers buzzed and her blood crackled. She had been right; there was more going on with the Wall than it appeared. Nothing about the Wall's magic had made sense when she examined it, but that had been when she believed it was just meant to be a barrier.

"Why would you do that?"

"Because the Wall cannot be fixed."

"But we have to try," she said, leaning forward in her chair. She thought she sensed him forcing himself not to recoil. "I went there, I saw the people. I don't want them to be stuck in East Berlin any more than you do, but it is going to be a massacre if we're lucky and a war if we aren't." But then her thoughts caught up with her words and she realized she had missed something in what he had said, something that communicated more than the words he had used. She wet her suddenly dry lips and asked, "Wait, how do you know the Wall can't be fixed?"

"Because I am the one who made the breach."

THIRTY

None of it was true. Not the Wall, not the tunnel, not Karen. They didn't exist; they had never existed. Figments of a rotting imagination. Ghosts of a world that had never been. It all had to be a lie, because if any of it was true, Jim feared he would go mad. Or worse. There were always worse things than madness.

"Good morning," the major said. Jim hadn't heard him enter. A moment ago he would have sworn an oath on his mother's blood that there wasn't even a door he could have entered through. "I trust you slept well."

Put sleep on the list. Another hallucination. Another fancy. It certainly wasn't real, not for Jim, not with his thoughts rattling in his head like a machine gun.

The major was looking at him. He could feel it even though he still couldn't make out the man's face. His eyes. His damned empty eyes.

"I was hoping you might be more willing to talk this morning," the major said.

Jim suddenly found himself thinking of Bill. Why was he thinking about him? It seemed important, but just beyond his reach.

Something Bill had told him? What was it? But the thought slipped away and refused to resurface.

"It isn't morning," Jim said.

"What's that?"

Jim felt his mouth twitching and words coming out. "It isn't morning. And it isn't afternoon or evening, either. They don't exist. None of this does. You don't exist and neither do I."

Then the major was gone. The desk, the room, the bone-white walls, all gone. He saw a door, but a different one: green with a burnished brass knob and a hand-painted sign hanging from a nail. He was walking toward it, reaching for the knob, pushing the door. (What did the sign say?) Smells reaching him as he stepped in. A roast in the oven. Biscuits. There'd be mashed potatoes too; he knew, like he knew his own name, that there'd be potatoes and gravy (the sign the sign the sign). And those giant green beans they bought at the market over the weekend: the one that just opened down on Walnut Avenue. Worth every penny. Now a voice calling out from the kitchen, calling for him, calling his name, calling him to dinner. He knew the voice, of course he knew the voice, like he knew his own name (like he knew what was on the sign), like he knew himself. Walking forward across the thick carpet, following his nose, following his ears, following his heart (off a cliff) into the kitchen where she waited, dressed in pink, hands lost in oven mitts as she materialized the pot roast like magic. It was her. Of course it was. Her name was on the sign. Like his name was. The Fletchers. That's what it said. Him and her. She and he. Together. Taking off the mitts, reaching for him, the glint of the diamond on her finger, in her eyes, reaching for him, her husband, just like he always wanted, her hair tied up behind her neck like his mother used to do, dinner ready when he got home, dinner and a smile and a kiss. Feeling her red lips on his cheek, on his mouth, skin on skin, a moan, smell of cotton and salt, heat building between them (the Fletchers) until there is nothing between them, there is just him and her and his name and the green door.

"Mr. Fletcher?" The major, the desk, the walls. All back. All closing in on him. "Are you alright? We lost you there for a moment."

"What . . . what is happening to me?"

"What did you see?"

"The door," Jim said, speaking because another instant of silence would destroy him. "I saw a door and a house. I went inside and . . . she was there."

"Miss O'Neil?"

"I don't . . . what is happening to me?"

"You can't blame yourself, Mr. Fletcher," the major said. "It is the magic. Her magic. It is still in your system, still working in your head."

"No," Jim said, shaking his aching head. "Karen didn't . . . she wouldn't . . ."

"I know this is difficult, but it is time to stop. It is time to be honest with me. It is time to accept what is happening before it is too late."

Jim felt anger rising like bile. He forced his eyes up into the blur of the major's indistinct face, despite the pain. "Why should I trust you?" he said. "You sound American, but for all I know you're as Red as Lenin. I trust Karen. I trust *her*. You? I don't even know you."

The major paused for a moment. Not just motionless, not just quiet; he was two-dimensional, a still-life painting of an army officer. Jim wanted to reach out and touch him, see if he could punch through the canvas, but then the major suddenly stood.

"Come with me, Agent Fletcher," he said. "Let's take a walk."

The request came as such a surprise to Jim that he was on his feet and moving toward the door before he had time to understand what was being said. Go out of the room? That made no sense; there was nothing outside the room, certainly no green doors or pot-roast-scented kitchens or inviting red lips.

They stepped out of the blanched white room into a blanched white hallway. Jim was amazed his legs even worked; it felt like he'd been sitting in that chair for weeks, months, all time.

"I understand your reluctance to trust me," the major was saying as he directed Jim down the hallway. "It is only wise in your position. But we are out of time for such things. I am the only one who can help you, and the sooner you believe that, the sooner we can see about setting things right."

The major stopped him in front of a blank stretch of wall. No, not blank; there was a window with the blinds drawn closed. Jim wanted to run. Flee. Never in his life had he been afraid of something like he was of whatever waited behind those blinds. It was madness waiting for him, madness of one form or another, like Russian roulette with every chamber loaded; didn't matter which bullet you landed on, they were all going to scatter your brains.

"I'm not sure—" Jim's voice started to say.

"I think you need to see this," the major said and opened the blinds.

What did Jim expect? The snowcapped skyline of Moscow? An ice-gray Siberian gulag? The endless void that we all stare into in the moment of our death?

What he saw instead were drab brown buildings, lush green fields, and unmarked black roads upon which marched blocks of young men in tan. He knew it at once, knew which bullet the hammer had landed on. Fort Bragg, in the good ol' US of A. An American military base. No Soviet conspiracy could fabricate that bright Carolina sky. It was time, he knew. Time to face the music (and the firing squad).

"Alright, Major," he said. His cheeks felt wet. "Let's talk."

When his fingers dropped the pocket watch, the colonel immediately reached up to his nose. The bleeding was significant this time. This subject was strong. The American fought with an admirable will, though he could not know what he was truly fighting against. It did not matter. They all broke in time, but time was something he had precious little to spare.

Leonid was at his side, pressing a handkerchief into his hand. He took it and held it against the flow. Magic was a high-priced whore; he knew that well. The headaches, the nosebleeds, the tremors in his fingers. You could not rewrite the rules of men's minds without spilling a great deal of ink, but that was why he had been sent. That was why he had been born.

"Did it work?" Leonid asked.

The American was slumped over in his chair, his whole body slick with sweat. The colonel's ears still rang from his screams. They always screamed, though they did not realize it. It was an animal reflex, the only part of them that knew what was really happening, the only part that understood the true depth of the violation.

"Yes," he said. "He is prepared."

He heard footsteps behind him: Kirill, returned from his task at last.

The bleeding stopped, so he tossed the rag aside and stood on unsteady legs. It was getting harder, or more likely, he was getting weaker. Age was the one demon no one could outrun. He knew this, had seen it work its terror on those who came before. But with the throb in his temple and the ache in his joints, he wondered how he had let the blasted thing sneak up on him.

"They are ready for you," Kirill said.

I doubt that, he thought. "Then let us welcome them."

The magicians waited in a musty room guarded by filing cabinets standing in ranks like soldiers. He wondered what delicate secrets were locked away here, if one had the time to sift the wheat from the chaff. In a way, that was exactly what he was about to do. He needed to know what caliber of men he had at his disposal.

When he entered, the magicians tensed as if preparing for a blow. This was bittersweet. It was important that they fear him if he was to make them do their duty, yet if they had come bearing good news there would be no reason to fear. A pity then.

"I will not keep you long," he said. He spoke quietly, forcing them to move closer to hear him. "I can sense that you still have much work to do."

They exchanged nervous, uncertain glances. Men without a leader. A sad sight.

"I do not need to tell you that things in the city are deteriorating. You can hear the mob yourself. If it comes to war over Berlin before your work is done . . ." He let those words hang over them like the noose at the gallows. "Moscow would be immeasurably displeased. And steps would need to be taken to vent this displeasure."

They swallowed hard. Some loosened their collars. Perspiration dabbled their brows, despite the late autumn chill.

Kirill, slouched in a corner of the room, snickered. He was barely watching the others, instead focusing on a large silver coin he was flicking higher and higher into the air, catching it each time with a meaty thwack on his palm. The magicians did their best to ignore him entirely.

At last, one of them stepped forward. "Comrade Colonel," he began, his quavering hands clasped tight in front of him, "we are doing our best. But Erwin took all our research with him when he . . . when he . . ."

"Betrayed us to the West?" the colonel finished.

"Yes," the man said, nodding vigorously. "His . . . departure has set us back considerably. We are months away . . . from even returning to where we were before . . . he left. I wish we could provide Moscow with better news, but . . ." The man stopped there. He looked like a spent shell casing, the bullet long fired.

The colonel sighed. He'd been afraid it would come to this. "Kirill?" he said.

The young man sighed and pushed himself off the wall. He caught the coin that was spinning madly in midflight and approached the magician who had come with excuses instead of results. Kirill stopped only a foot or so from the man and smiled. It was an unsettlingly childlike expression. The magician wiped the sweat from his forehead and glanced at the colonel and then back to Kirill, who was now holding up the coin.

"I am a magician too," Kirill said in almost passable German. "I would like to show you a special spell. One of my own devising. Would you believe me if I said I could make this coin vanish?"

"Comrade Colonel," the magician said, trying to look past Kirill, "I do not—"

Kirill flipped the coin one last time, caught it, whispered a few words in a forgotten tongue, and thrust his fist through the magician's chest. He pulled it back instantly, wary of the instability of incorporeal magic beyond a few moments.

"What did you—" the magician struggled to say, eyes huge with shock.

Kirill smiled and opened his fist. It was empty. "No more coin."

The magician clutched at his chest, his face red as blood. His mouth gaped open, but only pained choking sounds escaped.

His legs seemed to melt under him and he fell, fingers hooked into claws, face twisted with pain and dying rage.

There was silence then. The other magicians did not even look at their comrade on the cold concrete floor. They did not have to look, because they knew what they would see. They would see themselves. Kirill's demonstration had been effective, so the colonel chose to ignore how pleased he looked watching his victim twitch on the cold floor.

"It is important that you understand that I believe what he just told me," the colonel said to those who remained. "I understand the impact of the loss of Herr Ehle on this project. But it changes nothing. It is irrelevant. Only progress is relevant." He hoped his message was clear. He did not think he could deliver it any more plainly.

One of the magicians spoke. He was a thick man with a stomach that strained the buttons of his shirt and a mouth full of small, square teeth. "We will get it done, Comrade Colonel," he said, jowls quivering. "I promise you."

Ah, at last the glimmer of an opportunist. Germans were supposed to be conquerors, after all. Perhaps all the men of ambition had not died in warfires or abandoned the cause for the West. "I will hold you to that promise," the colonel said.

THIRTY-ONE

"It was you?" Karen was aware that she was speaking, but that was only to buy her brain time to process a reaction. Panic? Fear? Curiosity? Excitement? She felt them all tingling across her skin like a static charge. "The breach in the Wall . . . you did that?"

Ehle, for his part, appeared calm. His hands were still and his eyes downcast. "Yes," he answered. "And I would like to tell you why."

"I'm listening," Karen said, "and unless you want me to invite Arthur down here, I'd better like the answer."

Ehle exhaled, readying himself for the plunge, and then began to speak. "The end of the war was unpleasant for Germany. I do not say this to gain your sympathies but to explain decisions that were made. Our armies were crumbling and our enemies were out for blood. For us, it appeared to be the end of all things.

"When faced with oblivion, some men will cower and wait for the end. Others decide that if the world is going to burn, they will strike the match. Our illustrious Führer was among the latter. It was his direct order that if we were faced with an Allied victory, we would leave nothing behind for them to conquer. Bridges, buildings, roads—everything was to be destroyed before we let it fall into the enemies' hands. He would rather turn Germany to ash than let it be occupied by the heathen he had so nearly defeated. That was when I lost all hope for Germany: I knew we were going to lose the war, but when I read Hitler's decree I knew we had lost ourselves."

War had never made much sense to Karen, but such needless destruction seemed insane, and she told Ehle so.

"Insanity," Ehle said. "Yes, that describes it well. It was a time of madmen." Ehle's face twisted, as though he had a terrible taste in his mouth. "Hitler was no magician, but he had woven a spell over German minds nevertheless. He had no shortage of sociopaths and sycophants willing to follow him into the abyss, and chief among them was the head of the Reich's magicians, Reichsleiter Martin Voelker."

Karen nodded. "I know that name. We read about him at St. Cyprian's. He was an influential magician before the war. He died during the siege of Berlin, right?"

Ehle smiled sadly. "Influential, yes. Martin was the greatest magician of our age. In another, more benevolent world, his innate talents might have changed magic as we know it, opened up new frontiers, or solved the deep mysteries of our craft. In this world, however, his ability was a tragic failure of fate, as he became a devout Nazi," he said, adding, "and an utter bastard."

Ehle spoke of Voelker not as a figure of history, but someone he knew. Karen said nothing, but felt the muscles in her shoulders tighten. She wanted to reach for her locus, but kept her hands at her sides. What sort of man was acquainted with the Reich's chief magician? And what sort of person was she, standing here seeking help from such a man?

He continued. "Voelker was not content with just following the letter of Hitler's order; instead he embraced the spirit. Why leave only ruin when instead you could leave nothing at all? Mankind had their chance to submit to the will of the Reich. Since they had chosen otherwise, he was going to make them pay for their mistake. And he had the means to do so."

He leaned forward. "Everything I have said thus far is just history," he said softly, but with steel in his voice. "What I would say next is what they do not want you to know."

Karen swallowed. Try as she might, she couldn't quiet the voice of her father in her head, decrying that damned kraut magic. Maybe he hadn't been completely wrong. "Tell me," Karen said.

"When the German army sacked London in 1940, Voelker dispatched one of his most trusted assistants to obtain a particular artifact from the rubble. That man spared nothing in his search. Beatings, torture, murder: any atrocity was acceptable. Only his prize mattered. Eventually history would come to call this man 'the Butcher of London.' Sadly, he was successful in his task and returned to his master with the item in question: a book."

He lifted a book from her desk and ran a finger down its spine. "So much harm from such a simple thing. Perhaps Hitler was right to burn books by the thousands when one like this was in the world."

Karen snatched the book from Ehle's hand. "So if some knowledge is dangerous, all knowledge should be sacrificed?" She put it down, out of his reach. "Is that how you Nazis justified destroying words you didn't agree with?"

Ehle studied her for a moment. What did he make of what he saw? She stared back, but felt a chill looking into his careful eyes.

"I spoke too broadly," he said, averting his eyes at last. "But perhaps you should reserve judgment until you know more of the book in question. It had no author, no title. Rather, what name it possessed came from its opening words: *Concerning that which must never be . . .*

"The magic this book describes is not like any you or I have ever used. Even calling it magic is a corruption of language, like calling the machine gunner's craft an art. We have mastered many spells which can kill, but the magic in this book does more than that: it unmakes. It does not kill a man; it wipes away his very existence. It is, in short, the sort of magic no sane person would ever dare wield."

Karen squirmed at the thought. Throughout all her magical training, she had been constantly irritated at the number of spells they were taught that were just variations on smiting your enemies. One spell to set something on fire, another to throw someone across a room, another to block the fire spell so you could then throw someone across a room. Like war itself, it had all seemed like so much energy spent on breaking the world rather than fixing it.

But magic like Ehle was describing . . . it wasn't just destruction; it was magical nihilism.

Ehle went on, reluctantly. "There is little more I can tell of this book. It was written mostly in French, though some passages borrowed heavily from a dozen other languages, some remembered, some lost. And perhaps the most curious thing about this accursed book is that it was no musty tome from antiquity bound in unspeakable flesh. No, it was written by a steady hand in an accountant's ledger, which had itself been printed in 1903."

"This magic is a recent invention?"

Ehle shook his head. "It is as old as magic itself. Written on paper, parchment, or papyrus, by scholars, poets, or beggars. It has visited every great civilization in history, each time bringing death and despair. Until, inevitably, the book is destroyed. Yet without fail, time will pass and someone, somewhere, will again be inspired to put pen to paper and write: *Concerning that which must never be . . .*"

How had she never heard of such magic before? "The British had it?"

"A spoil of the First World War, we believe," Ehle replied. "But while they possessed the book for some time, they had no magicians who could decipher its spells. A small mercy. And so it waited in the Tower of London, until the German army invaded."

"But Voelker figured out how to use it."

"Yes," Ehle said. "When Berlin was encircled by blood-mad enemies and the Reich was breathing its last, Voelker brought the book to his headquarters in the Auttenberg district and made his preparations. Suffice it to say that magic of death can only be kindled with more death. Yet when he cast his spell, something went horribly wrong."

Unspeakable magic was supposed to descend on the Reich's enemies, Ehle explained, but instead it fell on Auttenberg, swallowing the entire district. Those stationed just outside of the magic's influence reported hearing screams coming from inside Auttenberg for an entire day.

And then silence. "When Berlin fell, Auttenberg was in the Soviet's zone of control, just on the border with the Western powers. At first they blamed their vanishing patrols on some hidden Nazi resistance, but eventually the magicians in the Red Army realized the truth: something terrible had been unleashed in Auttenberg.

"I cannot say how many lives were lost in the attempt to retake Auttenberg; if the Soviets kept such records, they did not share them with us. However, I know the number was staggering. And worse, those sacrifices accomplished nothing. In fact, there was a terrible suspicion that whatever lurked in Auttenberg grew stronger with each death. So at last an unthinkable decision was reached: they would ask for help."

Karen's mind raced to keep up. The existence of this horrible magic was enough to send her thoughts reeling, but she sensed the worst revelations were yet to come.

"An international conclave of magicians was assembled in secret. Each occupying power sent the best and most powerful to see what could be done about Auttenberg. The newly formed German Democratic Republic selected me, among others, to attend. There were, in fact, a number of my former colleagues represented, including the representative from the United States of America: the recently emigrated Dr. Max Haupt."

Dr. Haupt. Operation Hobnail. The document had mentioned a "senior magical asset" on-site just before the Wall was raised. America had few talented magicians at that time, and none as talented as Dr. Haupt. She pictured his kindly, studious face. He had done so much for her career, for her development as a magician. She shuddered at the thought that he had been hiding this dark secret from her, from everyone.

"What did this conclave decide?" she asked with a dry, thick tongue.

"To lie, Miss O'Neil," he said simply. "To lie. We all stared into that darkness and trembled. We knew we faced something that was beyond us, and so the decision was made to make Auttenberg disappear. Berlin was rebuilt around the cancerous district while every mention of it in any document or record or map was erased. Magical wards, the likes of which have rarely been summoned by men, were cast up around the district's borders: spells to contain, to obfuscate, to hide away.

"But in the end, even this could not hold. So much magic shines like a beacon and the last thing anyone wanted was for the attention of the world's magicians to fall on Auttenberg. It was not enough that no one could enter; humanity had to forget it was even there. So we had to hide our magic away, and what better silence than a roar?"

Karen couldn't breathe. She had a sharp headache; when had that started? She needed air; she needed to think. But before that, she needed to speak. "The Wall," she said, and the words sounded like thunder in her ears.

Ehle paused, and then nodded. "We needed to mask Auttenberg with something that had a believable purpose or it would draw too many of the wrong questions. The Soviets, conveniently, had a proposal." He excavated a map of Berlin from a nearby pile of paper. "Do you mind if I deface your map?"

She handed him a wax pencil.

"We should burn this when we are finished," Ehle said. "We would not want it discovered."

"Are you planning on writing something treasonous on there?"

"This whole conversation is treasonous."

Karen exhaled. Of course it was. "Do what you have to," she said.

Ehle nodded. He traced around the city in a black line. "Do you recognize this?"

"The Wall," she said.

"Exactly." He completed the circle and then placed the tip of the pencil on the eastern border. "Except, on a Soviet or East German map, it would look like this." His line deviated into East Berlin, carving out an island of space between the two markings. He tapped there. "This," he said, "is Auttenberg. For those who remember it, it is a lost casualty of the war, either destroyed or occupied by the other side, while in reality, it is surrounded by the Wall."

"But people cross the border," she said. "They would notice Auttenberg was gone."

"Magic is a powerful tool," he said, "but it works best when it works in conjunction with human nature. And it is human nature to believe what is easy to believe. For a conquered people trying to survive in the hollows left by war, it is easier to forget Auttenberg ever existed than to consider any alternative."

"What about planes? People could see it from the air."

He almost smiled, though his face seemed to fight the expression. "You should have been with us as we designed the necessary spells," he said. "We were weeks into planning before someone thought about airplanes. Another sortie in the long-lasting conflict between technology and magic. Let us simply say that Auttenberg is not a large district and that we applied a great deal of obfuscating magic upon it."

"You guys thought of everything."

"We were the best in the world," he said, with perhaps a sad touch of pride.

"The best in the world," Karen repeated. She looked down at her hands and watched them shake. "So the Soviets didn't put the Wall there just to blockade Berlin. They needed to hide away some terrible magic that no one could control." She forced herself to look up, to stare at this man who had trusted her with a truth she had sought, but now wished she hadn't. "And the Americans helped them."

THIRTY-TWO

A rthur had just been starting to feel young again when he saw the stairs. The problem with doing legwork again was that it required using his legs, who were presently lodging a formal, aching protest at the thought of climbing to the fifth floor. This was why he had a staff of eager ignorant youngsters at his beck and call. But this little detour had to be done alone. It was hard to delegate when you couldn't trust anyone. So for love of God and Country, he ignored his complaining joints and began the ascent.

It was more than likely that none of this even mattered. The reports he'd read coming out of Washington and Zehlendorf put the odds of this escalating to a real war uncomfortably high. It had always been a risk; they'd known that since the West had refused to abandon war-ruined Berlin. It had grown worse in recent weeks as the talk about rearming West Germany intensified. That was the real purpose of international borders: keeping a safe distance between you and the guy you never really liked anyway. But in Berlin, they'd never really had that option. The Wall had helped some, given everybody a bit of elbow room, but sooner or later it was destined to end up going to hell.

But even if Berlin was about to be put to the torch, Arthur wasn't ready to catch a plane westward. There were only a few things in life that mattered more than victory, more than survival, and one of those was catching a traitor.

He paused on the second-floor landing to catch his breath. There was one good thing about getting old, he realized: no one was going to ask him to sign up for the infantry this go-around. Leave the soldiering to the young. They thought themselves invincible anyway, might as well let them test out that theory. Then, unbidden, memories of 1945 and all the dead invincible young men he had known washed over him, turning the beads of sweat on his back to ice. After all he'd seen in his life, even cynicism wasn't satisfying.

Arthur eventually reached the fifth floor and found the right apartment. He knocked, one hand on the door, the other on the pistol in his pocket.

No one answered. He was met by nothing but silence.

Too much silence, in fact.

You learned something from a life of digging up what was meant to stay buried: the difference between the quiet of an empty apartment and the quiet of an apartment that someone wants to seem empty. You learned to read between the noise and the silence, to forget what you heard or saw and instead trust the less tangible senses. You learned to sense when a man was standing behind a closed door, waiting for you to leave.

And sometimes you just guessed and tried to sound confident.

"Open up," Arthur said, whispering just a little too loudly. "Or I'll have to make a scene. I doubt your neighbors will understand me, but they'll wonder why that nice young man in the corner apartment got a visit from a belligerent American."

He was rewarded with the sound of a turning lock, and then another, and then the door opened a crack.

"You are not supposed to know where I live," Dieter said softly.

Arthur shrugged. "I know lots of things I'm not supposed to." He gave the dour German his winningest smile; his wife had always called it ghastly. Dieter didn't seem to care for it much more. "I need some help. Now, you going to invite me in or should we talk out here in the hall?"

G oing down the stairs went more quickly than going up, but Arthur reminded himself that wasn't necessarily a good thing. Yet even as old, tired, and sober as he was, there was still a spring in his step. Nothing like a hunt to light the fire in a man's blood, and nothing started a hunt off better than the right bait.

They had known. The damn Soviets had known the moment Jim's little band had crossed into East Berlin, and now Dennis was dead and Jim lost. Someone had given them up. Someone betrayed them to Moscow. Someone sold out the West and traded away lives with some very specific secrets.

The problem with secrets, however, was that not everyone knew them. And these secrets, well . . . they were more secret than most. He hadn't cleared the border crossing with the director and certainly not with DC; it was his operational prerogative to control the flow of mission-critical information. Within BOB, there had been very few with a need-to-know. Very few indeed.

His driver was waiting for him in front of the building. Arthur didn't like loose ends, but he liked driving in Germany less.

"You get what you needed, boss?" the man behind the wheel asked as Arthur slid into the backseat.

Arthur considered what Dieter had told him, the trust he had placed in him. Nothing in life came without cost, but this was one he was willing to pay ten times over. For Dennis, for Jim.

"I did," Arthur replied, settling back into the leather. "Time for some international diplomacy. I've got a little friendly information I'd like to pass along to our brethren." And then wait and see what they do with it.

THIRTY-THREE

"Tell me," Karen said, doing her best to keep her voice steady, "why should I believe a word you've told me?"

Ehle almost smiled at the question. "You should not believe anything anyone tells you, not in Berlin. This place has become a city of lies." He intertwined his fingers and laid them on his chest. "And yet, I have forced you into a place where you must decide if you will take a leap of faith."

"You didn't answer my question."

"Your question has no answer," he said. "When I began this undertaking, I did not anticipate that I would require help. Therefore I have spent little effort in establishing credibility."

"And what undertaking is that exactly, Mr. Ehle?"

"Eventually someone will enter Auttenberg. They will take the book and they will use it. The Soviets, the Americans; the side does not matter. Men in power will always seek out more. And so that power must be destroyed. The temptation removed."

Karen studied his face. Unsurprisingly, it revealed little. If what he said was true, then he had spent years hiding his true intentions from his Soviet masters, and they were far better at this than Karen O'Neil. "But you are immune to such temptation," she said and watched for his reaction.

His lips twitched slightly, perhaps in annoyance? Or pain? "I would never use this book," he said after a long silence, "because I have seen its magic at work."

Karen narrowed her eyes. "What exactly was your job during the war, Mr. Ehle?"

Ehle took a breath before answering. "I was just a soldier, drafted from my home to serve the Fatherland," he said. "A magician, but the Reich had many magician soldiers. Hitler, and in turn his servant Voelker, knew well how to leverage magic on the battlefield. I will not defend our cause as righteous, but I am German, and it was war."

"And yet you were asked to help create the Wall?"

He shrugged his shoulders. "I was not without talent," he said, "and by war's end, there were few German magicians left alive."

"You know a lot of secrets for a lowly soldier."

"I lived through the worst of times, Karen. In doing so, I learned many horrible things. It is my burden. A burden I would lift, with your help."

Now here comes the real treason, Karen thought. "When you contacted me at the Wall, you said you could help me fix it. That's why we went over there after you. That's why Dennis gave his life bringing you back here."

"The Wall cannot be fixed," he said, shaking his head. "It all must fall in order to reach Auttenberg. The Wall's magic is like a tapestry: as you cut the threads, it all comes apart. And after years of planning, I thought I was strong enough to do it, but without a locus, I failed." There was something of a tremor in his voice now. "I thought the Wall was too powerful. But then a KGB colonel from Moscow came to Berlin and told me that the West had found a breach. A hole in the unbreakable Wall. My efforts were not in vain. The Wall could be broken. I thought, perhaps with help from another magician, I could finish what I started. I thought my chances of finding an ally on this side of the Wall were more advantageous, so I attempted to make contact with the West in order to defect."

"Through your prostitute," Karen said, eyebrow up.

"Yes," Ehle said, his cheeks a little red. "But I fear the Nightingale was one step ahead of me and my message never arrived. I was so close to my goal, but still too far. I had given up hope. In an act of desperation, I went under cover of darkness to find this breach. When I arrived, I sensed you nearby."

"So what you told me at the Wall about fixing it was a lie."

"I needed your help," he said, his voice tightening. "I caused the breach, but it wasn't enough. I helped to create the Wall; I know how to bring it down. I know the path to walk, but I need someone with stronger legs to carry me. I thought—"

"You thought I'd help you tear this city apart?" She heard the echo of gunshots and screams in the back of her mind; magical smoke hiding a massacre as refugees tried stupidly to rush the breach. "Have you seen the effects of your handiwork, Mr. Ehle? Have you seen the people dying because you weakened the Wall?"

Ehle's inscrutable face returned. His entire body was perfectly still. "There are fates worse than death, Karen," he said softly.

It was the war all over again. The fields of dead, the bombs raining from the sky. All for what? "How many?" she asked. "How many people have to die before it is all too much?"

There were cracks now, imperfections in the mask, glimpses of his true rage shining through like hot metal. Karen suddenly felt the gravity of her situation settle in the muscles of her shoulders, felt it tighten the tendons in her hands.

"You are young," Ehle said at last. He was not looking at her anymore; rather, looking beyond her, through the concrete walls around them. "You have not seen how dark the world truly is. You still believe it is a simple thing to value life above all else." He lifted the altered map of Berlin with the outline of Auttenberg sketched on it and tossed it onto Karen's desk. "I will see that damned book destroyed, no matter the cost."

Karen couldn't breathe. She stood and wiped sweaty palms on her pants. "Thank you, I think, for sharing all that with me," she said, moving toward the door. "Right now I need some air."

Ehle nodded. "I understand. But trust me, this is what must be done."

O ut in the hallway, the air was fresher, though still stale. No sign of her CIA minders. No sign of anyone, in fact, just empty whitewashed walls and the dull yellow of old lightbulbs. Karen had an aching head and a dry mouth. She'd come to Berlin to help, but she no longer knew what that meant. Part of her knew she should go to Arthur immediately and report what Ehle had told her. He would take care of it. Why shouldn't she? Why would she trust some strange German she'd just met over the CIA agents she had been sent here to assist?

But what if Ehle was telling the truth?

Air, that was what she needed. Air would clear her head, help her think clearly. Make good decisions. Not start any wars. But as she neared the stairwell, suddenly Emile was standing in front of her. She moved back, startled.

"Emile," she said. Magic was all too ready on the tip of her tongue, but she let it recede as the shock faded. "What are you doing here?"

The Frenchman offered her a guarded smile that she instantly did not trust. "I came to find you," he said. "I went to the room

Arthur said they had assigned you, but inside I heard only . . . a silence."

An odd way of putting it, she thought. English was not his native tongue, but he did seem fairly fluent. Had he noticed the silencing spell she had cast? "Yes," she said carefully. "We were having a rather boring conversation about the problem with the Wall. Magic is often more calculations and formulas than fireworks."

"So I have heard," he said, head tilted to one side. "And how is our guest, Mr. Ehle, finding his new environment? To his liking, I hope? I have asked for an opportunity to interview him myself, but Arthur has been reluctant to accept."

"We have been very busy," Karen replied. "Trying to fix the Wall."

"Of course you have," Emile said. "Still, I hope to have my time to speak with Mr. Ehle before too long. He is a man with a unique past. I am certain such a conversation would be . . . enlightening."

Don't trust any of them, Karen. You don't know what they want, but you know it isn't to help you. "You said you came down here to find me," she said.

"Ah, yes," he said. "I come with good news. The word just arrived through our diplomatic channels and I came at once to deliver it. The Soviets have agreed to return Jim."

THIRTY-FOUR

The bridge crossed the Havel River to the west of the city on the quiet forest road to Potsdam. In the old days it was made of wood, then brick, iron, and finally steel. It had stood to its duty for centuries, even after that strange summer night when the Wall appeared suddenly out of the river fog. Traffic still passed over Glienicke Bridge, though not with nearly the frequency of the prewar years and not without clearing the checkpoint the Soviets had placed at the gap in the Wall. But despite its prominence, its distance from the city lights and the restless mob provided it with a privacy that could be appreciated by the intelligence operatives on both sides.

The representatives of the West arrived at dusk in three black cars. Their headlights cut through the gathering gloom and the lightly falling rain as they rolled to a stop at the bridge's far end. Even at this distance, they could see their Eastern counterparts huddled against the wet under the green checkpoint huts.

Hours passed before either side moved. Bitter years had left them accustomed to staring across borders, not moving across them. Inertia held the sharp-eyed gray men in the cars and the huts in place, though they would have called it caution.

At last silhouettes could be seen amid the spotlights at the checkpoint, dark forms barely visible through the night and the rain. The men in the cars stepped out in long coats and wide-brimmed hats. And then, for seemingly the first time in an age, men on either side began to walk toward the middle.

Among the huddle from the East was a tall figure, walking stooped and dressed poorly for the weather. He fell in step with the others until they neared the center and then he walked alone. It was not clear if he noticed the difference.

He was met by his countrymen, his colleagues. They draped him with a coat, shielded him with an umbrella and with their bodies. He did not seem to notice. He went with them as easily as he had come with the others, a leaf on a foreign wind, propelled along by strong hands and a slack gait.

It was a perfunctory business that night. No words were exchanged East to West, only the patter of rain, the glare of headlights, and the question of this man, once lost and now found: a sheep returned to the fold by the wolves.

THIRTY-FIVE

Karen was half-asleep, her chin resting unsteadily in her palm, when she heard them arrive. She quickly blinked away three days' worth of fatigue and got to her feet. The clock hanging on the wall over the map of Berlin read 5:00 A.M. The bullpen was nearly empty, save for the night shift and the few BOB operatives who had been told about Jim's release. She was surprised to see Ehle waiting near Arthur's office; since his rescue, he had only rarely dared to venture aboveground.

Emile entered first, followed by Arthur. Behind them came Alec, who held Jim on his feet as they made their way inside. A cheer erupted among those gathered as Jim smiled weakly.

It was him. He looked terrible: wan, weak, and thin. But it was him. Before Karen realized she was crossing the room, she had her arms around him.

"Jim," she said. "I can't believe it. I'm so glad you're safe."

He tensed at her touch and so she let him go. Their eyes met and for a moment, she was confused by what she saw there. But then Jim's smile widened and he looked like his old self. "Of course," he said, his voice cracking. "Those Commies didn't know who they were messing with."

"Welcome home, lad," Alec said, squeezing Jim's shoulder. "Now someone get this boy a chair before his legs turn to pudding."

Jim sat at the table in the middle of the bullpen, flanked by a bevy of the typewriting mothers. One pressed a chipped mug of coffee into his hands. Another found him an old wool blanket. They fussed over him like hens, cooing and laughing. An unlikely family, reunited. Even Garriety, who came in last, seemed to be pleased. He wasn't quite smiling, but it was as close as Karen had seen. It was the happiest she had seen any of them, in fact, the first moment of relief in a time of trial.

Karen watched him, when she could see him past the bobbing heads. His eyes had spoken to her, a flash of honesty before the walls came up, if only she knew what they had said. She watched his hands, clutching the coffee he hadn't tasted. She watched his face, joining the others in the celebration when they were looking, and falling dark when they were not. What had they done to him? What had he seen on the far side of the Wall?

She found herself thinking of Dennis. Did Jim know what had become of his friend? It didn't seem like the right moment to tell him, though he would wonder soon if he hadn't already guessed. She had a hard time reconciling the two agents who had met her at the Berlin airport, so amused by their own banter, with what they had become. Either lost or broken. Not unlike the young men of their parents' generation. Maybe that was the fate of all young men, when the world decides for war.

"Karen?" She recognized the voice from one of the silver-haired women who tended BOB's tangled jungle of phone lines. "There's someone calling for you, dear. I couldn't make out her name, but she sounded upset. Arthur told us not to let anyone interrupt you, but I thought since you were already up here, maybe you wouldn't mind?"

Karen felt fear harden in her gut. Who would be calling her in Berlin? Some base part of her brain immediately thought of her sister. Why would Helen contact her while she was out on assignment? Had something happened? A series of possible tragedies, each worse than the last, flashed through her thoughts. Her mother fell and broke her hip; her father was in a car accident; little Martha was sick. Lost in all the possibilities, she let herself be led off to a corner of the bullpen and took the receiver in hand. She held it up, covered her other ear to block out the celebrations, and said, "Hello?"

At first she heard only the crackle of a thousand miles of static. Then a voice, familiar but unexpected: "Karen? Is that you? Can you hear me?"

"Allison?"

"Finally," Karen's assistant at the OMRD said. "I've been trying for over an hour."

"Allison," Karen said, fingertips tingling, "what is going on? Why are you—"

But Allison was already going on, her words about as clear as when Karen and Helen used to talk across the house using tin cans and string. ". . . as soon as I could, I promise. I'm not saying they were keeping it from us, but Gerald basically had to bribe one of the secretaries upstairs to get the details."

"Allison, slow down," Karen said, pressing the heel of her free hand to her ear to block out the celebratory noise. "What is going on?"

"Dr. Haupt," Allison said. "When he heard who you were working with over there, something about a German magician named Ehle, he went nuts. He said he never should have sent you. Started calling all sorts of people down in DC, lots of yelling."

Karen could hardly picture Dr. Haupt upset, let alone yelling into his phone. "I still don't understand," she said. "Why—"

For a moment, Allison's voice came in clear over the line. "He's coming to Berlin, Karen. He said he was coming to bring you back."

Karen's mouth felt like it was full of sand. She had been so wrapped up in solving the problem of getting into Auttenberg she hadn't really considered what the OMRD might do when she ignored Dr. Haupt's concerns. She assumed she could put him off long enough to do what needed to be done; she never thought he'd get on a plane to come collect her. And the more she thought about that, the angrier she became. She wasn't a child who needed an adult to come save her; she certainly wasn't a damsel who needed a hero to swoop in for the rescue. Sure, what Ehle was trying to get her to help him with wasn't even exactly legal, but Dr. Haupt didn't know that. He just thought it had become too dangerous for the dainty woman magician. If they had sent George, Haupt would never have—

"Karen? Are you there?"

"Yes," Karen said, blinking away clouded thoughts. "Yes, Allison, thank you. I need to . . ." Her eyes scanned the room until they found Ehle off to the side, silently waiting away from the cheerful throng around Jim. "I need to go. Thanks."

She dropped the phone back into its cradle. Allison had said Haupt had been upset when he learned who she was working with. There was clearly more to their shared past than Ehle had let on, and she wagered he would not be pleased to learn his former colleague would be coming to check in on them.

Crossing the room and weaving between the well-wishers, for a moment she caught Jim's eye. Everyone around him was laughing, slapping him on the back, squeezing his shoulders. Though he looked tired, he was laughing right along with them; that is, until he saw Karen. Then his eyes darkened, like an eclipse blotting out the sun. His face hardened and she felt a chill creep along her spine.

Then it was gone and he was sharing some old joke with Alec, pounding the table and grinning like a kid on Christmas morning. Had she imagined it? No, something had been there . . . but what?

"You look unwell," Ehle said, snapping her back to the moment.

"I . . ." she started to say. Jim's eyes, something about his eyes . . .

"What is it?" Ehle asked, his voice low.

"I was coming over to . . . to . . ." She forced herself to push Jim out of her head and focus. She needed to deal with one thing at a time. "I just got a call and . . ." As she was about to elaborate, she realized Ehle wasn't looking at her anymore; he was looking past her, toward the door.

"Whatever it was," Ehle said, "I am thinking you are too late."

THIRTY-SIX

Karen saw George first, his handsome sneer taking in and dismissing everything in the room in a single glance. And then came the stooped form of Dr. Haupt, leaning heavily on his cane. It was bizarre seeing them here at BOB, like characters showing up in the wrong book. She doubted anyone would be pleased with the outcome.

"Can I help you?" Arthur asked as the room fell silent. "Or maybe a better question is who the hell are you and how the hell did you get inside my building?"

George chuckled at this, a little mocking cough that made Karen's blood burn. He waved a lazy finger around the room. "This your fiefdom, Chief?" he asked with a smirk. "You CIA guys are always so impressed with yourselves, so I guess I was expecting something a bit grander."

"Son, I'm not sure who you—"

"I," Dr. Haupt said sharply, "am the director of the OMRD." He produced a folded letter from his suit jacket. "And I am here at the invitation of CIA director Dulles." He handed the letter to George, who held it out for Arthur to take.

"You spies should learn to answer your telephones," George said as Arthur read.

"We've been otherwise occupied," Arthur said as his eyes quickly took in the paper.

Then George's gaze finally landed on Karen and that damn smirk widened. "There you are," he said. "Our lost little lamb."

Before she could reply, Dr. Haupt turned toward her. "Karen, my dear," he said, touching his chest with his free hand. "It does my heart good to see that you are unharmed. When we could not reach you, we feared the worst had happened."

"I'm fine, sir," Karen said.

"*Guten Morgen,* Max," Ehle said as he stepped in front of Karen. *"Ich habe dich lange nicht gesehen."*

Dr. Haupt's expression changed then; disgust was the closest Karen could come to describing it, but even that was inadequate. Loathing, maybe, for having to face the worst part of yourself, the part you needed hidden from the world.

"Not long enough, Erwin," Dr. Haupt said. To the rest of the room, he said, "Arrest this man."

"Arrest him?" Karen said. "On what charge?"

Dr. Haupt did not meet her eye and did not reply, but George had no such reluctance. "Hadn't you heard? He's a war criminal."

"What?" Karen took a step back. "He fought in the war, but that doesn't—"

"I said arrest him," Dr. Haupt said again. When no one moved, he thrust a finger at Arthur and the paper still hanging from his hand. "You have read the report. You know with whose authority I speak. Arrest him. Now."

Arthur looked like a man with heartburn, but with a heavy sigh, he nodded to two of his agents standing nearby. They exchanged glances with each other, then at Ehle, then back to Arthur.

"Dr. Haupt, sir," Karen said, "you don't understand. He's—"

But Haupt ignored her. "Very well," he said, clutching his cane. "I will do it myself." As soon as he began to speak, Karen recognized the sort of magic her former teacher was summoning; it had, after all, been the subject of the most memorable of her studies at St. Cyprian's. Following long-standing tradition, the lesson came during her senior year, and though it was given to every senior class, it was never on the same day. Students would whisper about it, take bets on when it would happen, but inevitably it came when no one was ready.

Among the student body, it was called the Secret Lecture. It was the one and only time illegal magic was referenced, let alone cast, at the university. And for Karen's class, Dr. Haupt had been selected to give it.

Ehle let out a cry, more of surprise than pain. But the pain would be coming. That was, after all, the entire point of this spell. These insidious words sent shocks of fire through the body, burning every nerve, forcing air from your lungs and conscious thought from your mind. It was sadist's magic. It ripped at you, clawed at you, gnawed on you. Karen knew all this because in that lecture, for one fraction of one moment, the magic had been turned on her. It was the clearest way, the professors of St. Cyprian's believed, to impart a lasting lesson on the graduating magicians: some magic should never be cast.

"Dr. Haupt," Karen said as she felt the air curdle with that ugly magic, "what are you doing?"

Ehle groaned, on his knees now. There were some ways to fight against pain magic; they had been taught those too that day, simple incantations to ward off the worst of it. She was certain Ehle would know them, but he said nothing, did nothing.

"Sir," she said, "sir, he's down." Dr. Haupt did not look at her. "You're hurting him." Dr. Haupt continued to ignore her, continued to speak unspeakable words. Karen could almost feel Ehle's pain coming off his body like waves of heat. Arthur's men watched in mute horror. Even George looked uncomfortable, but did nothing.

Enough.

With a shout and an intricate wave of her hand, Karen sent a burst of force across the room, scattering folders and documents in its wake. It cracked not against Dr. Haupt himself but against his cane, which tumbled out of his grip. His spell instantly ceased, and he grunted and fell as too much weight fell on his crippled leg.

In the wordless moments that followed, Karen could hear only the gallop of her own heart in her ears. It had happened so quickly, she hadn't had time to think about what she was doing before the spell was cast. Using magic against another magician, against the director of the OMRD . . . how had she thought that was a good idea? But then she found herself at Ehle's side. His hands were still twisted, every muscle tensed like a bowstring about to break. His breaths came sharp, quick, and hard, but when he saw her, felt her hand on his arm, they began to slow.

Arthur's men appeared over her and helped Ehle to his feet. Across the room, George did the same for Dr. Haupt.

"Take him downstairs to the holding cell," Arthur said, at last breaking the silence.

"Arthur . . ." Karen started to say before he shot her a look.

He held up the paper Haupt had given him. "Orders," he said. "You go back down as well, Miss O'Neil. You've got work to do." Dr. Haupt began to protest, but Arthur stared him down. "Your memo addresses Mr. Ehle, Director, not Miss O'Neil, and I still have a crisis to avoid."

"Miss O'Neil works for me," Dr. Haupt said.

"Not today," Arthur said. "Today she's on loan to the CIA to assist in an emergency. If there's a problem with that, perhaps we should discuss it in my office."

Dr. Haupt turned to Karen, but she could not look at him anymore, not after what she had just seen. She had thought him to be the steady, generous man she knew from her time at the university and the OMRD. She knew his past was haunted, but he had been kind nevertheless. He had helped her, guided her. In turn, she had trusted him. But now she knew that man had never existed, not really; the true Dr. Haupt was something else entirely, a man of secrets. A man willing to use inexcusable magic. She turned away.

"Very well," Dr. Haupt said, nodding. His voice lost the edge it had gained when he saw Ehle; he sounded more like the man she knew, or thought she knew. "We shall discuss this in private. Once I am certain the prisoner is dealt with."

Arthur nodded. "Take him, boys."

Karen watched Dr. Haupt and Ehle disappear out the door. She could feel something foul burning the back of her throat. Jim was home safe; this should have been a morning of celebration in the midst of chaos. Instead it just added to the noise.

She was halfway to the stairs following Dr. Haupt when she heard George behind her. When he called out, she spun on him, finger raised. She was fairly certain she saw him flinch.

"You've got a lot of nerve," she said with twitching lips.

George held up his hands in mock surrender. "I'm not the one who just committed magical assault on our boss."

"That was illegal magic, George," she said. "Cruel magic. Used to hurt a man who posed no threat and is trying to help us stop a war."

George held up a hand. His thistle and branch ring, his locus, was on a different finger than usual; his ring finger was red and blistered: a reminder of their bout in Dr. Haupt's hallway back at the OMRD. "And what sort of monster would use magic to hurt an old friend, just to make a point?" he asked with mock seriousness.

"That was different," she said quickly, though her face burned at the comparison.

"Is it?" George asked. "You're awful quick to trust this stranger instead of your friends."

"Is that what you are, George? My friend?"

"This Ehle," George said, "he tell you what he did during the war?"

"Yes," she said. George was just wasting her time; why was she even bothering with him? "He said that he was a magician soldier for the Germans. If that counts as a war crime, then—"

"Wake up, Karen," George said. "He was a colonel in the SS. Part of the inner circle of Nazi magicians. For God's sake, he was the chief magical researcher at the Ravensbrück concentration camp."

Karen felt her face flush even hotter. Again her father's voice thudded in her head, like heavy boots on the stairs: *You weren't there. You didn't see what I saw.*

George wasn't done. "You look sick, Karen. Well, you should be. I've seen some of the pictures of what they did. The stuff of nightmares. And did I mention they housed mostly women there? That's right, your new pal is a torturer of women."

Of course Ehle had lied. Again. He had warned her not to believe anyone in Berlin, after all. Had any of his story been true? She'd known better than to believe him. A foot soldier, even a magician, wouldn't know the things he knew. So why had she trusted him? Why had she been so eager for him to be something better than what he obviously was?

"George," Karen said, "I can see on your smug face that you think you're riding in here to save the day, but let me be the first to tell you that nobody here needs you. You aren't some white knight; you're just a little boy whose feelings were hurt when he got left out. And before you show up here with your sanctimonious opinions about Ehle, maybe you should go ask the illustrious Dr. Haupt what service he rendered to the Fatherland during the war." She looked down the stairs toward the basement. "Actually, I'll go ask him right now."

Karen caught Dr. Haupt just outside the door to Ehle's holding cell. His skin looked jaundiced in the glow of the exposed bulbs. "Sir," she said, "about what happened upstairs . . ."

"Karen," Dr. Haupt said, surprised. "You do not need to apologize."

"I wasn't going to," she said. Her mentor seemed uncomfortable. His pale fingers tapped weakly on the head of his cane. He was exhausted, she saw; drained by the harsh magic he had summoned against Ehle. "What you did up there was . . . unacceptable, sir. You of all people should know that."

"Yes," he said, his voice distant. "Yes, you are correct. Erwin and I have a history together from the war. I let that cloud my judgment."

"What sort of history, sir?"

He pressed his lips together. "One I do not wish to relate," he said. "Now, if you will excuse me, there are matters I need to discuss with my former colleague. You and I can speak more on this later."

Karen stepped between Dr. Haupt and the door. "It's interesting. George told me you all think Ehle is a war criminal," she said carefully, "but then you also said you worked together. What exactly did you do in the war?" She'd wondered about this before, but never asked him. She had always given him the benefit of the doubt, as she had done to Ehle. But after seeing what Dr. Haupt was capable of upstairs, she was no longer willing to believe the best of any of them.

"My dear," Dr. Haupt said, staring at her over the bronze rims of his glasses with cold eyes, "I understand these have been trying days of late. This debacle is far more complex than I anticipated when I chose you for this mission. If you—"

"Would you have still sent me?" she asked. "If the CIA had been forthcoming about the problem with the Wall, would you have still sent me to take care of it?"

Dr. Haupt tapped his cane on the concrete. "Karen, I am sure you—"

"Or would you have picked George?" Her eyes narrowed. "Or would you have come yourself? After all, you must have a wealth of knowledge about the Wall's magic." She paused and watched every deep line in his face, every muscle around his mouth and eyes, for a reaction. "It is purely Soviet magic, of course. But I'm sure you must have had reason to study it in the years since it appeared."

Dr. Haupt licked his lips, a gesture she had never seen from him before. "You should be careful, my dear," he said after a long, heavy silence, "in whom you place your trust. There are those who would deceive you."

Karen let out a soft laugh. "If I had a nickel for every time a man told me that since I came to Berlin . . ." she said. "Seems everyone here is a liar, Dr. Haupt." His face was sour, but he made no reply. "Just one last question before I let you go, sir," she said. "You aren't really here for me or for Ehle."

"That," he said, licking those thin lips again, "is not a question."

"And that," she replied, "is not an answer." Karen smiled. She wondered if it looked real.

"I won't keep you any longer, sir. I know you have important work to do." She stepped aside. "And you do look very tired."

Dr. Haupt gave a curt nod. "We will discuss this later, Karen."

She turned on a heel and hurried down the hall and around the corner while the agents inside the cell room began working the locks. She heard the door start to creak open. Dr. Haupt had something to hide. Maybe Ehle had lied about everything, maybe just about his past. She grabbed her locus.

Either way, she was going to find out.

THIRTY-SEVEN

I t was not the first time Erwin Ehle found himself thrown back in a cell after a momentary release, but it was probably the fastest. The Soviets had kept him in prison for nearly a year after the war, but once they let him go free, it had taken six months before they changed their minds and threw him back behind iron bars. The Americans, it seemed, moved at a faster pace.

Or more likely, they acted with less singularity of purpose. Too many men with influence, too many agendas. Moscow had its share of each, but was far more adept at homogenizing its leaders. Everything for the Party, after all. The West could not decide on its highest virtue. Democracy? For some, possibly. However, Ehle doubted there were many in Washington who cared much for anything beyond reelection. Capitalism? Hardly. Capital, perhaps. They all wanted the destruction of the hated USSR, but that ambition was too nonspecific. Too many devils in too many details.

But burning former Nazis at the stake? Now that was something the whole world could agree on.

The CIA's cell was certainly more comfortable than the KGB's, though none of his Soviet torturers had ever used pain magic on him. The echoes of it still clung to him like fishhooks buried deep in his skin. The only solace he took was in the knowledge that such magic, while effective, was also remarkably draining on the caster. Max would be fighting a magnificent headache right about now.

For the first time that day, Ehle found his hand reaching for his lost locket. It touched, of course, on nothing but air. Old habits. He dropped his hand with a sigh. He missed the pictures it had contained, though the small, still images did little to capture the truth. And he considered how simple it would have been to blast open the cell's door, even with their valiant attempt at guarding runes, if he had not thrown his locus away all those years ago. It had been a vain gesture; you cannot discard the past as easily as you can its mementos.

So much would be different, if he still had his magic to draw upon. His work would already be done.

The lock on the outer door thunked and the door came open. "You have a visitor," the guard said. A moment later, Max Haupt stood in the doorway.

"Ah, Max. Have you come to finish what you started upstairs?" Ehle asked him in German as his visitor approached his cell. "I must admit, I had forgotten how skilled you were at such magic. Voelker was always very proud. Do your new masters give you as much opportunity to practice as did your old ones?"

The guard brought a chair for the director of the OMRD, then retreated, closing the door behind him. Max sat, his legs unsteady. His brows were pinched toward his nose, and his forehead dotted with sweat. "I am sorry," he said. He sat up very straight, as he always had, to compensate for his small stature, Ehle assumed. It made him appear as though he was always uncomfortable. "I do not know what came over me. I acted in haste."

Ehle sensed something then, something else in the room. It

was subtle but unmistakable, if you knew to look. A smear of color by the door, then in a dark corner. He forced himself not to smile. "Your German is terrible, Max. It almost sounded like you were apologizing," Ehle said, switching to English. "Let us continue in your new mother tongue."

"What are you doing here, Erwin?"

"You know why I am here."

"To help America defeat the Russians?"

"To right a wrong."

Max laughed. "You have become a poet in your old age."

"It is not too late," Ehle said. "There is little time, but it is not too late. Help me. Let us end this, once and for all. We both have debts in need of repayment."

"Do not speak to me of debts, Erwin. I have paid my dues."

"To whom?"

"The world."

"The world?" Ehle laughed. "To hell with the world. It was Germany we betrayed. It is Germany that we owe. And I doubt if your Western benefactors even know just how much you owe. Ah, I see it plainly on your face. They have no idea. It is truly a marvel you have survived this long when you write your secrets in every scowl. What would they think if they knew they employed the Butcher of London?"

"Erwin," Max said, tutting. "Do not be so naïve. The Americans, for all their public moralism, can be pragmatic when required. They know exactly who I am. What I have done."

"Your masters know your sins," Erwin said. "But what of those who work for you? What of Karen?"

Max cracked his cane on the concrete. "Enough. I did not come here to be lectured by you."

"So why did you come back to Germany, old friend?"

"I came here to prevent a war."

"How? You think you can restore the Wall? If you thought that, you would have been here days ago."

"It was you, was it not?"

"How could I unravel a spell mostly designed by the great Max Haupt?"

"You could not," Max said. "Unless the weaknesses were there from the beginning."

"But that would mean," Ehle said, "that while you and the other master magicians were determining how to hide away Germany's shame and divide its people, someone working alongside you was already planning to undo your work. That would take remarkable foresight and patience."

"Do you think I am impressed? If you were half the magician you once were, the Wall would be a memory now, and yet it stands."

Ehle came forward, pressed against the bars of his cell. "Help me, Max."

"Help you to do what?"

"Destroy the book. We owe Germany at least that much."

Max rested both hands on the head of his cane. The last decade had aged him, harder than the years warranted. His face was gouged by wrinkles, his hair thinned, his knuckles knobbed. Ehle wondered how much of the man he knew remained.

"You are without power," Max said after a long pause. "I envy you. There is a freedom in that. The freedom to be a poet. I have no such freedom. I only ever wanted to be a magician. Instead I have been made a politician."

"A dire fate indeed," Ehle said. "But you can use that influence to do what we must."

"Do you know what keeps the world safe, Erwin? Not poetry. Deterrence. The West has the atomic bomb, but we are not so foolish as to think the Soviets will not get their own eventually. We will build bigger ones, and then so will they. And we will have peace."

"That is peace?"

"Would you invade your neighbor if he had the power to burn your cities to ash?" He shook his head. "No. In all of our history, man has proven to be addicted to war. No virtue has proven stronger. Perhaps fear will be the answer."

"Then build your bombs. See what sort of world they usher in. But what Voelker unleashed in Auttenberg . . . it must be put to an end."

Max's grip tightened on his cane. "Do not lecture me about the book. I know it better than anyone."

"That is why you must help me."

Max scoffed. "If we take the poet's path and destroy it, what then? Wait for it to return in some forsaken corner of the world, for the Soviets or someone worse to stumble upon it? The book always returns. You know this."

Ehle felt his stomach drop. He had wondered how much of Max had changed with the years, and now he had his answer: very little. The only difference now was the flag he saluted.

"And what, old friend, is the politician's path?" Ehle asked. Max did not answer. "Ah. That is why you have come back to the land of your youth, not for the Wall or for me or for your pupil. You have come for the book."

Max stood. "The war was a long time ago," he said. "Perhaps you will find mercy for your crimes, as I have. Good luck, Erwin."

As the outer door closed and locked behind Max, Ehle closed his eyes and rested his forehead against the bars. We are all fools, he thought, cursed to replay our foolishness again and again, generation to generation. But not forever. No, only until we at last complete that task for which we are uniquely suited: our own destruction.

Ehle allowed himself the smile he had stifled earlier. He watched the blur in the corner start to move. It approached the cell. A moment later, Karen stood at the bars.

"Last time we met here," Ehle said, "you arrived in a more official capacity."

"Last time, I still trusted them enough to ask permission," she replied. Her voice was cold. "Luckily they haven't gotten any better at understanding magic in the last week."

"Men's minds change slowly," Ehle said. "You slipped in while the guard was getting the chair? Portuguese Light Bending?"

She nodded. "Crude, but hard to detect if you don't move around too much. Dr. Haupt is weakened by his little display upstairs or he'd definitely have sensed it."

"It was a risk."

Karen put her hands on the cell door. "You were no soldier. You were a Nazi bastard." She could not meet his eye. "And you lied to me. Again. That's a dangerous habit for a man looking for allies."

"I told you many things," he said. "The important ones were true."

"You wanted my help, so you lied."

"Did you speak to your friend Dr. Haupt before he came to see me?" Ehle asked. "How honest do you think he was with you? They are all lying, Karen: to you, to each other, to themselves. I lied to you in order to destroy something evil. They lied so they could obtain it."

Karen's face flushed. "I know what you did in those camps, Mr. Ehle."

"You know nothing of it," he said, too loudly. "You cannot even guess at the horrors we committed. Do not try. We did the worst things with the greatest of intentions. Like you, much of our work was dedicated to finding true healing magic. But in order to heal, we had to harm. In that, at least, we were successful beyond imagining. I shattered people, Karen. Broke them with magic just to see how they bled. Do not ask me how many died while I watched, because I simply cannot recall." He turned away, sick with fetid memories. "You know nothing. Do not pretend otherwise."

"How?" Karen asked with a dry throat. "How could you?"

Ehle sighed. "We were at war. If that does not explain it, nothing can."

"You were at war with women and children?" There were tears in Karen's eyes, tears and fire. "How many casualties did you suffer in that conflict, Mr. Ehle? Or did they deserve it, because they weren't German enough? I'm young and naïve, so help me understand, because from here it looks like you're a monster."

"Of course I am," Ehle said. She wanted him to help her understand, but that was impossible. "But what we did at Ravensbrück was nothing compared to what that book's magic could do." He approached the bars; Karen moved away an equal distance. "You called me a liar, and you were right. But here is the truth: Haupt, your mentor, retrieved the book from the fires of London, after killing so many he earned himself the nickname Butcher. In time, Voelker mastered enough of its mysteries to summon its foul power, but he needed to test his new spells. So he came to me. We thought it might salvage the war effort. We thought we could save Germany. But instead, we damned ourselves."

He wrapped his trembling fingers around the cold steel bars, holding himself steady, holding himself in the present. "I would say I remember the first person we used it on, but 'remember' is the wrong word. It was a woman. I think she was in her forties, maybe younger. I picture her now with auburn hair, but I know that is another lie. That I remember her at all is only because the spell was imperfectly cast. When the magic did its work, I watched the life ebb from her. Then she coughed out her soul like blood."

Karen turned away. Her skin had gone pale. "That's enough," she said.

"I thought you wanted to understand," he said, a little angry. She had demanded he draw up these old infections, but now she lacked the stomach for it. "In my time in the camps, I had seen pain. Unimaginable pain. But I had never seen agony like this, nothing like it. When it was over, she . . . what is the word . . . she crumbled, into dust. Into nothing."

There were tears on his cheeks now, but he paid them no mind. Perhaps now she would see. "In that moment, I realized I had already forgotten her face. Not like when a stranger passes you by, no, I had studied this face as it died. It should have stayed with me forever. But it was simply gone, like it had never been. Like she had never been."

He hated this, but the pain was purifying, a penance. No, nothing could make him clean again. "But it was too late in the war to bring the magic to bear in combat. Not long after we made our first breakthroughs, Ravensbrück was overrun by the Soviets. Voelker still had the book, and so he made his last stand. I do not know what that magic did in Auttenberg," he said eventually. "All I know is that I would do anything to see it purged from this world. Anything."

Karen was far away now, pressed against the wall.

"I am a monster," he said one last time. "What I have done can never be forgiven. But I am not asking for forgiveness. I am asking for your help. Auttenberg has been sealed for these long years, but no longer. If not the Soviets, then the Americans, or the French, or the British—someone seeking power, or safety, or knowledge will take that book and try to use it, and the world will suffer for it. Unless we act. Now."

She approached the cell then, her hands contracted into fists. "We should have left you on the other side of the Wall. I'm just glad Dennis didn't know who he died to save," she said, her voice soft but shaking with rage.

When she was gone, Ehle stared after her. He thought of his wife, his daughter. He thought of the women of Ravensbrück, those he did not remember and those he could not. And he thought of Auttenberg, waiting in darkness like an unconfessed sin. And he wept.

THIRTY-EIGHT

Old men have a curious response to waiting. To some, even the slightest delay is intolerable, whereas others can sit and watch the hours creep by undisturbed. Long life either makes a man covetous of the time left him or gives him perspective on the relative worth of a moment. The colonel had believed himself among the latter. He liked to think of himself as a patient man. He enjoyed the notion that he was the careful hunter watching the game trail, not moving a muscle, content for his prey to reveal itself when it is ready.

But Berlin was unmaking him. Too many pieces on the board, too many wheels turning, too many voices from Moscow in his ear. He just wanted this business done so he could return home. He wanted to watch his daughter dance. He wanted to smell his wife's hair. He wanted to be free of Germany.

He checked his pocket watch. Only a few minutes had passed. Patience. Let your plan work itself out. Let your quarry come. It will come. He will come.

"Sir?" It was Leonid.

"What is it?"

"The magician is here."

The bulbous German magician with the tiny teeth and ambitious eyes entered. Like all of his countrymen, he could not help but show fear when ushered into Karlshorst. The colonel did not blame them for their trepidation. The compound here was, after all, the clearest reminder that despite the trappings of a government and the never-ending masquerade that was international diplomacy, Germany was still an occupied nation. And yet this one seemed also somehow pleased with himself for braving these walls.

"Unless you have come to give me profound news," he said before the man could even take a seat, "your time would be better spent at the Wall."

The magician beamed a toothy smile. "I have come to report on our progress, Comrade Colonel."

"Progress?"

"Exciting progress," the magician said.

The colonel offered him a chair. "Tell me your name."

"Krauss, Comrade Colonel."

"Impress me with your progress, Herr Krauss."

The magician folded his blunt hands over his chest. With his fingers interlaced, they looked like pale pink sausages. "Sir, we have done more in the last week than we have been able to in the last year," Krauss said. "It is of course advantageous that the Wall magic is deteriorating—"

"I am not certain either of our governments would agree."

Krauss scoffed at this. "I am sure it introduces some political difficulties," Krauss replied, "but it makes the excavation of Auttenberg infinitely simpler."

People were dying in the streets of Berlin. Fools convinced of a better life in the West were facing down tanks and machine guns to break through the failing Wall under the watchful eye of American, British, and French soldiers. Political difficulties indeed.

"You see, sir," Krauss continued, "with the Wall diminishing we can focus on the other magical interference keeping us out of the district. There is a great deal there, more than we anticipated, but we have already begun to break down the outer layers."

"If it was so simple, why have we been waiting so long for any success?"

"Well, sir, I do not wish to speak out of turn," Krauss said, flexing those sausages until they shone white, "but I had offered a number of suggestions to Herr Ehle that he did not consider worth pursuing. With his absence, I have already put some of them to good use."

"And why did he reject them?"

"I suspect he was secretly attempting to keep us from meeting our objective, Comrade Colonel, undoubtedly at the behest of his handlers in the West."

"No other reason?"

"Well, sir," Krauss said, "nothing great is ever achieved without risk."

"What sort of risk?"

"We are dealing with dangerous magic, sir. The only magic we could possibly use to any effect must be equally so."

The colonel fixed his eyes on the round magician and said nothing. Sweat was breaking out on his pasty brow. Good.

"Well, sir, what I mean to say is . . ." Krauss sighed. "We have lost two magicians in the last three days, sir."

"Lost?"

"Dead, sir. Unfortunate accidents."

More casualties in their undeclared war. "These deaths," he said, "they were productive?"

Krauss grinned again. It was an unpleasant sight. "Yes, sir. Very productive. I believe we will have access to Auttenberg very soon. Very soon." The magician leaned forward and the chair groaned under his weight. "If I may, sir, what is the plan once we are successful?"

Now we have come to it. The cost of enlisting ambitious men. "I will lead a team into Auttenberg," the colonel said, "to recover the lost book, to be used for the good of Germany and the Soviet Union."

"Well, sir," Krauss began. Hunger was naked on his piggish face. "Again I do not mean to speak out of turn, but if it is possible, I would very much like to accompany this team and provide whatever assistance I may."

The colonel stood and Krauss scrambled to do likewise. "Get us inside that district, Herr Krauss, and I will find a place to use you in the excavation." He placed a hand on the man's thick shoulder as he led him to the door. He pressed his fingers deep into the soft flesh, and then deeper still. "But understand me when I tell you that if you fail to deliver on these lofty promises," he said, pushing in harder, "the terrors of Auttenberg will be the least of your concerns."

"Yes," said the sweating magician as he tried to hide a wince. "Yes, sir. Understood, sir. I will deliver Auttenberg. I swear it."

"More promises," he said. "Be careful what promises you give me, for I will hold you to them." The colonel watched the man go, and then felt an uncontrollable need to wash his hands.

THIRTY-NINE

There'd be no sleeping tonight, Karen knew, not with these jagged thoughts clamoring angrily in her head. She sat up, massaged her aching eyes, and sighed into the dark. Life had been so simple before, when her only job was to try to discover miraculous magic and heal some lab rats. That had been a manageable kind of impossible. Not like this.

She dressed and grabbed Ehle's bag, which had come to replace the one she lost in the tunnel. Maybe some night air would provide some clarity, if she could convince the men on guard to let her out. Probably a long shot, but just stretching her legs sounded like a good idea even if she was stuck wandering BOB's endless corridors. Anything but spending another hour staring at shadows, looking foolishly for answers that refused to come.

There could no longer be any doubt that Auttenberg was real and that Ehle had told her the truth; the conversation between Ehle and Dr. Haupt had proven it. The only question now was what she was going to do about it. Dr. Haupt and George had come to Berlin to get the book before the Soviets could, that much seemed clear. That was the best possible outcome, right? Certainly the world would be safer if the US controlled the book's magic.

Right?

She thought about George Cabott and the other men she knew at the OMRD: arrogant, careless men who would relish the thought of experimenting with previously unknown magic. All for the sake of world peace, of course. They wouldn't start out with the same vile ambitions as the Nazis, but would good intentions be enough? What were Dr. Haupt's intentions when he used illegal magic to subdue Ehle? The power was there, so he used it. Because he could.

Karen's shoulders slumped as she started up the stairs. This was not the sort of magic she had become a magician for. This was not the sort of problem she had been inspired to solve. And yet, here she was. The decision wasn't going away. Either she acted, or she did not. Either she helped Ehle enter Auttenberg and destroy the book, or she waited to see what fate had in store. Either she saved the world, or she hoped it saved itself.

She heard a door open a level below. Who else was wandering BOB's stairwells at this hour? Karen glanced down. Whoever it was, they were moving fast toward the basement. Had something happened? She leaned over the railing to get a better look and saw a figure disappear into the lower corridor.

It was Jim.

Karen's skin prickled. Why would Jim be awake in the middle of the night? He was supposed to be recovering from his ordeal. She hadn't been able to shake the strange feeling she had when he had looked at her. She couldn't know what he had been through, what that would do to someone, but in that moment he had looked like another person.

And now he was hurrying through BOB, at night, alone. Toward Ehle's cell.

She descended the stairs as quickly and quietly as she could, her locus pressing hard into her palm. It was probably nothing. Jim probably couldn't sleep. Just wanted to stretch his legs, like she did. This was Jim, after all. There had to be an innocuous explanation.

It was quiet as she neared the door to the detainment cell. Painfully quiet. There was supposed to be an agent on guard at all times, but the hallway was empty. She crept forward on silent feet.

The door was open.

The first thing she saw was the soles of the agent's shoes. He was on his side, his legs tangled up, just inside the door. When she moved closer, she saw the dark pool around the man's head. By then she could see into the room beyond. And there was Jim, kneeling over the fallen agent, two fingers pressed against his neck.

"Jim?" Karen said. "What happened?"

He looked at her as though she were a stranger.

"Where's Ehle?" she asked. She saw him now, down on his back on the floor of his open cell. Without thinking, she pushed past Jim and hurried to Ehle's side. He was still breathing, but had been dealt a hard blow to his temple. The skin was already swelling up in an angry wound, and blood matted his gray hair.

She reached into her satchel to grab a handkerchief to clean the wound. "Call for help," she said. "Hurry, I think he's hurt."

There was no reply.

She looked up. He was staring at her, only a few feet away, blocking the entrance to the cell. *No*, she thought. *Oh, no.* "Jim," she said carefully. "What did you do?"

"I have to take him," Jim said. His voice sounded flat. "They sent me here for him."

Karen's hand was still in her bag. It settled around something small and hard: the carved animal statue Ehle had used to lead her to his apartment.

"What are you doing, Jim?" she said. Ehle had shown her how

the old magic of the carving worked; she hoped she remembered. "Where are you taking him?"

"I . . . I can't . . ." Jim squeezed his eyes shut. In that moment, Karen slipped the carving into the pocket of Ehle's coat.

The next instant came as a blur of noise and pain. She saw Jim move; he came down on her too fast, swinging something black in his fist. Then an explosion behind her eyes, her skull cracking. And she tasted metal.

When her vision cleared, she was on her back on the icy concrete floor. She saw the bare bulb of the jail room above her. And then Jim's face. Or a man who looked like Jim, but with someone else's eyes. He was speaking.

". . . stupid whore," someone with his voice was saying. "What were you trying to do, huh? You going to break him out? Take him back to your masters?"

"What . . ." she said with a thick tongue, ". . . are you doing?"

"Shut up," he demanded. "I won't listen to you. Not anymore. I know what you have been doing to me. I know about the magic. You can't fool me again."

She swallowed and tried to ignore the pain that muffled her ears and her head. That look she had seen for an instant in the bullpen, that mask of hatred that had appeared and vanished in a blink, it was now all she could see.

"I don't know what you are talking about."

"Enough," he said. "I don't have time for this."

She realized it then: what was wrong with his eyes. She'd seen it before, when Bill returned from his mysterious absence: magic, snaking through his irises where it didn't belong. *Of course. What a fool. What a stupid, naïve fool.* She had been too distracted by the celebration of Jim's return, then Allison's message, and Dr. Haupt's arrival. The Soviets had a magician who could distort and manip-

ulate human thoughts. Bill had been gone a few hours and had
lost his memories; Jim had been gone a few days and had lost his
mind.

Karen pushed herself up to a seated position. "Jim, you have to
fight it," she said. "The Soviets, they are manipulating you."

He swung on her and raised a pistol. "Shut up," he said again.

"Jim, think," she said, her eyes frozen on the gun's barrel.
"What are you doing with him? They want you to take him back
to East Berlin, don't they? You have to fight it."

She should have known better. There was no reason left in
Jim's eyes. Not after what they'd done to him. He came over to
her, the gun stopping inches from her forehead.

"How could you? How could you do that to me?"

*Focus, Karen. There's only one way this ends, only one way to sur-
vive it.* But no words came to her. A lifetime of training crumbled
in her head.

"How could you make me love you?"

Even if she could remember a spell now, she knew it was too
late. She knew some she could recite in a rush, but as soon as she
started to speak, Jim's finger would move. But that only mattered
if she needed the words. She remembered the car ride from the
Tempelhof airport with two young agents eager to impress the girl
magician. She'd wanted to impress them as well, and had told
them about the theory of Universal Expression, the idea that
magic didn't need words or runes or hand waving; it just needed
the will of the caster. Spells were artificial limits on magic's true
potential. She knew it was true, had even experimented on it at
the OMRD, even at Martha's birthday party. She saw those lights
shining back at her in her niece's wide eyes.

Focus, Karen.

Focus.

Then Jim pulled the trigger.

FORTY

I t was raining.

Autumn, when the leaves turned red and orange and she could ride her bike through endless puddles until it got too dark to see.

Waiting for news from the war. Mom staring out the front window, trying not to cry in front of the girls.

Leaving home for the university. Clogged gutters, the smell of wet asphalt, the ringing of angry words in her head.

Why can't she be more like Helen? Why can't she just find a husband and settle down? Why does she have to study that damned kraut magic?

Her name. She could hear him saying her name.

And the rain.

The rain.

Karen's eyes fluttered as the water sprayed down from the ceiling. The fire suppression system. What had set it off?

She felt weak. Drained. Her ears rang and her mouth was full of iron.

Tried to remember. The door was already open. The agent's shoes. Jim. The gunshot.

Jim had fired only inches away from her head, but she was alive.

It had worked.

The exertion it required had knocked her out, but it had worked. She remembered now: the awful bark of the gun, then time slowed as her magic, no, her *will* reached out and shattered the bullet in midair. No spell, no incantation, just pure, raw magic.

Tears burned. *Oh, God,* she thought. *I'm alive.* There would be time later to consider her unprecedented accomplishment. But in this moment, huddled on a cold concrete floor under the shower of the overhead sprinklers, all she felt was relief.

Karen! Through her clouded ears, she heard her name. Someone shouting.

George stood over her, his suit darkening in the mist of water.

She pushed herself up. If George was here, then Jim and Ehle were already gone. She had to move, had to act.

"Karen!"

She tried to stand. George reached out a hand, but she slapped it away.

"What have you done?" he demanded.

A very good question.

"I knew it. As soon as I heard the fire alarm," George said, "I just knew you had gone and done something stupid."

Her legs felt uncertain under her, but they held. How long had she been out? She needed to move, to get after them, but George stood between her and the door.

"What set off . . . the fire alarm?"

"What do you think?" he asked. "Fire. All over the building. Probably set by your Nazi friend after you let him out."

"No," she said, swallowing. "No, no. I didn't . . . Jim took him."

"What?"

"They did something to his mind," she said. Her head was

numb and throbbed. "Jim must have set the fires as a distraction. We have to stop him. Before they get away."

"You aren't going anywhere, sweetie," George said. He grabbed her arm with hard, biting fingers. "I'm not sure what you are babbling about, but you've done enough already. Now we're going to sit here and wait for your CIA friends to come clean this up."

She looked down at his hand, then back up at his face. "Get out of my way," she said.

George gaped at her in disbelief. "You are nuts," he said. "Karen, this isn't playtime. I'm not going to just let you walk out of here. Look at your face, for God's sake."

She put a hand to her mouth and it came away red. Blood had poured from her nose and caked around her lips, probably stained her teeth. Too much magic, too much will. She smeared the blood on her wet shirtsleeve. "Move, George," she said.

He said nothing. Instead he crossed his arms over his chest. His thumb fingered his bulky ring; he could already be preparing to block any magical assault she could throw at him. She found herself regretting the trick she had pulled on him back at the OMRD, wishing she could use it now. George was a fool, but he wasn't that much a fool. That trick wouldn't work twice.

Luckily she had others.

"Fine, George," she said with a sigh. "You want to know what is going on? It's right there." She pointed to the far corner of the room. "It's all there."

He rolled his eyes, but couldn't resist the lure of curiosity. He turned slowly, patronizingly. "What exactly am I supposed to be looking at?" he asked, before turning back toward her just as Karen squeezed her eyes shut and raised one of Ehle's sunstones.

A blindingly white flash exploded in the room. Even with her eyelids screwed shut and her face pressed into the crook of her arm, Karen still saw purple blotches swim across her vision. There was no time to recover. Pushing past George as he stumbled, she cut through the hissing sprinklers and gray smoke and went up the stairs three at a time.

B y the time she reached the street, Jim was gone. The BOB staff had evacuated and were milling about, each with a different story about where the fire was and how bad the damage. They were wet, tired, and confused. No one paid any attention to the magician weaving around their huddled groups.

George wouldn't be down for long; the next few moments were critical. Jim would be heading for the Wall. There were a myriad of openings now for him to get through to make his escape back to the East, but the CIA could lock those down with a telephone call. But he had to get Ehle out of West Berlin tonight or risk getting captured, so whoever was pulling the strings must have a plan.

Karen reached into her pocket, grateful Jim had shown her the location of the motor pool office that first day. She hoped June wouldn't be too upset over the broken door or one missing car. She pressed the key into her palm; the cool, sharp edges biting into her skin were reassuring. Stay calm. Don't draw attention. She spotted the car parked on the far side of the street just down from BOB. Almost there.

Then she made the mistake of glancing back just as Dr. Haupt and Arthur appeared. Arthur was busy shepherding his people, but Dr. Haupt's eyes found her immediately.

How many times had she gone to Dr. Haupt for advice? How often had his wisdom kept her path steady and sure? She'd probably have never graduated from the university without his guidance. Her younger self—Dr. Haupt's eager pupil at St. Cyprian's—wouldn't even recognize her now. But it had been that wisdom and that path that had led her to this moment, fleeing from her mentor and about to steal a car from the CIA. Sometimes life took unexpected turns.

Dr. Haupt's old advice came back to her: *Trust your instincts, not your fears.* Now she had an addendum: *Trust yourself, and nobody else.*

She unlocked the car and slid in behind the wheel. Through the hazy windshield she could see Dr. Haupt; he was trying to get Arthur's attention. And he was pointing at her.

Sorry, Doctor. I'm not sure which side you're on anymore.

She turned the ignition and the car rumbled to life. In the cool autumn air, she could sense it, as she hoped she would: that same strange magical signal she had felt in East Berlin when they went to find Ehle. It was pulling her east.

FORTY-ONE

I t had all happened so fast. Too fast. He tried to stop himself, to stop and think and reason his way forward, but there was too much noise, too many voices, too many open (green) doors demanding he enter.

And then she appeared. How had she known he'd be there? She knew everything, that's how. It was all part of the plot.

But what plot? If she was working for the Soviets, what did she want with Ehle?

No, he knew it was true; he could still feel the cloying effects of her poisonous love magic in his veins, in his head. He knew it now. She had to be stopped. That was why he had done what he did.

He'd closed his eyes when he pulled the trigger. He couldn't bear to see her face . . . like that. The thought made his skin want to crawl right off his body and he couldn't blame it.

They had already put some miles between them and BOB, but he couldn't help but look in his rearview mirror every few seconds. When he did, he saw the prisoner bound and gagged in the backseat. He was still unconscious; Jim had hit him pretty hard back in his cell. He hadn't meant to do it. His hand had moved not out of anger but inevitability. How can you fight what you cannot stop?

In the distance ahead he could see the silver glow of the Wall, muted and pale like a clouded moon.

You killed her. You shot her in the head.

"Shut up," Jim said before realizing no one had spoken.

Returning to BOB had been strange, like walking across your own grave. None of it had felt real: the exchange across Glienicke Bridge, the drive through Berlin in gray dawnlight, Arthur and Garriety and all the others. They were images that belonged to another life, to some other man. Not like the green door. That was real. That was his. The green door and the look on Karen's face when he pulled the trigger.

They were close to the Wall now. He turned the car south, driving parallel to a part that was still intact, though nevertheless patrolled by West German and Allied soldiers. It was late, but everything was still lit brightly by spotlights and jeeps and tanks.

But Jim wasn't bothered by the checkpoints or the soldiers swarming over them like ants. No, his eyes were fixed on his rearview mirror. There was a black car following him. It wasn't getting close, but it had been back there too long, through too many turns. Another complication, like Karen appearing in the doorway. Another obstacle to be removed.

They were nearly there (where?). That building ahead, with the faded blue sign over the rolling doors, rotting with disuse. The tunnel was inside. He knew that, somehow. Just as he knew he had to take the prisoner through the tunnel to those awaiting them.

The thought of going into another tunnel made his hands tremble. He had not forgotten the last one. He could feel the sudden burning flash and the rocks and sand ricocheting all around him. Dennis was just ahead of him; then he was gone, vanished in the roaring collapse.

Dennis. He hadn't been there at BOB. No one even mentioned him. It was like he didn't exist. Had everything in his life before been a lie? Was anything true anymore?

He pulled up next to the building and slammed the car into park. His shadow stopped half a block back, engine idling. He recognized the car. He wasn't sure how they'd found him or what they were going to do. But that didn't really matter anymore, did it?

Jim grabbed the pistol from the passenger seat.

Keeping his car between him and his unwanted followers, he got out and swung open the rear door. Nap time's over. He prodded his prisoner with the barrel of the pistol until his hazy eyes opened. The man blinked and stirred, until his gaze focused on Jim.

"Let's go," Jim said, motioning with the gun. He didn't move. "We don't really have time to mess around, pal. We've got a schedule to keep."

Down the street, he heard car doors opening. The prisoner still hadn't moved. Jim's head began to throb; it felt like his brain was suddenly turning against him and threatening to blow. He forced his eyes shut, tried to ignore the pain, the icy, stabbing pain, but all he saw was the green door opening slowly, his own hand on the knob, cold against his palm, like the gun, cold and inert, then kicking back as it fired into Karen's face.

"Move," Jim heard himself say. "Or I will kill you."

Ehle slowly unfolded his legs and slid out of the car. Jim hazarded a glance behind them; four men had exited the trailing car and were moving closer. Otherwise, the street was empty.

They reached the rear entrance with the sound of footsteps behind them. Jim wrenched the heavy door open despite uncooperative hinges and shoved Ehle inside. He put his shoulder into the door and it groaned closed. He found an old chair nearby and propped it up under the handle. It would buy them a few moments at best, but maybe that would be all he'd need.

Jim switched on the flashlight he had in his pocket (how had he known to bring a flashlight?) and scanned the building's interior. The old air trapped inside smelled of oil and dirt. It looked like a machinist's workshop, with rusting tools hung on the walls and piled on steel tables, though it hadn't seen much use in some time. At least not machinist work.

They found the ladder down into the secret tunnel behind a massive tool chest, right where the intel (what intel?) said it would be. Jim slid the chest aside (grateful for its well-greased wheels—who had greased them, and how had he known to feel grateful?) and stared down into the darkness that opened up at his feet. He could feel cold damp rising like fog out of a grave. He swallowed. One more time. Just one last crawl through the abyss and then he would be free (from what?).

He heard the soft scuff of a shoe on the concrete floor and spun, pistol leveled. Three guns stared back.

"James," said the only man of the four who was not armed, "what are we doing here?"

"I wish I knew, Emile," Jim answered back. His eyes darted to each of the other Frenchmen; he didn't know any of them but knew enough from the looks on their faces that they wouldn't hesitate to cut him down in a hail of lead. He grabbed Ehle and forced him in front. "How did you find me?"

Emile spread his hands. "We were not looking for you, James."

"I get it," Jim said. He was close enough to the ladder to drop down, but he couldn't drag Ehle and didn't know how far he'd fall. "You had a man watching BOB who got lucky."

"It was an unexpected report," Emile said, "when my agent

told us that you fled the scene carrying your guest here over your shoulder." He took a step closer and Jim swung his gun to face him. That brought him up short.

"This doesn't concern you, Emile," Jim said. "Go home."

"Unfortunately," Emile said, "it very much concerns me."

Jim stared at the Frenchman. "Of course," he said. He shifted his feet back toward the tunnel opening, pulling Ehle with him. "That's why you had someone watching BOB. You want Ehle."

"He is going to help us retrieve something we lost," Emile said with an uncharacteristic smile, "before this city goes to hell and takes all of us with it. We would have preferred to work more openly with Arthur and Alec, but they are moving too slowly. On our little trek to East Berlin, I visited the site where the Soviets are working to cut through the Wall. They do not share our reticence. So please, have our guest walk over to us."

Jim wrapped one arm around Ehle's neck and placed the pistol against his temple. That made the Frenchmen tighten their grips on their own guns. "You're a popular man," Jim said into Ehle's ear. "I think my friends here would be very disappointed if my finger slipped, so they had better keep their distance."

Emile retreated and his men reluctantly did the same. "James," Emile said softly. "I am sorry you had to be dragged into this. I cannot imagine what they did to you. I have heard the stories about the Nightingale, but this is worse than I ever imagined."

"Shut up," Jim said. His head was hurting again (had it ever stopped?) and he couldn't think when everyone was talking.

"His magic has corrupted your mind," Emile said. "You are not yourself. Now put down the gun before someone gets hurt."

Someone had already gotten hurt. He'd shot her, after all.

"It's too late, Emile," Jim said. His hands were shaking; he pressed the gun into Ehle's head just to hold it steady.

"I am sorry," Emile said again. *"Je suis désolé."*

His heels were on the edge of the drop now. Could he make himself jump? The only thing waiting for him down there might be a broken leg, but that was at least a chance. The hard men inching ever closer to him wouldn't be so merciful. He'd failed, even if he survived. No, at least he'd taken care of that traitor, Karen, with her foul distorting magic that had nearly ruined him (before he had ruined himself). Karen . . . he could see her eyes: green, like the hills back home, like springtime, like the door that yawned wide beneath him.

Emile was speaking, but Jim wasn't listening. It was time. Move or die. He took a breath. Then he realized Emile wasn't speaking English. And he wasn't speaking French. This thought had no time to settle before the heavy tool chest, hefted by the invisible hands of Emile's magic, slammed into him and sent everything spinning, spinning into darkness.

FORTY-TWO

Karen slowed to a stop, fumbling quickly to turn off her headlights. She counted four, maybe five men coming out of the darkened building. Most were armed. One clearly had his hands tied behind his back. At this distance with such anemic light she couldn't be sure, but she did not think Jim was among them. She was fairly certain, however, that the man in the front, the one puffing away on a white cigarette, was Emile.

At first, she felt relief. Somehow the French had found Jim first and stopped him from taking Ehle to the Soviets. Disaster had been averted. But then her mind began to whir: Why were Ehle's hands still bound? Where was Jim? And how had the French arrived so soon?

The questions had barely materialized before she knew the answer: Auttenberg. Emile had seemed peculiarly interested in Ehle. They must know his background with the Wall, probably even suspect he was behind the breach. So they had eyes on BOB and had gotten lucky, and now were going to make a play for Auttenberg.

For that damn book.

Ehle had warned her about this. While she had been trying to keep the Wall up, the Americans, the French, the Soviets, the British, and probably even the damned Canadians were all maneuvering to get into Auttenberg before the others.

Just before they put the bound man in the back of their car, Emile stopped him and reached into his pocket. A moment later, Emile tossed something over his shoulder. They got into the vehicle and drove off.

Karen pulled up to where they had been as soon as they turned the corner ahead. Lying in the gutter was the artifact that had produced the magical trail she had been following. Emile had sensed it. That meant two things: Emile was a magician, and she couldn't let that car out of her sight.

Leaving the artifact and grinding her car into gear, she sped up the street after the Frenchmen.

Karen waited and hoped they would turn west and take Ehle back to the French sector or back to BOB. But they continued north along the Wall, skirting the more populous checkpoints. She knew now where they were going. Ehle had shown her on an old map of the city where the lost district of Auttenberg lay, and they were heading straight there. The Wall was still standing around what was once Auttenberg, which meant no soldiers or refugees to get in the way.

She slammed the palm of her hand against the steering wheel. There was no one to help her, no one she could turn to for advice. Just the decision to be made, and very little time to make it.

Act, or get out of the way.

Karen put both hands back on the wheel and set her jaw. Let's do this.

She did not see the black and chrome Volkswagen approaching from the left until its headlights filled her windscreen and she heard the agonies of steel smashing steel.

FORTY-THREE

Arthur had forgotten how cold it got in Berlin this time of the year. Rain or shine, the weather never made much of an impact on his daily pursuits, since he made it a point to stay inside as much as possible. He certainly didn't make it a habit to wander about in the middle of the night in October without an overcoat, but these were the times they lived in. He puffed out a mouthful of vapor and watched it disappear.

"So the fire's out?" he asked.

"Yes, sir. We were able to stop it from spreading much."

Well, that was something at least. "And the sprinklers?"

The agent swallowed nervously. "They're off now."

"How much damage did they do?"

"Well, sir, it is hard to say at this point . . ."

"Take a guess."

The man straightened up. "More than the fire, sir."

Figures. The cure is often worse than the disease. The agent's shivers were only reminding Arthur how cold he was, so he sent the man inside to warm up and continue the cleanup. Wasn't like any of them were going to get any sleep tonight anyway.

"If you don't mind me saying," said a deep, burred voice behind him, "you gents look like a nest of drowned rats."

As if the evening hadn't been eventful enough. "Have you come to help towel the place off?" Arthur asked as Alec approached. "Or just offer His Majesty's condolences for our misfortunes?"

"As an esteemed member of His Majesty's intelligence service, I can offer English condolences," Alec said, "and Scottish whiskey." He handed an amber bottle across to Arthur. The weight of the dark gold in his hand made his mouth go dry and his muscles twinge. He knew exactly how it would burn in his mouth, how it would feel going down his throat and into his veins. No, not now. He could run this place drunk or exhausted, but not both.

"Thank you for each," Arthur said, reluctantly relegating the whiskey to a nearby agent.

"Strange happenings on the wind tonight," Alec said.

"It's a strange world," Arthur said.

Alec grunted. "Ehle is gone?"

"Spirited out of his cell."

"By whom?"

"I think you already know, or this visit might have waited until a decent hour."

Alec grunted again. "Not sure this city has any decent hours left. Our boy Jim leave a trail of bread crumbs to follow?"

"That's what my magicians are trying to figure out now."

"Magicians? There's magic afoot?"

"Ehle was a magician, so it seems likely," Arthur said. And Karen too, but he decided to keep her vanishing act to himself for now. "Plus anytime something goes to hell, magic usually isn't far from the scene of the crime."

"Speaking of crimes," Alec said, staring off down the street, "you heard anything from our prickly French cousins this fine evening?"

Now Arthur wished he'd kept the whiskey. "No. Should I have?"

Alec shrugged his bulky shoulders under his heavy wool coat. "I wouldn't bring it up, certainly not with so much on our minds already, except . . . well, we've got word that the frogs had eyes on BOB these last few days, ever since the good Mr. Ehle took up his residence."

"You got word," Arthur said. This night was threatening to become memorable. "And you decided not to share this word with us?"

"We all keep our own secrets," Alec said. "But if the French were watching your offices, they must have seen Jim make his escape. And yet, here we are, standing alone without even a croak to be heard."

Because they were too busy making their own move. This was the chief mistake of getting old: you started trusting people.

"Come on," Arthur said. "Let's go see if these damned magicians have any bright ideas."

FORTY-FOUR

By the time her car had crashed into the curb and everything stopped moving, Karen was sure she was going to be sick. The sharp spike of adrenaline had punched her in the gut and the feeling of her car spinning sideways on mist-slicked asphalt certainly hadn't helped. Her hands refused to let go of the steering wheel even as she slowly began to realize she wasn't going to die. She was profoundly grateful for the heavy weight of her car and that the impact had been near the trunk, and not the driver's door.

She stumbled out of the steaming car on legs unprepared for action. She was met immediately by a rush of angry German words coming from the other driver, a gray-haired man in a suit, tie, and hat who was brandishing his finger at her like a rapier. She didn't understand a thing he said, but somehow she got the general theme.

Which way had the French been going? She looked at the street signs for help, but they kept moving, even as she tried to focus on them. How could they expect anyone to read something that wouldn't hold still? She suddenly felt an inescapable urge to sit down.

Then she threw up.

This at least silenced her verbal assailant.

North. They were going north. To Auttenberg.

She wiped her mouth and forced herself back to her feet. The man was out of his dented car now and jabbering at her with a slightly more compassionate-sounding but no less incomprehensible flurry of Germanic diphthongs and umlauts. She held up a hand to ward off his help, but now other cars were stopping. Police couldn't be far behind, or even soldiers.

North. It wasn't far. She hoped.

She looked at the two cars, caved in where they'd had their untimely meeting, and thought she might have the stirrings of a plan. With her stomach seemingly under control, she lurched back to her ruined car and retrieved her satchel. Then, ignoring the shouted protests and her own unsteady legs, she began to run.

FORTY-FIVE

It was not the path he would have selected, but he could not argue with its efficacy. This was, after all, the destination he had been dreaming about for longer than he dared to admit. They were at the edge of a park. It was no grand place, just a simple city park with a stretch of green, a few clusters of oak and linden, a pair of benches whose wood had long turned gray. It had been abandoned once the war came, then forgotten when the Wall was raised across it. In an earlier time, it had been the western entrance to the district of Auttenberg. As Ehle watched, the pale white Wall stared back at him, its length quivering like the flank of some great dying animal. His own hands had started this, and now it was time for the merciful killing blow.

The other men had moved away from him, in fear perhaps. If he were still a young man, such fears might have been warranted. But the magic necessary to subdue four strong men, armed with pistols or magic of their own, was long beyond him.

"Herr Ehle," the leader said in German with a terrible French accent, "it is time for you to prove your value."

Ehle laughed. He had not meant to; he saw no reason to provoke these men. But the very thought was too comical to let pass.

"I place little value on having value," he said, still facing away from his captors.

"Would you rather see the book fall into the Soviets' hands?"

"I would rather see it burn," Ehle said in French. "But somehow I doubt that is your purpose here."

There was a long silence, and then the leader said, "France has earned the right to safety. From you, from the Soviets, from everyone. My countrymen have earned the right. We purchased it with blood."

"There is no safety while the book exists," Ehle said. "Not for France. Not for Germany."

"It was not the book's magic that scorched our farms," the leader replied. "It was not this book that razed our cities and raped our women. I do not fear what lies beyond that Wall. I fear Soviet planes. I fear German tanks. I fear telling the next generation that we had the opportunity to obtain something that would keep us safe and that we did nothing."

"I have seen this magic," Ehle said. "It is no tame dragon you hope to capture."

The Frenchman paused a moment and then said, "Risk is of no consequence. I would risk the world for this."

"And so you are."

"I am tired of waiting, Herr Ehle. We have sought a way through Auttenberg's defenses a long time, and I know that you can provide us with just that. Do so now."

"If I could get into Auttenberg, it would already be done," Ehle said. "But I no longer possess sufficient magical power to do what is required. I am sorry, but you are going to be disappointed yet again."

The Frenchman smacked another cigarette out into his palm. "As I said, we have been at this for some time," he said, cupping the cigarette as he lit it. "We are not unprepared. If you require magical assistance, I can provide it to you."

"You have thought of everything," Ehle said. But then he shrugged. "You will have to kill me first."

"Emile!" It was a woman's voice.

Karen. She was walking toward them out of the dark Berlin night.

"Miss O'Neil," the Frenchman said, in English now. His guards started toward her, but he waved them off. "You are a long way from home."

"Emile," she replied as she neared. "And here I thought we were on the same side."

"That depends on the conflict," Emile answered.

"What are you doing here?" she said.

"We are preparing an expedition into a forgotten corner of this grand city," he said. "A place that, unless I miss my guess, you are already aware of."

"You're insane if you want to take it for yourself."

"I want nothing for myself. But for France . . ." He shrugged.

"When we went into East Berlin," Karen said, fitting pieces into place, "you disappeared. Turned off your radio. Were you investigating Auttenberg? Or was it you who betrayed us to the Soviets?"

"I am no traitor," Emile said. "I do not know how the Soviets discovered us, but it was not from me. But yes, I used the opportunity to observe the Wall from the opposite side, without an escort. We knew of Moscow's attempts to enter Auttenberg; they started work on the project from the first day after the Wall was raised. We hoped to learn more about their progress, and we found more than we might have hoped, in our German friend here."

"Don't be a fool," Karen said. "Nothing good will come of this."

"We have little time," Emile replied. "Berlin is on fire. We will not be alone here for long." He motioned forward and Karen was pushed toward the Wall. "I suspect our German friend has already asked you to help him break down the Wall spell. Please do so now."

Karen looked at him. There was dried blood on her face. One of her hands was bleeding and it felt like there was broken glass caught up in her hair. Her ribs ached. She wanted to sit down, to sleep, maybe even to cry, though she feared her long night was just beginning. She didn't fully understand all the steps that had brought her to this peculiar moment, but she knew she wasn't about to help anyone, ally or not, steal whatever waited inside of Auttenberg.

Emile sighed. A moment later he produced a pistol from under his coat. "Open the way, Miss O'Neil," he said, "or I will kill you."

FORTY-SIX

"Here," Haupt said suddenly. "Stop here."

The sedans screeched to a halt in front of what appeared to be an abandoned machinist's shop. There were no lights on inside, but then again, there probably wasn't much call for machinist work at four a.m.

"You sure?" Arthur asked, eyeing the place. Something about it was familiar, or at least reminded him of something he knew he ought to remember.

"I am certain," Dr. Haupt replied. Arthur watched as Haupt fumbled with the door handle for a moment before the smirking oaf called George took over and swung the door open for his boss. While Arthur found the OMRD director unpleasant, it was his sneering assistant whose teeth he wanted to punch down his throat. He'd met plenty of arrogant little boys like George who thought themselves invincible despite having been too young to take up arms against the Hun, and every one of them was worthless when it came time for an actual fight. Arthur had a litany of profane words to share with Miss O'Neil if they all made it through the night alive, but he certainly didn't mind that she had made George look like a fool on her way out.

On the street, Arthur could smell the river in the damp night air. They weren't far from the Wall; it shimmered just beyond the old machinist's shop, as impenetrable here as ever. Good. The farther they stayed from the killing fields of the overrun checkpoints and undermanned breaches, the better.

"What are we looking for?" Alec asked as he stepped out.

"No idea," Arthur said. "But I know that when I see it, I won't like it." At least he had his heavy overcoat on now, his last anniversary present. She hadn't loved him, but at least she had known his size. He waved over a couple of his agents: tall, able boys whose names he'd never remember. "Go check out the shop," he said.

There really was no good way for this to end. Maybe they'd find Ehle alive and bring him in, or maybe they'd find his body stuffed in a trash can. Maybe his face would end up on Soviet propaganda posters plastered all over buildings from Pankow to Treptow. Ehle didn't matter; Jim did. One of his own had gone rogue and would have to be put down. The Soviets got to him somehow when he was captive, probably with that twice-damned magic, and now he was a lost cause, even if he was still alive. Another casualty in a war neither side admitted to fighting.

And then there was Karen. When he heard the first reports that Ehle had escaped, Arthur had been ready to blame her. And while it was Jim who had been reported fleeing BOB with the prisoner tossed over his shoulder, Arthur still wasn't ready to let the girl off the hook. His old bones told him something was up, that she was playing notes from a different song; he just didn't know which key.

Or maybe his old bones were just telling him he was old, tired, and should have kept that bottle of scotch Alec had offered.

"Look!" George was kneeling in the gutter not far from where they'd parked. He picked something up and hurried to his boss's side.

"What have we here?" Arthur asked when he reached them.

Haupt held up a crude stone statue. "An ancient Teutonic signaling totem," he said. He almost sounded impressed. "I have not seen one in decades, but I am certain this came from Erwin."

"That was causing the magical disturbance you were feeling?" Alec asked.

"Undoubtedly," Haupt said. "He must have activated it so he could be followed."

"Followed by whom?" Arthur asked.

Haupt's face curdled. George, still a little singed after his run-in with Karen at BOB, looked ready to punch someone.

"So where is she now?" Arthur asked, not expecting an answer and not getting one. Something in the street caught his eye. He reached down and picked it up between his index finger and thumb. Crushed cigarettes certainly weren't uncommon in Berlin, though most of them weren't a French brand. Or still warm.

One of the agents, a clean-cut kid with a name like Thompson or Andrews, approached.

"How bad is it inside?" Arthur asked, still eyeing the cigarette.

"Signs of a struggle," the agent said. "Some blood."

"A body?"

Shook his head. "But there was a tunnel."

Arthur stared at the machinist's shop, then back at the cigarette. Damn. That was why the place had seemed familiar. He really wished he had had that drink, though he didn't think it would taste quite as good anymore.

FORTY-SEVEN

Under the waning silver light of the Wall, they laid out the requirements for Ehle's spell: chalk, beeswax candles, saltpeter, ground onyx.

"I did not expect you to come," Ehle whispered as the Frenchmen looked on.

"I'm not here to save you," Karen said. "I'm just trying to stop all this from going to hell."

Ehle nodded. "As am I."

It was complex magic, layers and layers of incantations precisely calibrated. Karen understood why Ehle had failed to cast this without a proper locus. It was masterful magic. She initially understood only about half of what he instructed her to do, but caught on quickly. After an hour, she could see the strands of logic in Ehle's work and marveled at it. What a waste for such talent to be spent in service of the Third Reich or the USSR. Maybe it was finally being put to good use.

When dawn stained the eastern sky beyond the Wall, Karen stood and dusted off her hands. "Is that everything?" she asked.

"I believe so."

"Oh, wait," Karen said, kneeling by the Wall one last time. She quickly traced out a few arcane symbols on the ground. These were deviations from Ehle's plan, but he watched without comment. "There, that should be enough."

Emile gestured with his pistol. "We are out of time. Do it now."

Karen looked to Ehle. He surveyed their work, and nearly smiled. "You are an able pupil. I am pleased that I found you, Karen O'Neil," he said, stepping out of her way. "Perhaps someday, you will feel the same."

She ignored him and moved closer to the Wall. Her hand touched her locus. Reading from Ehle's notes, she began the spell.

It did not take long. The Wall seized. Its gossamer threads turned brittle. Then a breach appeared and began to grow. It was a desecration, but no more than the Wall itself had been, a puckered scar on Berlin's wounded face.

Oh, God, I hope I'm not wrong, Karen thought. She pictured the refugees yearning for escape, and the soldiers waiting for them to try. She heard the echo of gunshots, tasted foul smoke. She had come to Berlin to prove herself; now she might be about to start a war.

Too late now.

The Wall in front of them was gone.

Immediately she felt the knifing tang of the defensive spells that had been set like battlements around Auttenberg. The Wall was just a distraction, but now came the barricades meant to keep Auttenberg lost forever. Unlike the Wall, this was not subtle magic; it was raw and sharp, ironclad. Hard magic. Deadly magic.

But they were ready for it. Her hands moved. Her palm ached as the points of her locus bit into her skin through the leather pouch, but she welcomed the pain. She heard the rush of blood in her ears and the thunder of her own heart.

And the magic. Such magic. It had never felt like this before. It came over her like a torrent and rushed out of her like a tidal wave. Ehle provided the knowledge, but her own strength was shocking and tantalizing.

The air around her shimmered and smeared, like heat, like light through melting glass.

And then she was through. A small opening appeared, a path forward wide enough for a person to walk through. Auttenberg waited beyond.

Karen stepped back, a little unsteady. Then her legs failed and she went forward, toward the growing breach. Ehle ran ahead and caught her before she collapsed.

"*Das war unglaublich,*" he said, breathless. "That was incredible."

She looked up at him, though her eyes struggled to focus. Everything was bright and hot. Fresh blood from her nose streamed down across her lips. She could feel the magic seething off of her like a fever; her skin hummed with it under his touch. Something called for her, wanted her.

And then the moment faded, the mists parted, and she was Karen again.

She blinked. "Oh, you liked that?" she said, voice a little hoarse. She winked. "Well then, watch this." Before Ehle could stop her, she whispered a brief incantation in a looping, vowel-heavy dialect.

The Frenchmen's car exploded.

It is hard not to turn and stare when a pillar of fire erupts around your method of transport, even when you suspect it might be a distraction. It is human nature, after all. Emile probably hated himself for falling victim to it, but even the French are human, in the end.

And in that brief moment, Karen grabbed Ehle's shirt and pulled him through the breach. Emile heard it and was spinning back toward them, pistol rising, when Karen cast her final spell.

The extra lines she had drawn in their magical diagram flared up, hissing like burning pitch. In an instant, a new wall, this one made of white fire, filled in the gap created by Ehle's spell.

"That was bigger than I expected," Karen said, her voice now almost gone. She stared at the flames. "Something must have been wrong with my calculations or with . . ."

"Miss O'Neil," Ehle said. "Karen."

The sound of her name brought her back. "Right," she said, shaking her head. She felt as though she could barely stand, let alone run, but she wasn't about to stop now. "We need to go. That won't hold them long."

They were tired, spent, and soon to be pursued. She was a traitor now, perhaps; at least a fugitive. She was scared: of death, of success, of failure; that she had made a terrible situation far worse; that she had made the wrong choice; that she had made the right one. But there wasn't any room left for fear or hesitation or doubt. It was time to act, and to see how the knucklebones fell.

Behind them, the Wall's collapse spread in all directions.

Together, they limped into Auttenberg.

FORTY-EIGHT

He did not sleep well on the best of days, and these were far from the best of days. Moscow was not kind to heavy sleepers, but it was more than caution that kept him awake. Age ached in his bones and regrets stalked his dreams. Some nights he stared for hours into the dark, wondering if this was what death would be like: an endless, restless sleep. So when he saw Leonid's somber face at the foot of his bed, he was not sorry to be interrupted.

"Krauss?" he asked, already reaching for his uniform.

"He is here, sir, waiting for you," Leonid said. "Arrived moments ago."

So the terrible little man had come back in person. What did that foretell?

He had been dreaming, but of what? He could only remember flashes: cracked reflections, the illusion of memories. He saw a great open hole before him, black as death, empty as a newly dug grave. The earth around it sagged inward and called to him, not with words he could hear, but with a voice his body knew. And could not deny. As he tied up his boots, he tried both to remember and to forget but succeeded in neither.

His new pet magician was pacing the floor when he entered. He looked less like an official of the GDR and more a wild itinerant prophet, calling the masses to repent or face the fire.

"Sir," he said, quickly coming over. "There is news. Tremendous news."

"Out with it," he said.

"The Wall," Krauss said. The man's voice was so eager, he sounded almost childlike. "It is collapsing."

"That is hardly news."

"No, no," Krauss said, waving his hands. "More. It is collapsing more. And quickly. And the collapse is centered on Auttenberg."

That name stopped him. He knew what the reports said about the forgotten district. He had read the evidence, the theories, and the fears. "Is something from inside Auttenberg causing—"

"No, of course not," Krauss said. His excitement was great indeed, as he apparently thought nothing of his interruption. "Sir, it is not just the Wall. The rest of the magic that surrounds the district is failing. Someone has undone the spells." He paused, staring at the colonel as if he thought he was a fool. "Do you not see? Someone is entering Auttenberg. From the West."

Pieces were coming into place. The enemy was on the move.

"If the Wall is failing . . ." the colonel said.

"Yes," Krauss said, eyes gleaming. "My men are already at work." The German magician offered a hungry, porcine smile. "The way will soon be clear."

He already could feel the crackle in his veins, the cold burn on his skin. It was the hunter's rush as he watched a carefully stalked prey emerge from the underbrush; it was the validation of patience.

"Show me."

FORTY-NINE

They stopped beyond the park on a quiet avenue lined by empty houses. With the Wall safely behind them and no sign of pursuit, this deserted corner of Berlin felt strangely serene, like they had wandered unwittingly into a painting. The rough scrape of her shoes on the street and the rapid drumbeat of her heart made Karen feel like an interloper, like she was violating some sacred calm.

"The statue you put in my pocket," Ehle said when they had both caught their breath. "That was clever."

"I knew he was going to take you," she said, brushing a strand of hair back from her sweaty brow. "And I needed a way to track you."

Something about Auttenberg unnerved Karen. After Ehle's descriptions, she was ready to be on edge here, but this wasn't just caution; something was wrong in this place, something that tickled her spine like a warning. Karen remembered something her mother would say whenever she got a chill: *like someone was walking over my grave.* Staring into Auttenberg, those words echoed in her head like a stranger's footsteps.

"I remember Agent Fletcher coming into the room, he unlocked the cell, and then . . ." Ehle touched a red welt that had sprouted just above his hairline. "How did you escape?"

Karen heard the jolt of Jim's gun. And then felt the surge of power that had stopped the bullet mere inches from her forehead. "Just lucky, I guess," she said.

Ehle did not look convinced, but he did not press.

Something else bothered Karen as they continued deeper into Auttenberg: she should be feeling worse. She had a headache, sure, and she knew she still had dried blood around her nose and mouth. But between the bullet at BOB, the spell to distract George, deconstructing the barriers beyond the Wall, and stopping the French from following, not to mention blowing up Emile's car, she had used more intense magic in the last few hours than she would normally in a month. She should be spent. She shouldn't be able to walk.

And yet she felt mostly fine. In fact, she felt better with every step. The magic she'd done tonight had been easy. Too easy.

When she expressed this to Ehle, he did not seem surprised. "Magic has behaved oddly around Auttenberg ever since that day. There is a great surge of energy here. It is what we used to fuel the Wall."

"But where does that energy come from?"

He shook his head. "Any answers lie farther in," he said.

As they traveled eastward, the marks of the war on the city became more apparent. They passed shops that had been burned to black bones and stone buildings that had been bombed to rubble. Old newspapers fluttered in the road like wounded birds. The rest of Berlin had done its best to recover from the Allies' onslaught, but ragged Auttenberg had been left to fend for itself.

Karen took a deep breath and realized what felt so strange: there was no smell. In her experience with Berlin, West or East, the air had been heavy laden by cookstoves, tailpipes, and chimneys. It had been hard to breathe at first, though she had gotten used to it since her arrival. Each city block had its own scents, pleasant and otherwise, a pungent patchwork made up of overflowing trash cans, disheveled street vendors, and wet cigarettes. It could water the eyes or the mouth and it made the city feel alive.

There was none of that here. Nothing, not a whiff of smoke or dirt or decay.

They kept forward, pausing at every corner to watch for any sign of movement, ahead or behind. They saw none. It was as if the whole world was empty except for them. It made Karen want to scream, but she feared the sound of her voice echoing hollowly back. The silence was like a physical thing, a dark watcher stalking them through dead city streets, and Karen could not abide it anymore.

"I need to ask you something," she said, only able to manage a whisper.

"Go on," Ehle replied.

"You said at Ravensbrück," she said, sensing him flinch at the word, "that you were trying to discover the secrets to healing magic."

Ehle did not look at her, but eventually said, "Yes, I was."

"I don't want to know what you did," Karen began. "Those secrets are yours. But I need to know if . . ."

"If we succeeded?"

Karen nodded.

Ehle sighed. It was the only sound that stirred for miles and Karen felt the weight of it settle on her shoulders. She wanted to regret asking him, to regret digging up the sorrows of his past, but it meant too much to her to stay silent. Her research excited her, challenged her, motivated her; but it had turned up nothing. Not even a single moment of possible progress. Since man had first begun to wield magic, he'd wanted to use it to live forever. Her goals might not be so lofty, but she still believed in a world where such power could bind up wounds as well as it created them.

"No," Ehle said, breaking the silence and her heart. "We did not. I wish I could tell you otherwise." She did too. She wished he had something to offer in exchange for what he'd done in that place. The scales would never balance, but it seemed worse that one side remained utterly empty regardless.

She felt tears stinging their way to her cheeks. "Do you think we'll ever find it?" she asked, erasing the tears with a thumb.

They stopped at the edge of a brick building. An empty intersection awaited them ahead, still draped in the gloom of the end of night. Karen wondered why dawn was so long in coming to Auttenberg. Briefly, she thought she could smell smoke in the cool air.

"I fear," Ehle said, his voice dropping low, "that magic was never meant for anything other than to destroy."

Karen didn't want to accept that; no, she couldn't accept it. She was ready to say as much to Ehle when he held up a hand.

"I have a final lie to confess," he said. His voice was barely audible, but the words cracked like gunshots in the still air.

Karen wet her lips. "Tell me."

"My wife and daughter," he said. "I told you before that I lost them in the war, so I threw away my locus. Another lie. They survived the war and were even in East Germany. I could have gone to them. We could have been a family again."

"Why didn't you?"

"I wanted to," he said. "I tried. Once I was freed from a Soviet prisoner-of-war camp, I found where they lived. I went to them as quickly as I could, but when I arrived . . ." His voice was shaking now, a dry leaf about to fall. "I saw my wife from some distance off. My daughter, she appeared a moment later. I had not seen them in more than a year. I should have been overjoyed. They were so beautiful; I should have wept in delight. But do you know what I saw when I looked in their faces? The women of Ravensbrück. The women I hurt. The ones I killed. The ones I wiped away."

He was crying now, silent, swift tears. Karen felt an unexpected pang of pity. Ehle was the cause of so much suffering that she had not stopped to wonder how much he had experienced himself.

"In an instant," Ehle said, recovering his voice, "in a moment of clarity, I realized that it would be better for them if I had not survived the war. The best gift I could give them was the chance to start over, to move on, free of my shadow. Better a forgotten father than a monstrous one."

"I am sorry," Karen said, though her feelings could not be so easily described.

"Do not waste any sympathy on me," he said. "I do not deserve it." He coughed, trying to regain his voice. "I left. They never saw me. I hope they never do. Magic," he said, "is no good thing, Karen. It is like gold, something we pretend has value, so that we can kill for it."

It was easy to miss it, masked by his unrelenting ambition to come to this forgotten place and right an old wrong, but she saw it clearly now: Ehle was broken, barely holding water. She wondered how he had remained sane, or even alive, all these years.

"How much of this," Karen asked, waving a hand to take in Auttenberg, the city, their entire quest, "is your attempt at atonement?"

"All of it," he said without hesitation.

She too saw the faces of forgotten women lost in the vain search for impossible magic. Born in another time, in another place, she might have been among those girls who stood before Ehle and wept. "It will never be enough," she said. The words were out before she realized it, but she did not regret them.

"Of course not," Ehle said. "Even if we succeed, there is no atonement for what I have done."

"Then what are you hoping for?"

Before he could answer her, Ehle turned his head sharply and looked down the side street. "Do you hear that?" he said. "Voices."

FIFTY

I t was quiet as the colonel and his men cut through lifeless streets, rifles high and ready. It had been nearly morning when they passed through the Wall, but it remained dark here, dark and still. It reminded him of the war, when he had led such men through the ruins of Europe, always hunting their accursed enemy. The thought set his blood to race in an unexpected mixture of fear and excitement. A part of him had never felt more alive than at the siege of Leningrad or Breslau; how does a man truly return home to a loving wife and adoring children when he has held the mortal blood of brothers and avenged their deaths with his own crooked hands?

"Sir." It was Leonid. His scarred face loomed white in Auttenberg's strange darkness. "Scouts reporting in. Still no sign of movement. The way forward appears clear."

He had not known what to expect. He had read the reports, of course, and knew the stories: no one who entered Auttenberg after the fall of Berlin had returned. Hardened soldiers and powerful magicians alike, all lost forever in this place. Yet so far it appeared to be nothing more than an empty shell, a long-dead limb.

"Give the order," he said, nodding. "Move ahead."

Yet there was something here. Now away from the crackle of the Wall and the chaos of failing magic, it twisted deep in his chest. Glancing over, he saw that Kirill felt it too: a queerness in the air, like a scent that defied identification, alternating between the sublime and the putrid.

What did you do in your darkest hour, Germany? What did you summon?

Krauss waddled along at the rear of the column. The colonel had not wished to bring him, but he could still prove useful. They were marching into the unknown and he would use any advantage he could, even the unpleasant German magician.

He heard it before the others, he and Leonid. The rest were too young to recognize it, being fresh-faced veterans of a war without battles. But for him, it was unmistakable: the echo of German boots on asphalt.

"Hold!" he ordered, too late. The road ahead was suddenly full of gray and black—German soldiers, not East German or West German, but German men of the Reich. Their frantic shouts and the rattle of their guns echoed back a decade, stripping away years of his life just as bullets began to tug at his clothes.

Leonid tackled him and pulled him to cover before returning fire. The others were doing the same, except for a few who were already down, bleeding out silently in the road.

"What is this?" he asked Leonid with a voice that sounded far away.

Leonid reloaded his rifle with casual, automatic movements. "I do not know, sir," he said. "But I know how to kill Nazis."

It lasted only a few minutes. His troops were fresh, well trained, and well armed. Kirill's magic had played a part as well, breaking apart the Germans' paltry defenses with mystic fire. They lost four men, but that had been in those first confused moments. Once the soldiers of the USSR brought their strength to bear, few could withstand it.

The colonel walked among the enemy dead. His boots crunched on broken asphalt and scattered empty shell casings. The soldiers' uniforms were tattered, not by time but by hard conflict. The insignia on their collars had not been worn by anyone since Berlin had fallen. Their weapons too were years out of date, though looked new. The war had never ended, not for these men. He had thought they were entering a lost district, but he saw now they were in a lost time.

"What do we do, sir?" Leonid asked.

He knew he should answer. He had to answer. But what was there to say? This was not magic; this was madness.

"Sir?" Leonid gripped his arm. "Orders?"

"Send out the scouts again," he said, regaining himself. He nudged a nearby body with his foot, rolling the man over. Blood had dripped into the man's now-empty eyes. "And tell them to do their jobs this time. If there are more of the enemy about, we cannot blunder into them at every turn."

Now the air smelled of war: iron and black powder. His skin trembled with drying sweat and fading adrenaline. As he moved away from the enemy bodies he realized that in the exchange, he had not fired a single shot.

How was it still not morning? He reached into his pocket and fumbled with his watch. But when he got it open, he saw that it had stopped. He tapped its face, tried to wind it, to no avail. It lay in his palm like a dead songbird: inert, profane.

What sort of place was this? What sort of magic had they come for?

He had seen his death in those Germans' faces. Only Leonid's quick action saved him. When had he become such a fragile old man? If this truly was the war of his youth summoned back to life like an avenging spirit, would he have the strength now to withstand it? Or was he destined to end up like those young men bleeding in the street—

Gone. They were gone. His own dead remained, but the Germans were gone: bodies, rifles, casings. All gone. It was not possible. Had he imagined them? No, of course not. They had fought. Men had died, just moments before.

"What did you do?" he demanded of Leonid.

"Sir?"

"The Germans," he said. "Why did you order them moved? And when?"

Leonid's brow creased. "Sir, I do not—"

"There," the colonel said, pointing to the empty ground. "Where are they?"

This time, Leonid said nothing.

They turned to the sound of running feet. One of the scouts appeared from the way the Germans had come. He ran straight to them, panting.

"They are coming back," he said between gasps.

"More Germans?" the colonel said.

"No," the scout said. "I mean, yes, sir. But no."

Leonid grabbed the man. "Speak sense, soldier."

"They are coming. A German patrol. The same German patrol. I saw their faces, sir, and their uniforms. It is the same men. The same men!"

No. None of this was as expected. None of this was possible.

Then the scout looked past the colonel and saw that the bodies had vanished; all sanity fled. "Holy God. This is hell. Sir, you have brought us into hell."

The colonel could not refute him.

FIFTY-ONE

Two blocks east, they heard the voices again. Louder this time, though still indistinct, and not just voices: boots, moving in near unison, crunching across broken concrete. Soldiers.

"Soviets?" Karen mouthed to Ehle, who frowned in reply. She hadn't known what they'd find in Auttenberg, though most of her fears were abstract: a shadow looming across the wall, an unspeakable terror lingering in the dark. But the Soviets were very tangible. And very dangerous. Her skin crawled in the cool air. She tried not to think about what they'd done to Jim and to Dennis, and tried not to decide which fate would be worse.

They hugged the buildings and tried to move away from the sound, but it grew inexorably louder. Karen was about to decide if it was time to fight or run when Ehle stopped and nodded across the street. There was a figure there, huddled in the doorway of a slouching apartment structure: a woman, beckoning to them with thin fingers. With a glance back down the street toward the approaching sounds, they quickly crossed over to her. As they neared, she waved more furiously, gesturing into the building behind her, whispering rapidly in hoarse German.

"She says it is not safe out here," Ehle said.

The woman spoke again, and then disappeared inside, leaving the door open for them to follow. The building's interior was dark. It reminded Karen of staring into the tunnel under the Wall, a memory she had no interest in reliving.

"Who is she?" Karen asked. "Who is left in Auttenberg?"

Ehle shook his head. "I cannot say. No one who entered after the war ever returned."

"Because some ghost woman lured them to their doom?"

Ehle was looking down the empty street ahead of them. "We cannot afford to be caught by the Soviets."

"If they're already inside Auttenberg, we can't afford to hide," Karen said. "We need to get to that book."

"Our French friends are behind us," Ehle said. He nodded in the direction of the soldiers. "And they are ahead of us. We cannot go farther until they move on."

"Fine," Karen said. "Let's wait for them to pass inside the creepy haunted death house."

They found the woman down a hall and through a broken door. It was a large room, its original purpose unknowable. Smashed remains of furniture were scattered across the floor or stacked against a wall. The windows were mostly cracked or shattered and boarded over with wooden slats crudely nailed into the frames. An anemic fire struggled in a small fireplace, painting weird shadows along the ground.

The woman who had invited them wasn't alone. There were four of them in all: two women, a young boy, and an old man. The women couldn't be anything but sisters, with the same angular nose and wide-set eyes. The boy, quiet and fair, huddled around their skirts, a handful of the simple fabric gripped tight in a small fist. The old man stood away from the others, staring eastward. Their clothes were dark with dirt and ash, nearly torn to rags.

Ehle greeted them in German and they responded. When Karen gave him a questioning look, he held out a hand for his leather satchel, which Karen wore over her shoulder. She passed it to him, all the while keeping an eye on the shadowed Auttenberg residents. Ehle shuffled through the bag's contents, eventually retrieving a ring of tightly wound copper and silver wire, about the size of his palm. Karen inspected the ring in the faint light: it appeared mundane, but she could feel the enchantment stored within, thrumming like a plucked violin string.

"Hold it to your ear, like this," Ehle said quietly. Karen put it in place and he instructed her on an invocation. She said the words, but nothing happened. She was about to complain when suddenly there was a crackle and then her ear was flooded with noise: a rush of unidentifiable sound, like a thousand voices whispering a hundred languages at the same time.

"It will improve," Ehle said by way of apology. "Give it a moment."

Karen winced against the cacophony, but it did begin to die down. It was soon replaced with a metallic buzz, and then a softer murmur. She blinked hard, her head still spinning. She heard Ehle speaking, but it sounded far away. He was saying something in German, something . . .

". . . for taking us into your home." The words sounded right, but wrong somehow, like through a strange accent.

"We must help one another, in these dark days." The woman was speaking, still in German, but somehow Karen understood.

"We were not certain who we would find remaining here," Ehle said.

"Where would we go?" the woman's sister asked. "How could we leave? This is our home."

The woman said something else directed at Karen, but she could only catch every other word, the sentence lost in a Teutonic muddle. The woman produced a rag from her apron, dipped it in a bucket of dust-covered water, and held it out to Karen.

"For your face," she said, motioning.

Karen took the cloth and tried to smile. She had forgotten the dried blood that still caked her cheeks and mouth. She must look frightful to them. The rag was coarse, but the cool water felt good on her hot skin. They hadn't known what they'd find inside Auttenberg, but Karen certainly hadn't expected hospitality.

"The soldiers outside," Ehle was saying. "Are they Soviets?"

"No, no," the woman said, shaking her head. "Not yet. They are coming, but not yet."

Ehle's frown cast dark lines over his face. "Then who did we hear?"

"Those are the brave sons of the Reich," the woman's sister said, gaunt face beaming. "The Soviets will come, but our sons will keep us safe, even now. They have to."

"Ehle . . ." Karen started to say, but he raised a hand to stop her.

"How soon," he asked, "before the Soviets arrive?"

"The radio broadcasts have stopped, so we cannot know. A matter of days, perhaps," the woman said. "Maybe hours. The shelling, at least, has stopped for now, but we no longer know if that is a good omen or ill."

"Dark days," her sister repeated.

Ehle turned to Karen and she saw her own suspicions written across his brow. "Are they talking about the war?" she asked him in a whisper. "How is that possible?"

"The world moved on," he said, as if in a trance. "But not here. This place has been stuck in that same day ever since. This is the day. The day Voelker used the book."

At the sound of that name, the old man at last turned toward them. His faraway eyes suddenly became lucid and he raised a finger toward Ehle. But before he could speak, one of the women came forward, blocking him. "Come and sit by the fire," she said, gesturing for them to approach. "We have little left, but we will share."

Karen reluctantly moved deeper into the room. As she neared, the little boy looked up at her and rattled off a flurry of words while Ehle's magic struggled to keep up. She smiled at him, but he did not return the expression. Karen thought he looked very sad.

While the women prepared a meal from their meager supplies, they sat by the weak fire on unsteady stools. Karen caught Ehle's eye. She spoke softly so the others didn't hear her speak English. "You didn't tell me this book could stop time."

"It cannot," Ehle said. "Nothing can."

"And yet . . ." Karen motioned to the Germans and their ruined home.

"The book's magic," Ehle said, "or at least the part Voelker understood, manipulated reality. Unmade existence. What it could do was never meant to be." He nodded toward the women. "There were bound to be . . . consequences."

"Like distortions in time."

"Like distortions in perception."

"And you still want to keep going?" Karen asked.

"More than ever," he said.

She couldn't argue. Ehle had never tried to hide the fact that something was wrong in Auttenberg, something worth hiding away. And in fact, she'd actually expected worse. As long as bombs didn't start falling from the sky.

"This," she said, tapping the metal ring, "is remarkable magic."

Ehle flushed at the compliment. "It took me years to create," he said. "And it is far from perfect. In the end, translation from German proved rather simple. *To* German, on the other hand . . ." He shrugged. "I was never able to master its linguistic subtleties."

"You said you made these enchantments as a young man,"

Karen said. "How old were you when you created this? I know magicians back home who'd be satisfied with something like this as their life's work."

"The hypothesis came to me as a student in university," he said, "though I did not finalize the design until . . ." His voice died, as did the brief glimmer of pride in his eyes.

Karen's head began to hurt. "Ravensbrück," she said as she lowered the ring.

Ehle's face had gone sour, but he took her hand and returned it to her ear. "Please. No one was harmed in its making," he said. "It is the product of my idle time, not my work for the Reich."

That distinction didn't really seem to matter, but before she could reply, the women appeared with cups of steaming watery coffee and a tin of crumbled stale bread. Karen took what was offered her, but did not eat.

"What was your service to the Fatherland in this awful conflict?" the woman asked Ehle as they sipped. Karen felt sick as the magic translated the words; she could not look at her companion as he replied.

"I served on the eastern front," he said softly.

"Are you a soldier?" asked the boy.

"Of a sort," Ehle said. Karen's mouth tightened at the too-familiar lie.

"My father is a soldier too," the boy said. "He is out there now fighting our enemies, but he will be home soon."

"Quiet, child," the woman said. There was something in her voice, something nearly lost in the arcane translation, but Karen still heard it: the woman did not share the boy's optimism about the return of his father. Whatever these people were—ghosts, echoes, or souls trapped by Auttenberg's magic—they were German. The end of the war carried no joy for them.

"Just a soldier?" The old man spoke at last. His voice, low and weak, made the ring's magic hiss and spit. "Surely you do yourself a disservice. A man such as you must have done great things for the Fatherland."

Ehle shifted uncomfortably. "We have all done our part, every man, woman, and child."

The old man shuffled a step closer. His wet eyes gleamed in the firelight. "Yes," he said, "we have all served. But not all of us have earned the German Silver Cross for our service."

"Who are you?" Ehle said sharply. "How do you know me?"

The old man laughed. The sound rattled in Karen's head. "We are dear friends, you and I," he said. "Have you forgotten already?"

Ehle stood. "Karen," he said in English, "it is time to go."

But the women were there, somehow behind them now, blocking their way out. When the woman who'd invited them inside spoke, it was not with her own voice, but with another's: masculine, deep, cold.

"Leaving so soon, Erwin?"

Ehle replied, but the words were breaking up, the letters of English and German smashing together like a car wreck. Karen tightened her grip on the translation ring, but could feel its imbued magic failing.

"Why are . . . here?" the old man asked. ". . . nothing . . . Auttenberg now, except death." Then the magic was gone, the ring silent.

Karen looked to Ehle. He met her eyes, then glanced at the door they'd come in, and then to another on the far side of the room.

"What is going on here?" Karen said, standing at Ehle's shoulder, but he said nothing. "How do these people know you?"

The sister pushed the other woman aside, laughing, and barked out a challenge in that same strange voice. Her careworn face folded into a creased sneer as someone else's words poured out of her.

"What is this?" Karen said, voice shaking with the first hints of panic.

"It is him," Ehle said. "Voelker."

"What are they—what is he saying?"

"He welcomes us to Auttenberg," Ehle said. "He is pleased I have come to his domain so that I might see him wipe Germany's enemies from the earth."

Now it was the boy speaking with a voice far too old. The women came behind. They were all speaking now, the same jeering, boasting words coming out of three strange mouths. "How is he doing this? How is he speaking through them?"

"I can feel it now," Ehle said. "Can you not? Such power . . ."

Karen did feel something, but she could not name it. The quiet of Auttenberg was gone; maybe it had never been. Now there was a murmur, a growing rumble like the ocean made mad by the wind, permeating everything. And the unmistakable, undeniable sense that there were eyes everywhere: in every shadowed alleyway, behind every empty window, in the night sky that still refused to give way to the sun.

Then the old man elbowed his way to the front. The others fell silent as he pointed again at Ehle. When he spoke, it was that same unnatural voice, and yet not the same. It was weaker, strained, aged. It was the voice of the same man—Martin Voelker—but with none of the pride, none of the haughtiness. He sounded broken, weary, and desperate.

"What did he say?" Karen asked, cursing herself for not picking up more of the language.

"He . . . he is asking me," Ehle answered softly, "to help him."

"Help him do what?"

"To help him stop himself."

Before Karen could consider what that could possibly mean,

the old man crumpled to the floor, his bone-thin legs suddenly turned to water. Facedown in the dust, he looked more like a jumble of dirty clothes than a fallen man. One of the women stood over him, a bloodied brick clutched in a delicate hand.

The little boy ran over to him and began to kick him. This was not a child at play; the blows fell hard, splintering ribs with each terrible, snapping strike.

Karen, aghast, reached out and grabbed the boy's arm. "Stop! How could you?"

The boy turned slowly to her. Unblinking eyes stared hungrily at her; not the eyes of a child, or even of a human, but dark, seething pools from which no light escaped. The boy was smiling, the slit of his mouth too large for his face, revealing a mouth sharp with fangs. Karen shoved him back as hard as she could and he fell, tripping over the fallen old man. But then the women started toward her. The closest one dropped the brick as she reached out for Karen's throat with clawed fingers.

With a shouted word of magic, Karen sent a wave of force out and into the woman's chest. It should have only been enough to stun her, but instead it picked her up like a discarded toy and sent her body careening across the room. She smacked against the far wall and tumbled down to the ground like a bundle of broken sticks.

The magic had come so easily. It lit up her veins, loosened her joints. She hadn't meant to use so much power, but it had been ready for her call, eager. She felt her lips tugging into a grin.

Then the second woman was suddenly in front of her, less a woman now and more a bony knot of talons and teeth. The little boy was just behind her, his skin now lifeless gray and his eyes wide with black malice. Karen summoned a kinetic shield just as the woman lunged for her; the magic seized up but held back the assault, if only for an instant: long enough. They ran for the far door, slamming it behind them as they passed through into an empty hallway.

"Hold it shut!" Karen said to Ehle as she scrambled for her chalk. Claws raked the other side of the door, but Ehle's shoulder held it in place as she quickly traced symbols around the frame.

"I do not—"

"There," Karen said, stepping away. Her magic began expanding quickly, creeping over the door like ethereal vines, sealing it. Ehle moved back. A moment later, the monstrous things inside the room crashed into the door with terrifying force, but the barricade held.

"See?" Karen said. The magic tingled in her head like too much rum. "You Germans aren't the only ones who know how to make a good wall." Inhuman voices raged behind the door, but Karen was smiling. Her skin tingled with energy. They'd almost just died, but she had never felt more alive.

Ehle did not share her amusement. He pointed down the hallway behind them. Something was moving in the dark. Coming toward them.

"Run," Ehle said. "Run!"

FIFTY-TWO

He followed. He did not know why, but he followed.

The earth beneath his feet felt solid, but nothing else did. He didn't know why he was here, what he was trying to do, or for whom. He wasn't even sure of his own name anymore. His head hurt, but maybe that was another illusion, another trick. He was limping but couldn't remember why. Something in his head told him he'd been attacked by a frog (a frog with a gun . . . no, a flying tool chest!), but that thought only left him more convinced than ever that he'd lost his mind.

But it didn't matter if he was crazy. Because he had seen her.

He had stumbled out into the night just as a car pulled away out front. Something in that car mattered (or was it someone?), but he didn't remember what. He watched it go, head thumping, trying to remember the right emotion: should he be angry? Sad? Lost?

And then she had appeared.

She pulled up in a car. She hadn't gotten out, but he had seen her plain enough. Karen. That name he remembered. That name, and that face. He saw it in a photograph paper-clipped to her file while he (no, they; someone else was with him) waited for her airplane to land. He saw her face smeared with dirt and smiling when they snuck into East Berlin. And he saw it waiting at the end of his gun.

He'd killed her.

But she was still alive.

When she drove off, he hadn't stopped to think; he just ran. He wasn't so nuts that he thought he could keep up with an automobile, but that didn't really matter. He just had to follow. He was sinking under the waves and she was a rope dangling in the water.

He almost caught up with her when she got hit by another car, but she had run off before he could reach her. He hoped she wasn't hurt, but if a bullet to the head hadn't done the trick, what could a little car wreck do to her?

She was going north, which felt wrong (though not as wrong as west). He needed to go east, but couldn't do it alone. Memories, orders, desires, and commands piled up in his head, filling his thoughts with twisted metal and broken glass. There was no sense to be made of it, no order left in the chaos.

So he followed.

He found her as she and another man prepared something on the ground in front of the Wall. He had enough sense left to wait and watch rather than face the frogs again. He huddled in the shadows until the night erupted in light and she vanished into the broken Wall. She was going east. He followed, through a park, through the broken Wall, and into the silent streets beyond.

He tried to think what he would say to her when he finally reached her.

Karen, who am I?

Karen, why aren't you dead?

Karen, does this mean I can come home?

Her name was an anchor, a thin thread holding his sanity in check. He had to find her. He had to speak to her. If she knew him, if she could see him, then maybe she was still alive, and if she was still alive, maybe this had all been a terrible dream, and maybe he could still wake.

The city beyond the Wall was empty. The sky was dark (too dark for this hour) and the streets abandoned. Where was this? He expected to see Soviet soldiers on patrol, or refugees waiting for a chance to escape through the failing Wall, or at least signs of life. But this felt less like East Berlin and more like a graveyard, the gray buildings looming like tombstones, the grimed street signs like forgotten epitaphs.

And Karen was nowhere to be found.

Had she been the dream? The vain hope of a doomed fool?

Did it matter?

He went east on numb legs. There were tears on his cheeks.

"Are you lost?" The words crashed violently into his thoughts, stopping him midstep. The echoing solitude of this strange place had enveloped him so fully that another voice almost finished his rapid fall into madness.

"Sir?" the voice asked again, coming from behind and to the left. "Did you get the summons too?"

Somehow he turned toward the sound. There was a girl (maybe twelve or thirteen) standing there, in the doorway of a grim-looking house. Her face was white, her hair brown, tied up under a blue shawl. She looked hungry, he thought, and then he realized she was speaking German. This surprised him, but why? Wasn't this still Berlin? Wasn't it?

"I am looking," he said in halting German, "for a woman."

The girl didn't seem to notice he had never quite mastered the hard-edged language. "I see. She probably got the same summons," she said, holding up a scrap of paper. "She is probably at the church."

"Church?" He wasn't sure he'd heard her correctly.

"The soldiers came. They want us all to come to the church," the girl said. She came closer. "The Reichsleiter has a plan. He is going to save us."

He didn't understand some of her words; she was talking too fast. His mind was stumbling over itself trying to form words in English, so responding in German seemed impossible. But he did not have to respond, as she reached out and took his hand.

"You look afraid," she said.

"I am," he replied. "I am afraid I have done something that cannot be made right."

"My mother told me not to be afraid, that everything will work out."

His chest ached; his memories burned. "I hope she was right," he said.

"Will you take me? My parents . . . they are gone," she said. He saw now that her resolve was a facade, a faltering one. Beneath the cracks, he saw sorrow. "We have to go. Everyone will be at the church. The woman you are looking for," she said, carving a rough smile onto her face with no small effort, "I am sure she will be there."

What is this forsaken place, emptied of everything but an orphan? Where have you led me, Karen? Are you here waiting for me on one of these quiet streets? Am I chasing a shadow?

He squeezed the girl's hand. It was light to the touch, almost airy. "Lead the way," he said, and thought her smile looked a little more real.

FIFTY-THREE

Karen and Ehle burst out of the building through a back door and ran for an alleyway, death close at their heels. As they scrambled into the narrow passage, Karen stumbled over the words to a spell, then corrected herself just in time. Her magic shot out at the building at the head of the alley and it exploded, burying the nearest creatures in a shower of rock and mortar. More came, and she sent broken shards of brick through the air, cutting them down.

Something with clacking fangs dropped just in front of her, but the words came easily now, the combat spells she'd learned dutifully but never expected to use outside of a fencing bout: fire and force and power. The creature yowled as Karen's magic pummeled it. Karen raised her voice louder, summoning even more of the latent magic running through Auttenberg, one hand outstretched, the other clasped white-knuckled around her locus.

There was a sudden tug at her arm. The magic stopped, dammed up by the distraction, and she gasped at its absence. It was like someone had punched her in the gut. She turned toward the new threat, but it was Ehle.

"Karen, come," he said. "You destroyed it. But we must go."

He was right; the thing was nothing more than a stain on the cobblestones. She nodded, relaxing her grip on the leather pouch. "Let's go," she said, breaking into a run.

She did not bother to glance back for fear of what she'd see. Ehle reached the alley's end and rushed out into the road, but just as Karen was about to follow she felt something grab her. Claws knifed into her shoulder and pulled her off her feet and down to the unforgiving ground.

She twisted and scrambled up. It was the boy, his shape almost unrecognizable. His jaw had unhooked, his mouth opening impossibly wide to show row after row of yellowed teeth. Sinews strained against his skin like trapped snakes. Talons, red with her blood, clicked sharply on the asphalt.

Words came quickly to her lips, but the boy came quicker. She dove under his mad lunge, rolling away as he crashed into the building with a shuddering thud. He was on her in an instant. She fell back, pushing his claws and fangs away. He snapped at her, but at last she got her feet up into his stomach and heaved. The boy grunted as he lost his grip and went airborne.

He was on his feet and coming for another assault in an instant. Behind him, more nightmarish things skittered down the alley, howling for blood.

The creature that had once been a little boy threw himself at her, mouth open wide enough to swallow her whole.

And then he evaporated in a torrent of fire that erupted from Karen's outstretched hand.

The horrible black shapes behind him were soon consumed as well, leaving nothing behind but ash on charred brick. The fire did not stop; it tore through the alley and spouted out the far end like an incinerating tidal wave. It scorched the street, the buildings, the air.

All her life Karen had dreamed of power like this. When the

examiners first came to her school and tested all the students for magical aptitude, she'd been afraid. Magic wasn't natural. Magic was dangerous. What if she passed their tests and they came and took her away from her family and her friends?

But then she had passed. The examiners had been kind and complimentary. She was selected, not to be stolen from her bedroom in the middle of the night, but to take extra classes, to read interesting books, to prepare for college and beyond. Magic wasn't something to fear; it was who she was, and it was who she was going to become.

Even from the start, the rules had seemed so arbitrary. When her instructors described the purpose of a locus, she assumed it was a training aid, not a requirement for even the most skilled magicians. When they were taught to memorize spells that had been written in the 1400s, she had asked when they would learn to write their own.

Magic was supposed to be freedom, but all she was taught was conformity.

But now that freedom filled every cell in her body with a fire hotter than the one that had burned away their pursuers. This was how magic was always supposed to feel: untamed and wild. Feral. Man had tried to domesticate it, but now it was showing its teeth. With this fire, she could cleanse all of Auttenberg, all of Berlin. What could stop her now? Who would dare? She was grinning like a fool, laughing like a drunk fool, before she realized that she had just killed dozens of people.

The fire stopped.

Its absence threatened to drown her. Her head buzzed; her ears roared with silence. The power was gone and without it, she felt hollow, like a brittle china doll.

What was this place? What had it done to those women, that boy? And what was it doing to her? A small taste of some untapped strength and suddenly she goes mad? That wasn't her. She suddenly felt very cold.

Ehle was gone. He probably was still running, probably thought she was right behind him. She looked around; there were probably more of those things lurking. Worse, the man behind that terrible voice was out there. Voelker, Ehle had called him. The chief Nazi magician. The one with the book.

She was on her knees. *Get up. Move.* Her body didn't obey. Her limbs felt like concrete.

Somehow she found her way to her feet. Her legs trembled; her muscles ached. She felt like she was going to throw up. But there was no road back, only forward. She might be hurt, tired, and afraid, but she had to see this through. *If I can stand, then I can walk.* She shuffled her feet and took a step. And another.

Whatever this place was, it wasn't going to stop her. Not when there was work to do. The world wasn't going to save itself.

She did not know which way to go or what she was looking for, but she knew she had to keep moving. So she went east, watching for anything moving in the dim twilight. She saw nothing and no one, until she turned a corner and walked right into an oncoming patrol of Soviet soldiers.

FIFTY-FOUR

Ehle did not know how long he had been running before he realized Karen was not with him. It was only the sound of his own feet he heard echoing, mocking. His hands hardened into fists. Another failure paid for by someone else's sacrifice. He reached in vain for his lost locus, hoping to draw on its refining power to tear this whole city down and salt the damn earth.

But it was gone, of course. He had no magic with which to sate his fury, just memories and regrets.

I am sorry, he thought. *I am sorry.*

If only anyone was left to hear it.

He looked up at the old night sky. Somehow it was still the same day Voelker used the forbidden book. It was an impossible thought, but a helpful one. That meant he knew where Voelker was: the headquarters for the Reich Office of Magic. In a perfect expression of Nazi hubris, Voelker had converted a seventeenth-century Lutheran church to house the Reich's magicians. Ehle had been there more than once, even then marveling at the Reichsleiter's gall. They had been the princes of the world then, fated to rule it by divine fiat. Victory had been more than a certainty; it was theology.

But then the world had thrown down their would-be Aryan gods, smashed their idols, and laid waste to their temples. Except for Auttenberg.

The memory of Voelker's words spoken through the old man left an icy touch on his skin: *Please, Erwin. Please. It is becoming too much for me. I can only hold it back for so long. Help me.* That too had been Voelker, somehow; some splinter of that great, doomed man awash with panic and regret.

Whispers and madness, that was all Auttenberg held now.

But those were not the most chilling words he had heard from his former leader. No, those had come from the strong, assertive voice that rang with an arrogance unchecked by the last ten years of defeat.

Thank you, the alien voice had said. *This could never have been possible without you. It is right that you see how it ends.*

Yes, it was right that he be here. And it needed to end.

The church was not far. It would not be long now.

FIFTY-FIVE

The strange, stale Auttenberg air suddenly shimmered with spent magic. The colonel felt it hot in his lungs, like the acrid smoke from a cheap cigar. It came from the next block of houses, where he had sent Kirill to lead a scouting party. He locked eyes with Leonid and together they ran toward the sounds of shouting.

Kirill was down, dazed and leaning against a building. His assailant was on her feet, surrounded by soldiers. She started to speak, but the colonel's men were not inexperienced with magicians; the butt of a rifle to her stomach stopped her spellcasting cold. The magic slipped away.

Though he did not recognize her face, the colonel knew who she was at once. She was clearly not one of the unfortunates stuck inside Auttenberg when the world had sealed it away, nor did she have the look of a refugee who had wandered into the district when the Wall began to fall. No, she had the imperious bearing of an American and the coiled energy of a magician; there could be no doubt who this was.

"Your friend over there might be good," she said at him in English, nodding at the defeated Kirill, "but his magic is slow and predictable. Are you any better?"

"Much, Miss O'Neil," he said softly. Her struggling stopped immediately. No reply was forthcoming. The colonel took no little pleasure in the unchecked shock on her face at being so easily identified. At last, something good from this accursed place.

But her silence did not linger. "You," she said. "It was you." She no longer looked shocked; she was angry. "The Nightingale, right? That's what they call you. What did you do to him? What twisted magic did you work in Jim's head?"

"Jim? Ah, yes. The boy caught wandering where he did not belong," he said. "I must admit, I am surprised he did not kill you."

"He tried." Her anger was sharpening into something more dangerous: defiance. "That magic you used against him is a war crime, you know."

"A war crime," he said, listening to the sound of this curious English phrase as he repeated it. "Are we at war?"

"If we aren't, then let me go."

The colonel frowned despite himself. This woman would be a problem, if he allowed it. He could not. "Leonid," he said in Russian, "disarm her." She barely had time to react before Leonid's thick hands pulled the small leather pouch from around her neck and handed it to him. There was the shock again. Good.

He opened the contents of the pouch into his palm. A children's toy. "You think you are safe here," he said, shaking his head. "You Americans think you own the world. You think you can stick your finger into the fire and not be burned." He upended his hand. The silver stars scattered on the ground. He brought his boot down on them.

She flinched as if struck, sudden pain written across her defiant face. A magician's locus was a sacred thing. If she had been polite, he might have merely taken it away from her.

"Your foolish CIA friend learned he does not own the world. I taught this to him." The colonel scraped what was left of the girl's locus into a gutter drain and tossed the pouch in after. "I see I must teach you the same."

She was staring down after her ruined locus, saying nothing. No more anger, no more strength. Emotions always betray, in the end. He had broken many men in his lifetime, more than he bothered to count, and the key to breaking each of them was through their emotions. Make them fear, or make them weep, or make them angry; it did not matter. Once they began to feel, they would break. Every time.

And women were nothing but emotions. No control, no will. This was why they made terrible magicians, why they made terrible soldiers. They were simply too easy to break.

"You came here with Erwin Ehle, did you not?" he asked. She said nothing. There was no time for this. He slapped her. "Ehle? He helped you take down the Wall and enter Auttenberg. Where is he? What is his plan?"

Her eyes slid up and met his. He could not read the thoughts behind them. He considered using his magic to pry into her mind. He even put his hand to his pocket watch, but then remembered the watch had stopped. Something about Auttenberg. Could he still work his magic without the tick of his watch? Certainly the power was in him, not in this brass bauble. But he knew he did not believe that.

He wanted to be free of this place.

The girl would wait. She was of no consequence. Ehle was of no consequence. Only the book mattered.

"Ehle isn't the one you should be worried about." Her voice

surprised him as he was turning away. There was a smile on her face now, and a coldness.

When he hit her this time, it was no slap. Yet still she smiled. *Very well*, he thought. *You leave me no choice.* When he struck her for the third time, bone cracking on bone, she crumpled to the street and did not stir.

"What do you want to do with her, sir?" Leonid asked.

He massaged his hand. He had not meant to get so upset, or to hit her so hard; he was no brute. Yet she had left him little choice. They were too close now to have everything undone by a woman who did not know her place.

"Bind her," he said, shaking out his hand. "We will take her back to East Berlin when we leave."

As Leonid did as he was ordered, he saw scouts returning from their reconnaissance to the north.

"Sir," one of the men said as he saluted. "We found people, sir."

"More soldiers?"

"No," the scout said, "civilians. German."

"And?"

"They are all on the move, sir," the scout said. "They have been ordered to gather at a church about a mile from here. We reached the site. It is heavily guarded."

The Reich Office of Magic. More ghosts of the past. The Reich, like any infection, was proving harder to eradicate than first believed. Whatever hell they had wandered into, old enemies were waiting for them. The colonel did not want them to have to wait long.

"Leonid, assemble the men," he ordered. "The church is our objective. Kirill, take four soldiers in reserve and wait for us here."

The young magician scowled. "Sir, will you not need my help?"

Kirill was angry. Expected in a young man who had suffered a defeat, however minor, at the hands of a woman. But unacceptable in a magician. Anger caused mistakes, and they had made enough of those already.

"What I need is to keep our path of retreat clear," the colonel replied. His eyes fell on the American. It was a risk, keeping her alive. Much easier to put a bullet in the back of her head. But he understood the power of appropriate leverage, even on a country as confident as the United States. He had been forced to return his last prisoner, but he felt that this might have proven an opportune trade. "And I need someone to watch over our guest. I would not want her to come to harm, and more importantly, I would not want her to affect our plans."

Kirill was not pleased. For a moment, the colonel recalled the fury he had seen in Kirill's eyes when he had recruited him from that labor camp. The boy's talent had been evident from the start, but so also was his rage. Even then he had wondered if the boy could be tamed, or if he would one day turn his teeth on his master. But no, once again, Kirill bowed and went about his duty. Good.

"Come," he said to his remaining men, "I know where we will find our prize."

FIFTY-SIX

I t loomed up out of the never-ending dark like a phantom, like a regret. From the outside, it looked as it had for hundreds of years. The Nazis had done little to the facade when they appropriated the building, its terrified priests all too willing to offer it as a gift to their Aryan overlords. After all this time, it still looked like a place of worship. And it still was, Ehle knew, though one that offered a vastly altered liturgy.

All of Auttenberg was being herded into the building by the black-clad soldiers under Voelker's command. The people looked tired and afraid and hungry; they looked like the forgotten casualties of war. Thankfully so far none had sprouted fangs or taunted him in the Reichsleiter's voice.

It had been many years since Ehle had last visited a church. The idea of God had fascinated him as a boy, bored him as a young man, and terrified him now. He was not afraid of being judged for his sins, but of an all-powerful being who would allow him to commit them. A God who would create a world that could give rise to Nazi Germany was a terrible creature indeed.

"Hey, you." A German soldier with a gaunt face and a leveled rifle was approaching. "Inside with everybody else. Move."

Ehle had heard stories from men returning from the doomed eastern front. They spoke of utter cold, bone-snapping cold. Even when the sun was high overhead, your body never warmed, they said. You slowly became increasingly numb until you closed your eyes and drifted into the fog. Your comrades would find you, dead fingers still clutching your icy gun, head bowed as if in prayer. The only peaceful death for a soldier, they said.

He felt that numbness now. Eternity seeping into his veins.

You came here for this. You pursued it. Like a fool, you even prayed for it. Now go. See that it is done.

"You hear me?" the soldier said, jabbing Ehle in the chest with the barrel of his rifle. "Get inside."

"No," Ehle replied.

The soldier blinked. Then narrowed his killer's eyes. "What did you say?"

"I do not take orders, Sergeant," Ehle said. "I give them. Consider yourself blessed we are in a time of war, or I would have you whipped for insubordination."

The gun lowered an inch. The soldier looked him over. "Who are you?"

"My name, Sergeant," he said, brushing dust from his lapel, "is SS-Standartenführer Erwin Ehle. You may address me as 'sir' or not at all. Is that understood?"

"Sir, of course, sir," the soldier said. "I did not recognize you out of uniform, sir."

"Understood, Sergeant," Ehle said. The church waited for him up ahead, but still he hesitated. "What is the situation inside?"

"Reichsleiter Voelker has ordered the remaining populace into the main hall, sir," the soldier said. "We have been sent to round them up."

"Why?" Ehle asked. "What does he need them for?"

"I do not know, sir."

Blood. Life. Death. Powerful magical catalysts, Ehle knew. Too well. "Escort me inside, Sergeant. Your master is expecting me."

The church was dimly lit, except for the raised pulpit, which was bathed in golden light. Even as the Reich Office of Magic took over the building, Voelker had demanded the sanctuary remain untouched. He often liked to address his subordinates like a priest, sharing the word of God from on high. Now the pews were mostly full, but Ehle knew the huddled congregants were no more real than the spotless church or the soldiers standing guard or the monsters who had attacked him and Karen.

"You came." The voice echoed in the murmuring room, but sounded only in Ehle's mind. "I so hoped that you would. I have been waiting a long, long time."

"What is this, Martin?" Ehle asked. The soldier had led him to the front of the church, but there was no sign of Voelker. "Why are these people gathered here?"

"Power like this . . ." the voice said, ". . . demands a sacrifice."

"What have you done here?"

"It is not what we thought," the voice said again. "We were fools. Not in my most fevered dreams did I guess at its true nature."

"I saw its true nature," Ehle said. He felt exposed, naked. "That is why I am here."

Suddenly the Reichsleiter stood before him, glorious in his officer's regalia, not a thread out of place: medals gleaming in red and gold, creased pants tucked into spotless boots, pistol strapped to his hip. He had not aged a day since the war: still young, vital, full of pride. Ehle had admired this man once, idolized him even. But now the sight of him as he had been, the great German magician, dressed in Nazi black and silver, made him ill.

"This is the only way it could have ended," Voelker said. "Do you not see?" There was something odd about his voice now, as though two men were speaking; not two, but the same man, speaking across a decade, across a lifetime. "Magic was never the salvation of mankind. It was always our undoing."

"Martin," Ehle said, "it is not too late to stop this. Where is the book?"

"The book," Voelker said. "The book is nothing. It is a symptom."

"It is corrupt magic," Ehle said. The room was filling with the last of Auttenberg. Outside, through the smear of stained glass, he could see the first light of dawn. "We can destroy it. You and I."

Voelker shook his head. "You do not understand. This book is not corrupted. It is purified. This is the essence, do you not see? Magic is not the gift of fire stolen from Olympus. Magic is a loaded pistol placed in a playground. We are schoolboys toying with danger we cannot understand."

"I came here," Ehle said, "to help you. You asked me, do you not remember? You asked me to help you stop all this. Martin, please, I know there is a part of you that wants to put an end to this. Let me help."

Voelker blinked, looked away. In profile, he seemed older. There were deep lines fanning out from tired eyes, a sunken quality to his sharp cheeks, a thinning grayness in his blond hair.

"I wanted to stop them," he said after a pause. His voice wavered. "They were closing in on Berlin. The army was in shambles, the Reich in ruins. The Führer, that coward . . . I had to do something, Erwin." He turned back quickly and locked his gaze on Ehle. "But this magic cannot be bound," he said. "It has its own will, its own purpose."

"What did you do, Martin?"

"I . . ." Suddenly he could not speak. His eyes were fixed behind Ehle, on the congregation. Ehle turned to where he was looking. The ghostly soldiers suddenly raised their rifles. The machine guns flickered in the church like candlelight. The people of Auttenberg, betrayed in their final hour by the man they hoped would save them, cried out as if in prayer as the bullets cut them down, and then the room fell silent. Voelker's magic moved among the dead like a scavenger, drawing unspeakable power from the offering of blood.

Hovering above them all was a breach in the world.

"I thought I had pieced together some great spell," Voelker was saying. "I thought I had mastered the secrets of the book. But they had mastered me."

The breach twisted and thrashed like a living thing. Beyond it lay a darkness so complete that Ehle felt ill after just a glance.

"Do you feel it?" Voelker said. "Magic . . . not as we know it, but as it truly is. It comes from there," he said, pointing into the void. "The source of all magic."

Man had always wondered from where magic's power came. Theories and speculation abounded, but no one had guessed at something as terrifying as this.

"It is a trap, Erwin," Voelker said. "Set by God, or something worse. Life is an aberration. Creation is a flaw. Magic is the corrective. Magic is supposed to wipe the slate. That is why the book always comes back, even when destroyed. Because its work is not done. Because we are still here."

Ehle could not look at the breach any longer. He focused instead on the wan face of the Reichsleiter. "That was ten years ago, Martin," he said.

Voelker nodded, though he seemed to barely be listening. Instead he was staring into the face of it, the dead unlight reflecting on his creased skin. "When I saw what I had done, I knew I had to stop it. The power coming through it is unfiltered magic. I have never felt anything like it. With that power I have been holding the breach in place, all this time. The world has been bending under the strain, repeating itself, an endless cycle of my gravest error."

"Where is the book, Martin?" Ehle tried to keep the urgency from his voice, but knew he was failing. Now that the breach was visible he felt its insidious touch, heard its dark whisper. This was what was poisoning Auttenberg.

"I . . ." Voelker said, confused. "Yes, yes. If we can destroy the book, perhaps that can buy us some time."

Voelker was growing weaker, but also stronger; the young, damned part of him reasserting control. They had to act, before it was too late.

"Where is it? Tell me, Martin."

"It . . . the pulpit," he said, eyes brightening. "Hurry, take it and—"

As Ehle took a step toward the pulpit, his body convulsed in sudden, familiar pain. He tried to fight against it, to somehow ignore the feeling of dull blades tearing into every muscle. But it was too much. He fell to his knees, hooked fingers reaching in vain toward the book.

Dr. Haupt walked up the center aisle, his hands wrapped tight around his cane as he channeled the agonizing magic. Ehle stared at him through bloodshot eyes. A fool to the last. Max could not see: the breach seethed as his magic ripped through Ehle. And grew.

"George," Haupt said to his assistant. "Recover the book, please."

FIFTY-SEVEN

She hadn't been knocked out, but she had enough sense to stay down. *So that's what getting punched feels like.* Her skull rang like a cheap brass bell. Not so bad, really. Her eyes were cloudy with tears and her mouth tasted like blood, but otherwise she didn't see what all the fuss was about.

What hurt far worse had been watching her locus disappear under the Nightingale's boot.

She and Helen had exhausted many summer sidewalk hours with those jacks. Bounce, grab. Bounce, grab. It had never really mattered much who won or lost; most of the fun had been in making up new rules on the spot. Once they had left them out on the floor in the living room and their father had stepped on one in stocking feet. Karen had never heard him swear like that before or since. She thought of him, a world away. Would he come to her rescue, if he knew? Would he fight for her?

Even if he would, it wouldn't matter. This was a mess beyond Roger O'Neil.

A tremor ran over her skin. Panic threatened to crawl up her throat and scream. She was alone and in serious danger. She might not make it home.

No. She set her teeth and forced the fear down. *We didn't come this far to lose it now.*

Most of the Soviets were leaving, heading off to the north. Only a few remained. Her bodyguards. They were young men, younger than her maybe, and they looked afraid. She wondered if Auttenberg had shown its true face to them as well. No, she thought not. They would not be so calm.

One of them, the leader she guessed, worried her. He had tried to use some attacking spell on her when she stumbled onto their patrol, but it was clear he had little actual experience fighting other magicians. Even surprised as she was, Karen had broken his concentration with a quick burst of light, then knocked him back against the bricks with another unexpected surge of magic. So it was not his magical prowess that frightened her, rather the ice burning in his ever-moving eyes, and the way he wore his stoic expression like a rubber mask. Whatever was waiting behind that mask, she did not care to know.

They had tied her hands and gagged her, effective means to cripple a magician. She pulled against the rope, but that did nothing other than alert her captors that she was awake. Most of them glanced at her and then went back to watching the shadows. All except the one with the cold-fire eyes. He approached.

"You are mine now," he said with a dark smile and a heavy accent. "You understand? Mine."

She did not reply, though it was not the gag that stole her voice; it was the sudden realization that she was about to die.

Fight it. The panic was back. *Not now.*

His eyes glinted at her. Anger filled them. Humiliation. In besting him, she'd wounded something worse than his body: his stupid, masculine pride. He waved his hands, taking in the nearby buildings. "This is strange place, no? Easy to be lost in such place.

You have friends here? Hm? Somewhere? Easy to disappear. They look for you, but not find you."

It hadn't been many hours since she had stared down the barrel of Jim's pistol. She had been afraid then, of course, but there hadn't been much time for it. Now she felt the fear burrowing into her heart. The Soviet magician was right; they'd never find her body in a place like this. *Missing in Action,* the report would read. They'd probably send people out to her parents' house, maybe Helen's too. There's always hope, someone might say, though they wouldn't believe it.

"He says to wait," the magician was saying. "I do not like to wait. I am tired of waiting. Been waiting all my life." He reached into his pocket and pulled out a large silver coin. He was smiling again. "While we wait," he said, "I show you real magic, yes?"

The bullet. Remember the bullet. Only a few inches from her head but she'd stopped it, not with some spell she learned in school, but her own magic.

But she'd had her locus then. Something to channel her will.

He flipped the coin high in the air. It turned and turned, and then he caught it. "Special magic," he said. "I make coin disappear."

Up the coin went. Turn, turn, turn. Then fall.

You don't need your locus, like you don't need the words of some old spell. Remember what you did to those monsters, remember that fire.

That fire that had almost consumed her.

Focus on it.

Up. Turn, turn.

She wasn't going to die like this. And she didn't need someone to save her.

Focus.

She thought about George's ring, back in the OMRD. The surprise on his face.

Up. And down.

Time to make up new rules.

When the Soviet opened his palm the last time, instead of a coin he caught a handful of molten metal. He screamed in sudden, bright agony. He grabbed his wrist and held his smoking hand out ahead of him like a beacon. The mask had been banished from his face, replaced by very real anguish.

Oh, God, what had she done? And it had been so easy . . .

The other soldiers were getting to their feet. *No, no. Think, Karen.* They blocked the only way out. Could she break through the wall? The magician was writhing around his ruined hand.

He was still screaming, screaming. Rifles were moving toward her.

Her bonds fell away.

Magic arced across her fingertips.

She heard gunshots. Saw muzzles flash. The bullets came closer, spinning slowly, twirling like dancers. And she reached out with her magic and then they were gone.

It was inside her now. Years of powerlessness, of holding herself back; years of derision, of contempt, all washed away. Now she understood. This was what magic truly felt like. This was her true potential.

The rifles were next. She wrapped her will around the metal stocks like a vine, and tightened. They resisted, then buckled, then collapsed.

Then she reached for the riflemen.

A moment later they were alone, she and the magician with the smoldering hand. He looked up at her. He was afraid. He should be.

She silenced the man's screams. Enough of that.

Why had she been so afraid of this power? Why hadn't she let it consume her before?

Her eyes, crackling with white light, turned. What was that? She could feel something calling to her. Yes, of course; she knew it now. It was the source. The wellspring. A passage to another world, the only world. That was why Auttenberg mattered, not some silly book. The truth. The essence.

Power. Waiting for her.

The ground splintered like failing ice beneath her feet as she started north.

FIFTY-EIGHT

"Max." Voelker's voice was growing stronger. Younger.

Haupt lessened the spell on Ehle, but did not release it. "Whatever you are," he said to Voelker, "you are not the man I knew. He is long dead. You are an illusion."

The Reichsleiter laughed at that. The sound of it boomed in the church like artillery. "You were always a man of certainties, Max. But you do not see. This is all illusion," Voelker said. "Life is nothing but a mirage. A mistake of the eyes."

"George, the book," Haupt said. His assistant hesitated, unwilling to approach.

"Max," Ehle managed to say through the pain, "look . . . up."

"Erwin, I did not want it to come to this, but you have left me no—"

"Look!" Ehle shouted, the force of the word wracking his chest with fire.

Haupt stopped. And looked. Seeing the breach looming above him for the first time. Seeing his magic feeding it. Seeing the blackness beyond. He lowered his cane, the spell broken. Ehle collapsed, his breaths coming in sweet, terrible gasps.

"What . . ." Haupt's face was pale. "What is that?"

"It is the end," Voelker said approvingly.

"Get the book," Haupt said again. His eyes were fixed on that horrible gash. "We must leave this place."

"No," Ehle said, pushing himself up to his knees. "The book caused this."

"I will take what I came for," Haupt said. "I have my orders."

"This," Ehle said, flinging an arm toward the pulsing breach, "this is what happened the last time you sought out this book under orders. Or have you forgotten?"

"Silence."

"How many did you kill to get this book for Voelker? How many, Max?"

"Do not speak to me like you have no blood on your hands."

Ehle held his hands up, palms out. "Mine are soaked in it. They can never be clean. That is why I am here. To make this right."

"The world turns," Haupt said. "America—"

"America, France, Russia," Ehle replied. "It does not matter. No one should have this book. It is beyond all of us. Can you not see that?"

"Men of such little faith." There was no trace of doubt in Voelker's voice now. He looked again like the triumphant magician-lord of the Reich, more powerful, more feared than the Führer himself. "I taught you both better than this. What has become of the proud warriors of Germany? Am I the only one left with the will to do what is necessary? Am I the only shield against the foe?"

"Martin . . ."

Then the book was in Voelker's hands: that simple ledger, filled with impossible words, such a small thing to bring about the end of all things.

"They are at the gate," Voelker said. "Rome burns, while our leader cowers in his bunker, our men throw down their arms, and you stand in my way. Even if I must go alone, I will walk this path."

Ehle saw Haupt begin to prepare another spell. "Max, no," he called. "The breach. You cannot risk it." Haupt faltered, the spell lost, and Ehle recognized the look on his face: terror.

"The time for doubt is over. Now is the hour of action. You will see for yourselves the cost of defying the will of God."

Voelker stepped toward the breach and opened the book. Ehle's body still trembled with echoes of pain, but there was no time. He was on his feet and moving. Voelker turned, but too late. Ehle crashed into him at a run, slamming them both to the hard wooden floor.

The book slid under the first pew, and Ehle scrambled after it, his fingertips nearly brushing the cover, when he felt Voelker's hands lock tight around his throat.

"I will not be stopped," Voelker hissed through his teeth. "The Reich will be avenged."

Ehle clawed at him, gasping, but in vain. His lungs burned, his chest heaved, and his vision darkened. Above them, he could see the breach dance with wild abandon, reveling in the ritual done in its name.

Haupt raised his cane and chanted something in Latin, but Voelker was still too fast, too powerful. A single word from the Reichsleiter knocked Haupt's locus from his hand and sent him sprawling backward. His assistant, finally able to act despite his obvious fear, ran forward then, only to be thrown aside by another spell. Ehle saw him tumble through the air, feet over head, until he crashed into the pulpit in a spray of broken wood.

It was over in a moment. The grip on his neck was iron, even as Voelker dispatched the others. There was no chance to break free.

But for a moment, Voelker turned his eyes away, and so he did not see Ehle reach for the pistol strapped to the Reichsleiter's hip.

The shot was deafening. The recoil felt like it might have broken his wrist. But when Voelker's fingers went slack and his eyes wide, Ehle knew it was worth it. His lungs ached blissfully as he rolled to the side, drowning in air.

He rose on shaking legs. Voelker stayed down. Blood bubbled around his lips as they opened and closed wordlessly, shock replacing speech. The bullet had entered low in his gut, angled up toward his chest. It would not be long now.

"Farewell, Martin," Ehle said, his voice a quiet rasp.

The Reichsleiter's angry, disbelieving eyes focused on Ehle. The light behind them was quickly fading. Breathing fast now, he managed to say, "Thank . . . you."

Ehle dropped the gun. He had not come this far to kill a man, to put another soul on the scales weighed against him. But he had come to do what he must. And if he had to measure the balance, he knew at last he had done something worth remembering.

He looked up toward the breach. He had no desire to look upon that black otherworld again, even if it were, as Voelker suspected, the source of all magic. Whatever it was, it was nothing for mortal men to see, nothing that deserved to continue, even in memory. But he wanted to watch it close, to see his work finally at an end.

But it did not. Even when he heard Voelker's last struggling breath, the breach remained.

No magic could outlive its caster, not without another . . .

The book. Voelker was not the key; the book was.

The barking of machine guns filled the church. The phantom German soldiers that ringed the room like statues sprang to life, fueled by instinct, as their dreaded enemy poured through the main doors. Ehle watched in horror, but it was over almost as quickly as it began. The Soviets were too many, too well armed.

When the shooting stopped, a tall man in a Soviet officer's uniform appeared at the doorway.

"Herr Ehle," the man he knew as the Nightingale said, stepping over immaterial bodies. "You found your way into Auttenberg after all."

FIFTY-NINE

He pulled the little girl close when the shooting started. She stifled a scream and he held her, shielding her with his body. They ducked behind the stone wall that ringed the church on all sides and pressed against the cold brick as though they might melt into it.

"What is happening?" she asked, her voice a quaver.

"Wait," he said. He held a finger to his lips, removed his arm from around her, and crept toward the corner. The guns had stopped. He heard voices.

There were men around the church. A dozen, maybe more. Their uniforms did not look German. He knew them . . . somehow. He could not concentrate, could not remember. What were they saying? It wasn't English, wasn't German. The pain in his head was worse, had been getting worse as they neared the church. He didn't want to tell the little girl, not when she was so intent on going, but he hadn't been sure if he could continue on much farther. Not when every step was like walking barefoot across broken shards of yourself.

A big man approached the others, giving orders. They were

close, only ten feet or so from where they were huddled. His face . . . he knew his face. That scar, those big hands.

His mind twitched, like putting too much weight on a bad leg. He tasted dirt. Sand. A rush of heat.

He remembered. Dennis had been just ahead of him in the tunnel. The mission had been a success. They got the asset, made it to the Wall, were almost across the border.

Then everything had gone too bright. Karen yelled something. Dennis grunted.

The dirt, pressing down. Choking him.

Like the world had fallen.

Strong, hard hands pulled at him. Dragged him out of the dark.

A face loomed. A big, scarred face.

Soviet uniforms.

A bag over his head. The back of a truck.

Karlshorst. No question about it.

A dim cell.

And a Soviet colonel. With a pocket watch.

The green door, traitor, Karen, Ehle, the major, Fort Bragg (and that blue Carolina sky), BOB, the green door, another tunnel, escape back to the east, a mission, the door, but then the French, and Karen . . . staring into his gun.

"Oh, God," Jim said. His hands were shaking; his whole body was shaking. He remembered. Finally, he remembered.

And wished he could forget.

What did they do to me?

The haze had lifted, like when the sun decided to burn off a morning mist. He saw it all now: the walk across Glienicke Bridge, his return to BOB, waiting until everyone was asleep, going to the basement, knocking out the guard, knocking out Ehle, and Karen.

In his mind, Karen stared at him. Stared at his gun. On her knees. He could feel the weight of the gun in his hand, feel the pressure of his finger on the trigger. He'd hated her in the moment; the weight of her imagined betrayal smothered him. Why had it been so easy for them to turn him against her? Why hadn't he fought harder? But he had seen her, somehow still alive. He'd followed her. She wasn't dead. He couldn't explain it, but she was here, somewhere. That meant it wasn't too late.

Please, he thought, wiping away tears that had appeared on his face. *Please let it not be too late.*

The Soviets were laughing. They had two men on the ground, hands behind their backs. One of the prisoners was older, thicker in stomach and chest, and the other was a big man, with a beard black as midnight.

It was Alec. And the other was Arthur. What were they doing here?

There was a tug at his sleeve. The little girl, her face pale with fright.

"Do not be afraid," he said softly, holding her close. "I will keep you safe."

In the distance, he heard a rumbling. Thunder? No, the sky was still mostly dark but pricked with lingering stars, no clouds. It was getting louder. Then he realized he felt it in the ground beneath them: shaking like the little girl, as if in fear.

Something was coming.

SIXTY

There was almost too much to consider in a single glance: hundreds dead in the pews, shot where they sat; the fallen German soldiers crumpled along the border of the room; the traitor magician Ehle standing at the front with the body of a Nazi Reichsleiter at his feet; and the gaping hole in reality hovering above it all. It was too much, too much and not enough, as the colonel saw no sign of the book.

"It seems I have arrived at an auspicious time," the colonel said as he neared where Ehle stood. He turned over the body there with his foot. "I must guess this to be Herr Voelker, no? What a peculiar place. I trust the two of you worked out any lingering disagreements."

"It is not here," Ehle said. The man's neck was already blackening with long bruises, his voice a broken whisper.

"Herr Ehle," he said, shaking his head. "We find ourselves at odds, but still you must be commended for your effort. You have done what you could. Secretly delayed us for years, no doubt. And that escape of yours into the West. So unexpected. But you see now it was always leading here. Fate, perhaps. Or gravity. Or bad luck. So let us not play more games. Where is it?"

Of course he knew; the colonel could see it in the man's unnatural stillness, in the enormous force of will he exerted to not even blink. But of course he would not tell them. That was not in his nature.

Krauss was at his side then. "You have lost, old man," Krauss said to Ehle. "You ignored me, pushed me aside, but now here I am. I thought you were just incompetent, not a traitor, but that does not matter now. Just give us the book."

Ehle waved a hand toward Krauss. "This is your new chief magical adviser?" he said, laughing; with his damaged throat, it sounded like the gasps of a dying man. "My condolences to Moscow. I did not realize times had become so desperate."

"Tell me!" Krauss shouted.

The colonel heard a groan; they were not alone. There was someone else, waking up in the ruin of the church's pulpit. He motioned to his men and soon the soldiers dug him free and brought him forward. He was a young man, dressed in a ripped suit and unarmed. His head was bleeding, but he was alive.

"Who are you?" the colonel asked in German. When the man did not reply, he asked again in English.

"You . . . you can't be here. You hear me? Let me go," the man said when his eyes focused enough to see who stood before him. "This is an act of war."

Americans. Always condemning the world for what they did freely. No time. The colonel unsnapped the holster at his belt and drew his sidearm. He pressed the cold metal against the man's forehead.

"The book," he said. "Where is it?"

That instinctual American bravado shriveled. The man's eyes immediately dropped, but not just out of fear. No, he was looking under one of the pews.

And there it was. The colonel knelt and picked it up. The cover was smooth under his touch, worn down by decades of reverence. The item long-sought, at last.

His first thought was that his daughter had a ballet performance at the end of the week. He had been prepared to write to her, to beg forgiveness for being away, but now he did not have to. Even if he had to run from the train station to the theater, he would be there.

"Thank you," he said to the shaking American. He placed the book in Krauss's hungry hands. So much work, finally at an end. "Thank you."

"Destroy it." It was Ehle. The man's persistence was laudable, if not his loyalty. "Look at that up there. If we do not close it, nothing matters. Destroy the book, close the breach, and make certain another madman does not open it again."

"The book is a matter of national security for the Soviet Union," the colonel said. "We must keep ourselves safe from the ambitions of evil men. That," he said, pointing upward, "is German handiwork, not Russian."

"Have you seen into the breach?" Ehle said, that ruin of a voice stretched to its limit. "This is not about countries. This is not about war. This is about existence. Destroy that book, or there will not be a world left for the politicians to carve up."

The colonel thought about his daughter. What sort of world would be left her, when her forebears were gone? What sort of world were they building for those who would come after? The question made him uneasy, not because he had no answer, but because he did.

And yet.

And yet the needs of the current world often outweighed the needs of the next.

"Shoot them," he said in Russian.

But before the order could be carried out, the front wall of the church exploded.

Standing where the doors had been only a moment before was the form of a woman.

SIXTY-ONE

I t sounded like the world was breaking apart. Jim held on to the little girl as the noise grew, telling her not to be afraid, all the while wondering if terror was exactly the right response. Then they heard it (whatever it was) hit the church, blasting through old stone and brick, showering them with a jagged hail.

He risked a look.

Karen. It was Karen!

But not Karen. Wreathed in heat that distorted the world around her, eyes lit up like magnesium flares, she looked more like a creature of myth than the wry girl he had picked up at Tempelhof. Something was wrong, terribly wrong.

There was movement to his left. Some of the Soviets guarding Arthur and Alec were running toward the front of the church. Toward Karen.

Jim only had a moment to make his choice. He wanted to go to Karen, but something told him she had little need for his rescue, not from Soviet soldiers anyway. So instead he ducked back behind the wall and took the little girl by the shoulders. "Wait for me here," he said slowly, certain to get the unfamiliar German words correct. "I have to help my friends."

She nodded, chin quivering, and though he was loath to leave her, he was up and over the wall before he could stop to question his plan.

He landed in the soft grass of a decrepit cemetery. Between him and the Soviets a field of weathered white stone marked the lives and deaths of generations of Berliners. Three men remained with the prisoners. The first man had made the mistake of taking off his helmet and so he had nothing to protect him from the hunk of broken tombstone Jim crashed into the back of his skull. The others were looking away, toward the chaos at the front of the church, so didn't turn back around before Jim wrested the first man's gun free. One of them got a shot off, but it went wide and disappeared into the dark as Jim hit both men in the chest.

"Jim? Is that you?" The rough Scottish burr was music to his ears.

"Yeah," he said, panting. He dropped down to the ground by Arthur first. "Sir, I . . . I can't even begin to explain. They did something to me before they sent me back. Magic, I think. I . . . I am so sorry."

The CIA Berlin chief was looking at him like someone might a cornered animal, uncertain if it was about to bite.

"Sir, I—"

Arthur stopped him with a shake of his head. "I always said magic couldn't be trusted," he said. "But no one listens until it's too late. Now, untie me."

Jim got Arthur loose and was working on Alec's bonds when the big, scarred Soviet soldier appeared. He shouted at them in Russian, harsh, angry words that needed no translation. The man had a machine gun cradled in his arms. Jim's rifle was just out of reach, so instead he threw himself at the man.

But the Russian was too quick, too strong. He turned Jim's rush aside and cracked him on the back of the head with the barrel of his gun. The world swam in flashes and darkness, but Jim did not go down. He swung wildly, his fist connecting with the scarred man's ear. The Soviet grunted and staggered. Jim pressed forward, reaching for the gun.

And found it. The butt of it, at least, right between his eyes.

Almost, Jim thought as his legs melted under him. *I almost did it.*

The scarred face was over him now. Then the muzzle of the machine gun.

There was the crack of a gunshot, almost inaudible with the noise from the church, but it did not come from the Soviet's gun. Instead the man stumbled back like he'd been pushed. Another shot and he fell against the side of the church, eyes wide.

A moment later Emile stepped forward, his pistol leveled. He was alone and bloodied. His clothes were torn, like he had passed through a thicket of thorns, and his brow was wet with sweat.

"Où diable sommes-nous?" he said. "What the hell is this place?"

"Emile," Jim said, watching his gun, "Karen is in trouble. I don't know what's going on, but she just went inside the church and—"

"She went in there?" Emile asked as he helped Alec to his feet and shook his head. "Then she is braver than I." He turned to Jim. "You seem different than when last we met, James."

"They did something to me," Jim said quickly. "No time to explain. We have to—"

Alec's big hand rested on his shoulder. If not for the weight of it, Jim would have jumped at the touch. "We heard you, lad," Alec said, nodding. "Lead the way."

SIXTY-TWO

I t was intoxicating.

Like lightning in her blood that made adrenaline seem tiresome.

Like standing on a cliff edge, knowing you could step off and fly.

No, like knowing you could step off and force the ground to rise up and catch you.

Or that you could tear the whole cliff down with a thought.

And the closer she got, the stronger the feeling became. Something was waiting for her, calling to her. Offering power. Not the paltry children's games she had been taught, memorizing timeworn incantations in old languages. True power.

Soldiers shouted and fired their guns, the latter no more effective than the former. Why had she been afraid of men and their toys before? What could armies do against her now? They pretended at war, feinted at destruction; they knew nothing of ruin. Nothing of unmaking.

She would show them.

When she reached the church, she knew she was getting close. Her bones hummed. More men, more bullets to bat aside. The church was closed shut. So she tore the doors from their hinges, then the hinges from the wall, and the wall from its moorings.

At last.

The breach swelled at the sight of her, further ripping open the paper-thin veil to the world beyond. No, not another world: no world. Nothing. Not even emptiness. Nonexistence. The inevitable destination, the origin and the apex, the beginning and end of all roads.

This was why she had come. This was why she had been born. To end.

Bullets buzzed around her like insects. She shooed them away and dismissed the men and their guns; they were not needed here.

The breach grew.

She felt its breath on her skin.

Then agony. Like being torn apart.

The breach cracked wide, like a lunatic smile.

She roared in pain. Something was slashing at her, cutting away at her. Magic. Foul magic. One man was on his feet. A squat man with a pig's face and a weasel's eyes. And something in his hand.

A ledger.

The book.

What a fool, using a spell against her, like a child trying to race a champion.

With a thought, the book leapt into her grasp, and the sweaty, pig-faced man gaped at her with openmouthed surprise. But she was not done with him. With another thought, he was off his feet, dangling madly in the air, and then flying headfirst into the wall.

No. She stopped him just before impact. She could break him, easily. But there was another option.

He screamed as she threw him into the breach. And then he

was gone; truly gone, as though he had never been. She could not remember her anger, or the pain of his spell, or how the book had reached her hand. He had never been.

Good. No more distractions.

E hle watched Karen enter the church with a soul-rending dread. Her magic fed the breach like nothing had before, and it grew, spreading across the high church ceiling like the voices of a choir. She was mad with it; he had never seen magic like this, magic without words or spells, magic of thought, of pure will.

The sort of magic that could end everything.

Krauss tried to use the book against her and for a sickening moment, Ehle thought it might work. Worse, he hoped that it would. But she was too strong, buoyed by the breach, beyond all limitations. It was like standing on the shore and trying to hold back the waves.

Waves that were going to wash the world clean.

He started to get to his feet and then saw it: Voelker's pistol, only a few feet away.

J im froze as he entered. Inside the church, madness reigned. The room was full of the dead: civilian and soldier, German and Soviet. The few tattered survivors huddled near the pulpit and cowered before Karen. Some terrible power irradiated the air around her. The glow lit up her face. And above her, something else waited like a thunderhead.

"Karen!" His voice seemed to die in the room, swallowed up by things a whole lot bigger than he was. But he had to tell her. Before it was too late. "Karen!"

She turned.

———————

Jim. She vaguely remembered him, enough to be surprised to see him.

Had she not killed him yet?

"Karen!" he called. There were others with him, but he broke free of their ranks and ran toward her down the center aisle. "You're alive!"

She ought to thank him. He had forced her hand, forced her to commit to this path. A bullet is powerful persuasion. As he neared, she could see that the wild magic in his eyes was gone. The madman who'd attacked her was gone, replaced by . . . whom? The self-assured spy she met at Tempelhof? No, that man had died in the tunnel with Dennis. This was someone new: not mad, but not whole either.

"Karen, I'm so sorry," he said. He fell to his knees, just under the swelling breach. "I . . . that wasn't me. I would never . . . I'm sorry. I just had to tell you."

This didn't matter. Jim was in the way, but easily removed. She raised a hand, prepared the magic that was aching to be released. He just stared at her with blank eyes. He didn't understand; none of them could.

Good-bye, Jim.

Ehle's arm felt encased in concrete as he lifted the pistol. Karen was facing away from him, distracted for the moment. The tear between this world and whatever dark place lay beyond had given her untold power, but Ehle doubted it would be enough to stop a bullet this close, not when she did not see it coming. Just a bit more pressure against the trigger and he could stop it.

The end of the journey.

Just one more step.

Just one more life.

Just one more ghost.

Above them, the ceiling beams of the church groaned and then split, and then were gone, as the breach suddenly gaped wipe, devouring the air above Auttenberg.

Why had she raised her hand? The movement was vestigial; a remnant of juvenile magic that required coaxed incantations. Was that all it was? *Then finish it*, she thought. *He's waiting for it; he needs it.* Absolution for his crime. Send him beyond, through the widening gap. Obliterate his sins.

What was this voice? It didn't sound like her.

Because she was different now: fully realized. They had been stopping her all this time, keeping her in her place, stunting her. Her locus had been a leash, her spells chains. Because they were afraid. Afraid of real magic. Of losing their grip on power. Afraid of her. And now they could no longer hide that fear.

But Jim wasn't afraid. He should be.

Magic ignited on her fingers.

Yes, he should be.

In another moment, it would be too late. Everything sacrificed, for nothing. Better that he had faced the Soviet firing squad than to have strived for ten years to reach this place only to falter now.

Pull the damn trigger!

Liesel . . . she would be about Karen's age now, if she was still alive. What did she think of her papa? Did she remember him fondly? Or curse him for never coming back from the war? She believed him dead; a better fiction.

End this now, or that sacrifice was in vain.

But perhaps it should be.

For what did it profit a man to gain the world at the cost of his soul?

He lowered the gun.

And it was torn from his hand.

"You idiot," Haupt's assistant said, pushing him aside. "She's going to kill us all!"

George raised the pistol.

What was happening to her? The power . . . she coveted it like she did her own life, but it was doing something, changing something. Deadening something inside of her.

The sneering Soviet with the coin.

The men shooting at her in the streets.

The soldiers inside the church.

Oh, God. How many people had she killed? And with each one, the magic grew hungrier. It was in her now. Magic, like a cancer: her, but not her. Bent only to destroy.

No . . . she could not let it.

". . . going to kill us all!"

George's voice. Behind her. She began to turn.

Then the gunshot.

SIXTY-THREE

The bullet hit Jim square in the chest. He didn't feel pain at first, just shock. When he saw Ehle with the gun, he'd tried to reach Karen, push her out of the way, but he'd been too slow. Maybe this was better. Maybe this was the only way to make amends.

He looked down. Blood was blossoming across his shirt.

Then the pain hit him and his legs gave out.

No, no, no.

Jim . . .

The idiot had stepped in front of the gun. She'd been in no danger from George, not with this much magic at her command; she could have caught the bullet in midair or burned it to ash or sent it flying back the way it had come.

But Jim had to be a hero.

He collapsed to the wooden floor. His red-stained hand reached for her, then went still.

What a fool. A beautiful, dying fool.

Because of George.

George stood over Jim's body, gaping at what he had done, the gun limp in his hand. Karen's magic snapped out and wrapped around him, lifting him off his feet. The pistol vaporized. Power gathered in her, roiled up from her marrow like her fury. Jim's dark blood pooling around her feet sizzled with it.

Yes, George. Time for you to see. Time for you to pay.

She sent a shock of pain through him. It gnarled his body and compelled him to his knees. A whisper of guilt brushed at her as he cried out, but it was hard to hear over the roar of magic in her ears. She narrowed her eyes; he screamed again.

Then she saw his hand, still burned around one finger.

Back at the OMRD, after she'd beaten him in their bout, she'd let the magic go on a little too long. She could have just shocked him, distracted him, but instead she'd used her magic to hurt him. He'd made her so angry, then and so many times before, that it had felt good. Justified. He would have done the same.

But that wasn't who she was; or at least, it wasn't who she wanted to be. It wasn't what she wanted magic to be.

She had always been proud of the fact that while the rest of her colleagues were off battling rogue magicians or discovering new ways to wage magical war, she'd dedicated herself to something noble.

And now here she was, dead men in her wake and another in agony before her.

She pulled back her magic. George gasped in relief.

No, she thought. *I'm not like them. They can't make me be like them.*

She could be something else.

Karen knelt beside Jim, touched his hair. He still wasn't moving.

Her research had found nothing, not a single spell in all of magical history that could heal even a paper cut. Ehle had failed in his own search, and his methods hadn't been bound by any morality or ethics. But they had both been searching while blind-folded. Magic, after all, wasn't what they believed it to be.

With a sigh that became a cold shudder, she gathered up her strength like a final breath. All that rage, all that fire: she brought everything to bear. She mustered every ounce of arcane vitality she drew from this strange place.

And channeled it all into Jim.

Arthur didn't like to admit it, but he didn't have a clue what the hell was going on. Ghostly Germans, very real Soviets, and too much damned magic all over the place. Not to mention a giant black hole floating over their heads. It was enough to make a man wish he were drunk.

He'd frozen when they first entered the church. The sight of Karen all lit up with fire and light had quickly made it clear to him that he was out of his element, like a deer hunter who stumbled into the path of an angry bear. These were some of his people, but this wasn't his fight.

And then Jim had to go and get shot.

"Damn it," Arthur said. That boy had been through enough; he wasn't going to leave him to die like this. Not in this hellhole. He was halfway down the center aisle when he saw Karen kneeling by Jim's body. She was still burning like a pagan goddess. Then she did something, something he couldn't see. And whatever it was made that breach overhead roar to life. As he got closer, his skin felt like it was broiling. His clothes steamed and smoked. But he could see Jim and Karen amid the shimmer of magic; indistinct forms in the haze, like overdeveloped photographs. He called out to them, but his voice vanished into the storm.

Hands grabbed him. Pulled him back. He swatted at them, but then more wrapped tight. "Let me go!" he heard himself say.

"Come on, Arthur," Alec's rough voice shouted in his ear. "We've got to go."

"Not without Jim. He's been through enough."

"Arthur," Emile said, a hand on his biceps. "Look." He pointed up.

The breach blotted out the sky. There was barely anything left of the church; there was barely anything left of the stars. And still it grew.

"We have to go," Emile said.

Arthur looked from the breach back to Karen. He couldn't see her or Jim anymore. Just the void and the void beyond.

It felt different. She knew what using her magic felt like, even before it had burst out of her like water from a busted dam. Her magic was familiar to her by now, a timeworn reflex. But this was something else, like the difference between a shout and a breath. No, that wasn't right; it was like she was speaking a new language, one that somehow made more sense than her mother tongue.

Jim opened his eyes.

His shirt was more red now than white, and his blood was still arrayed around him on the wood floor like a corona, but the wound—

The bullet wound was gone, as if it had never been.

"What—what did you do?" Jim's voice trembled.

"Jim . . ." Karen said, furiously blinking away tears. There didn't seem to be anything else to say.

"Karen," Jim said again. "What—?"

"Don't speak," she said. "Save your strength."

He lifted a finger and pointed up. "What is that?"

Her eyes lifted. The breach surrounded them now. The magic that had saved Jim's life had ripped the breach wide; it was now an ocean, an endless sea of oblivion. Even healing magic, it seemed, fed the breach's unyielding need.

Karen thought quickly. There must be a way to stop it. If she could use the power to seal flesh and bone, she could close this terrible rift. But that was just it: she hadn't saved Jim. The breach had. Raw magic. Absolute power like that only ever did one thing. She helped Jim to his feet. He could barely stand, but then Arthur was there. "If you don't mind me asking," he shouted, "what in the blue hell is going on, Miss O'Neil?"

"Arthur, take Jim. Get him out of here," she said. Her voice sounded distant in her ears.

"Karen . . ." Jim started to say.

"Go!"

The CIA chief nodded. He threw an arm around Jim and pulled him away, against his own weak objections.

She spun back to face the emptiness. It took her breath away. Suddenly terrified and small, she stumbled back a step and her foot kicked something on the dusty floor.

The ledger.

Voelker was gone, but still the breach remained. There was power coming through it, but what power kept it open without the caster? Something else was at work here; a single magician would not have had enough energy for magic like this. That energy had to come from somewhere else.

She heard Professor Goldberg's squeaky words ringing from another life: *Now, class, what is the best way to upset an existing magical spell?*

Exhaust the spell's source.

She gripped the book. Jim's blood from her hands marked the cover in wet brown lines. It was such a little thing.

"You aren't supposed to be here," she said. And threw it into the breach.

But nothing happened.

Distantly she was aware that the others were running. Of course they were; it was the sensible thing to do, when the world was ending. She'd be doing the same, if she believed it would make a difference. Karen stood tall. She would face it, whatever it was, on her feet.

Then the breach exhaled. And began to collapse.

But before she could let out a long-held breath, Karen felt the breach reach for her. It thrashed about wildly, like a dying animal. Broken church pews vanished. Boards from the floor were torn up and consumed. A Soviet soldier, too slow in fleeing, was lifted off the ground and then was just gone. The breach's expanse was shrinking, but its fury was at its peak.

Karen was about to run when she saw Ehle. He wasn't far from her, standing still and facing the fading breach. She called out to him, but he didn't seem to hear her. The breach's foul magic tugged at his clothes, his thinning hair. She yelled for him again. Again, he just stared.

With one eye fixed on the breach, she ran for him. It was only a matter of feet, but felt like crossing a great expanse on legs too tired to move. When she grabbed his arm, at last he turned.

"We have to go!" she said, pulling him away. "It isn't safe here."

He smiled at her; he looked like a different man. "Thank you," he said.

"Thank me later," she said. The breach gaped in front of them. "We have to go."

"I never thought," Ehle said, his voice barely audible over the noise of the disintegrating church, "that after all this time, after all I have done . . ."

"Mr. Ehle, we—"

". . . someone like you would help me." He put a hand over hers. "Thank you, Karen. It is better this way." Before she realized what was happening, he pried her fingers away and turned. Karen opened her mouth to scream, but by then he was through the breach.

And gone.

A moment later, she closed her mouth. She couldn't remember his name. Erwin . . . something?

Then she forgot the shape of his face, the color of his eyes.

And then . . .

Why was she still standing here? What was she waiting for? The whole place was falling down. *Time to go, Karen.*

Time to go.

SIXTY-FOUR

The colonel watched the breach until it was no more. He had watched the strange scene unfold, oddly powerless before forces that were clearly beyond him. After what he had seen in the war, he had thought this world could hold no more horrors for him. He had been wrong.

His mind was muddled, his memories untrustworthy. And yet he knew his mission was a failure. He had come here for something, something important, but he could no longer remember what it was. He doubted the gray-haired man would be so forgetful. There would be a reckoning waiting for him; in Moscow, there was always a reckoning.

Only a few who had entered the church remained. Most of his men had been killed by the magic-mad American or consumed by the hungry breach. There was no sign of Leonid; with the arrival of the girl, he doubted he needed to bother to look for Kirill.

No matter.

The colonel looked at his pocket watch. The hands had started moving again.

He skirted the edge of the ruined building, eyeing the other survivors as they huddled together. They had seen his face, which was unfortunate, but it could be overcome. He still had his pistol, but this was not the time for violence. He just needed to stay low and hidden. East Berlin was not far and he doubted there would be much left of the Wall to stop him.

A smile tugged at his mouth. Perhaps he still might return in time for his daughter's performance.

He heard the click and froze. It was an unmistakable sound: a hammer pulled back.

"What a night," said a voice, speaking English with that absurd American accent. "Didn't exactly go the way I hoped either, if that's any consolation."

The colonel turned slowly. The man facing him was older, a bit too thick in the stomach and jowls for his suit, and looked like he had not slept well in a long time. He might have been handsome once, or at least vital. Now he was on the edge of exhaustion, with sunken eyes and a sweaty brow. And yet he also had a black pistol aimed steadily at the colonel's chest and looked like the sort of man who would not miss.

"I am an officer in the—" he began.

The man with the gun stopped him. "Trust me, I know who you are. It's my job. Can't say I've had a great track record with that job these last few weeks," he said with a shrug, "but you do what you can." He glanced over at the empty church. "And maybe tonight doesn't need to be a complete waste. Let's take a walk, Comrade Colonel. And have a little chat."

The little girl waited for Jim, right where he'd left her. As the sun began to brighten Auttenberg's streets with a (very late) dawn, she was already starting to fade. Jim could see the outlines of the buildings beyond her, through her. Whatever magic had held Auttenberg in place for ten years was going fast.

She smiled when he neared, but then her eyes grew. "Are you hurt?"

He looked down at his shirt, at the hole, at the blood. "Not anymore," he said, without really understanding, without really believing.

"I do not hear the shelling," she said. "Have we won?"

He knelt down. What really happened to her, that dark night when Auttenberg became stuck in history? Had she been in that church with the others? Or had she escaped, maybe making it to the western side of the city to greet the Allies when their tanks arrived and halted the Soviet advance? Maybe she was out there now, a free, happy woman enjoying a world without war.

"It is over," he said softly, grateful he knew the words. "You can go home now."

She clapped her hands and laughed, but when she ran to embrace him, all he felt was a brief breeze and the sun on his face.

Her laughter held in the air a moment longer, and then it too was gone.

Karen stood near the church, or what remained of it, for a long time. Whatever their purpose had been was accomplished: Auttenberg was free from its endless night. Now it would wake to see the world that had left it behind.

Arthur was there, rounding up those who were left. Alec helped Dr. Haupt, whose cane had been lost in the church. Emile hovered at the perimeter, watching eastward. Jim was closer, but did not approach. He looked dazed, as one might expect from someone who had been brainwashed by illegal magic, and then healed by impossible magic. Two bullets in the same night, Karen thought, both denied their killing purpose.

She closed her eyes and breathed in the chill morning air. She'd done it. After years of wasted research on pointless spells, she'd found the magic she had always believed in and had saved Jim's life. Nearby, she saw a fallen Soviet rifle lying in the street. What had happened to the soldier carrying it? Had she killed him? How were her scales balanced now?

How was she supposed to feel? Because she felt cold.

Some of the tombstones of the church's cemetery remained. The names were faded by time, some almost unreadable. Empty markers of forgotten lives. The thought made her sad. She felt as though she should be in mourning herself, but could not remember why.

They reached the park at the western edge of the district just as the sun reached over the buildings. Another glorious day in Germany.

Arthur needed a drink. Badly.

But his work wasn't quite done; it never was, in fact. What a terrible job he had, a thankless, low-paying millstone around his aching neck, one he'd be much better off without. And one he planned on doing till the day he finally croaked. Or they fired him.

Though he wouldn't mind fewer days like this one.

He'd had a good chin-wag with their Russian guest on the walk from the gutted church and he was pretty sure they'd reached an understanding. His English was pretty good for a Russki. Arthur still couldn't help but wonder if the right course of action was to put a bullet in the guy's skull and leave him for the crows, but he was supposed to be one of the good guys, after all.

At the park's border, Arthur held back and addressed the man known as the Nightingale.

"You think you can convince them to back down?" he asked.

The Nightingale nodded. "We are all reasonable men."

"You sure about that?"

"No," the Russian said. "But we like to think of ourselves as reasonable men. That is enough. There was something we wanted here, but it was not war."

Arthur patted the gun in its holster. "I need to tell you what I'm liable to do if you ever grab one of my boys again?"

"After today, I do not expect I will be in a position to hinder your work."

"I wouldn't be so sure," Arthur said, eyeing the man who made all of Western intelligence shiver. "You look like a survivor to me."

The Nightingale nodded, and then turned to the east.

One down, one to go. Arthur waved Alec over. The Scot approached, shaking his head. "You're letting him go? That's a high-value target walking away from us right now. Not sure how the President or the Prime Minister will feel about that."

Arthur shrugged. "I'm in a generous mood."

"Better you than me," Alec said.

Arthur's stomach was turning sour. Mistake or no, he'd made his decision. Time to follow through. "You'd better hurry," Arthur said, "if you want to catch up."

Alec stared at him. "What?"

Arthur jerked his head back behind them, toward West Berlin. "That shop where we tracked Jim earlier tonight," he said, "you ever see that place before?"

"No." Alec was scowling.

"Me neither," Arthur said. "So it took me a minute to place it."

"Arthur, what is this—"

"After Jim and Dennis's little trip to East Berlin went south, I had some weight on my mind. How did the Soviets know we were coming? How did they know when and where?" Arthur rubbed his cheek, listened to the rasp of a day's stubble against callused palms. "Keeps a man up at night."

Alec shifted his weight back. "I don't—"

Arthur held up a hand. The others were waiting for him, too far to listen in. "Let me finish," he said. "I knew we had sprung a leak, just had to know where. See, very few knew about that operation. Not something I was looking to advertise so I kept a tight guest list. You, me, the Frenchies, Garriety. And one had gone bad."

Alec said nothing.

"So I went to our old friend Dieter," Arthur went on. "An industrious man, our Dieter. Turns out the tunnel we collapsed wasn't his only one, not by a long shot. Being a persuasive sort of fellow, I convinced him to give me the locations of a few more. Then I offered that intel up, one location to each of you. And then lo and behold, the Soviets try to sneak our boy Jim back east using one of those very tunnels."

The Scot looked away. "Damn," he said. His voice was quiet, quieter than Arthur had ever heard it. Alec sighed. "You were there in '43," he said, looking anywhere but Arthur's face. "You saw what those Nazi bastards did. Everyone talks about how they sacked London, but I stood on Calton Hill and watched Edinburgh burn. There was nothing left when we finally threw them out. They salted the earth and killed a lot of good people, very few of whom were soldiers."

"And we paid them back," Arthur said.

"Not by half," Alec said, his voice strengthening. "Not by half, Arthur. Now everyone in the West talks about peace and harmony with the Germans in Bonn, like any of them are worth trusting. They're going to rearm them. We're still finding bodies in the rubble in Scotland and they're going to give the Germans an army, to 'protect against the Communist tide.'" His laugh at this wasn't a pleasant one. "The Soviets might be cruel SOBs, but at least they know that the only good German is a dead one."

Arthur suddenly felt a need to be anywhere but right here, right now. "I was there," he said. "I saw what happened. And I won't tell you we've always done right by our fallen, but there still are good ways and bad ways, Alec." He shook his head. "You don't go against your own."

Alec's face was dark. Without his usual chasm of a smile, his beard reminded Arthur too much of the emptiness that had almost swallowed the church.

"So what now?" Alec asked.

Arthur nodded east. "You've served king and country well enough," he said. "So get going."

"You're letting me go too?"

"My mood is turning less generous the longer we stand here yapping."

Alec glanced back at the others. "What will you tell them?"

Arthur shrugged. "I'll tell them you needed a vacation and heard Siberia was nice this time of year."

This seemed sufficient for the big man. He looked like he was going to say something, but then thought better of it. "I won't offer you my hand," he said, "but I will offer my thanks."

"Good luck," Arthur said.

As Alec started after the Nightingale, Arthur decided it was time for that drink. Anything but scotch. He didn't think it would taste the same anymore.

"Should I ask what that was all about?"

Arthur turned at the voice. "Miss O'Neil," he said. She looked terrible. Her skin was white as fog, her hands were twisted together to keep from shaking, and her eyes had a faraway look that Arthur unfortunately recognized. "You here to apologize for stealing one of my cars?"

"Sorry about that." She smiled, barely. "It was in the service of a good cause."

"Any cause can look good, if you squint hard enough."

"You really believe that?" she asked.

Arthur shrugged. "Uncle Sam doesn't pay me to believe in things, Miss O'Neil."

She stared after the way Alec had gone. "You going to be alright, Arthur?"

"I could ask you the same," he said. "Though, as a gentleman, I'll refrain from doing so."

"Thanks," she said, her voice brittle.

"You weren't lying before," Arthur said, "when you called this a lonely business."

"And you said on the good days, it was worth it." He tried not to notice how her shoulders were trembling as she spoke. "Was this one of the good days?"

Arthur exhaled. Damn, was it cold. "I'll let you in on a secret, Karen," he said, his words echoing back toward Auttenberg. He pulled off his jacket and draped it over her shoulders. Looked better on her anyway. "I just pretend they're all good days."

SIXTY-FIVE

MEMORANDUM

SUBJECT: De-escalation of Military Force Following Berlin Wall Collapse
TO: Director, Central Intelligence
FROM: Chief, Berlin Operating Base

Forces at border remain on high alert following the total collapse of Berlin Wall. Estimated fifteen thousand (15000) refugees crossed between hours of 0500 and 0800. Processing has been set up at Tempelhof Airport. Expect will take weeks.

Reports of Soviet aggression against refugees widespread. However, following orders from Soviet and GDR high command that arrived early morning, military strength was reduced at every border crossing.

Seems they decided it was not worth World War Three (3).

Can confirm reports that during the night following collapse of magical Berlin Wall, Soviet and GDR forces began construction on concrete barriers at every major crossing between East and West Berlin.

Unrelated fire at Berlin Operating Base during same night
was contained. Damage from fire suppression system widespread, but manageable.

Tempelhof was awash in activity. Even though the sun had
gone down an hour before, the airport still hummed with the
rumble of truck tires and a choir of refugee voices. The lucky ones.
How many others were still stuck in the East, barred now by concrete and tanks rather than shimmering silver magic? Too many,
Jim thought. But it was a start.

The military plane was running late (no surprise), but it would
be taking off soon. He wasn't supposed to be here, wasn't supposed to be outside, but Arthur's mercy was apparently without
end. He tried to ignore his escorts. At least they'd taken off the
handcuffs. He rubbed his chest where the bullet had hit him, an
unconscious habit he'd picked up. No scar, not even a mark. Like
it had never happened.

The coffin was rolled out onto the tarmac without ceremony.
There'd be time for that when it landed Stateside. All the time in
the world. The family would be waiting, impatient after all the
delays, but Jim was for once grateful for the slow-moving wheels
of bureaucracy. Otherwise he would have missed his chance to say
good-bye.

Jim put his hand on the polished wood. He could feel the grain
under his fingers, almost imperceptible. He tried to think of
something to say, one last joke for his friend, but nothing seemed
all that funny anymore. "It should be me," he said. Distant rotors
scattered his words into the German sky. "I should be in there and
you should be out here. I think you'd have done a better job."

"Jim." He hadn't heard her walk up. He knew she'd be here
(this was her ride home after all), but hadn't decided if he wanted
to see her or not. She looked good, or at least better. More like

herself. Less like the woman with dead, blazing eyes who had been about to kill him. Not like he could blame her for that, though; he'd earned it.

Jim steadied his quavering legs with both hands on the coffin. "When you land, his sister will probably be the one to meet the plane," he said, staring at his whitened knuckles. "His parents are older, probably won't be able to make the drive. If you see her, tell her . . . tell her Dennis was a good guy, good at his job. Tell her . . . that he's a hero."

"I'll tell her," she said.

"And tell her that he was terrible at poker," he said with a cracked voice, "and that he couldn't hold his beer, and made dumb jokes. And that . . . he was a good friend."

She put her hand on his. "Jim."

He forced himself to look up. She was crying too.

"It wasn't you," she said. "Trust me, I know. It was the magic, not you."

He wanted to smile for her, to put on that mask in the hopes of raising her spirits, but somewhere along the line, he'd forgotten how to. "That would be easier to agree with," he said, "if I knew who I was anymore."

"You're still you," she said. "We both are. It's the world that changed around us."

"Not sure if that's comforting or not."

He earned a tiny smile for this, one he'd cherish.

"You saved me," he said before he could stop himself.

"It seemed like the thing to do at the time," she said softly.

"Thank you."

"You're welcome," she said. She glanced at his hovering baby-sitters. "What's next for you?"

"Debriefing," he said. The euphemism sounded ominous.

"It wasn't you," she said again.

"I'll be fine. Arthur understands," Jim said, as if that mattered. If they needed a scapegoat, well, he knew they wouldn't have to dig around much. He suddenly needed a cigarette. He patted his coat and produced a crumpled pack and offered one to her. She took it carefully, but steadily. Not a two-pack-a-day gal, but this wasn't her first smoke.

"A light?" she asked.

This made Jim laugh, despite everything. "Sure," he said. "I've got a light." He spoke the incantation in Latin (accent on the last syllable) and snapped his fingers. A warm little pool of fire illuminated their tired faces. They lit their cigarettes and exhaled out over their heads.

The flame turned her eyes to gold.

"Hardly anything impressive," he said, a little embarrassed. "Just a little trick, one of the few I still remember."

"No," she said, mesmerized by the glow. "This is what magic is. Mankind's great endeavor." Now she laughed, but the joy had gone out, like a snuffed candle. "We spend all our time trying to steal fire from the gods, and when we succeed we have to find something to burn with it."

Jim said nothing. There didn't seem to be anything to say.

She dropped her cigarette and put it out with her shoe. Leaning over, she kissed him on the cheek. "Good-bye, Jim," she said. "And thanks."

They loaded the passengers and the coffin into the rear of the plane. The huge engines spun to life, drowning out everything else with a bored roar. Jim felt a firm hand on his arm, his cue to go, but he stayed put, watching, watching until the heavy green door was all the way closed.

SIXTY-SIX

"Sorry, Elvis," Karen said as she hurried the bandaged rat back into his cage. The little creature scurried out of her hands and into the sawdust, nose twitching like mad. If he begrudged her the incision, he showed no signs.

Another bust. She'd actually let her hopes rise for this one, but it turned out to be just another fool's errand. Gerald apologized, but it hadn't been his fault. She jotted down the last of her notes in her research notebook and sighed.

Sometimes, she wondered why she bothered.

And then she'd remind herself that it was possible. The magic was there, somewhere.

When she returned to the OMRD after Berlin, she could have had any job she wanted. Her report had become required reading for all field agents. Everyone wanted to hear about the strange magic she'd found in Auttenberg, but she didn't have it in her to tell the story again. She just told them it was classified.

She didn't say that there were entire chunks of it she couldn't remember.

Dr. Haupt had called her to his office on his last day. His retirement was long overdue, he said, and would be a welcome chance for rest. She hadn't argued. They hadn't spoken once while in West Germany, nor on the flight home. The only one less chatty than Dr. Haupt had been George, who'd resigned from the OMRD before their landing gear had touched down. She wasn't sure if he'd quit because he didn't want to work with a woman or because he didn't want to work with a woman he'd tried to murder. Either way, he wasn't missed.

"Tell me," she'd said to Dr. Haupt as he packed away his things, "why did you send me to Berlin? You knew that we'd helped erect the Wall, you knew about Auttenberg. Why send me? Why didn't you go yourself?"

When he stared at her, he'd never seemed so frail. "My dear," he said, his voice a tired whisper, "I did not know the Wall was involved. I thought it would be a good experience for you. Give you a chance to learn, to grow. I never meant for you to be hurt. I never meant . . ." He trailed off. Since Auttenberg, he looked less like the fearsome director of the OMRD and more a fragile old man who had stepped out into the street only to forget where he lived. "You were always like a daughter to me," he said eventually. "I only wanted what was best for you. I only wanted to keep you safe."

I already have a father, she had wanted to say. *And I don't need him to protect me either.*

"I thought the Wall would stand for a thousand years," Dr. Haupt said, shaking his head. "I thought Auttenberg was buried forever. I thought the past would stay where it belonged."

"It rarely does," she said as she left.

She'd turned down the offers from the other department heads, though she didn't fail to notice the newfound deference they paid her. She just wasn't interested in fieldwork, weapons research, or whatever else they offered her. None of that mattered. She had glimpsed the true face of magic; she knew its voice now. The rest could still choose to believe it was some unexplainable force that existed for men to harness for a brighter tomorrow, but she knew better.

It wasn't man's future; it was his end.

Except, it didn't have to be. Jim was alive, somewhere, after all.

Now she had Gerald and two other magicians for her research. As it turned out, being a celebrity meant a bigger budget. She'd even found a woman willing to join, fresh out of St. Cyprian's. The next generation, the next turn of the wheel. She left the actual spellcasting to them. She was too busy, she told them, and they needed the experience; they, of course, were honored. She didn't tell them she hadn't cast any magic since Auttenberg. She didn't tell them her locus was gone, a pain she felt every day, like a lost limb. And she didn't tell them that the very thought of trying to work magic without it filled her with stomach-turning dread.

"Don't look at me like that, Frank," she said as the other rat eyed her from his cage. "You're up next."

There was some solace to be found back in her research, back in routine. There were times she even felt stable, like the ground under her feet wasn't about to give way. Like her legs could still hold her up. Those times didn't last long, but she appreciated them when they came.

She realized she was holding it again; the ring had come back with her from Berlin, a souvenir for the forgotten moments of her time there. It had been enchanted once; the spent magic left a faint echo she could sense when she tried. The ring had translated words spoken in German to English: powerful, unique, startling magic. And it had been given to her by the man who had enchanted it. And she had no memory of who that man was.

The door opened. Allison's head poked in. "Karen? You have visitors."

A moment later, Martha burst into the room. "Whoa," she said, taking it in.

"Say hi to your aunt," Helen said, coming in after.

"Hi, Aunt Karen," Martha said. "Is this where you do the magic?"

Karen shared a glance with her sister. "This is where I do research," she said. She set the metal ring down on her desk.

"That sounds boring," Martha replied.

"Magical research," Karen amended.

Martha shrugged. "That sounds a little better. Oh!" She rustled in her knapsack and came up with a red leather book. "I read your birthday present!"

Karen took it from her and smiled. The cover announced, in fading gold leaf, *The Discovery of Magic*. It had been her first textbook. After she had passed the tests in school, her father had forbidden her to consider the extra studies, but one morning she had found this book wrapped in thick brown paper at the foot of her bed. A simple note had been attached. It read: *Change the world, darling*. Her mother had signed it, for her and her father.

"And what did you think?" Karen asked.

"It was neat," Martha said. "I mean, I want to read it again, and Mom says it will make more sense after I take the tests, but I can't believe the stuff in here. Can you really do all these spells?"

"That and more," Karen said, suppressing a wince.

"Neat," Martha said.

There were times she found herself back there, staring into that void. In the lab late at night, where she found herself often these days when she couldn't sleep, or looking into the mirror, or when she passed by a church or a park. It whispered to her, even now. But in those moments, she tried to focus and remember the man who had given her the ring.

She saw him in other people's faces. A glimpse, nothing more.

Like trying to grip a vapor. And then there was the bag: an old, tattered leather satchel she'd carried back from Auttenberg, from Berlin. Someone had given it to her, she thought, along with the enchanted items inside. Whose magic was it infusing wood and stone? It seemed unknowable, a word in a foreign tongue. But this mattered. Something was missing until she could recall his face. Something was broken inside until she knew his name.

It was hard; probably impossible. But she'd made progress. It was becoming a new obsession, not unlike her research. Sometimes it seemed even more important. When she narrowed her thoughts, truly forced herself to think, she could believe it could be done. She knew only one thing for certain: she had forgotten someone who was worth remembering.

It must have happened again; Helen was giving her that look. The blackouts were brief and manageable, she tried to tell her sister, but big sisters were experts in not believing a word spoken by their little sisters.

"Come meet our friends," Allison said, ushering Martha over to the rats' cages. That was a bad sign; that meant her assistant was noticing it too.

Helen came over. "Are you okay?"

Karen smiled. It felt tired, but genuine. "I'm great. Really."

"You look like you haven't slept in a month."

"You look like you haven't slept since Martha was born."

"I haven't," Helen replied. "Just wait until you have a daughter. Then you'll understand." She put her hand on Karen's arm. "Really, you can tell me."

"Really," Karen said. "I'm good."

The look again, mastered by big sisters everywhere. "If you can't have lunch with us, Martha will understand."

"I wouldn't miss it for the world," Karen said, and meant it. "Let me just tidy up a bit and we can get going."

Martha was telling Allison all about the hamster they kept in their classroom at school. Helen looked like she was doing her darnedest to avoid touching any surface in the lab. And for a moment, Karen felt a glimmer of the peace she'd been looking for her entire life.

She grabbed her research notebook and dropped it into one of their filing cabinets. As she did, something inside caught her eye.

"You coming, Aunt Karen?" Martha asked eagerly from the doorway.

"Yeah," Karen said. "Just a minute." She reached into the drawer. At the bottom was another research notebook, like any one of a dozen she had spread throughout the lab. But unlike the rest, this one didn't have a title on the cover, just a blank spot where she'd normally write it in. But the spine was worn and the pages already a little ink-spotted and dog-eared. It was clearly in use. She flipped through it: it was full of strange formulas, spells, and incantations. It wasn't anything she recognized. Maybe it was from one of the other departments and got mixed in with hers by mistake.

She knew none of this but knew that she should, she definitely should. It was like she'd forgotten her own name. This mattered, like her research, like him. She turned to the first page. Something passed over her like a chill.

The words were there, written in fresh ink. They were at once unfamiliar and well known, foreign and intimate. She felt like she should be shocked to read them, scandalized. And yet, they also seemed as inevitable as time.

She ran a fingertip across them, as if to confirm they were real.

The first line of the curious book, written in her own handwriting, read:

Concerning that which must never be . . .

Photo by Kimberly Goodwater

W. L. GOODWATER lives with his wife and son on the coast. He designs software, teaches fencing, and writes novels—though not necessarily in that order. *Breach* is his debut novel.

Ready to find
your next great read?

Let us help.

Visit prh.com/nextread

Penguin
Random
House